# Never Ever Days

## WJ MORIA

**PP**

Publishing Place LLC

*PP*



Published in the United States by Publishing Place LLC, Skowhegan, Maine, United States



Book Cover by Kris McKenna

'Never Ever' and the *'PP'* colophon are trademarks of Publishing Place LLC

ISBN: 978-1-969343-08-7 (*Hardcover*)

ISBN: 978-1-969343-09-4 (*Paperback*)

ISBN: 978-1-969343-10-0 (*eBook*)

LCCN: 2025924047

Printed in the United States of America

First Edition 2026

Publishing Place
Skowhegan, ME 04976

www.publishingplace.net

# Contents

# Prologue

## THE LOST NOW FOUND WRITINGS IN 2009

Our house hunt led us to this old home, built in 1869, located on Main Street in the Town of Skowhegan, with a wrap around porch, reminiscent of my beloved Grandmother's home in Milo, Maine. Upon entering the home there was an undeniable aura of peace like quiet, whereas each room was like entering anew. My antiques were the perfect fit. It was as if, the house itself, opened up to say,

"Welcome to your new home."

The house is a modest two story building, plus attic with an attached shed leading to the barn with pine finished ceilings and another attic. This new place has lots of nooks and crannies perfect for poking around to investigate. I'm in the barn's attic loft thinking what to do next, when over in the corner I spotted an opening leading me to reach for my trusty flashlight, which is a necessity tool for searching and finding household treasures. Shining the light in the opening I saw old looking big green shutters standing upright on their sides, and on the floor at the back was a leather strap tempting me to go into this space. I then thought better of this idea as being by myself, and my cellphone, being charged in the kitchen of the main house. This is how disasters happen! Maybe I can reach the leather strap allowing to pull whatever it is to me. It's awfully heavy to slide along the unfinished pine board floor at the angle it is wedged, around the corner. GOT IT!

It is an old worn brown leather satchel type bag. What to do now? Open it? This thought made my heart race, and of course my curiosity won over my good sense leading me to unleash the bag, while all the time watching for a mouse, or some critter, or the dreaded spider. Instead of reaching inside the full bag, my thoughts of dumping it out would let me see what was in there quicker, not to mention safer. Out came small white crystal rocks, seeds, leaves, and flowers all dried and flaky, feathers of all colors from many types of birds. All this I was fascinated by, as they were what I would have gathered to be keepsake from Mother Earth. I wished I had known the story of it's owner.

Touching the soft brown leather of the bag, then picking it up I noticed it was much too heavy. Feeling around inside my fingers found an unusual slit in the bag. It was a secret pocket full of papers, and antique tools for writing. I went over by the window to get a better look, and took out what appeared to be stories as all seemed titled. What a find! My curiosity was piqued. I will take all into the house to sort through, reading immediately, with many cups of coffee.

The stories were of our recently purchased house when the Stevens bought the home in 1871, and how important it became to Sarah's survival. Reading her stories led me to think of my Great Grandmother with thoughts of what her life must have been, just to live each day, and everyday to survive. My heart felt saddened; for along with the survival struggle she also had to endure the hardship of living all her days in a repeated void.

Sarah's words spoke as to enlighten my knowledge of the unfairness of what was the life of most women, whose only option was marriage to a man, perhaps one she did not even know or choose, and to take the role of housekeeper of his homestead. We owe our very lives to these women, who endured the hardships. All the work expected of them to upkeep a home along with having to bear the many children, in a time of solitude.

We, men and woman were all born, with a thinking brain, lest we forget, arms and legs to do more than housework. Sarah was born in a time of life; when women had no voice, no freedoms and no rights to own property or to vote. Women were to be household possessions, belonging to the head of the house. Women were – only to be housekeepers —slaves of yesteryears.

Sarah's stories brought me to research the deeds with facts to collaborate her words, which brought the true weight of her words. I found Sarah memorable.  Writing her stories of "life's — ups and downs" within the deep secrets she lived.

"Never Ever" as Sarah expressed was she able to share her words on earth, with exception of one. Sarah also wrote in secret; of the families, their lives, their secrets. I wanted to know Sarah's story. Now, over two decades of fact finding I am inspired to share her journal —

"Never Ever Days"

Now I am thinking...

Careful for what you wish as you may get much more!

Hope you enjoy reading the penned words of...


Sarah Fletcher Pitts Stevens — 1836-1909

Presented by WJ MORIA (2026)

# *Introduction*

## THE 19TH CENTURY WORDS

In Maine, women were married to take up what was as expected, endless housekeeping. They also knew their place in society which was to be seen doing women's work, and not to voice their thoughts. The menfolk handled the thinking and speaking, they were in charge of the church and the towns, whereas only men voted, and they alone owned the land. In fact they made all the rules that society followed, such as women do not belong in the workplace. We women did as we were told. I too was married only not so much a proper wife because we lived with many relatives and it was not my job to run the household. This job of housekeeper belonged to the elder woman, who was my mother-in-law, until the day she would relinquish it to the next in line. All the while she worked tirelessly to keep life in our household strong on the farm. I did my part as, "Many hands make the work light" This was what was needed to keep order of the household on the farm.

Women were not encouraged to be writers of stories; be the stories true, or not so true. At a young age I liked to tell stories, then started to write down stories about my life I have come to have, including the goings on around our home, and within our quiet town. This writing I do in secret. Not my first secret, no one knew or could imagine shy quiet Sarah writing down every word overheard from private conversations. This was a hard task. Walking up and down hills always carrying my leather bag, a satchel for my rocks, twigs, leaves, bird feathers (my favorite) and many nature collections. My bag would become heavy leading me to sit at the base of a tree to rest.  Here in my bag I created a hidden opening where I kept my paper with writing utensil to use for jotting down memorable moments in nature, along with the words of the colorful town folks. Mostly I use this writing as an untold means to speak. I am an eccentric nonconforming woman, acting out childlike, wanting to live life my way, yet all the while I knew full well this needed to remain and was my secret. Writing gave me a memorable life, as if, to be speaking.

Not knowing how to openly live this unheard of life I was born into, or how to fight for my way of living life, with my beliefs. I just sneakily wrote stories using my childhood voice, and never ever showed anyone, except for one, yet not even my husband, as I continued to write in secret.

I was born to be me. Writing is my way of being authentic. My words are thoughts from my mind, sparking my soul, lingering in my heart, until they become an unbearable burden, of not being free to express who I am, and what I believe through vocal words, as to communicate with others. Writing gives me peace, without bringing strife to those I love. I know it is very important not to be owned by anyone, also to be able to speak freely...

As freedom to be ... is life...

Never Ever Days


These stories will tell of the days in between and before, all times of my life, the ones, I made time to pen.

In the barn I will get up the wooden stairs to place my satchel in the corner under the rafters. There my stories will remain until the right curious special person finds my treasure of my heart's joy, written over the decades of my fast-moving life. Here are my written words to be found. I know there are no coincidences in our universe, so my writings will never ever stay hidden. At the perfect time my journal will come into the light of day.

Today I know this insight is to help another, whom I do not know. Most likely I will never ever lay eyes on any reader of my writings, because these are remaining my secret. It is strange to write such interesting bits of life's prophecy, and know it is not for now, but for some future reader.

Somehow, someday, someone, who feels rooted in guilt where they can not move forward, nor back, will get a needed message from my stories of life in the days of old. My voice will always find a way to be...


Written by Sarah Fletcher Pitts Stevens  1836-1909
Presented by WJ MORIA (2026)

# Part J

**Poetic Justice**

If only there was a recipe to follow
to enjoy all of our short fragile life...

Would we seek out just the right ingredients
as to make a fulfilling perfect life...

Knowing the essence of life is in living
each and every present day...

**Never Ever Forget Life's Lessons...**

# CHAPTER ONE

# Sarah's Forever Home

We need this house. I do not know exactly why?"

I, Sarah say to my reluctant husband, James. My mind is racing with many thoughts knowing James will soon be meeting with John Bailey to make an offer for the house.

The kitchen of the farmhouse is cold from the fire burning down overnight, whereas the black cook stove is snapping from the heat of the freshly built morning fire. The kitchen still cool, yet the water in the teakettle is steaming hot, as if ready to wash up the few breakfast dishes. Reaching to clear the dishes from the table I felt an urge to further convince James, "No matter the cost." This desperate tone is so unlike my demeanor and unnecessary.

James said, "I prayed. Our God is looking over us. Always know and remember we have our promise, we have made this pledge to each other."

'What will be- shall be'

He is calm and so centered in his faith. James can live freely practicing his beliefs in his everyday life. What I believe and know to be true, today it is not an accepted way in life. I look at James—my heart swells—he is truly the love of my life. I feel so fortunate to be growing our life together. We know we will be fine no matter where we live, but please, let it be my choice in the new village at the house on the corner of the two contemplated streets which both lead to the burying ground.

It is February the shortest month of the year, whereas most times the hardest month, being it is the coldest coming just before the March winds usher in the changing of the seasons from Winter to Spring. This is my favorite time of the year when life comes back...

Look to the bare trees, they have been as sticks, for all the long winter. Spring gives them back their green fullness, becoming a display alongside the fields, which are filling out quickly with meadow growth, leaving us all with a touch of spring fever making our hearts flutter with new purpose to life.

What a perfect time to be buying our new house! The one on the new contemplated street that leads past our church to the burying ground, where my baby Asa, age 3 and big boy Willie, age 6 are permanently gone from their father and I. We have one child, Nathan, age 12, who is book smart without any interest in our life on the farm. This new trend excites me too, as I want to own the house that does not require constant farm work, also in this neighborhood.

This way of life working for funds to buy what you need is so foreign to us. We are a family of three who have lived conservatively all our lives joining with other family members to preserve and grow the farm. Lately, as if suddenly my eyes saw, bringing the feeling into my heart, that we are totally suffocating within the walls of our farm. We have worked and toiled leaving nothing accept blisters with sore muscles to show for our labors. We cannot unproductively continue farming, by working from sunup to sunset, without making us prosperous, only surviving to live each day with the same results, year after year, without promise of better days to come.

James has always farmed with each year becoming harder, it is fickle in nature depending on the weather, and if, there are hired hands to help with the crops when the time comes. Farming takes a toll without having lots of children to help out, to then one day taking over the family farm.

It is the year 1871, the County is Somerset, the small town was called Bloomfield, recently to be known as Skowhegan, which is an up and coming town in the western part of the State of Maine, with the Kennebec River passing through leaving prosperity in its wake. This house is a newly built place in the middle of all, which is being constructed to make a new village, whispering of progress. Houses are being built close together as people like living in villages, in contrast to sprawling farms. This house becomes a promise of a new sort after, independent life allowing us to leave the farm life behind.

A new way of life is scary to live, mostly for James, who has farmer's blood flowing through, and through, although he has accepted that we cannot survive by farming. Our hair is graying, and there is no denying, our youth has been spent. I will not let getting older make me sad. We have another chance to grab onto a new way of life with an easier existence allowing us to learn of living our lives anew.

Seems like yesterday we were married. We are nearing our 25th Anniversary. How can that be? We will be half a century old soon. Where has our youth gone?

We have laughed, cried, and spent these years, we can never ever get back. This house will guide us into old age within a community filled with people living in houses built close together, one after another with no land for farming. To live here you must work for hire and purchase your food at the dry goods store, also barter, and buy from farmers. No more tending animals. No more tending gardens. No more sunup to sundown work on the farm.

I am so excited! We will have freedom to come and go without finding someone to keep care of the farm animals, even though we are not travelers it is comforting to know, we will be free. James and I have always lived with relatives as was expected when we married twenty-four years ago. We have lived with parents, brothers and their families, uncles and aunts, without a home to call our own, even if we owned the very farm.

Times have been hard, now at age forty-six, we need to independently live, existing on our own. The wife leaves her family and moves within or near the family of her husband bringing, along a dowry to keep her needs met. I had nothing tangible only very few newly made clothes by my Nana and Aunts, who also taught my housekeeping skills learnt as a child of twelve, whereas I was good at my tasks. It was second nature for me to be confident in the work of the household once I set my mind to the plight of knowing this was to be my life.

Looking back my mother seemed to always be busy in the kitchen. Then she had a day to wash, whereas her summers were consumed with canning and gardening. Everyday the floors were swept, the wood smoke dust was wiped from the mantles, stove, and furniture. She never ever complained even when becoming ill. It was my little sister, who tried to help. I would have, I know I should have, but to me she was sick because of so much work. This was not going to be my fate until, here I am, well trained and worrying I will not get my own home, but this is different it is not a farmers homestead with endless chores.

It is a house in town with no land to till as there is no space for growing crops. We will live there and not work our fingers to the bone. No fetching water as there is a cistern in the basement to collect rainwater for washing. I have never ever wanted anything like this house. It is a place of freedom with no one telling me what to do. I am forty eight years old, and since getting married have never ever made any household decisions on my own, while in all this time there was no space to be mine. There is no backing away from this house of which I want to be our family place of liberty, to live as we wish.

James would be content to live on a farm with all the family. He lost his father when he was twelve putting his childhood aside to help his mother run the farm. He is happy with his family, their values are his; loving God, as he was taught, and working hard. I too lost my mother at twelve years of age whereas I learned housekeeping to care for the farm of my father, my sister and I.

When we first met he was helping my father gather hay, and it was then, at first site, unbeknownst, we exchanged hearts. So he knows my heart. He can see how important this house is to me. so why did I say,

"The perfect place for us to live." Then I added, "We will pay the price. We no longer own the farm on the Middle Road way down, this is your brother's farm now. We are without a home"

James is not drawn to the house leaving me a strong feeling that I need to push him into being interested. Then adding,

"The first time the house was seen by me I knew it would be our home."

James took my hand saying, "If only we had known when the carpenter, Mr. Cushing was selling. We could have bought it then for less. Bailey however is from New York, and will want much more. This is a, could of, would of, should of, moment."

I squeezed his hand saying, "Just remember, currently we are living on the farm with your mother and brother, his wife Phebe, their daughter Sarah, 12; their sons, Joseph,10; James, 8; our son Nathan,12. This is a houseful with three women all wanting to be in charge and only one of us is the housekeeper, your Ma, Effie. It is true and very acceptable to say; I need a break from this situation."

Dyer as it may sound, ' Housekeeper' is a married woman's only identity without this there is only doing what you are told by the matriarch of the house. Obeying as if a child, obeys their parents, making a woman never ever free to make any choices or decisions. Not being in charge of the household leaves a woman with no voice.

"Remember Nathan and I are looking forward to our new home in town. You will grow to like it there too. Soon we will have our new home located right near the center of the small growing town. We will have big windows to let in lots of light and to see out to watch the going and coming of the folks. We can walk to the dry goods store, the church, and think of Nathan walking to school. Everything we need will be handy and nearby. We will not need to keep livestock to pull carts, as we can walk up and down, to the town, buying what we need."

James is not ready to move he has always been a farmer of the Stevens farm, yet with the body of a tired man. On the other hand, I am excited beyond words. This is the beginning of our new Life's Journey. We have never ever, had freedom.

Desperate to make the tense conversation light I said, " I think we should go to the Contra Dance at the Dance Hall this Saturday to celebrate our newly bought house." We both laughed as remembering when I shied away from the dance.

"The best part of owning this house, not the farm, is we will just take care of ourselves which reminds me I put your coat by the stove to warm for your ride into town."

"Thank you, Sarah.  What will be; shall always be."

Where is James? He has been gone for some time. This day is cold, but not extremely cold, looking out I see there is still snow on the dirt path from the skiff that came in the night. Enough snow to make everything fresh and clean just like our move from the farm, as we sold our farm to James's brother. They were living with us anyway since returning from Australia, when our families mother, Effie became very ill. It took their ship six weeks to get here, making the local news paper. They remained at home on the farm.

I could walk to the Village as waiting here is making me uneasy and impatient to hear those words, "The house is ours, let us move in." We know and like the people of the village, this gives us, a nice feeling of home. I cannot stand still, so I wrapped my scarf up around my face, with my coat buttoned up to my neck, boots on, and out the door I went, to walk away from the farm, to our new life; our beautiful humble home built in the new village.

I am walking up and down the so-called road, waiting to hear from my husband, who is with Bailey, the current owner of the house; this perfect place for us to live.

I now think of the last desperate words I said before James left to buy our house. "I made up my mind; we will have to pay the price." I told James, "No matter the cost; this house is to be ours. Under no circumstances will we settle for not moving into this house." I needed him to be really interested. What if he does not pay the price?

I need this house. I do not know, exactly why? The first time the house was seen by me, on that very day, I knew this house was meant to be ours!

Walking along my mind begins to think of all the changes which will be in our life as we live in town. Skowhegan is a well maintained little town, with old farms and emerging businesses. We are content and orderly people that busy ourselves; the women with gossip, the men running the town.

There is a lot of land to survey making land available to sell for building new houses. These houses have no growing space; no land for farming. It's a tight-knit community on the cutting edge for those who choose to labor not associated with farming. How encouraging to think of a life without laboring by day and night, to keep the farm going, to survive.

People buying these houses are laborers. Some at the Oil Cloth Factory, owned also by Bailey, and located on the makeshift road that runs on the north side of our soon to be house. There are carpenters, butchers, shoemakers, dressmakers, merchant plumbers, butter makers, finishes of wool, landlords, spinners, teachers, miners, we also have loggers due to the river. Some workers became borders and lodgers.

We are a town getting on our feet, struggling to build the town into a place where people will want to come, to stay in this small town with a welcoming atmosphere. The town has growing pains, building houses close together making for quaint neighborhoods, allowing us to go out our door of our house, whereas, our neighbors are in houses up and down the street. We will be near our town folks and pass the time, with a chat, a nod, or just a smile, to say hello.

On the farm there were no people. The farm was isolated due to the land it consumed leaving neighbors far away working their own farms. Life goes on without interruption, and under isolation. So our house in town is like a dream of inclusion. We will have a home in town with all the freedom. No more farms with the animals needing constant care, no crops to grow, no firewood to be cut, sawed and split. This new life seems like a dream come true for James and for me, with no more isolation where information does not exist.

There are people walking on streets going here, who knows, going there, who knows where? Some of the travelers live on our street, some I know from church, most I do not know, and sometimes I can feel their stares. They seem to know me as "The wife of James Stevens, can not remember her given name. She is kind of a quirky one, to be always on the move walking here and there, then sitting on the ground at the base of trees."

Can they tell I am listening and writing? Matters not as moving into a neighborhood makes me feel very happy!

The house makes me happy!  People however when seen clustered in a group talking about the people, who are not present sharing personal information, such as the amount of money Nathaniel paid James for the farm. This news would unequivocally give Bailey an idea of what James could afford.

People in neighborhoods would be all around to know your family, know where you were, when you work, who is at home at different times of the day. In our family, the church folks have talked of James selling the farm to his brother, Nathaniel. They all know we are planning to move into town. We also have been seen at the corner of this house, as it took awhile for us to get our money in order, while this property had been bought and sold. Now it is for sale again. Under no circumstances will we lose our chance to own this house.

Anything I asked of James, he would do and this house is so important. We have sold the farm. We cannot even think of living with all of our family in the small farmhouse. This has been our life. We need a place of our own, a house to call our home. All this waiting has me on edge.

Nathan is twelve, he will be going to the new school just down the street, down over the hill, called Bloomfield Academy. I can just picture our life being so perfect.  I was in that frame of mind, when I heard James calling,

"Sarah, Sarah,  we got the house!"

He climbed down from the wagon, there, both with our feet on the ground, we were feeling filled, with our good news. We locked hands and saw the joy in each others eyes, then in the middle of the so called road, we jumped up and down filled with excitement, not  unlike children.

He said, "I had to pay a lot for it, but we got the house."

I was taken back when he told me he paid, two thousand and fifty dollars for the house.

"I know the cost was more than we never ever imagined."

James explained, "Please no worries now, it is what it is, as we own the house; and if need be we can mortgage the property as our investment."

He said to me, "When he would not come down I negotiated to have the furniture, curtains, carpets, and all to remain in the house."

I was then sad to think, he had to pay double the price. Sad to think, Bailey had taken advantage, by knowing from the talk around town how much we had from selling the farm. After all, Bailey bought the house with no desire of personal ownership or for community connection; it was bought as a money maker, an investment of proportional profit. I felt sad for James, the true farmer purchasing a house for only shelter. Now, he will feel the pressure of laboring for funds to purchase our livelihood.

"The farm is not but a walk away and you can go back any time to help. Farming was always, your way of life, now you can choose to do a craft, to build our nest egg for our old age, which is not today by the way we are dancing around here on the snow covered carriage road."

"You are a good man and I am fortunate to be your wife. We have a lot of life, to be with a new way of living our life together."

Our home is to be an oxymoron; sadly James's burden, and equally as Sarah's joyful gift, and to become Nathan's birthright.

I was crying happy tears and looked James in his eyes and spoke, "Oh, thank you James, from the bottom of my heart. In two years we will have lived five decades, the time has ebbed away our youth, leaving us on the downhill side of life. The years have been short, and the days have been long, teaching us time is a precious gift, as our life is brief."

" In time our new home will be a blessing for our family."

"We will be fine, you will be fine."

"Sarah, as you always say, 'What will be, shall always be.'

"I love you, dearly, Mr. Stevens and every time I see you I know all is going to be alright in our life."

"I love you Mrs. Stevens. Now what do you say, are you ready to go look over our investment to see what kind of house we have purchased?"

"Yes, I am eager to go to our new house."

We are in the buggy filled with excitement to be going to our new house!

I am daydreaming of our life at this new house located past the church, on the road that leads to the burying ground, the perfect place for our new family home.

How excited I feel!

We have our own, new built house, at last, for just the three of us.

My spirits dance with pure joy,

making my heart cling to this house, some would call,

a less than perfect, ordinary house.

In my mind the house represents a glow of freedom.

It feels like an adventure,

while our homeland is on the outskirts;

of this new community.

I pinch myself to make sure this is not a dream.

*Up ahead is our house;*

*I do not own any of this land,*

*yet, the house I see is also mine.*

*"Home at last!"*

*All will be right,*

*in our world of Freedom to be...*

**_MORIA Thoughts:_**


_Sarah your happiness of being a family of three living in your new home with freedom to be, is happiness tripled._

_This is the house we recently purchased, and where I found your stories, read them, became inspired, knowing they would someday need to be published. Wisdom and knowledge protrude from within the journal of life from the past, with innovation to the future._

_All your thoughts of your days, resonate profoundly true and could, or perhaps, should, be implemented into today._

_Your words let me feel as though I know you, Sarah._


_I would be honored to have a friend like you._

_Yet, not in your_

**_'Never Ever Days'_** _of survival._


_Perhaps, here and now, in this home,_

_we have shared, over the decades of time._

# Chapter Two

# Our Dream Home

James and I are smiling, bringing on laughter as we both, at this very moment are so happy. Together our feet reach the wooden plank steps leading to the door stoop for us to enter our house laughing, knowing our future is to be lived out here in this our new home. We are blessed, also thankful beyond words.

Moreover this house is stirring up all my hidden emotions, as if, being here allows me to be myself. It is like a whirlwind of feelings. I find myself happy with the excitement of my renewed emotions. Being myself I reached over to give James a tight hug, then kissed him, not the peck, but a long kiss of love stirring up the feelings of our courting days.

James seemed stunned commenting, "Where has this Sarah been? I could get used to spending time with the girl I married."

"I know, right. I am free to be me in our own home. It is like I was in a cage, where just survival, used all my energy and became the only important element in my life. Being here in this cozy quaint place is like being let out of the cage, free to go, free to do anything I want within our own walls. This is what it feels like to be free. I am being myself." Adding,

"In this house I will be doing many of the same things I did on the farm. Here it all seems new with the purpose of being our family. If you will excuse me, I have much to do. I feel like a little child in a candy shop, going from the beginning to the end, and back again, to take it all into my thoughts, as to figure out where to put our things making a near perfect home, for just you, me and Nathan."

"Mr. Stevens, shall we, together investigate the heart of this home."

"Right here are the stairs, Mrs. Stevens."

"Albeit, you know full well the heart of the home is the kitchen. This is where we, mostly I, spend a good part of my day investing in all things cooking. Therefore you, my dear husband have always had good timely meals."

James agreed, "You are right, Mrs. Stevens."

We enter the kitchen where there is a prominent black iron cook stove with a large warming oven and a filled wood box. I said, "Nathan will be happy as bringing in the wood shall be his job."

There are plenty of floor to ceiling cupboards with big plank doors that are oiled and natural, whereas in the middle there is a long black slate sink. This gets my approval because it needs much less time consuming work than an iron one which needs constant oiling. Also over the sink are high double windows, which seem perfect for me to peer out seeing the back path where people walk, confirming I am not alone, how comforting. This room is finished off with an oil clothed linoleum of brown print design.

Off to the side is a little pantry room with a small cupboard for potatoes and onions, also a standing icebox. Built into the cupboard top is a pastry board, whereas the top of the cupboard lifts up leaving a space for rolling crusts, cookies, or kneading bread and biscuits. After each use the counter top closes to be cleaned when time permits. Anyone who cooks knows a good deal of time is cleanup whereas this will save me from rushing when cooking meals.

"I am very pleased with the heart of our home, Mr. Stevens."

"What do you think?"

"Actually I like the tin ceiling, Mrs. Stevens. Where does this door go?" He said as opening it. "Why look here, Mrs. Stevens, we have a stairway off the kitchen to the bedrooms."

"Shall we check it out? Mr. Stevens."

"Thought you would never ask, Mrs. Stevens."

"Yes we are going to be very happy in our home."

"You have heard that old saying, Mr. Stevens."

"Happy Wife — Happy Life"

"This is us today."

The kitchen stairway takes us into a room with slanted walls on both sides, created by the roof. There is one window facing west and a brick chimney, whereas the kitchen stove is under this room. The door of this room leads into a hallway with the attic door and across from this is a washroom door, along with two more doors. One leads to a bedroom with fireplace with one slanted wall, the other door opens to a hallway at the top of a stairway, where there is a closed door on the left. Opening this door is another bedroom with long windows facing east to view the road, along with the sunrise, also adjacent to a hidden closet with two steps up. This I thought as charming. We, together, chose this as our room.

Down the front stairway there is a square landing with a stained glass window, and turning the corner, go down two steps, another landing, then four more stairs into the entryway space. Entering into the next room through a wide doorway is a sitting room for guests, with plush furniture, and scatter rugs in front of the couch and the chairs, along with wall lights for proper lighting.

"Look, this room has a tin ceiling, Mr. Stevens. I cannot often recall, you sitting to talk or read. Perhaps, in this house you will find more time to sit in one of these overstuffed chairs, and relax, although this does take a great stretch of one's imagination to see you motionless."

We have a dining room quite common in the houses built in the village. It has a built-in cupboard with a glass door. The room closes off from the rest of the house with panel doors made with small glass windows, and a regular wooden door to lead into the kitchen. Now back in the kitchen there is a door that goes into the shed. Here the south wall has a door to go outside, along side of one to go into the barn, which has pine ceilings, and a makeshift workshop perfect for James to organize to turn into a place of envy. Even the barn has windows to let in the daylight. It is comforting to look out windows and see people. This place is perfect for us to grow old together, in the middle of a busy community. I am content with my happiness in life, free, to be me.

I am glad my emotions are surfacing as they have been quiet within, now they are springing up with intensity, that surprises. I had forgotten what it felt like to be me.

*I will make this house — my forever home...*
*I know this home, is the place, I am to be...*
*I will bring my white quartz rocks,*
*from my magical meadow...*
*These will hold the aura of space,*
*in this place where my spirit will reside...*

# Chapter Three

# Nathan Hates New House

I do not like this house. I want to live on the farm with Sarah and my other cousins." Nathan said to me, his mother, as if, expecting me to agree. Instead I asked, "Are you going to mock out the animal's stalls to be of help for your Uncle Nathaniel?" He looked thoughtful saying, "Sure if Sarah does."

Leaving me to reply, "That is a no then, for we all know Sarah does not do these works as she is a girl."

I knew and understood why Nathan wanted to stay at the farm with his Grandmother and his newfound cousins, who have come to Maine from Australia. Now, he has children at the farm to join in games to spend hours playing.  We only want to take him away. This is what he thinks as his childlike self awareness can only focused on himself. Nathan was angry. He did not try to hide his anger, as he was yelling,

"I am not living here in this house! I want to stay on the farm."

"Nathan, please come sit here on the stoop with me, and lower your voice as your mother is not, yet hard of hearing. I want to tell you what happened to me when I was the age of you, and your new cousin Sarah.

I had a big life change.  My mother died suddenly leaving my sister, my Paw and I, to take care of ourselves. This was my part. I was to learn to be the keeper of the house. My job was to learn how to take care of the household, my younger sister, and to run the house for Paw. I was twelve years old. I had no dreams or thoughts of what my life should be, as girls are not encouraged to do or be anything. Girls back then same as now are trained in housekeeping. Are expected to join in marriage; their life is all about having and raising children, church, clothes, canning, cleaning, also candle making, and growing small crops for food."

"The larger each family could grow with many boys the less they needed to barter, which meant a more prosperous life on the farm. Farm life is full of compromise; with change not always by choice, depending on the situation, but most often forced by mishaps. Wherever we found ourselves, we always pushed onward facing our fears, and learning to master the new task at hand. The alternative was death. Only when all was said and done did we look backward to understand how close we were to the final disaster, while all of our time we were mastering the toil of life, and moving forward."

"A real farmer knows the key to farm life is to be vigilant, to become a very determined worker, and never ever lose sight of survival. Now, I remember you have expressed many times how much you hate farm life. Is this still so?"

Nathan squirmed and answered reluctantly, "Yes."

"Nathan it is sad to be as I was at 12 years of age with no dream, and no reality of life outside of the farm. I cannot be disappointed in my life for I never ever imagined to be anyone, but what I was told, the housekeeper, wife and mother. I went from playing in the woods and my meadow to being fully responsible for my Mother's household by learning housekeeping. In fact, my whole grownup life I have been a helper of a farmer's housekeeper, learned and told as a child. Years went on, and I cannot know the darkest month or the day, that I accepted my job as a challenge. I became stealth in daily movement becoming master of the craft. After many years it became my passion to do all things of housekeeping right and on time. I was the center of the household, the master of the fate of my sister, my Paw and myself. This took much strength with determination along with teaching from Aunt Harriet."

"My poor Paw labored on the farm, feeding us and the farm animals. We felt the end was to be in the near future as it takes a family of boys to keep a farm going. Doing the best we could, we kept it going as we had no other choice. I never ever thought to how hard it was for my Paw, but I gave a lot of thought to my unfair situation. I had no friends to miss, no one, as the nearest farm was miles away. There were no playing games, no time for fun swims in the summer, barely time for a quick bath. Leaving me to quiet days filled with work to learn, then relearn, what was the 'art of housekeeping.' In the beginning, I had no idea or any knowledge of this job, I was called to do."

"Just thinking back to this daunting task makes my heart race, as it did when I was a child, full of fear. I was scared of doing mostly everything wrong, and I felt paralyzed, as I tried to remember all the steps of the household chores taught to me by Aunt Harriet. This was a time where the long shadow of grief prevailed. Grief for the quick abandonment of my mother, by death, and grief for the abandonment of my childhood freedom. No longer was there time for carefree nature journeys, even though all things of nature captured my heart as they do till this day."

"I was nervous about all the jobs I needed to do and conger, especially the wood burning black iron cooking stove. I can tell you many funny facts about the twelve year old housekeeper, and what a sorry, sad, silly choice for survival, was this scared little girl. No one has any idea what it feels like to do all the work each day of your life, and have no other choice. I was needed, as I was the only one available to learn the routine of running the farm. I cried myself to sleep each night, and was heartbroken to be alone all the long day, while trying to master my fate of housekeeping."

"One day my mother was here, and the next I was to replace my mother's job, her role she chose as housekeeper, which was filled with pride. No one ever expected me to be perfect like my mother, but there were certain expectations; the biggest and hardest one tending the stove, to be able to cook meals on time. Never ever did she teach her daughter how, and without my Aunt's teaching, I would have given up, although she showed me no pity. We had very little time with lots to learn, as winter was approaching."

"Imagine the change from being a carefree girl running through the meadow, into a serious young girl learning to be a housekeeper, without any of the knowledge needed to do justice to the job. It was what it was. It was my time to be there for my family, so my sister and I would be together, and not put in the workhouse. The air catches in my chest just now, remembering the hardship on us all. We all got thrown into this time of our lives, this time I would never ever again choose to live. I know what being twelve years old can be, and what it should not be."

"You have a mother and father looking forward to watching you grow into a young man. We are here for you, we love you, and cannot let your need to play throw us away. You can visit cousin Sarah and the boys on the farm, perhaps stay overnight with the approval from your grandmother. Your home will remain here with us. Long as we are all on this earth, we will be honored by our son's presence in our home."

"I love you Nathan. Let us go in and fix up your new room. A space all your own. What do you say?"

He looked so sad and muttered, "Do I have to?"

"My answer is — yes. This sadness will pass, and you will learn from the unhappiness of moments in your life. They will spur your thoughts into growth. You will learn your strengths, and find a way to do the things in life that will give contentment. We all have times when we need to do things which make us feel unhappy. It is these times which help mold our determination to leave behind the unhappiness, then this sad unhappiness, leaves within us a strength, to tell us we can overcome all, by facing the problem, excepting, and living out the trial. This is why Nathan, you must always be ready to accept where you are in life."

"Now, see the problems, as steps up to where you want to be. Make plans for your best life even in the darkest saddest moments. The life you want will grow out of the life you are living. Through it all, keep your dreams alive even when you are not able to feel the grasp of them. See your life's desires clearly, and hang onto this dream tightly. Then when asked, what you want to be when you grow up? Say clearly what you want out of your life. I want you to follow your dreams, which will grow into many different realities as you mature."

"Living here in town is convenient to school, and you will make many friends. This will be a different life for all our family, but a very necessary move. Please give it a steadfast try."  Nathan breathed out heavily and muttered "Alright." I did so much want to hug him. Nathan was not receptive to hugs, even as a young child, and now he is more standoffish. Is this karma? As my mother and I were not familiar with hugs.

"For years I worked and questioned not, as I was too tired to dream.  I was trained, even as, I did not choose to be a housekeeper, yet never ever questioned my place in life. I did not know what to do. I was a child, whereas I did what I was told. At first my best was not perfect. It was a horrible time in my young life; when I seemed alone with long dark shadows over me, changing me, and claiming my life, all for the good of our family. Then I met your father and started to dream of love, then my life as a girl, that I thought was long lost. Next I became his wife, and of course then your mother.  Today I am, also the housekeeper, for the good of my family. The biggest difference is, it is my choice made with love and my freedom of choice."

"We love you. We will help you grow into a successful young man, with all your dreams coming true. Choose wisely, as if, your whole life awaits your choices. To achieve, dream big, as life moves quickly, and time awaits, none."

"Your father and I have a saying to explain our strength of love. "What will be, shall be —As of late, I have learned to add 'as long as moving forward' and your father adds 'always be."

"If love was tangible wealth; you my son would be the richest!"

***MORIA Thoughts:*** *Sarah, you are a wonderful example of love to your son— by sharing your young life so full of hurts and disappointments, telling this tale to the angry boy, who was set on only what would make him happy, in this moment. Your sharing helped him see you as a person, who understood from your own unpredictable childhood. As parents, your love and caring will lead him onward.  Sharing with your son, his parents, life long promise, is priceless...*

**'What will be, shall always be, as long as moving forward.'**

# CHAPTER FOUR

# Supper Time

I remember as a child spending time outside playing with my younger sister. On this day we were drawing pictures at the edge of a mud puddle with a pointy stick. We drew the sun, the trees, flowers and I attempted a bird, but birds and people never ever were identifiable when drawn by me.

My mother opened the door calling, "Time to come in and wash up for supper. Your father will be coming anytime from a hard days work in the fields, and he will want his supper."

We always went to the sink to wash the sweat off our heads and the dirt from our hands, today that included our arms, then looking cleaner we would await Paw, who would do a makeshift wash up before eating. I looked at our mother stirring the boiling pot of stew, on the old black cook stove, so it would not catch on the bottom causing a burnt taste. Her face was flushed, also she looked hot and tired, after a long day of housekeeping.

In came our Paw all washed up and sat at the head of the table. Mother took three big scoops of stew, setting the plate in front of Paw, while he was drinking a big glass of water. Then she took two small plates, putting a small scoop in each for us girls. Mother had a medium plate for herself in which she placed one scoop. It smelled so good as steam rolled off the top. "Eat before it gets cold."

This was too hot and it bit my tongue. No one talks whilst we eat. I looked at my mother, and kind of stared to get her attention.

"What is it Sarah?"

"I think it is too hot for my mouth." I said.

"Oh then, just eat around the outside edge of your plate, as Paw and I do." This was perfect, still hot, not too hot, to burn.

After the meal mother cleared then washed the table top, where she instructed us girls to sit, to work on school tasks, while she cleaned up by washing and drying the dishes, and putting them away. The stew that was left had a heavy iron cover put on top of it, to save for us if it did not sour, or the pigs, if it was uneatable. Pigs, I think can eat anything.

I am surprised my sis and I can speak clearly, as no one in our family never ever had much to say. After eating Paw would routinely go outside to check on everything. Tonight he said, "Good meal, Mary."

I thought I saw him wink, but then I always have been told I have an active imagination.

When it begins to form twilight, this is the most beautiful time of the evening, when all of nature glows. We start lighting candles, as darkness creeps quickly inside. Mother comes to inspect our work, and us on the side to see if more washing up is needed. Soon we will put on our night clothes because at dusk, we are all headed to bed. Early to bed, early to rise; makes a man healthy, wealthy and wise. Or in our case more time to toll in the daylight hours.

Mother says to us often at daybreak when she awakens us, "We are gifted to begin a new day, to enjoy." Today she added, "This is a new Spring day with a growing season just to begin. We are blessed with a mackerel sky which is telling us less than 24 hours dry. This will be perfect timing for our newly seeded gardens."

This is how life is for Eliza and I. In the morning we do a few chores, which I think was Paw's idea, as it has to do with watering and feeding the animals and chickens, after which we are free as a bird till lunch time.

So anyone can see we did not have much upbringing, and no work which could give us the satisfaction of being needed, which would have given us confidence to deal with what life always expects from all who belong in a society.

We live in isolation as only our family. We are not attending school or church goers. We are good people with survival being our main focus. My paw is strong allowing our family, not to fear for the future. We just keep on doing what is needed, to keep our lives on track by any means available.

You could say our family is blessed. We have the necessities; food, shelter and cleanliness. We are blessed, if you do not notice, there are no male children to help grow the farm, and perhaps to help face a life that can be cruel. Paw never complains, never ever says much at all.

Paw is up at sunrise to feed and care for the farm animals, then a quick breakfast and out the door till the evening meal, near the time just before sunset.

Before he starts his long day he fills his saddle bag with food to eat that need no cooking or utensils, canteens  filled with fresh water to last all the day long, and off he goes to do whatever needs to get done, as there is a season for all works, to keep a farm alive.

On Mondays, if the skies are clear Paw hooks up Molly to the wagon and lugs out the clothes to go with us to Nana's to be washed and hung in the sun to dry. All the Aunts and children get to visit on this family wash day.

Paw stays home on the farm and does not seem to miss not being able to go along, none of our Uncles go either, yet I can tell he misses Molly.

On our return, when he hears her hoofs coming he comes quickly, taking her into the barn making sure she gets comfortable with food and rest. So anyone would see my Paw as caring, hard working and a man who looks after our Mother and us, all on the farm.

Whatever he knows or thinks is perhaps a secret...

I think of quiet people, as secret keepers, to be private thinkers of a life not lived, and or, shared, in public, as they remain to their selves. Never ever the less, but not with the same fear of discovery, as a protective secret keeper. Instead, could be an attempt to avoid notice, in a manner characterized by quietness, as to prefer to be alone to foster deep profound thoughts.

This is my Paw.


***MORIA Thoughts:***

*I lived as a child in a country neighborhood, everyone knew each other, and these people built our childhood memories. Our community was one of different folks, yet we knew if in need, we could count on each other. This was our hometown with our family of neighbors.*

*Our father worked, sun up to sunset cutting wood in the woodlot with his brother, then trucking it to the mills. The rainy days made working to cut pulp wood to hard with mud and puddles. Dad would be home and this was our day to go somewhere in the car, a rainy day adventure. These were unexpected days to spend with our parents, riding in the rain.*

*They both worked, yet we ate our meal together as a hungry family awaiting suppertime, as snacking before a meal was frowned upon, as to spoil your appetite.*

*Have not thought of this family time in a while now. Your words bring back memories, to be as gifts, thank you, Sarah.*

# CHAPTER FIVE

# Winter Storms

The sky is gray with the air cold and within is a dampness that permeates to your core. Could this be the beginning of a Northeaster storm?

We will not want to be surprised. All will be affected by how well we prepare. First and foremost will be to take care of the farm animals. The horse needs to be blanketed, fed extra grain, and forking in hay throughout their stalls. The cows will be milked, fed and given extra hay. The pigs also can be fed, and given hay to lay for their bed, as they also will be moved inside. The chickens are not free to run, as all will remain in the barn awaiting the storm to diminish from the winds and snow. I helped my Paw by getting pails of water, one at a time because I am not strong like a boy.

There is a chorus of sounds; as they are neighing, mowing, oinking, and clucking, all in simultaneous rebellion of not being free, even though it is for their own good. Later they will settle down. Paw decides to run a rope line to the barn, in case, it is necessary to go feed the cooped up animals in a white out of a blizzard.

In the meantime we must gather in the wood for the stove. When the wood box is filled, we continue to put wood along the wall, and also just outside the door in case we get snowed inside, as could happen in a big storm. This feels like a storm maker with all the signs supporting a big storm. We look and see, there are no birds or squirrels in the farm yard. They know the signs, which we have learned, to abide by their natural instincts of nesting, putting us on track of our survival.

Our folks were making sure all preparations were put in place to preserve and protect the people, animals, and the farm.

Blankets are gathered and some are nailed up as a curtain for a temporary wall. This is done to allow the wood stove to heat a smaller area. We also have dragged a mattress onto the floor to allow a sleeping place in the warmth of the kitchen.

Mother has been filling big kettles with water at the sink with the hand pump. If it gets real cold outside the water would freeze, so it is best to draw enough water to cook and drink. It is not for washing up or doing the dishes, the water is saved for survival. We must also gather candles and oil for the lanterns.

We are organized and await the storm as Paw says,

"Snug as a bug, in a rug."

It is fear of the out of control wind and snow that raises us to transform our way of life into this mode of survival, for we have known people who have died by not being prepared. Even if this is not a big life threatening storm the fact, it could be gives us the strength to prepare. So far the signs have been right, allowing us to sit out the storm comfortably by the warmth of the fire, with hot drinks and freshly cooked stews. This is the adventure I remember.

We were fortunate to have our parents, who made our lives one of great substance. We did not have money or fame, nor did not have the church family. What we had was a sense of belonging, to parents with common sense, to protect us from the dangers of life. We, children never ever felt the fear, laying claim to our parents, of the possible loss, as the storm could cause damage claiming their livelihood. Our folks constant thoughts of survival of the farm meant the well being of us, all, as they continued the fight of survival.

Who would ask for anything more than to have a warm cozy place to stay during a northeaster. These memories are of when we were warm, and all together in a small room listening to the windy northeaster blowing the cold snow outside. For us girls this out of control weather became an adventure. Our Mother and Paw, played cards with us. We were a real family with talking and inclusion. These have become my most heartfelt memories; at the same time the storms became my parent's fight for survival.

Responsibilities claim the wonder of life...

### *MORIA Thoughts:*

*To have 'out of the box' experiences with your parents creates a fond memory as they happened outside of the everyday homelife. Leaving many to want to capture the feeling, of gathering together within different surroundings. Perhaps this is why today camps at lakes are popular places to spend our summertime.*

# CHAPTER SIX

# Summer Woodland Friends

My summertime friends were Arwen and Aspen. I never ever spoke any words to tell of the fairies near the forest, not to my Mother, my Paw or my sister. The fairies won over my alliance to keep their secret life in the woodland to myself.

At the edge of the meadow, I closely observed my friends—the lovely, beautiful beings whom I never ever, even once touched. Their concerns for me went beyond caring; they truly impacted my life by taking me under their wings, so to speak, by helping me decipher life. I will write what I know of their existence, as they were a large part of my meadow life, and I am ever so grateful.

The Fairies are woodland creatures, whom befriended me as a young child. My first sight was in the rose bush, I routinely stopped to smell—one of my favorite scents to this very day. First, looking closely for bees, while reaching for a fully opened blossom of the pink rose, this one was perfect as touching the petals felt smooth as silk. Holding this beautifully formed pink rose made my thoughts dance to sunrise and sunsets, as they too give such a feeling of awe.

Bringing the rose to my nose inhaling the scent allowed my thoughts to be still, leaving me transformed as a part of the flower. I had the rose cupped in my hand, breathing in deeply while closing my eyes, to enhance the scent without any distractions. My busy mind brought thoughts creeping into this perfect moment. Mother's words interrupted: "I am anxious to leave early to go to Nana's to do the wash, as there are signs of afternoon rain storms. Do your chores quickly. Do not dottle about."

Upon opening my eyes, I saw this most beautiful being of the same color of the pink rose. On its back were wings like a butterfly, also pink, and seemed to be glowing without any movement. This creature was in front of my eyes, speaking,

"You caught me watching you. Please do not tell of me. No one will believe you. We all, the others like me, are the Fairies, whom live at the edge of the woods, at the back edge of the meadow. We would like to be your friends. Come visit us. See you later..."

The Fairy was gone from my sight. Where did it go?

I was not scared. Instead I was intrigued by this talking creature, who was to be found by the edge of the woods in the meadow. When at first I saw this pink fairy there was an enchantment with a connection to this beautiful winged creature, whom I felt was kind and friendly. It was not strange, just an event where we immediately liked each other. I was excited for tomorrow to go into the meadow to play, even though knowing, I would need to bring my sister. We were allowed to go to the meadow as long as we came back to the house when Mother rang the bell.

So I searched and looked in all places, and never ever saw one sign of their being where it was said they lived. Then it dawned on me, my sister was not asked to visit. Eliza noticed the circles of very green taller grass asking me, "Why is the grass growing in circles?"

I looked and despondently said, "I do not know. Shall we go back? It is hot up here."

"Sure, it is also boring," she replied.

That very night Paw hung a swing from the old oak tree and my sister, Eliza claimed this as her own. This was fine by me as I felt the call to go into the meadow, all by myself to see the fairies. Whom were beautiful, and awaiting my appearance. I was sure they would be watching for my visit. None were to be seen. I could not find them. I saw not a one. After many days my hunt became tiring, whereas my attention was transformed to the birds with their fluttering wings and musical songs.

I was sitting in the shade of the trees being content with my surroundings, thinking: This will be my 'Magical Meadow.' How enchanting are the birds' songs. My senses were full, I was relaxed, and feeling a part of all in this very spot in my chosen place.

I heard a voice, "Life is good, yes. You are happy within?"

"Yes, where have you been? I have missed seeing you."

"We have been here awaiting you to stop looking.  We, fairies can be invisible to the eye unless we choose to be seen. We, the fairies only appear to those who genuinely believe, and were chosen. We wish to share with you in your love of nature."

"We will spend time with you. I answer to the name of Arwen."

I saw another, "You may call me Aspen, and shall we call you Sarah?"

"Yes, please. I feel special. Is that alright?"

"Yes, but of course. You are special holding a place within all the Fairies Realm. We are protectors of children we choose."

"Those who genuinely believe are within our realm. We know the lie in belief of those not genuine."

"Why me and not my sister?"

"You, Sarah, have a strong sense of nature. It is like our strong connection to the forest, flowers, trees, and where we communicate with all animals and plants."

"We will help you develop and inspire your creativity and imagination, to pleasure all..."

In the distance, I saw another beautiful fairy and more were appearing. They were talking in a speech whereas I knew not what they were saying, my voice was not their natural speech. I was overwhelmed by their grace, and how beautiful each one appeared.

"How exotic you all appear within your many colors. I feel inferior to be here."

"Nonsense, you are in our realm because we welcomed you. We see you from the inside, which is like us, to the outside of a growing child, who will then become a beautiful fully loving woman. It is the child in you, whom we are befriending to tend to your every need, bringing good fortune in this time of your full life of happiness within your meadow life. We will prepare you to handle the opposite; the sadness all cannot escape throughout their long life. We will help you to be strong, knowing peace from within your beautiful soul."

I grew to love Arwen, who was pink as a rose, and Aspen, who was green as a grasshopper, and always did as they asked.

One Summer time I collected white quartz rocks because "I will need them in my future," for what I knew better than to ask, even though I knew not why, I trusted them to have a reason.

The day I found a piece of rock that sparkled in the sun pleased them so much. They asked me to place what they called shale, near the edge of the woods. My rocks were placed always in a pile next to the big rock where I sit in the magical meadow.

The next day at the edge of the woods there was a circle of darker greener taller grass around the glass-like shale pieces. I have seen these circles of patches of grass which grew faster and greener, also mushrooms growing in perfect circles.

When Arwen and Aspen came over I said, "I was surprised to see the growth around your shiny shale rocks. My big pile of white rocks has no such growth." They laughed, and in the background there was a choir of laughter, then was said in unison, "We were dancing!"

Arwen continued, "In a circle in this special place of magical happenings. This is joyous and gives life, creating the grass to grow faster and greener, or mushrooms sprout in the perimeter of a circle. The great amount of shale created fairy dust for the fairies to fly. We call the circles 'Fairy Rings.' We dance in the dark of night, and we are involved with magical properties to create."

"I wish I could dance," I said.

"If it makes you feel good to see our end results, remember we also dance at times to benefit you."

"Knowing you dance for me makes me feel special."

"No, it makes you special!"

"I have seen you collecting bird feathers. Look to your right, my left and walk until you see more than enough feathers."

"What color are the feathers?"

No answer, as she is gone. This happens all the time as they can be here, there, then nowhere, to be seen...

My Magical Meadow has become an enchanting beautiful place, a land of Fairies...

Fairies taught me — of my deepness within —a place for  belief.

Told of how I am special— to be ultimately who I was born to be.

The Fairies taught me— to be worthy with my gift of Joy.

To promote the ability— to perceive what is good and true.

Have common sense— to be with sound judgement.

Have possession of much knowledge — to be as wise.

To one day have my desired life filled with love — To Be

**FAIRIES REFLECTIONS :**

So this was the beginning of my Summer days spent with the Fairies, my friends, and guardians as they were watching over me assuring my well-being. They were not always within my visual sight, still I felt their presence. They were on the earth and spiritual so always with me, helping me to learn the many lessons of life, without interfering in my childish ways...

**Arwen spoke:** "Deep within each person there is a secret place to hold belief, the core is who each one was born to be, so this place, no one else would fully understand. Focus your attention on not fighting the old ways you were taught, but in living the new ways, will lead to dreams brought forth to reality. Innocent children hold the key to life. It is not imaginings..."

**Aspen added:** "It is the truth. Most children are convinced they have a great imagination, then told not to speak of what they think, they know. Innocent children hold the key to their life, then lose their dreams by listening to others."

**Arwen spoke of choices:** "We must talk of choice, to choose the right path to have the key to know life, bringing forth the power  that lays dormant until you accept to know all, as you are known."

**Arwen continued:** "There is nobody like you. Looking to be other than self, is not going to be who you are at the core. This is to be your task— " To Be."

**Aspen reflected:** "A star danced at your birth, instilling a full sense of nearness to the mysterious fountain of Joy. You take pleasure in the little things, perceiving the world as it is, thus perceive your modest place in it, with a feeling of gratitude for what is yours, and never ever longing for what you have not..."

**Arwen advised:** "The foundation of life is to believe in work, not apathy, have faith, know your God, know your worth. You were born with purpose; of being. Find your place in life on earth, whether it is big or small, it will be blessed with success, only if you take the path prepared for your life."

**Aspen continued:** "All journeys are connected throughout the Universe, most never ever know or suspect. Think of this as you look to the sky. There is not a moment of any day when nature is not showing a perfectly beautiful scene. Picture the beauty of all, everyone, wherever, and however far away, are able to just look up to see the view. The sky is there for all to see and appeals to the immortal in us. It is essential to the spirit of life and yet, people never ever attend to the beauty of the sky. Extraordinary skies of darkness do cause all to notice as a warning to take cover. The sunrise, or sunset, or the puffs of clouds, in all ways are there to be seen and or, lost in our apathy..."

**Arwen whispered:** "God fills the Universe silently without noise; Nature fills the heart and soul of children."

**Aspen added:** "The sign of the Universe is love in a perfect world all humans are each connected to one another through love. Those who have lived in your heart, will remain as loves within the heart and in your mind, are their words and deeds to comfort."

**Arwen spoke of darkness:** "We must talk of death with the sense of darkness that floods all the heart and mind, shadowing the love that never ever leaves. The light of wisdom gives power to gradually overtake gloom, leaving the darkness, to be overcome by the early dawn. The sunrise becomes day, with the full light of the sun, our life is exposed with a call to move on, as we live our life..."

**Aspen concluded:** "Hold these times in your 'magical meadow' as 'happiness memories' alive in your heart, in your very soul; for they will endear life, and give a lifetime of love for all the days, yet to be... all your life is to be with you always, you are Sarah..."

**Arwen reflected:** "Sarah say, and remember. Yes, these memories will be with me always, and nothing will take them away from the life they have shown to my heart and soul."

**Arwen concluded:** "Daydreams help the fulfillment of visions, hopes, wishes, to become reality. Let your mind wander with wishful creation of imagination, enjoying imaginary thoughts as real."

**Arwen spoke of choices:** "We must talk of choice, to choose the right path, to have the key, to know life bringing forth the power that lies dormant, until you accept and know all, as you are known."

**Sarah reflected:** "Fairies are not only beautiful, they are wise, kind, helpful, and disposed to do good. The fairies of my 'Magical Meadow' are the guardians of the natural world with a strong connection to the forest where they communicate with all animals, plant life, also children like me."

*My loves forever are... Arwen and Aspen.*
*I, Sarah remain ever grateful...*

# CHAPTER SEVEN

# Words Of My Mother

Today started the same as every other day. Feeding the chickens, to then getting each and every hen off her nest to easily collect their eggs, and give them fresh water. Next, move on to the pigs with food scraps. It rained overnight, leaving the ground wet, so they had dug holes to roll in the puddles that had formed. Here they are completely covered with mud, and they were oblivious to their stinky smell. This means when the sun dries out the pen I will need to pitch fork in fresh hay before nightfall, giving them a dry place to sleep. For now, they are content to roll in the mud and the muck. We raise pigs every year, this year we only have four pigs; one for us to winter over by salting and canning, and three to barter for other needs on the farm.

Done with all chores I am free to go visit the meadow until time for lunch, when Mother rings the bell to come eat. Eliza is swinging on her swing which Paw put up on the old oak tree, and when looking for Eliza we go there first, as this is her favorite pastime. As for me, I walked to my rock pile. The rocks are all white quartz and form a big pile since I started collecting. They were plentiful at first, lately, I never see as many. Perhaps I have enough. The fairies told me, "I would collect as many as I need."

The day is becoming warm with happiness everywhere in my Meadow. The birds are singing, while the squirrels and chipmunks appear to be dancing over the grass while going to the wildflowers for their gathering of seeds. Their cheeks are stuffed full, and I think they make the job of survival seem like fun. My time has passed quickly making me feel that I have just arrived, when I notice the sun is high in the sky signaling noon has arrived. I must go eat lunch. This is Mother's one rule, so I turn to run towards home, when in the air I hear the ringing of Mother's bell. I must hurry, knowing if I am late, I will not be able to return to the meadow today.

We washed our hands and faces, to appear as children who have breeding, not little rascals of the field. My life is  perfect. Good food to fill me when hungry, even if, I never ever felt hungry before beginning to eat. After eating we put our scraps into the pigs' pail, putting the cover on tight as not to have fruit flies in the pantry, our plate is placed in the dishpan, as was the household rule.

Then I turned to run out the door to run back to my sanctuary of nature. My mother called out, "Not so fast young lady. We have the business of schooling. Go to the bin for paper and a writing tool. Sarah, write a story of life on the farm. Make it one page with proper printing, punctuation, and spelling."

I quickly wrote about my Paw, and the horses working in the garden and how he grew most of our food and that he looked tired at supper time and mother was the best cook ever. There, done in no time. My mother read this, looking disappointed. I was trying to remember what I had written as she looked sad.

She said, "Sarah Pitts, this is the most outrageous spelling of words, with worse grammar and your printing is not legible. Many run-on sentences, without proper punctuation. Your afternoons or mornings, your choice, must be spent learning proper writing."

All I heard was no afternoon, or no morning in the meadow, so I said, "I do not like learning. It is keeping me all locked up in the house."

"This is never ever the matter if your writing skills are dreadfully bad. The story could have been quite enjoyable, if I did not spend my time reading to decipher the words, with such incorrect spelling. We will start with spelling. We will get your Aunt Harriet to give me a proper spelling list for your age. After spelling we will go to proper use of words  you can now spell."

I do not want to hear her describe how awful my words are, so I spoke up with defiance, "I wish I was deaf and then I could no longer hear your words."

"Perhaps you should save your wishes for something you desire, and or, hope to happen. Deafness is not a wish  anyone wants to happen. A wish is something you want, something good. My wish is one day you will succeed with your learning, leading to one day being able to write properly, so anyone can read your thoughts. Have no fear of you not learning, as all can be taught the basics of the printed word."

"Sarah, you on the other hand, have a gift of painting a picture with your words by seeing clearly the events around you. It would be a shame if you do not learn to write properly. Perhaps, when you conquer spelling, sentence structure, punctuation, and neatness of print, you will rewrite the story of your Paw on the farm."

"For now, until we get the list, when you go up into the field I want you to take a book to read. This will act as a guide for you to see the proper way of writing. Through reading even if you never ever write another tale, you will learn. There will always be letters, notes, and lists, no one would take the time to decipher. They will never ever read what you have written leaving an important tool of expression lost, not to mention the expression of communicating, or by telling a tale about a farmer."

"This learning will seem hard, but not too hard for my smart Sarah. Learning will bring you the discovery of the joy of expression, whereas someday you may pin a book."

Writing is hidden for my personal joy, while I write without hesitation. Thanks be to Mother.

Rewritten for my Mother

**My Paw—-by Sarah Fletcher Pitts**

Looking off into the field that seems endless... with straight rows of freshly growing crops, my eyes see Paw stopping to drink from his water jar. The sun is high in the sky, making the air seem too hot to take a breath. Then I noticed he took out a pan and gave the horse some of the water.

Soon they will stop to rest and cool down in the barn. Paw will wipe down his helper whom we call Molly, and give her fresh hay. Sometimes when I walk by the barn I hear Paw say, "Thank you, girl. You did a good job today. You rest now, as it is too hot to work."

My Paw has not much to say with trivial talk. When he speaks it is from his heart, and he is a man of his word. The animals are like his family, whereas they love and trust my Paw.

My Mother seems to be at ease when Paw comes in from the fields; tired, thirsty, and hungry. This is where my Mother shines the most, with her big wonderful meals which are hot and ready on time. My Paw never ever needs to wait on his supper, as we are all seated for the moment he appears. No matter how hot the weather, we have a freshly cooked meal, fit for a King.

*"Our King, Paw..."  Love, Sarah*

# CHAPTER EIGHT

# Mother Leaves

On this night our Mother became ill. I was saddened without tears as I was mad. God did not answer my prayers. I had been on my knees all night long, leaving my legs feeling tingly and stiff. I do not understand 'why' my Mother died.

My Paw went in the wagon to my Mother's family, and they came and took her away.

I felt unseen and unheard. The house is still and now feels as if abandoned, all is quiet, without the movement of the broom, or dishes, and the stove is burning down. In this room is just my Paw and I, as Eliza is swinging under the old oak tree. I think the stillness is closing in on Paw, as he said, "Sarah, could we sit outside on the door stoop in the sunshine of this day?"

I knew he was sad, as his face was drained of color. I also was sad, but I did not want to cry. Instead, I felt the anger taking root in me.

"I have some family things, I promised your Mother, I would tell you. This will be a lot that I never ever wanted to talk about ever again. Even though I told your Mother we would talk, I probably would not bring these things up that have been left unsaid, if I was not so worried about your anger."

I felt I needed to defend myself. "It is just I prayed hard because I wanted Mother to get better, but instead the horrible fact is Mother died. It is as though my love for my Mother was not enough to have her stay here at home with us."

Paw looked so sad, as he spoke. "Sarah, I know you love, and need your Mother, and the sad truth is you only have your old Paw so bear with me. First, we are not responsible for others death, when their time comes to pass over. We can love them, help, and pray for them, but we have not been given the power to prevent their deaths. We must accept their time for life, by letting them go."

"This is what I must share with you. Let me start at the beginning of my life when we lived amongst people in a community in the State of Massachusetts. We, my parents, three brothers, and I had to leave what was our home because my father signed up for free land in Canna, quite a few acres, whereas the only thing required was to homestead the land."

" My father was a drinking man, my mother a church goer, and us four boys had no say of what happened in our family. My Pa, bought a still to make moonshine with some of the funding, that was part of the homesteading plan. We were to buy wood stoves, chimney bricks, then cut trees to build a house. We would need axes and saws along with a good deal of knowledge. My brothers and I built this house where we now live. We were in pain each and every day from the work of cutting the logs and moving them by hand."

"When my father dipped into the drink he would become as angry, a man, as you would ever see. He was mean and argumentative. We would get knocked around and punched, for no reason, other than his internal anger. My brothers were talking of leaving, just walking away, which was what they did when the house was built, and the barn was raised by the help of our town folks."

"I was left with this drunken lunatic, and my Ma, who spent her days up in the field at 'The Prayer Rock' as she so called it.  The work of the farm was all on me. I knew better than to talk out loud of anything, as he would become angry, so I never ever spoke after my brothers left. When my father was in a bad angry spell, I would hide in the barn with my animal friends."

"My mother was able to quiet him, and get him to lay down to sleep it off, until this one day he became enraged, afterward I never ever saw my mother. I do not know if she left, or if she died. One morning she was there, and at night she was gone. My father never ever spoke one word of explanation or expressed any worry or wondering about where she was."

"My days were guarded, due to my father being unpredictable, and if he saw me he would holler loudly and angrily, coming after me. The only thing keeping me from a beating was how fast I could run. Sometimes he would sneak up on me, swinging a board, or a stick, or anything, to take me down. Times were hard."

"One night I noticed no smoke in the chimney. The next day there was no smoke in the chimney. I needed to check his whereabouts, so I went into the house. I looked around and he was nowhere to be found. Later when I checked his moonshine still, it was gone, along with bottles—everything was gone."

"I lived alone farming from fourteen years old to a young man of eighteen. Then I put a notice in the church saying I had a farm and I needed a wife, and this is how I found my helpmate, your dear Mother, Mary. Before she became part of my life on the farm, I told her of my life alone for four years, which was lonesome, yet not as hard as always watching over my shoulder. I suspected he was capable of killing me when he was drinking, for I knew in my heart my poor mother never ever would have left me alone with this man full of brew. I still miss my Ma. She being the only reasonable sense, or resemblance of love, in my young life."

"I hope she ran off like my brothers, but deep down, I felt he got out of control with the moonshine taking away his senses. If anyone was to meet my father they would have seen, he was not able to keep order on this farm. I made sure that the farm looked as attended to ward off those unscrupulous persons from taking over all that I had left."

"I am telling you this to have you understand anger. I want you to know that anger unabated, can control your life, allowing for destruction. I promised your mother I would tell you of my life. I am sorry your mother passed away. She was the life of our home. I will miss Mary so much...

Paw paused for a time.

I have been alone. I can survive. It was nice to have a companion. It is you and your sisters I fear will resent our struggle to survive here on the farm."

Paw looked sad saying, "Your Mother's family are hoping to prepare you and Eliza to take care of the household. Aunt Harriet has said she will come, and stay to teach you housekeeping. You both are healthy and smart. It will all work out, and we will have each other. We will all do our best. Any questions?"

My answer, "No. I am sorry you have lost your mother and now your wife. You do not seem angry. Thanks, Paw, for teaching me your life. It is a shame that love leaves. I will never ever leave."

Paw took my shaking hand. "Sarah, no one knows what will become of their future. We can always only do our best with the time we are given. My Mary is gone and life must go on. Please do not worry—your Paw will protect all which becomes important to you. The nature of change makes life impossible to predict, just know I love you girls. Even though she has passed, her goodness lives on, and this makes me feel hopeful. We never ever forget the people who loved us, then made us feel, and be special."

"Never ever let go of the collection of memories from the life she gave you, including the lessons in writing she knew were in your heart. When you look back, look not at the hurts and the wrong decisions. Trust yourself—it starts from within, then move forward with your trust, as was given in the beginning with your Mother."

Paw then said, "I know I am quiet. Just remember you girls are all I have as family. Now I need to go to the barn and tend our livestock, as their needs are always present, no matter what goes on in life."

"Are you going to be alright, Sarah?"

"I am fine. I am not angry. I love you, Paw."

Giving my Paw the longest ever, tightest ever, hug, I said, "Give our Molly this extra hug from me."

This is day one, of our struggle to loom ahead. I already miss my Mother.

Paw left, and I stayed, listening to the sounds of the farm animals as they got excited when Paw went to the barn. They know he is going to care for all their needs each and every day, just as he depended on them when he was all alone.

My sister and I also will be looked after by Paw, although it is not the same, as Mother who is always available. Last week when I fell, scraping my knee, Mother was in the house, and in no time, it was checked, the dirt washed off. She said, "I think you will live," and out the door I went feeling happy.

If my no-nonsense mother had lived, she would have helped me overcome my fear of people, which is noted as shyness. It freezes me into silence, even as I learnt to spell and use the words to describe all the activities in my life. I have never ever had the confidence to share any of my words. All of my stories lie dormant. This my Mother would never ever have allowed. I have lost my champion who thought I would pin a book. I may write a book for my mother who believed in my ability, although without her, there will not be the confidence to share my story.

Then I think of my poor Paw, who was alone most of his life. He had a Paw who was obsessed with drink, which brought forth demons, and a Ma who was obsessive with prayer, allowing no room for the real-life needs of her boys. Three of the boys escaped, leaving my Paw to fend for himself. In all of his life, he stayed diligent to overcome the hardships of being an orphan, even though he had a makeshift family that was not there for him.

My Paw needs Eliza and I to be a family of three, now that Mother has passed. It is more important than ever we stay together on this farm Paw helped build.

I know Mother was important to Paw, as she brought him an acceptance of life. She somehow knew to accept the life you are given, and to rise above the limitations. She helped Paw feel, as if the weight and burdens of the world were now theirs to share.

Paw feels alone again as his Mary is gone, and we girls feel all alone, as our Mother is also gone from our sight.

Her dependable, never ever changing ways of no-nonsense love has been taken away, leaving a life of uncertainty for all that was in her capable care.

All our lives will be changed forever.

On this the first night without Mother, Paw built up a fire, cooking up fried eggs and canned green beans there was no bread or biscuits. We ate then Paw said,

"You two go to bed and after I settle in the animals, I will be down here. So worry not, this will take time to become used to us finding our way without your mother."

In our bedroom, I first tucked in Eliza saying, "No worries I will take care of you. We have each other and our Paw." I reached down and gave her a hug. "It will be better later on, tonight the first night, without our mother, is the hardest. I have been sad too, all the day long. You can come into my bed, if you need to know you are not alone."

The core of my being is to deny Mother died, yet to this long day, my mind travels back in time, bringing tears for Mothers death and Paws sad past, whereas I have no one to tell. Eliza is too young and Paw is done sharing the sad tale of his abandoned youth. I must live with this truth of the past, as if a secret.

The night was long, and restless, with sad thoughts, and feelings encroaching my mind, then I heard my mother's sensible nonsensical voice,

"Sarah this will not do for you to dwell on the same conversations over and over, put them away, by writing them down. This will be as putting your thoughts to rest."


So this is when I began to write,
to quiet my thoughts,
to have a voice through out my life.
To write is to have a friend to listen,
then hold your truths.
Thanks be to Mother...

# Not A Fairy Tale Aunt

It was my Aunt Harriet who came to our aid, as our mother had died, leaving my sister of 8 years, and me of 12 years. We saw her coming with her satchel handles tucked under her arm, and she immediately began talking. "It is my duty to help my sister's little orphans. You need to be shown how to take care of yourselves and your father. This will be a task, monumental and necessary, if you are to survive by living on this farm."

"I will stay only one week to teach you what I have learned in a lifetime of doing. You will need to be at my elbow as I will work swiftly. We will begin with the fire, which is the heart of the home. All must pass through this kitchen stove. The food will be cooked. The water is heated while we eat so it is ready for doing up the dishes soon as the meal is through, so they do not stick on, and or, bring about bugs or mice. This stove is essential for life, and a much-needed heat in the winter. Later on this week, I will show you how to blacken the stove to stave away the rust. I am going to teach you the things your mother should have shown you."

"Your Nana taught us, girls all things housekeeping to last us throughout our lives." She paused and took a long deep breath. "I remember fondly of getting the hang of building a fire. When you are young, fire building is not such a chore. It is fun! Our game was to see who could build the best fire in the shortest time. Your mother was the winner most times, as she knew instinctively how to tend fires. Why on earth, did she not teach you two such a necessary skill? I will never ever know. What is done is done. We can not change the past."

She set down her satchel, and proceeded to the old black cookstove. Taking the covers off while saying, "We will knock the ashes down. What is this unburned wood? Now, we will clean it out and you will learn proper, how to lay a fire. In the summer we cook up our breads, cakes, and let it go out like this, then we clean the oven, and blacken the stove, fixing anything loose or broken, but now we need to get her going. Your father must have gone off to work the farm without any breakfast, poor duffer." She paused. "We will put an end to that."

"Let us begin by cleaning out the fire box. Move the grates back and forth so the ashes can be dumped. We will have a fire in no time, a hot one, as we will next make up some biscuits. You girls have so much to learn!" She went through the steps of building the fire. First with the placement of kindling,  the lighting, the timing of adding more wood. It was overwhelming, making me feel nervous. "The damper will be open to start the fire, and with more coals the damper is closed a little more. This will become second nature. It is just new to you so it seems like a lot. When you understand what the fire is doing, you will know how to tend the stove."

"Sarah, you will be alright." She gave me a long hug. It was unfamiliar to have a hug. How did she know I was feeling uncertain?

It was then I wanted to learn this "Black Iron Contraption" to make my Aunt Harriet proud of me. In time, the contraption, called the Black Kitchen Stove will be under my control, or my name is not Sarah, who is known to be stubborn. The basics are easily understood, yet my timing is not right. I burn things, or I am not putting enough wood in, so not enough heat. Perhaps it is the damper control setting. It is hard, and not an exact science, and my Aunt says, "It must definitely become second nature, and you will need to perfect this skill if you are to learn to cook.'

She was trying to help us survive as a family, otherwise we would be put in the workhouse for hired hands. We know a family of three will find it hard to work a farm. Living life will be one big chore. Paw's job will remain the same. My sister and I will do Mother's job along with our feeding of the animals. We will be alright.

Not enough time for trips across the field. No more life as I knew it to be. I want to be back in my 'Magical Meadow.' I long for timeless peace, but I cannot go back. Not only is there not enough time in the day to play, now I feel so very lost, trapped, weighed down, and so alone, in this grown-up world where all of life revolves around time. The breakfast should be done at the right time, as everything has a time, and everything is timed by the daylight hours.

If I hurry to do the dishes, sweep up, and mix up the bread, while it is rising I will scoot out to my meadow. I can relax with my birds, animals, and my fairies. I was becoming excited at the prospect of being outdoors. The freedom of being in my lost meadow. I went to tell my sister, "I am going out back. You want to come along?" She was swinging, and had no interest in leaving, so off I went on my own.

I was becoming excited at the thoughts of freedom. Then in the back of my mind, I was thinking the bread needs to be punched down soon. Life used to be so carefree and predictable. Would it ever again?

My world was tempered by twinkles of joy. I was walking and I stopped to listen. There were no birds joining in, and the animals were nowhere to be seen. Where are the fairies?

At that moment, I knew my life had changed, and not for the better. All that I knew was upside down, as I now had responsibilities and worries. I was no longer the carefree child my mother allowed me to be. So much has changed, and I do not like this change. This is doing my part; helping my sister and Paw to survive on the farm. This now, is my life; one I know not, where I have no choice. It will do no good to allow myself to be as sad as I feel. I need to push through and work hard. My Aunt has been a godsend to help me learn. I will do my best to please her. My future I know not...

I only know the hurt of no longer being a part of the meadow life. All that was, has ended, as this serious Sarah is no longer to be recognized. I can never ever go back. That child has ended. I must go and punch down the bread. My mother died, she was ill, and this changed all we knew of our family's life.

My heart has turned a corner and all the things have become veiled. Now there are serious life-saving jobs which are my responsibility. It feels like a heavy burden.

So much so, I can hardly recognize myself, as the playful Sarah, that was my life.

*Not only did my mother die; so, also, did I.*

*All that was — has ended.*

# CHAPTER TEN

# Wait It Through

The challenge is to get through," said Aunt Harriet. "There will be a beginning, middle, and an end. Wait it through, do not become discouraged. This too will end, and you will master all I know and have taught to you. This will also be done as good, if not, a bit better by you than me. There will be pride in all your new abilities of helping those who count on you."

"Next summer we will learn how to make jams, jellies, and all about the canning of vegetables. We will start with dandelion greens. There is a need for what we do. It's called survival. This will become bigger than yourself. You will be the master of the farm household. Never ever the 'Master of the House' — that is a man's place, and rightfully so. You are 'The Giver of Life.' Take pride in all you know, and what you do to provide for your family. This sheer belief in yourself is a gift that allows women to give as the need is real. Food is essential, cleanliness essential. Housekeeping is essential."

"We have only months to prepare for Winter's weight, of gloom and doom, with freezing cold, short day that will be filled mostly with darkness."

My life as I left it in favor of helping my family stopped, leaving all thoughts of freedoms behind. Joys were no longer mine. Instead, mine was a world of hard work, uncertainty, and trying hard to remember only what my Aunt taught me. Then my Aunt would say, "Dear, dear, your mother should have taught you this. These are things a five-year-old now does. Let us get on with it."

I tried hard knowing there were so many unfamiliar things to learn. My Aunt was kind, she was a good teacher and I learned fast. This is what she said: "It is good for us both that you are a good learner." I needed to impress her as she was all there was in my life. The only one I could count on to help me. My father was always working the farm, and seemed to need to be alone. My sister enjoys swinging under the big oak tree, which was fine for now, as Aunt Harriet said she could not teach two at once.

"You are a good student and you can teach your sister to keep house. Starting this winter, teach her the workings of the stove and the wicking of candles, sewing, cooking, cleaning up the dishes, and all the cleaning to make it a full lesson. You can never ever have too much knowledge on how to keep a house. More than likely this will be the life for you and your sister: caring for the family, and preparing food, keeping the home fires burning, while your husband works, then comes home to rest. While you work around the clock. It is, what it is, there is no changing it."

The more farm life took over, my life became smaller. My fingers were cracked from water and stove wood. No idle moments, no time for childlike thoughts. There was me learning how to take the place of my mother in her house, she seemed to love. Yet, did she? How could she? As each day, became the next day, then the next, leaving always more than enough for one to do.

My thoughts go back to my Mother. I find myself thinking of her doing all of these chores. I am learning about her ways, living in her life. We were never close, now I know she had given me and my sister time. The time to play, to be a child, to explore — all of this household drudgery would have taken over our lives, like it did my Mother's life. Soon enough, it will end our lives too. I have no time now, but I made a secret promise to my mother: "I will visit the meadow this Spring. Today there is no time to call my own."

"Feeding the farm animals is essential, keeping the fire is essential, sewing is essential, canning food is essential, cleaning the house is essential, washing the clothes is essential, keeping the pantry in stock is essential, candle wicking is essential. Tending to the small crops is essential. Cooking meals morning, noon, and night and having them ready on time is essential. It is more important than ever to continue 'The Art of Housekeeping' as this is essential for the farm to exist."

My Aunt Harriet smiled at me and gave me a wink, saying, "You will see, someday soon, you will be known as a catch."

"Let us sit down here at the kitchen table just for a minute, and I will tell you of my sister, whom our family loved very much. This was her secret. Your mother was sickly as a child. The family always thought her adult life would be bedridden, but she was stubborn  pushing herself daily to do normal everyday tasks. She learned to survive, even thrive in her work of housekeeping."

"When she married, her two girls were born. It was thought a miracle as each time she recovered regaining her strength. Your Nana attended to you and Eliza, until your mother could navigate walking, and be able to get up out of the bed. Your Nana took care of you for a long time. It broke her heart to give you two back to your mother, even more so you, Sarah, as you lived with Nana twice. Once when born and again with the birth of Eliza. In a sense, you became Nana's little girl, whereas she loved you as her own. There would be no talk of this, however, as you had a father and mother at home awaiting the return of health to make it possible for you to live with your parents. How hard for your Paw to be watching and waiting, with the ever-looming fate of losing his wife."

She gained back enough strength to function in the farm life she created for herself, living each day as a housekeeper after spending her childhood with full focus on her health — or I should say lack of health. Your Nana never ever knew what was the cause of Mary's ill health, spending endless hours to nurse her daughter to match the wellness of her other children. Each day she would have no nonsense talk of Mary being bedridden; in fact, Nana's sheer will of bringing wellness brought about your mother. Not as a strong woman, but a capable person able to perform her chores throughout her life. She married and became a great independent housekeeper."

"You remember we used to help her with spring cleaning and canning also on the wash day. This we did at the request of your Nana as she feared the extra work would take a toll on your mother, who would not stop to rest — as this is much-needed work in the standards of housekeeping. In Nana's way of thinking, if it was important to Mary, then we all needed to help. We as sisters always did as Nana requested to lighten Mary's workload. We took care of Mary to the best of our abilities, even though we had much, too much work of our own farm life. Yet, I would gladly do more for Mary if only she would have remained with us."

"Our dear sister taught us to never ever surrender your will. She pushed on to do the things in life that made her feel the same as everyone else, leaving her thriving to do all the works that were chosen. Mary chose housekeeping as this was what all young women did when they married and had a family. Nana sewed a few of the clothes and curtains to alleviate some of the burden of the task of housekeeping."

"Your mother was a miracle brought forth by the love of her mother. Your Nana never ever gave up on her child spending endless days doing all she could to strengthen Mary. They both were stubborn, and when Mary came to our mother's way of thinking, this became a strength doubled. In our thoughts, she was altogether better and healthy as the rest of us, leaving us grateful, giving all the credit to our mother and all the thanks to God. She always said this child was meant to live and thrive. Yet, I know your mother's health was her struggle all through her life. She died young, leaving two young girls alone and untrained. This should never ever happen,  life goes on, only if the knowledge of survival is taught."

"Your Nana sent me to you to pick up the pieces by teaching the skills needed for living our lives. I am so glad I came for I have gotten to know Mary's girls. You were stubborn, not unlike your mother and in the beginning surely thought me a hard taskmaster. There was so much to show you before the weather turned cold. I am not a teacher at heart. I see myself as a no-nonsense, very serious-minded person, when it comes to housekeeping, which if done right can make a difference in survival."

"You were a joy learning all quickly reminding me of your mother, Mary." My Aunt tenderly went on to say, "I also noticed you are unfamiliar with affection. Mary never ever showed love by hugs or kisses; it was as if she instinctively knew her time was to end too soon. I think she thought in her mind she would not leave longings of sadness behind if she kept to herself. Your Nana, being Mary's Mother would have none of this and would give her daughter a long hug. We sisters were well trained by Mary, and would not dream of giving her hugs. I never ever dreamed she was disciplined to the point of not allowing hugs and kisses to give love to her girls. I am so sorry, as she loved you, indeed."

" My wish, for you as a young person figuring out life, is you will be self-assured from knowing deep within that you are an important part of life because of the love from your mother and father, also their mothers and fathers. Their love transcends living on through you, making you special, to be with great love."

"Come over here and give your old Aunt Harriet a hug. You are our family's special girl."

As I hugged Aunt Harriet tight, in my mind I saw my mother always busy working so hard in her role of housekeeper, and now I realize this is what kept her striving to be the very best ever. This job became her life; as it gave her life, by allowing her to be wholly able, to be as others. She strived her whole life to be able to keep up with the many tasks of life.

My voice was shaking as I took my Aunt's hands in mine. "Thank you for telling me of your Mary, my Mother. Knowing her story has helped me understand her choices. I want you to know even though my mother let us as children be free to run and play, it was to not have us be tied by the apron strings that take over a woman's whole life. She wanted us to have what she never had as a child: the freedom to play. She gave love without hugs and kisses by giving freedom to be in' nature's school of life' sharing her wisdom of life in her discerning words."

"Remember, she had a saying for everything pertaining to events in life."

"These are a few of My favorites— Heard in childhood and echoed today. I am sure you also heard them."


*"Red sky at night, sailor's delight;*
*Red sky in the morning, sailor take warning."*

*"If spiders are many and spinning their webs,*
*the next spell will be very dry."*
*"When dew is on the grass,*
*rain will never ever come to pass."*
*"A ring around the sun or the moon,*
*means rain real soon."*
*"Mackerel skies, less than 24 hours dry."*
*"The love we give away is the only love we keep."*
*"The road to hell is paved with good intentions."*
*"If wishes were horses, beggars would ride."*
*"All in good time."*
*"Patience is a virtue."*
*"You cannot rush a good thing."*
*"This too shall pass."*
*"Love dies; like an untended garden."*
*" If your heart is in rule, more attention*
*should be given to your mind."*
*"Life must go onward. Do your chores,*
*just move about one day, then the next day,*
*to the rhythm of life, this will bring you back*
*to heal your broken heart and wounded spirit."*

*AND*

*"Remember if you want anything done right,*
*you must, do it yourself."*

"This is the Mother I know and I will never ever forget.
Her words are embedded deep in my heart, along with
our love... forever and ever... Your Sarah"

# CHAPTER ELEVEN

# The One In The Haystack

As a young girl, I was told by my Aunt Harriet, "I would be married, meaning I would have a family, keep a household running to preserve our lives, and live in a farming community of people that are living the same exact life." I am twenty-two with no man in sight, no one who looks promising for my foretold destiny. I am currently eligible, although shy.

James came to help with the haying season. Paw said, "James is a steady hard worker, who works quite cheerfully. Not only this, he also liked fishing and hunting." My father praised him as if a long-lost son he never ever had, but Paw said he could still be part of our family. This would be a dream come true for Paw. He continued to praise James when saying, "Comb your hair and clean up because after you make the hay drink, I want you to bring it out to the men in the field. Not to put it off onto your younger sister."

I am sure he promoted my single girl image to any of the eligible men who would listen. The first man I approached with the drink was paying attention to me by smiling. I gave him the dipper.

He said, "Thank you, I do not know your name." Giving me a bigger smile. He was polite. I like to be thanked even though this was my part of the process of haying. I was just doing what my Paw said to do.

"My name is Sarah," I told him. He smiled again, and the third time was a charm.

"Well then, I must say thank you, Sarah," he bantered back.

"You are welcome, Mister Stevens," I said confidently, remembering my father saying to me the Stevens brothers were going to help hay this year.

"This old hay field does not require formality. Call me James."

So this is my father's favorite worker, James.

"You are welcome, James." I realized I was smiling ear-to-ear, as I turned to serve the next worker. In my mind, I was hearing "Thank you, Sarah." It was, as if, it was the first time in my life, I had heard my name, as Sarah.

My heart was so happy, and I was smitten, leading me to go happily from man-to-man serving the "Haymakers Switchel" always being aware of where James was on the field, until I then became aware of my shyness, and my co-ordination became stiff, allowing my movements to be clumsy, causing me to think I cannot deliver any more of the brew. I only wanted to go. I set the pot with a ladle on a big rock, turning quickly to run off through the field to my special place in the meadow. This is where I go if I want to think. I will think over my new feeling of joy.

Listening to leaves, they sounded much like paper, as the breeze is gently shaking them overhead, as I look up seeing they are curled up ward seeking rain. I hear the Crickets chattering, also asking for rain. All my animal friends and birds are busy with activities that are unchanged. Everything in the meadow was all the same. It was me, Sarah being different; I have a happy heart and a blushing face.

Is this what love is? Is James thinking of me also?

I am in my twenties, and folks say an old maid. It is funny I do not feel old. I have always felt the same, yet not like when I was a child as a wild recluse running through the fields, staying in touch with my animal friends, within all the solitude nature provides — this allows no one ever to be or feel alone. Today a crack has entered my space in the form of wanting to know more of James. My refuge spot has become my hiding place until I make peace with these new feelings that are making me smile.

My conclusion: If it is to be, it shall be...

All I know is he is from Bloomfield, which is about eight miles south, and he hires out to farmers for haying. We all know haying is a sweaty, hot, dusty, itchy, hay-chafing job of gathering the hay into the barn for use all winter to feed our grass-eating animals.

All of our lives exists by planning ahead. We would enjoy our fresh vegetables, then vegetables were canned, also some types were put in the root cellar to be buried in sand to preserve them for the long winter. We would eat fresh fruit in season, and then, to save for the time of no growth in the dead of winter they were canned, also berries were picked then preserves were made, helping to ward off scurvy. Our survival depended on planning ahead to a time when the need was always more of a dire need, when all was barren. This was our way of life with this time for self-preservation to save us during the long desolate winter.

The meadow brought me back to being myself, plain everyday Sarah. I have developed no talents, or gifts. I cannot sing, cannot play an instrument, or draw, maybe a little drawing. I like to write words that attest to feelings. No one knows, as this remains my deepest secret, and has become my silent voice.

I like to cook fast and plain much-needed food. I also like to make up recipes letting me be adventurous with food, particularly baked goods. If it is good, I write it down, to bake again.

This recipe book is not a secret, and just makes me happy, as does the smell of the fresh-cut hay that is now the smell throughout the meadow, reminding me of James.

I wonder if he is helping himself to another drink.
Is he thinking where is Sarah?

***

**Haymakers Switchel** – *"Serving this drink I fell in love."*

1 quart water
2  spoons apple cider vinegar
add: ginger, syrup or spices
1 spoon molasses, honey or maple syrup,
stir and serve cold — with a smile...

# CHAPTER TWELVE

# Our Time For Courting

James asked my father if he could take me to a Contra Dance at the Grange Hall in Canaan, making arrangements for him to stay the night in the barn, to go home the next day in daylight with the horse-drawn buggy rather than in darkness. My father readily agreed.

When my Paw told me, I was not sure this was what I wanted. Yes, he was in my daily thoughts, and I heard the saying 'love at first sight.' I am not in love. I think of him a lot each day. Where does he live? What is his life like? How many in his family? Is he thinking of me daily?

"Yes, I would like to see him again. I am not sure about the Contra Dance. I have never ever been to a dance, and I have no clothes for dancing. Could he just come for the evening to eat with us, we would spend time talking, and getting acquainted, for now? Perhaps we will not like one another. I would be more comfortable at home. Have him come Friday, and stay the night. I will make a special supper meal, and a pancake breakfast with Maple syrup."

I thought to myself this being Wednesday, it will give me two days, to cook, clean, and calm down.

I wish I had something nice to wear. We stay pretty much to ourselves, so I have no pretty outfits, although I do have a long skirt. Maybe Aunt Harriet could help. I really like James, and need to feel pretty. These are foreign words to me as having no friends, being schooled at home, and never ever leaving the farm. Most girls my age are married with many children. Maybe he will be disappointed about not going to the dance. I tell myself, "Stop laboring over your choices as you cannot dance, plus you have no clothes. You can not go even if you wanted. If he is the one, your destiny, it shall be."

Eliza will help me make all perfect. We are no longer children, and have bonded, whereas, there is nothing we will not do to help each other.

What to cook? A tried-and-true meal or one of my new dishes. It would help if I knew him, since I do not, I shall have to please myself. First thing Friday morning, I will put the jars of milk down in the well to become cooled. Milk goes good with Brown Sugar Chews, which are my newest made-up receipt, a favorite of mine and a perfect combo. We can eat them later while talking. I wish I had a week to prepare. I have only got two days. I need to talk with Aunt Harriet at her farm.

"I feel silly now that I am here."

She looked worried, and started talking fast,

"What is it? Is everything going fine?"

I said, "Very well," adding, "James, a boy from Bloomfield wishes to come over to visit with me, and I decided to cook him a meal."

She started, "Oh how exciting! He is courting you. I told you. You are a catch."

Taking her hand, I pleaded, "I am a nervous catch. Can you help me? I want this to be good for James, as well as for me. The food will not be a problem. I can cook now, thanks to you."

Taking a deep breath, I confessed, "It is me being nervous, and not used to being around boys."

She patted my hand with her free hand, released her hands, putting them one on, each side of my face, then said, "Listen to me. If I was as pretty as you, I would lead with my face, instead, I have had to depend on my well known, 'Gift of Gab."

"Make him welcome. Be yourself. This is who you will be in the end."

"Trust it is your turn for happiness. God knows you deserve to be happy. You have been a great blessing to your Paw and Eliza. Now, it is your turn."

"If you like this feller, grab hold with both hands, and enjoy your new life. You are the sweetest most loving person I know. I love you to pieces."

She hugged me tight. There in her arms, I found my courage knowing all was to be alright, also taking advantage of the pause I said,

"I love you too, Aunt Harriet."

She looked at me and said, "Let me know if he is the one. If so, we will start straight away on your trousseau. Never ever forget your Nana, my sisters, and I, we are here for you, and want only the best for you."

I went home feeling especially loved. Full of daydreams, of our entertaining evening. We can play cards, whilst we talk, then we will eat the Brown Sugar Chews, with cold fresh milk, perhaps a short walk under the stars, to get the milk out of the well. Now I am looking forward to James's visit, and planning a feast for us all. Our Friday night get-together will be a memorial occasion, of this I am confident.

In the morning, by daylight, I will write out the meal details so I have everything needed. I could not sleep for happy thoughts, plans, and visions of our time together. All was prepared in my sleepless night. I am glad today, there are only two days to get through. I would not last a week!

**Ratatouille: Meal Plan**

Canned pot roast heat, make gravy, set aside

Add lard to fry sliced onions and potato

Top with beef

Bake

Place in warming oven

Canned green beans alongside

Sliced tomatoes (picked in the morning)

Milk in well to cool

Bake Brown Sugar Chews and rolls

***

Today will be for cleaning the house, extra clean. This should dispel some of my nervous energy. Tomorrow I will be cooking, and getting myself ready for supper. Time was going slowly, as if waiting for a pot to boil. Thinking of a boiling pot reminds me I need to wash my hair to make it fluffy and full. I will do this when the rolls are rising. I think I will also make Molasses Cookies. In this house, we all like cookies. My hope is James does, too. Everything is done. James will be here soon. I do not know if I can eat, with all these butterflies, in my stomach!

There is a soft knock on the door.

I wink at Eliza and whisper, "Thank you sis for all your help."

Then I was at the front of the door, not remembering walking there, and I knew I needed to open the latch inviting James to come in. Taking a deep breath, I said, "Welcome! Mister Stevens."

He smiled and said, "Good Evening! Miss Pitts."

"Please call me Sarah."

"Only if you call me James."

I was in front of the door, beginning again, saying,

"Do come in, James." He said, "Thank you, Sarah."

This was the beginning of "James & Sarah."


***


We ate supper which tasted even better than I had imagined. Paw and James talked while Eliza and I did up the dishes. It was becoming dark, and we lit the lanterns, said good nights to Eliza and Paw, leaving us alone to talk. I had so many questions, as did he. We talked most of the night.

We were both at ease with each other, and a distinct fascination held us captive. I never ever realized how much I was missing by not being around people my own age. We ate Molasses Cookies, then Brown Sugar Chews, with cold milk retrieved from the well, on this perfect, star filled night. Playing cards, we shared our lives through words and laughter, so when morning came it was a surprise. Leaving this night behind, filling us with the feelings,

we have known each other our whole lives.


Thanks to my Aunt Harriet's love, and words of advice;

"Be yourself — it is who you will be in the end."

# CHAPTER THIRTEEN

# Wedding Dress

Whenever, James was free from the work of farming we would spend our time together never ever running out of conversation, and still feeling as though I have known him my whole life.

James said, "Sarah, I would like to ask you to share in my life on the farm in Bloomfield. My mother will live with us at times, being that I will always be there for her. I have come to think about, you and I, marrying, then growing the farm. I am hoping this is also what you want. You make me feel like there is nothing I cannot do. I have been walking high in the clouds with my thoughts of you, and have been falling behind on my farm duties. What do you say, Sarah?"

"I am going to say, yes. Marriage is the next step, into the next chapter in our lives. I feel the same as you. Life may be hard, and if we are going to have to navigate the ups and downs, we should do it together. For us, a good life will win out. Thanks be to your strength, love, honesty, humility, and your fine life of goodness. This is how I see you, and I would be so honored to be your wife."

"You may kiss the bride-to-be, as long as there is just you and me." Our lips touched briefly, and I knew it was as I thought. We were meant to be together. We are perfect for each other. We are destined, although we are two people that are walking on different levels of faith.

His is a commitment to God, and I am thankful to his fine life of goodness. Mine is a secret belief. I acknowledge everything which happens in the world connects, and everything affects something else. Black and white with all moments connected in between. Therefore, I have known powerful fairies, and I believe in the power of the Universe, past lives, rebirth, and innate second nature. We come at our beliefs in different ways, nevertheless, we both have humanity and God at the core. My beliefs are never ever to be spoken aloud, as my death could soon follow. Now with our soon-to-be nuptials linking us, I cannot allow any harm to come to our household. I will continue to believe my truth in my heart. I will not turn my back on my truth, and I will not allow my truth to affect James. He wants to be married in the Church.

So it begins!

The next day, I ran over to speak with Aunt Harriet. I was calm till reaching her door stoop, and then the excitement took over, whereas the more I said, the louder and faster I talked, "I said YES, we both want a life together. We are getting married!"

Aunt Harriet took my hand, quietly saying, "Good, very good indeed. Now tell me when, where, and what, can your family do?"

"Oh, thank you! I cannot marry in the church in my work dress and apron."

My Aunt Harriet smiled and asked, "How about a Wedding Dress worn by your Nana, then me, Aunt Norah and Mary, your mother? This is the most beautiful dress. Nana and I, will fit it to you perfectly. Let us go to your Nana's. I cannot wait for you to see, your Wedding dress."

Nana was so happy. "I wish your mother was here. She always said someday her girls would wear this most beautiful dress too. Let us go up and get it out of the old chest."

The first layer in this chest were hand-stitched quilts, made from colorful scraps of wool, embroidered around each piece with flowers and birds. Embroidered in a lifetime of work, with the beginning and end dates embroidered in the corners. There were other wool blankets not so fancy, also doilies and tablecloths.

Almost at the bottom was a wooden cedar box, inside was something wrapped in cheesecloth. When Nana opened this, I could see the lace, then the satin all of a cream color. There were loose pieces that had been removed when altered for my mother, and now it was my turn. My heart was beating fast as I exclaimed wholeheartedly,

"What an heirloom treasure! I am so happy and surprised! I never dared to dream, I would have a dress, and here is the 'Perfect Wedding Dress' waiting in my Nana's old chest!"

We three hugged and cried happiness tears of pure joy.

"Best yet, my mother, will be with me all through my wedding."

Nana spoke up, "Yes, I will too, and Aunt Harriet and Aunt Norah."

"We will get your trousseau ready, mainly some clothing for your new church life along with some personal things for your pleasure."

"We want you to be happy."

"Let us go make some tea and discuss what is needed for your new married life, and of course, write up a 'to do list' so all gets done."

"It goes without saying we will be at the wedding with bells on!"

"Well, pearls anyway."

Come over here and hug your old Nana and aunt, before we make plans for our girl to be, a most beautiful bride.

"Nana can we bring the' Wedding Dress' downstairs, so I can see, and know, I have the perfect 'Wedding Dress', as we make plans. I need to know this special dress is here, where my own Nana, is my dressmaker to make all perfectly fit. How fortunate, and how loved, I feel on this very day, to have before my very eyes, the most beautiful of all, Wedding Dress to transport; love, and joy, to our wedding."

I feel special; to be so loved by my family, to have met my one and only, my soulmate. All the love I feel swells my heart, which has remained empty, as my life was overcome with aloneness, as each of my days have been spent alone, with the one purpose, of keeping our family together, on the farm.

Today, has been all about my hopes, plans, and dreams. Imagine how thankful, grateful and blessed I feel, to love and to be loved, then all to be shared with my family.

No one never ever could imagine how so much love feels...

### *FAIRIES REFLECTIONS:*

*Aspen reflected: "A star danced at your birth, instilling a full sense of nearness to the mysterious fountain of Joy. You take pleasure in the little things, perceiving the world as it is, thus perceive your modest place in it, with a feeling of gratitude for what is yours, and never ever longing for what you have not..."*

# CHAPTER FOURTEEN

# Wedding Day

## 5TH SEPTEMBER 1847

James is special and soon to be my husband. My heart is so full I can hardly catch a breath. This is what young love is, new love, best love ever known in all my twenty-four years of living. My 1st love, my only love. I feel like I am walking on clouds in a dream.

I glance at his face and the words fall from my lips, "I trust you to be my love for the next twenty-four years or more, my destiny. We were meant for each other. Your love is written forever in my heart. I believe in us, and our exciting future. There is not anything we cannot do together. The days are flying by till we will be married, together forever."

James laughed echoing my sentiments with a quick reply, "Tomorrow would not be too soon."

We sit there outside the house content to listen to the crickets, and breathe deeply the fresh cool air. We were joyful, awestruck of all this love, together looking up at the stars. It was as if they were shining brighter, in the glow of our love.

Breaking the silence, James said, "I have picked up some extra work to raise money to help pay for our wedding, therefore I will not see you much until our big day. Ma said to tell you she will help, to do whatever she can. I will come get you every Sunday, so we can go to church. This will be only four days out of the whole month that we can be together." James spoke sadly, "Just the thought of being apart, I already miss you."

"I feel the same. It helps as we will both be busy. All my awake hours are consumed with our wedding preparations starting with the family bridal dress I never ever knew even existed. You can not begin to understand how glad I was to lay eyes on my Mother's dress. It is being made to fit by my Nana, who wore it originally all those years ago. Do not worry, it is most beautiful. Then there are the invitations of which your mother could address some, once we choose a calligrapher. If we had six months this would still be a challenge. We have one month, to gather all together, to make a wonderful, special and spectacular 'Stevens Wedding' for all."

To clarify and let him know I would count on him for the religious parts of the ceremony, I said, "In the Church there will be the ceremony. I trust, this will be all up to you and the minister. The rest will be up to me and my small family. We are stretched to the limits. Aunt Harriet is the organizer. Aunt Norah and Nana sew beautifully, so Eliza and I will be perfectly dressed in our wedding outfits. I cannot wait for you to see my splendid Wedding Dress."

"We will all, including Eliza, write out invites and plan the cakes of which there are three. Bride's cake is bundled with charms attached to ribbons, then baked into the cake with the ribbons hanging on the outside to be pulled by each member of the wedding party, to release the gift of each charm. It is said to foretell the future and bring us good luck. The best is a groom's cake, a dark fruitcake with white icing. The guest's cake is precut in pieces and put into a cloth bag, to give away as the guests depart. Many sleep with this under their pillow to bring on dreams of new love."

"Paw needs his suit cleaned and freshened to be ready for our big day. Eliza, being maid of honor will need a dress sewn. We will need to make a wreath of flowers for my veil. I have made a list so as to remember all that needs doing and why."

He said, "You will not have time to miss me."

I whispered in his ear, "I will miss you, owing to the fact of we will be working on all things for our wedding, which ends with me on your arm." Seriously, I spoke up, "I do the housework and go to Nana's and work all day. She sends supper home with me so Paw, Eliza, and I, can eat without as much effort as starting from scratch. Each day is so filled with more than any one person could do, although together, we are getting all things to be accomplished."

James then remembered to tell me, "I asked my brother to be Best Man."

I said, "Is he available?"

He said, "Sure."

Prompting me to ask, "No, I mean, is he single?"

"You realize Eliza will be my 'Maid of Honor' and he as 'Best Man' will be together and spend the wedding together."

"Love is in the Air."

"Just think if they catch love there is no known cure." We laughed in spite of ourselves.

"It would be heaven-sent if Eliza and Benjamin, also found love. We could remain a close-knit family. My sister and I have shared the same sorrows, and lived together all our lives. We are different, yet sisterly close. It would make me happy, if they got together and she remained in the Stevens family. I am going to miss, plus I will worry about my sister most of all. We have always been together."

"Sarah, what is it you are always saying?"

"What will be, shall be."

"Remember this as our pledge for always in all ways, my love."

"What will be — shall always be. No worries."

Then James was serious, as if to make sure I understood what was in his heart, so he spoke slowly and softly,

"I want you to know, I have waited all my life for you to share my life, to make my life, right and complete."

" I knew the moment I saw you, that you were my one and only. The one I was meant to spend my life with sharing everything in life with you, Sarah, bringing me only happiness and joy."

"What would I do without my Sarah?"

" I truly love you, more than words can say."

"Soon you will be, Sarah Stevens."

Tears tumbled from my eyes, as we were looking in each other's eyes, and I took his hand in mine, sighed as to catch my breath to say,

"Our love is invisible to the outside, as it lives deep within our hearts. I feel safe, cherished, and blessed, that I, Sarah, found my perfect mate, one whom makes me feel special."

James said, "People say, 'There is someone for everyone.' I am ever, so grateful and thankful, we have found our true love."

"I love you, James, with all my heart."

James put his arm around my shoulder, I leaned my head upon his chest, sitting there together, time was standing still, all was peaceful.

Our starlit sky was twinkling,

I felt all was to be right,

in our world of love...

## Wedding Invitation

***Mr. Frank Pitts*** *requests the pleasure of* ___________________ *'s Company*

*At the marriage of his daughter*
***Sarah Fletcher Pitts***


*To:*

***James Corbeil Stevens***
*Saturday the 5th of September 1847*
*Eleven O' Clock at The First Baptist Church*

***

## Wedding Day Preparations

**Marriage Ceremony (Church) {James}**

**Accompanying Festivities {Aunts, Nana, Sister & I}**

**Wedding Dress**

**Maid of Honor Dress**

**Paw's suit (get ready)**

**Wreath for Veil (pick flowers morning of)**

<u>To-Do List</u>

Write a few invitations

Bride's cake (bake Wednesday)

Groom's cake (frost Thursday)

Cake cut, bagged to give to departing guests

Nana to sew cloth bags for cake slices

Buy ingredients 2 weeks ahead

Pack my clothes


**Wedding Day Traditions——**


**Something Old**: Wedding dress (connects to family of Bride)

**White Dress**: Stands for Joy

**Something New**: Beginning my own new family and journey — **(?)**

**Something Borrowed**: Handkerchief from happily married lady (Aunt Harriet)

**Something Blue**: Ribbon; Faithfulness, loyalty in relationship ——- True Blue (Nana)

**Sixpence** (from James): In shoe for Good Luck


**Our Promise —**


**"What Will Be — Shall Always Be"**


**Our Strength — Our Forever Love**

# CHAPTER FIFTEEN

# Wedding Ready

This day at Nana's I was sharing, "James will be only coming by on Sundays before the wedding, whereas he will be working extra time during the week to save up some money for our wedding. Now this Sunday will be my first day in the church. I can hardly wait to see the church where we will be wed."

Nana looked at the others and commented, "So soon, this Sunday? Now these next days will be spent, getting Sarah ready to go to the church!"

My thoughts were confused, consequently because I knew nothing of the real world, existing away from the farm. Nana went on, "First we will start with a proper church dress. Let us see what we have for cloth which would do for sewing a 'Sunday Best' outfit." She went on to say, "This is to be part of your trousseau from Aunt Norah, Aunt Harriet, Eliza and old Nana."

"We all love you, so much. While we are making a dress and bonnet for church, let us express our wisdom gained over the years to make, a formal introduction to church."

I piped in by saying, "He goes to church. I will learn how to fit in with his family, to look at this new life as an adventure."

They talked except for Eliza, who was in awe, as was I, to think the church was so complicated. My old house dress and apron were all I knew of dressing. Who knew there were clothes, saved for church, known as "Sunday Best" not to mention special manors, that most put on with their Sunday suits, that were aired out Saturday to make them presentable. Also, the people bathed Saturday night, due to Sunday becoming the new beginning of the week. To start out the week at church, clean and looking fine puts us all on the right path. The church was the highlight of the week.

The Doctrine was put in place by men, just as men run the town, the banking, real estate, business, they were head of every endeavor, as the superiors. Considered smarter and stronger, than women, who had no voice, so women talked only to each other about other women. This superiority was shown by the men, leading to when women talked, not one man listened. Men were trained to be head of households, whereas, women were trained in housekeeping, the backbone of life on a farm.

Stemming from their talk it made me feel inferior, as deemed useful to a new superior husband. Do others feel this way?

Our place as a married woman is to run the household, without complaint, cheerfully. No wonder Mother did not prepare me for this life of sacrifices with service. This will destroy my freedom, and my choices will be taken away in the persuasion of the good for all. This is what marriage is and what it is not, as we do have love.

I clear my mind and Aunt Harriet is still talking, "To have and to hold; is to receive without any reservation. The total self gift of one to the other. It is not a statement of ownership, but a promise made of unconditional acceptance of one to the other. For better, for worse, for richer, for poorer, in sickness, in health, to love, cherish, and obey, till death do us part. On this you make a vow of solemn promise In the presence of God and family. Therefore a man shall leave his father and mother, hold fast to his wife and they shall become one flesh. Two become one. This explains your vows."

I was thinking to be honest: James & Sarah to become one, my thought, if you are fortunate to be born a boy, all the people will give you the freedom to speak. My Aunt Harriet sure can talk and knows about everything, "Sarah do you understand?"

"My eyes are wide open. I know there is no endless joy, to make a life. Life is a combination of all; Peril, Utopias, and Grief. Life is a test of strength and fortitude. I will not be one who cannot cope. I will push on to better myself while learning  how to exist in unfairness. I will stay true to the girl who enjoyed, just existing in Nature. The awe of what was true shall never ever leave. Today I feel natural love in untethered Joy, as a woman who is to be married."

"I am entering my married life with insight thanks to my family. What would I have become without you. I love you dearly.  I can accept, the husband will be head of house. The wife is not considered in legal matters. She is a much needed part of the household; is it not she who keeps the household running, to bear the children, and all the hard work which is her duty, also to honor and obey? This is the rule of the day and the way things are for all who marry. It is a man's world."

*Note to self: 7C's & more After Marriage a woman's life consist of House-keeper... Children, Clothes, Church, Cooking, Cleaning, Crops, Caregiver, Candlestick making... Canning fruits and vegetables...*

It is going to be hard to spend so much time doing what I dislike, mainly Housekeeping. My desires are with writing. This no one knows. I am going to marry, and fight for this new life, and win. I will navigate our marriage for my life, our life, and our family. I am strong willed and stubborn. I trust in James, his strength, his commitment to God, his honesty, his humility, and his love for me. I am thankful and recognize his fine life of goodness. We are people walking on different levels of our faith. We both have our beliefs. James is religious, and the doctrine taught by the church are his principles. This is proper and expected of all people. Mine are kept secret, as they are not proper in our society.

I believe in God, feeling the greatness of His powerful Universe, with fairies, past lives, rebirth, and second nature, where everything happens in the world, connects in everything, and affects something else in the world. All moments are connected, as we are connected by our love. Both of our faiths share humanity, goodness and truth. I only know of and can connect to both; this is very unfortunate.  I can not share my belief with anyone, as I have experienced there are powers coursing through the Universe, and in each one of us. I think of our marriage, as the next step into a new chapter with one step closer to religious freedom, with God's true love, at the center.

At Nana's we worked on my new outfit, as I learnt of church and my new church manners. My new outfit is sky blue trimmed with white making me feel so put together. I cannot wait for Sunday to show off to James. My new bonnet will, also be blue. I never have felt so loved, so human, and or, felt this connection of my own family.

Today is Sunday, my day to spend with James. Perhaps, next week we can make a dress for Eliza, so she can attend church with us to see all which is the church, and get acquainted with the Stevens. This would make me happy because I feel like I am leaving her behind. She too, needs to be happy and loved. I am ready, therefore I keep a vigil at the window to run out the door the moment he appears. The more time that goes by my mind becomes overactive with doubts leading to my questioning myself. What did my mother say?

*"An unharnessed mind leads only to trouble."*

There he is and he looks so handsome. How blessed I am to have a family to help me understand my new role in life. I would have been so embarrassed to have worn an old house dress. May they ever keep me on the right path. James paused making me immediately think there was something wrong with my church outfit. He climbed down reaching for both my hands and said, "You look so different, and always amaze me with your sense of proper clothing. Sarah, you are beautiful."

I happily said, "Thanks to my family in more ways, than this one."

We laughed and hugged. He took my hand saying, "I have so missed you, all week I do not remember laughing once."

I wholeheartedly said, "I agree we make each other laugh."

James said, "I cannot wait for you to see the church and to show you off as my bride to be. You make me so happy, Sarah."

He looked so handsome and proud. I was content with just, James and me, in the horse drawn buggy. I got nervous as we entered the church. We were greeted by the minister. Upon walking down the aisle I could hear whispers of talk by the seated congregation. We took our seat, not a minute too soon, as I felt like my knees were about to buckle. Hopefully the worst is over, and I will not become an embarrassment to James. So this is our church we will attend. I knew right away, I could not fit in. I have no known talent, can not sing, play a musical instrument, and do not know the Bible facts well enough as to teach Sunday school, and I doubt if they ever have needed to teach volunteering to a parishioner. I will sit and observe the church and the people, as they watch me, this seems fair.

Over the next few weeks I learned, that the churched people were a breed of their own. The churches were run by boards and committees, made up by men of prominent families, along with the banks and communities. If an outsider came in they remained always an outsider, unless they had deep pockets and were of a generous nature. So I would be pushed into a small life within the church. I was known as James's soon to be, shy wife. This was good for I would be left to myself, and they would not want to know how the church skeleton looks to someone coming into their fold, who has no experience of the church's ways.

It was unbelievable how self-serving people could become when on a mission to be the upper crust, the so-called respectable. We all have heard the phrase 'Sweeping it under the rug' I believe this misjustice became common in the church. In my small home we knew, whatever dirt went under the rug would be swept out. The church left things hiding, and just got a bigger newer rug. All looks fine on the surface, yet as an impartial observer, I could see clearly how deep the church buried many secrets. I lost respect for the church's ways, as a consequence, the reality was not what one expects from those in the mission of spreading God's Word.

This church life was James's world, so I chose to be silent and respect his beliefs. If he discovers the church I see, it must be through his own eyes by observant watching, to understand the coming and going of the parishioners. The man truly loves God, and this is what matters most. I will remain James's shy wife. No need here for a Pollyanna.

Religion like all beliefs, should be open to acquire helpers, and involve fairies, as well. To believe in the goodness of people by not what they think, or not what they say, it is what they do. James I believe in you.

James asked, "Sarah, what do you think of our church?"

I knew my answer, "It is fine, all is fine."

"To dress up each Sunday, spending the day with family and friends, to recommit your love to God, while all the time spent, is replenishing your spirit."

"Could you use this verse during our wedding?"

*For I am convinced that neither death, nor life, neither angles, nor demons, neither present, nor future, nor any powers, neither height, nor dept, nor anything else in all creation, will be able to separate us from the love of God that is in*

*Christ Jesus; Our Lord.*

*"To love, cherish and obey. I give thee my faith."*

***

Today is the Day! I need to go into the meadow to pick flowers for the wreath to be pinned on the veil, other than this all has been done. We have done every detail on the list.  Today I can not believe that I, Sarah is soon to be wed to be; 'Mrs. James Stevens.'

"Tell me, how are you and Benjamin getting along? Do you like him? Does he like you?"

Eliza looked at me with the same annoyed expression, she used, as a little girl saying, "Are you writing a book? If so, your next question will be, Are you getting married? This is what you are trying to find out. This is what you want."

I say, "Sure this would be great if we stayed in the same family, but only, if, there is true love."

I walked out the front door and into the field with a basket to carry all the flowers. My last day on the farm where I have lived my whole life. I am going to miss my family. Tears trickled down my cheek. Stop this crying, you have found what you wanted, a man to love, who loves you back. It does not get better than this. This union is a blessing to be cherished, you are just feeling sentimental today. I am happy my feelings are overflowing with tears from emotions. Wonder how James is doing? He will not be leaving his family, or home, only I will move. I will leave Paw and Eliza, for the two to be a family.

Thoughts close in of my Nana, my Aunts, my Mother, soon it will be time to go to the church to put on our, beautiful Wedding Dress, thus driving in the buggy would soil it, with all the road dust. Eliza also will change at church. We gather up our things stepping out the door, for one last time at my home, on the farm, in the town of Canaan.

Paw looks nice in his suit and gives me a hug. "Seems like yesterday when your Mother and I married. I gave her this heart locket on our day. I want you to have this in her memory."

"Paw I was looking for something new, to represent beginning on 'my own journey' and this is perfect!"

I started crying again and hugged him tight. Saying in his ear, "You picked this guy, and I am glad. I love you, Paw and thank you for walking me down the aisle. I will be in the next town over. If you need me, I will be here. Promise me, you will find me, if need be, and always stay close in touch. I never ever want to let loose, of my one, and only, Paw."

We never ever talk, for some reason emotions of the day helped us share what was always left unsaid.

"Always remember, I love you Paw, so much."

He hugged me smiling in a satisfied way, and said,
"I was right. He will make me a great son-in-law."


***


*May we note the marriage of James and Sarah,*


*on this Day—*


*5th... of September 1847*


*"May God bless and keep."*


Our Wedding in the First Baptist Church, with an ongoing preparation taking many weeks, was now official, in just a matter of a few brief minutes. I was so scared to be standing at the front of the church. I hardly remember any of what was said, and when I spoke it was with softness, being sure no one could hear, except James. The one thing I do remember, was James looking so happy. On his handsome face was the broadest smile making his eyes shine brightly.

We are husband and wife—Together we, stood,
*as if in a warm cloud of love...*

# CHAPTER SIXTEEN

# Married Life On Our Farm

This whole day was not built for a girl, who spent her youth alone except for the meadow life, including the fairies. This is a secret I promised not to share, so no one knows of my childhood special companions. Then when twelve my mother died, leaving me to take care of Eliza, who was eight and to become the housekeeper for Paw, who worked hard to keep the farm. This was the time I was all alone, day in, day out, each, and every day. I was a misfit when it came to society and speaking with people.

This is also my strength in a way as I am just as I present. I am a person with no hidden agenda, or with a plan to be fulfilled. James can see my innocence spurring him to be protective of my feelings. I do love this man, who is my self appointed protector.  I cherish our time together.

Today we are married, an adventure for our time together begins.  I never ever dreamed of how happy I felt to belong side by side with James. We deserve happiness and Joy, how fortunate to marry one I love.  Who would not love James? He is perfect.

"Let us go to the farm to change into our walking boots and old comfortable clothes." James was grinning while saying, "First thing we will survey the Stevens Farm, so you can see just what you have married into today." James changed quickly saying, "Come down to the barn when you have changed. I will ready the horse and buggy."

I tried to hurry, but taking care of the dress, then finding my skirt, blouse and sweater in my valise took time. I felt so disheveled with my face was becoming flushed, hurriedly I dashed down the stairs almost running into Effie, who smiled and said, "I have put together a picnic for you both, hence even you two cannot live on love alone. You will find it in the kitchen on the table. It is a beautiful day."

"Thank you. I fear I have kept James waiting."

I found myself running to the barn, and there was my husband, James leaning on the buggy, waiting. Leading me to say, "I am sorry I took so long, Mr. Stevens."

He was in a teasing mood saying, "Tell me is this what I should expect each time we decide to ready ourselves for an outing or church, Mrs. Stevens"

"By the way you do, look beautiful."

After hours of walking, and riding in the buggy we checked the land which was one farm with several places situated for the family members. This was fascinating, also an eye opener, for I never ever dreamed their farm would be so vast. James took my hand announcing, "Our farm house is where my mother will continue to resides. She will remain 'Head of Housekeeping' for now."

I spoke from my heart with empathy, "This is good as I am a stranger to the farm, of course, I will help her anyway she needs. I am one more in the mix and I do not want to be a burden."

He winked saying, "With your nature of fairness, my mother could not have picked herself a better daughter-in-law. Even though it was clearly me who did the picking." I laughed telling him, "Yes, my father found you, for me or though he thinks. You are his perfect son-in-law."

James spoke with pride, "We are a match made for each other. Today proclaiming our love in front of all at the church."

"Our day was a wonder filled day with twilight ending our trip about the Stevens Farm, where I learned more of who and what is your life. This trip about the farm is my most memorable, as it was the two of us, not to mention a picnic, my favorite."

At night I could not sleep, as I lay awake listening to the different sounds the house held. James, lying next to me was fast asleep, breathing deeply, and there was a smile across his lips. Then I heard his mother cough. My thoughts began anew. I am married, we have a farmhouse on the Stevens family farmland. This is where James has lived all his life. This place is a comfortable memorable home for him. His days are filled with farming and plans for us to fill our lives with many children, preferably boys to inherit their birthright. The girls will have a dowry to take upon marriage.

Our home will continue to be kept by Effie, as she has always been in charge of the household. This I agreed is the way it should be, still I feel so out of place. I am like a visitor in my own home. Eliza and Paw live on our farm where Eliza is Housekeeper, since of course it is no longer my home. I married and jumped out of my nest feeling like I landed on the ground, as I know not how to fly here, where all the care of our dwelling is no longer mine to do. This makes me feel awkward like I need to invent a new purpose to make my existence, somewhat reasonable. I hear the birds outside chirping already to begin their new day of purpose. Laying here I think, if I was home I would be getting the morning started with biscuits and fresh eggs. Then I think you are home. It will take time for my heart and mind to adjust to this new way of being married.

James and Effie are comfortable on their land in the farmhouse, due to this life has always been their way to live. I will need to strive to fit in, without so much of an interference in their ways. I restlessly listen to the birds' songs leading me to know everything will be fine. My days will be full of challenges which could lead to woes, if I allow myself to feel as not useful, or not authenticated. This I promise to control, perhaps by beginning to sew, as my Nana is a seamstress. I could get a few lessons or hints from her and who knows maybe sewing runs in my bloodline. "Sarah the greatest seamstress on earth." I will create wool quilts, tablecloths with napkins. I will learn to crochet doilies. Then I will continue to write the cookbook, for all my girls to add to their dowry. I should have lots of time without the constant job of housekeeping. Just think, I can go for walks and write. All good thoughts.

Now I am perplexed about my shyness and wish not to be shy. When as a little girl my Mother and Nana would say, "My you are quiet. What is the matter cat got your tongue?" I could not tell them it was my way, which I learned to identify as shy. This shyness has me anxious for morning's breakfast, also the long days all week alone with Effie, while James works the farm.

This is a new chapter in my life. I will be curious to watch who they are together and why they are happy on their farm. This will help keep me from self reflection allowing me to stay in the moment, instead of worrying about what Effie is thinking of me. James and I, together, with Effie will share and make a comfortable and happy home, for all who inhabit the farm. I am strong willed and confident.

This is the first day of the rest of my life. For now this life is hidden in an unknown way.

I am in my mind comparing myself to a flower bud, of the deepest crimson red, that opens up, without so much, as a fanfare, into a magnificent captivating flower, for any to behold. Then to fulfill its purpose the flower dies to become seed, this plant then begins anew, producing another perfect bud, where people walk by and do not notice. Most of my life I am not noticed. This unfolding happens over and over again. I like comparing my purpose in life to nature. This nurtures my mind to 'hope making' as perhaps my wishes to belong without feeling shy were to someday be true. Others will see me, I would be accepted, as I accept, and see myself, to become accepted, then fully Sarah.

I have come to the conclusion that I was born with my shyness which is a burden by leaving me locked inside my body without knowing how to be free, to be me. The person I am, cannot freely communicate with others leaving me all alone with only myself. I listen to others, and learn many things having no desire to share them aloud, only sharing through my writing. I believe writing is giving me a voice that will someday be heard. In my desire to be free from being shy I have learned to be compassionate to all, as I sense we all have a deep seated Achilles' heel. Mine happens to be shyness.

I am not shy with James as we share a life with the foundation of love. He is not shy, and a freedom has developed with him, I have yet, to have with any other person as I keep the world at bay. In our love I am free to be my quiet self and this is enough.

I accept who I am and James loves me, as I am.

This is the first day of the rest of our lives.

**_MORIA Thoughts:_**

*Shyness is a feeling creating awkwardness to be around others making conversations with most others difficult. I can understand why you, Sarah, who spent your days alone, would find co-existing around others as not natural.*

*Remembering myself as a child being self aware of my bashfulness, as a red faced girl when asked to come up in front of our class. I was shy. Then the many times of going in front of the other classmates where I was uncomfortable within my own space taught me to feel less discomfort, until one day my shyness was gone. After many  red faced embarrassing events, repetition conquered my shyness.*

*Sarah your time was spent without others as in a time warp void. You missed the every day lessons that taught all the skills to live life. You had to rely on yourself without knowing the knowledge, that comes from the lesson of repetition.*

*Perhaps children who are alone get an audience with the fairies, to guide their lives, to be.*

**_FAIRIES REFLECTIONS:_**

**_Arwen spoke of choices:_** *We must talk of choice, to choose the right path to have the key to know life, bringing forth the power,  that lays dormant until you accept to know all, as you are known.*

# CHAPTER SEVENTEEN

# Remembering With Stories

Today I find myself reading our wedding stories. It reminds me what I knew and did not tell Paw. He was right when he said, "He will make me a great husband." My role of wife is starting out as a nontraditional journey for me, being on the Stevens Farm living with his mother in the lead role of 'Housekeeper' is leaving me free for the fulfillment of my life. I have chores to do, and by working the farm together we each have time to enjoy our days. Effie spends time crocheting, knitting and making presents for all she loves. I started sewing finding it not enjoyable, also not as easy as others make it look.

I choose not to stay inside when my jobs are done leaving me free to travel around walking the fields of nature where I gather 'Nature's Art.' I find special rocks, leaves, seeds, and search for my treasures of bird feathers of many colors. On the days when there is more time, I walk to town on the so-called dirt streets lined with people mostly women gossiping about the town folks. These are the overheard conversations, I wrote down on paper in pursuit of saving for prosperity, as documents of our time.

Today, townsfolk make taking walks never dull, all out and about, up and down the streets, making me wish I could be in two places at once. The folks have many tales to tell, some of their own to share, yet many and the most interesting about others and their plights.

Enjoy their stories, I heard then wrote down.

My hope is someday, someone, somehow, will read:

**"The Days Of Our Times In the 19th Century"**

Recorded by Sarah Fletcher Pitts Stevens

***

**Flossie's Way**

Think of this. Flossie was a little old woman, who lived in a small weathered shed of a shelter, being the only building in a large open field. She was alone except for lots of her feline friends which had adopted her. It was a good fit as they needed a home, and she was in need of companionship.

All through life she was struggling without funds, until the people of the town helped her acquire enough to survive, by making and then selling her handmade doilies. Town folks brought to her crochet cotton, of the color they would like their dollies. They also purchased the finished works, which of course had cat hairs throughout, that had to be removed. This is how they took care of Flossie's needs because she had no family, or no way, to survive on her own.

Flossie would save this money for a time of need, so she hid the bills in books, in furniture, in covered dishes, under the rugs and all throughout the house, and who knows she may have buried some outside. This was her secret.

After many years, she passed on. All her things were scattered throughout, and mostly thrown out as trash. It was then, that people started finding the hidden money as they were talking, "What a waste, such a loss of hard-earned money, all those unused doilies. How much do you think was thrown away?"

What do you say? The truth is it was Flossie's choice. This was her secret, which brought her peace of mind by having the security of the hidden wealth. She knew eventually she could find enough money to buy whatever she needed. This hidden money served her purpose in her life, her choice brought her, just what she wanted, 'Peace of Mind' with no more money worries. She did not count the money. There was no need for it was not hidden to be rich. It was her way to survive.

***

## Town Folks Say

Now I have heard it all. This is a plausible event.

The large Farm in Canaan had an equally large family, who all worked the farm, sunup to sundown. They grew it into a profitable farm with many large buildings, and the latest working tools. The drawback was of all the children were now born, not one was a boy. All were girls, who were not allowed to inherit land. This farmer was upset beyond words. Then his wife was once again expecting a child for the 13th time. The farmer joked, and was heard saying, 'A Baker's Dozen' this will be my boy."

The baby was born at home. The father filled out the birth certificate, as his namesake. He was a Junior, finally an heir to the farm. The child was masterful at farm life. He was their pride and joy, inheriting the farm and growing it bigger.

Junior made sure all the family was taken care of, due to all their needs were met. It was not till death of old age that the sex was noted. No one could believe or comprehend that this boy was their 13th girl.

This was something done, that could no longer be changed or reversed; they all got what they wanted, the farm with its prosperity. Or did they?

It was a colossal secret right to the end, as no one divulged the secret. I overheard one of the sisters talking in front of the grain store. She wanted all there to know she was as surprised as anyone, no one in the family, other than the parents, who raised Junior, knew of this strange secret., yet a necessary secret in order to keep the farm for the survival of the family.

***MORIA Thoughts:***

*Your story Sarah, peaked my curiosity to check timelines.*

*By the 1900's every state gave a married woman control over their property, but women still faced a gender bias when it came to financial matters, It wasn't until 1970 before women were able to get credit cards, before then women needed her husband's signature, to open an account. Property was inherited to the son, until 1925.*

***

## Father Put To Pasture

"How is your father? He must like you taking over the farm." I recognized that grimace so I said, "I know my mother was so misunderstood by me. Over time I have come to find out, it was not her being irritated with me, it was my perception of irritation that took over our relationship. I only saw what I thought to be true, and acted accordingly, reacting as being unfair to my mother, as she was only doing what she knew. She was only trying to do her best to live her own life."

"So I guess what I am saying is, if you are irritated by others, first look at yourself, more than likely they have not changed, they are pushing on in the same way. It is you who have changed, finding less time in your life to enjoy the people who live with you. The less time you have is because there is too much work to do running the farm. Leaving you with less patience to deal with each everyday criticism."

"Look at your father to see the farm was his life, and still would be if he had the physical strength. Now, he is asked to step down, told he is supposed to sit and rock the rest of his life away. Not his farm, the new owner, his son, is doing things differently. Your father is not happy at the farm. It is not how you are doing things. It is that he is not. We call for much empathy to the father, who has lost his life's work, as this is what he knows best."

"In such, a short time this will be you. Remember to look to your son, as owner and give him all the dignity you seek from your own father. Continue to make your decisions as the success of the farm, now lies with you and your sons. You are doing a good job."

"I hope this helps you see your father more clearly. I wish I could have known this when my mother was alive, as we were strangers in the same house. I will not keep you from your work. Look to your father, to see his secret desire for his life. Know in your heart, 'being happy is an act of courage' for you and yours."

"My Paw needed to leave the farm he helped build, the only home he knew. This place was where he lived his whole life. He moved to the Stevens farm with my sister. This could not have been easy, yet his horse, Molly died and he could no longer live alone as when a boy. Life is always changing, sometimes the way we envision change, can make all the difference, on how hard, or easy it becomes."

As I walked away, I was thinking, me sharing my thoughts took amazing courage. I felt happy. Hope it helps the farmer and his father.

***

## Not In Our Town

Today is a wonderful sunny day being the kind of day making a person glad to be alive. Walking across the bridge I find myself pausing to watch the rushing water of the Kennebec river, finding the sounds of the movement of the water captivating, adding to the perfect day. I had errands to get done in town, and this thought was encroaching on my moment with nature.

Up on the dirt street in the middle of town there was a crowd of people gathering around this woman, who was standing on a wooden box speaking. The people were tentatively listening to what was being said. I thought, what is she saying to attract so many people? I moved closer to hear.

"The Bible does not mention wedding vows being required or expected for marriage. There are no vows for him or her. To have and to hold is to receive without reservation. It is not a statement of ownership but rather a promise of unconditional acceptance of which there is no division. Even though it is thought a wife's duty is to Honor and Obey."

"The wife is not considered in legal matters and the single woman cannot work as equals so she must marry to have a home."

"She is a much needed part of the household. Is it not she, who keeps the household running, bearing all the hard work that is her duty under the man-made title of Housekeeper. Women stay home doing all the chores, cooking, cleaning, bringing children into the world to add another plight to her workload."

"The Men on the other hand work on the farm or bring in funds working in towns, they have all power as Head of House. They are stronger physically and they believe mentally stronger than women, therefore they control and keep their way of life brought forth by perpetrated rules, such as women should not have a voice of matters of importance and not to be allied together to speak of opinions. Women cannot vote or own land or even work in factories. Women are Housekeepers."

"We are the slaves of the Head of the House, our husbands and the fathers of our time."

"Fear and routine freezes us from being brave to break away to live in a time of freedom. The slaves have been freed. Should not women have freedom to live a full life within their community?"

"Women's roles are formed as children and through isolation they did not know any other way to live, or any need for change."

They got her down from her makeshift stage.

Men said, "Nobody takes her seriously."

"This speaking of things she has no part of, is uncouth, and proves her impureness as a worldly woman from a big city."

"If we listen to this blasphemy or adopt this premise, the walls of virtue and morality would be breached leaving our society to have no further defenses against the forces of change."

The men in the immediate crowd began shouting in unison, "Does not know her place! Does not know her place!"

"Spoke up about anything, that came to mind even that of which women are ignorant."

"This is inappropriate for a woman."

"The woman is clearly ignorant and insulting to our townsfolk."

"She speaks with jealousy of our unity."

This was the rule of the day the way things are for all, it is a man's world and fear of the unknown keeps us bound...

### *MORIA Thoughts:*

*This is 'A Man's World' is as to say, 'life goes on in a known way' —taught to us, as children, as the way.*

*I am ever thankful you recorded the harsh ways of unfairness to women— to be good for housekeeping and to bear children. No freedom, yet no knowledge known in the population, of the fact that women needed to overcome and break free of the false bonds keeping them bound.*

*The women with courage, speaking in loud voices —*

*— could not even be heard.*

*It is discouraging to know women would not get*

*the right to vote until 1920 ( the 19th amendment)*

*Black men voted in 1870 ( the 15th amendment)*

*Equal rights under the law for men & women in*

*1923 (ERA) — then it was 40 years —-1963*

*before passing (The Equal Pay Act)*

*A fun fact: Lady Diana Spencer deleted*

*'Obey from vows' ( 1981 )*

*before wedding Prince Charles*

## Rules Of Time

I was sitting behind a tree, near a contemplated Street and I overheard women talking. Looking around the corner of the trunk I saw three women standing and their voices I could hear plainly, as their pitch carried much better than the deep tone of a man's voice. They seemed excited stemming from what they had recently learned, saying the school board was soon to be questioning the rule of the representation of women working as teachers when pregnant, and not with a husband. This teacher was married, had two other children, her husband died, leaving her pregnant with her third child. No husband, pregnant, no job, this was the rule.

One woman spoke, "I cannot fathom a world where this is just."

Another one broke in excitedly saying, "I know the family. She has always been a good teacher. Now the family is responsible for her and her family, because she has lost her way to earn a wage."

The next woman spoke, "The town has been fortunate indeed to grow under her wisdom of learning."

Another broke in saying, "The students do not want her to go. How will she get by with three children and no husband? That rule needs to change."

The oldest woman of the three said, "You are right. It is now more important than ever that the trained teacher teaches the 3 r's. Just think, she cannot hold a position of teaching because her husband died."

Another broke in saying, "She needs the teaching funds, more now, than when he was alive. I hope she stays and teaches our children."

Another then said more quietly, "There are teachers, who have complaints against them. These complaints are overlooked and they are allowed to teach, for one reason or another. This one they are letting go is a well-respected teacher."

Another said, "She should teach."

They were in agreement with the last statement, speaking together they said, "I wish I had a vote."

James is on the school board, and I shall ask him about these disgraceful words I heard today. This dehumanization of the teacher by having her leave her position due to no fault of her own. To lose a husband due to an accident, then to lose her teaching position due to a pregnancy. A pregnancy that was fine when her husband was alive, now that he is gone it becomes a reason for dismissal. This is no more than treating her as property. Makes little to no sense.

The old timers are firmly planted in what they know to be the rules throughout their lives. The others are molding to a nuance of change. The two; rules and changes are trying to coexist. How will they respect each other's opinions that are versed?

The catalyst of change is now, as we all live together in a community. The demands of the new forward terminology over old rules are changing from the "Boxed-in Way" of living that we have been accustomed to. They are changing the old schools of thought, as it is being challenged by us as citizens who live in close-knit villages or in towns.

My husband is on the school board. What is my part in this? In society owing to a woman with no voice, and a husband with a vote. Do I continue to look the other way? Are rules not to be honored? Can they be changed? Should they be changed? Some say, "Rules are to be followed and there can be no middle ground to take precedence, due to it is the rules that keep order in society. Without rules life becomes a chaotic mess." We have a standard of rules that can sometimes be unpopular and unfair.

To vote against a rule of doctrine, instead of applying the rule blindly, is also not popular amongst the community. This is when men must go back to the doctrine to change the rule, at the root.

This will not help our pregnant teacher and her family. Yes, it will mandate another's plight. Justice is slow, yes, there are people who speak up to change rules. The makers of the rules are men, not women. We as women must familiarize our men with the unfairness of some rules. These words that I heard today are "The Voice" of the women to help the people.

I do not believe every man is guilty of the work he did not do; however, now we must move on, to move forward to a more conclusive life of common sense fairness.

The future is full of hope even as our struggle remains, our journey is never ever going to end...


### *MORIA Thoughts:*

*Sarah you were born (1823) my year (1947) your writings are of a different century, yet the angst in humanity is the same now, as in your 'Never Ever Days' today the rules are lost to a circumstantial thought process that involves details, and sometimes repetitive thinking, that delays reaching the main point of communication. This is leaving delays in decision-making, due to lack of logical thinking, where leaders should, could, and would know the real difference of; left from right, and or, up from down. It is frustrating to see those in charge of laws, circumvent legal requirements, for policy changes.*

# CHAPTER EIGHTEEN

# Changes Are Coming

We have been married almost three months, it is late in November with the beginning of Winter. Effie and I are no longer strangers. She has welcomed me as James's wife, encouraging me to think of her, as our mother. She has a warm, easy manner, always ready with a smile reminding me of my husband's ways. They love and respect each other, therefore I have become like another daughter as part of their Stevens family.

It does not seem real, today is Saturday, the week has gone by quickly with me walking and secretly writing. At first I felt apprehensive of not being in charge of Housekeeping, thus I was taught by my aunt this would more than likely be my plight in life, as with all who marry. I have never ever felt so free, helping out as I am told, being careful not to overstep by doing things on my own. In the household we do our chores leaving free time to do what brings our lives joy. This will change very soon as Winter is at our door and one morning soon it will be cold with snow.

James's winter jobs on the farm change after the fields are fertilized with manure leaving them to await Spring, just like me. When the weather turns cold James enjoys working inside the barn where everything is looked after as he counts on it lasting for years of work ahead. He prides himself on having a neat well-preserved barn, where the tools of growing the crops are oiled and placed in an order to be used in the cleanest barn in the County of Somerset.

Sometimes when I go to the barn he is talking to the animals, he says, "They are a big reason the farm and we survive." He is like my Paw in this way. I take him a snack,  an excuse to go to see him. It is good to have him near the house with the weather cold on a typical winter day. All my days of walking are on hold. It is an acceptable change although my spirit of adventure will be awaiting spring.

I was picturing us working side by side making the work go by more quickly, like when I work with Effie. I said, "In the Spring my Mother would have her sisters help her thoroughly clean her house."

He said, "Then she would help out at your Aunt's?"

I said, "No, and it is odd. I never ever thought of the trade-off before, until my Aunt told me after Mother's death, the sisters helped because she was ill. Is there anything I can do to help?"

He said, "No, Sarah this is man's work. Thanks for bringing me a snack. This is good. I get to have an extra kiss hello and goodbye added to each of our days. I like the winter months leaving me where I can be close to home with the people I love. Today, I am enjoying the solitude of organizing my barn."

I was thinking thoughts of maybe this is man's work and when I was a child of twelve I was asked to do woman's work of being the housekeeper. I said, "I have been so busy all my life knowing not how to have free time, so if you do not need my help, perhaps I will continue to write my cookbook."

His comment, "That sounds like a perfect worthy chore. With the long winter you may finish the cookbook for our girls' dowry, and Ma will do some sewing."

Then I laughed saying, "I know I pictured myself sewing beautiful blankets, table cloths, even crocheting doilies, in my mind I was a great seamstress. I just have to laugh, as my real sewing skills are non-existent. Thank God for your mother. The cookbook I can accomplish before we have our first child be it boy or girl."

James put down what he was doing, searching my face looking for a clue. I had his full attention. He spoke softly, "Sarah, are you saying we are expecting our first child?" I leaned in close, taking his hand and putting it on my waistline while saying, "Not now, how about June?"

He gently hugged me. Held me as if afraid to let me go. Out of the corner of my eye, I saw tears on his face. It was a moment seemingly stopping in time, two people grasping to enjoy the thrill of becoming parents. My plans of parenthood would be a mother with lots of hugs and kisses. James is filled with awe at becoming a father. He will be ever so proud of this little one. When we released our hug, dried our tears it was as if our life became all about the baby.

James spoke first, "Does my mother know?"

"No, I thought you would like to tell her our news, then on a clear day we will all go to Canaan to tell Paw, he is to be a Grand-Paw and Aunt Eliza. Depending on the weather I would like to tell my Aunt Harriet. She has shown me so much love, and taught me so many things."

"Let us go tomorrow. We can go after church because once the family knows, I can start telling our baby news to anyone and everyone. I am excited beyond words to think of us with a beautiful child. This has given me so much to think, and plan for the day I will be a father. Sarah I did not think I could love you more, yet this commitment adds a lifetime of caring to our love."

I felt teary-eyed again, and hugged him with all my might, speaking from my heart of what I knew to be true, "We will have beautiful, smart, healthy and happy children starting with this one in June."

James said, "The anticipation is going to slow down time making it seem so much longer before the baby comes."

"I feel the same we will need to practice waiting patiently, while our little one is becoming ready to meet us, as Mother and Father Stevens. Seems like yesterday we were Mr. and Mrs. Stevens. We will get through this time by preparing for parenthood. We will make a list of things we will need to properly care for our child."

"I know my mother, who will be a big help with our list and possibly have some clothes already made." We both laughed.

I said in agreement, "The Effie, I have come to know, will do all that and more. I definitely have come to love, and appreciate your mother. I could not ask for a better Grandmother. We are so blessed."

James answered, "Our life is good.  It is more than I ever thought of it being. May we always be so down right happy with all our dreams coming true."

"Want to go up to the house tell Ma?"

James was elated, he was to be a father, he was 'proud as a peacock', as the saying goes. I too was trilled at first with the thoughts of us becoming parents, yet not so much, as the time draws near to baby's delivery. Over the long days of winter, we were busy preparing all the things on our list. This child would want for nothing.

Time marches on and springtime arrived, but not with my regular routine to greet the awaited season of spring. Instead of taking nature walks, I was expected to stay close to the farm, as I was with child. My life was no longer mine to choose, what I would like to do, it truly was all about our baby with safety of mother and child. This was good in the beginning, now a burden to bare.

Occasionally at first, now more often my thoughts go to the birthing process and I am developing a fear of the unknown which will come to be, in June. Effie will be there with a midwife. To them it is 'old hat' for me it will be embarrassing, painful, and hopefully uneventful, with all ending with a healthy child, and an elated mother and father, especially if a son for James.

***Boy born to Sarah and James Stevens, June 3rd,***
***named Asa, after James beloved father.***

All is right with the world if you do not notice, that I, Sarah am not to be up out of bed for a time, to be determined by the healing process. James says "No worries Ma will take care of Asa, all you need to do is feed him and recover, Ma can do the rest until you get stronger."

So I lay in bed not daring to get up, without help from my mother-in-law or husband. Time drags onward with nothing to do, as sleeping day and night is not my way, so I read some during the light of the day, yet not into the darkness of the night because the oil lamps and candles would not be safe, if I should somehow fall asleep.

Time heals all, and life goes onward, where our little one becomes the center of all we say and do. Everything representing our life, is focused on the well being of Asa.

We are growing our family — on the Stevens Farm.

Life is, just as, life should be, wonderful!

James, Sarah and baby Asa, We are Blessed...

# Chapter Nineteen

# Asa At Age 3

He is so hot with rosy red cheeks and he breathes in slowly and then out, often with a moan. My heart breaks and I am fearful as the doctor says, "If he makes it through the night." He was continuing on speaking of what was to come. I only could hear "If he makes it through the night." Why my child?

He is our baby. I love his perfect little face. The way he laughs when we play hide and seek. The way he laughs when I say, "Here comes Papa."

Asa is our joy; our perfect little one. As I think back to when he was born, each day we loved him more and more. Our baby has become our world, and our very lives. Nothing matters but him getting better. There is no way God will take him away, he will remain here with us. This I know as Asa is so loved by us. "You are part of us, and you will always be part of us. Please be strong. Fight this fever. I pray with all I know. To God be the glory."

In the background I heard the doctor saying, "Keep a vigil with steam under the sheet tent that I have formed. Stay close keeping the steam up, to help him breathe." He added, "Stay vigil. I will check back in early morning, as tonight there are many to be seen."

He is leaving! He is leaving, James and I to watch over our little one, and asking us to nurture him back to health. I am so scared. He is so little, and so sick. I will find the strength to care for my son. I will not let him down. He has never ever needed my care more. It has never ever been this urgent to do everything right all through the long night. My heart aches.

I hear James praying softly, "Oh God help us. We need a miracle to make him well. Keep him comfortable."

I started singing, "Lullaby and goodnight, little one sleep tight. In the morning when it is near I will wake you my dear."

"Little baby Asa, your Mata and Papa love you."

James was tending the fire to heat the water, then bringing it to me so I could keep the steam just right. In between runs to the stove, he would fall to his knees, taking Asa by the hand, and pray quietly to God. My heart broke watching this man do all he knew to stave off death.

It was like I was out of my body unable to think. When alone with Asa my mother came to mind. My mother was strong-willed, determined, and gifted in leadership with knowledge of survival. She was a perfect wife and mother if you wanted someone to take care of you. She was safety in motion with no time, or need of showing affection. Why does my mother come to my mind? She does not even know the real me. Sure she washed the clothes, the dishes, even the whole house, fed our bellies and encouraged Eliza and I to read and write saying, "Get you ready for life." Our parents took care of our needs; food, clothes, house and manners. We knew when to be quiet, "Children should be seen and not heard."

There were no kisses or random hugs, given from my mother or father, to be remembered. I knew of hugs as I saw with my own eyes, my mother with her mother hug. First I saw their eyes meet, they looked at each other, broke out into a smile, and hugged. Then mother reached over, and patted Nana's hand three times, not slapping. It was beautiful, gentle, and made my chest tighten. I also thought I felt like crying. I looked away to not let anyone see. This was the summer when I knew I was what mother called, "Tender-hearted, with the need to be careful you do not become taken in by your heart. If you are strong in your heart, then more time must be put into your minds development. This is what will sustain you in the end."

Asa was taken from us. The baby boy never woke up, I never ever again saw the love in his blue eyes. His hand went limp. I heard screaming, "Asa wake up! Come back!" James was shaken me, I was brought to the present, and realized I was the one screaming, "Why was he taken from us? Why? We loved him!"

"We only had three years. Why?"

I lay awake, as every time I close my eyes, I relive the worst night of my life; the night Asa left, and God took my heart. The night I fell across the bed crying, "Why? Why? Why Asa? Come back!"

In my mind, we share looks of love with smiles that turn into laughter. His little arms would hug me tight around the neck and I would say, "Mata loves you more than life itself."

or "I love you as far as I can reach, with my whole heart."

then, "You are my little one, and I will help you to have everything in life, keeping you happy."

or "My son, we are blessed. I have never ever been so happy."

My heart only knows our unbreakable love through the hugs and kisses we have shared, where we hold each other tight and we say, "Mata loves you more!" "No! Asa loves more!" You laugh. "Mata loves you more, today, tomorrow, and forever." You hug tighter with all your might.

My son, Asa, you were too good for this world. Asa is still my little angel. This I believe. I will always miss those little arms hugging around my neck, and the smell of his little head as I hugged him back. He knew my love, I felt his innocent love and Asa took this with him. I know this much is true we planned so much around our child starting with the perfect name, Asa.

### *MORIA Thoughts:*

*Sarah your loss was quick, leaving complete despair after reading my heart is sadden, and sorry for your loss of your much loved child.—why?  This upheaval of death seems unjust, as the loss of an innocent little one, who needs you to love and protect him. I too, as a mother would have felt the burden of loss, thus, also would have proclaimed why?*

### *MOTHER'S WORDS*

*"If you are Tender-hearted you need to be careful, you do not become taken in by your heart. If you are strong in your heart then more time must be put into developing your mind. This is what will sustain you in the end."*

### *FAIRIES REFLECTIONS:*

***Aspen added:*** *"The sign of the Universe is love in a perfect world all humans are each connected to one another through love. Those who have lived in your heart, will remain as loves within the heart and in your mind, are their words and deeds to comfort."*

# CHAPTER TWENTY

# My Life As I Know It To Be

Each day laying in bed, I lay awake, breathing in, breathing out. The rhythm of life is present leaving my mind in constant perpetual motion.

Never ever, will I understand how our sweet baby boy, Asa, of only three years of age can die.

We had Asa, and were thrilled with our new role of being parents to our beautiful boy. James would ride him on his shoulder as soon as he was sitting up, and take him everywhere to show him off to family and friends. We were so happy, and filled with joy. Life was good.

We were good as the Stevens family; James, Sarah and Asa, namesake of James's father. Then the unthinkable happened. Asa became ill with the fever, and died, taking with him our joy.

How to go on now each and every day. I rise up early, slip on my wool sweater, and pull on my sheepskin boots to go down the back stairs into the cold dark kitchen. My candle flickers showing a white design, as if the frost danced on the window panes. I no longer care to see these arts from nature. Instead I grab the lid lifter for the stovetop, and open the covers to use the stove poke to stir up the coals. Next, I put in the kindling, and wait for it to catch on fire so that finally the wood can be added. With this done I go to the sink to fill the tea kettle. Grabbing the handle of the sink pump I push it up and down a few times to prime the pump of air. Then fill the kettle, also a big pot to heat water to do the dishes later.

Now I stand very close to the stove to warm myself, especially my hands. Once again, I lift off the covers to add more wood. The room does not feel much warmer, yet the cat laying behind the stove is content. Most cats are barn cats, when I became friends with this one "the no cats in the house rule" was dropped. It was thought the cat would help me abandon my grief. If the truth be told I always liked cats. The cat will not make me forget or help with my grief. In my mind there is the cat, I love as a person loves an animal. In fact, I first knew and experienced death with the loss of my childhood kitty, Peaches, I was heartbroken as she died. My mother grew tired of my long face and said, "If this is the worst thing to happen, you will be very fortunate indeed."

Then there is Asa, the love of my life. The center of my being, by losing him, at only age three, we never got to the point of distancing ourselves. He never ever became independent from us, now his memory will remain one of a sweet, innocent, wonderful baby.

Effie tries to help me move on saying, "We will have Sarah put her talents to work by organizing our morning meal, helping her get on with the rhythm of life." Break of day is fast approaching, as I, each and every day prepare coffee and tea. When the tea kettle whistles, I hear the upstairs floorboards squeak telling me they will soon be coming down for breakfast. Quickly I finish up the biscuits, by putting them on a wooden board to cut out, then they will rest in the baking pan until the oven is hot. Biscuits take a very hot oven to cook quickly. I raise the stove lid, and add more wood. James first to come down saying, "I will go fetch the eggs." I was already putting lard into the heavy black iron frying pan to bring to the stovetop to heat, while I set the plates and silverware around the table.

Coffees were ready so I quickly ran upstairs to our room to dress, being sure to put back on my wool sweater. James is sipping coffee when I come down. "How did you sleep?" I heard myself say, "Fine. All is fine." This is easier than admitting I cannot. So the day has begun, as each day.

I lit the fire to warm us, and ready the meal, clear the table of breakfast remains, and washed up the dishes as the water was heating while we were eating our fried eggs and hot biscuits with lots of butter and molasses. Now, to sweep the floor. Next a quick run up the stairs to make the bed covers smooth, and get the chamber pots to dump, also clean with creolin. Next to gather the compost as the chickens need feeding, they are always feeding. James has milked the cows. I need to pour the milk into jars right away allowing the cream to rise so I can skim it off the top, as today is butter churning day. This should be done when the day is cool, as it will set up faster with less churning time. The men folk are off doing chores, always an endless list of things that need doing. Today is also bread making day so we need to keep the stove stoked. It will rise well when the kitchen is warm and the wool sweater can be hung on the hook for later. The stove is fed again as the bread has risen, and is ready to be baked for supper. The heels will be saved for bread pudding.

We, now the women of the household, act as a team, peeling vegetables, setting the table, and getting the pickles from the cellar pantry. Life on a farm is a "Feast or a Famine." I hate the uncertain nature that is our life. Each day hours of cooking will be gobbled up quickly as there is much to do before it gets dark. As the sun sets daylight will soon be lost. We gather the lanterns to fill with oil. The inside of the house becomes dusky right away as the windows are small. The men come in each carrying an armful of wood to fill the wood box.

They look tired and hungry. We get the food to the table. Few words are said. We women hurry to wash up the dishes.

I grab my wool sweater for 'early to bed, early to rise.'

Each day is 'a cookie-cutter day' of the last, on the farm.

I climb the stairs to our room, knowing James will be along soon. It is a quiet time. I quickly put on my nightgown and steel a glance out the window to check the sun going down, to be, twilight on the earth below with a twinkle from the stars above. All is perfect within nature It is me who seems upside down and sideways.

I hear the steps creek and quickly get under the covers of the bed with no movement, as to be asleep. This started after the loss of Asa, leaving my heart guarded, so I no longer feel interested in sharing, or verbal conversations. I just want to be left alone. This is understood by my demeanor of hiding, in plain sight. This does not feel right.

I just know not, how to be within my changed life, without baby Asa.

***FAIRIES REFLECTIONS:***

***Arwen spoke of darkness:*** *"We must talk of death with the sense of darkness that floods all the heart and mind, shadowing the love that never ever leaves. The light of wisdom gives power to gradually overtake gloom, leaving the darkness, to be overcome by the early dawn. The sunrise becomes day, with the full light of the sun, our life is exposed with a call to move on, as we live our life..."*

# Chapter Twenty-One

# More of Mother

As your child you let me run in the meadow where I had all of nature to show me love is contentment in life filled with awe."

"Then it was James and I, as we were married. You would have loved him as did Paw saying, "He chose him for me." We were so happy and content sharing life by talking and hugging, always there for each other in the good and the bad times."

"Mr. Stevens and I, had a lovely wedding day. Paw gave me your heart necklace, which I had never ever had seen, telling me it was his gift to you on your wedding day. I wore the 'family treasured beautiful gown' same one you had worn, and I felt your presence. After the marriage vows we spent the day in perfect harmony, with a tour of the Steven's farm, including 'my favorite' a picnic."

"Then there was the bad time, the death of our first son. It was your voice, I would hear, giving the same advice as when I was little. Never ever was there a hug from your arms, not because I pulled away, so with baby Asa I loved him right to death, and this left me alone, longing for his innocent love. This is known to my eyes from the life we shared. There are many ways to show love. I remember never ever seeing my Paw and you hug, or for the real matter talking about anything at all. My father was a man who spent his days outside of the house farming, came in prompt for his meals, then skedaddled elsewhere without a conversation or anything."

"Until the night you left us. When alone Paw told me of his life to help me quiet my anger of unanswered prayers. He helped me accept we have no control over death, we only can do the best we know in life."

"Then my Aunt Harriet told me your secret.  You lacked good health allowing me to make sense of our family dynamics. I was twelve when my world fell apart, allowing me to see everything that was neatly hidden. It was so much to process, to know all was not as it seemed, leaving me to grasp onto events, then to see with my new foggy vision the events, allowing me to know nothing in my life, was never ever real or true."

"Why did I not see? I think of myself as knowing. Paw always seemed uncomfortable around Nana and Papa, along with your sisters who came to help. I thought perhaps they were keeping company with a woman who literally had no one, as it was miles to the next neighbor. No one to talk to of everyday chatter. Those days of shared work were more than helping to get the work done; they were almost just an excuse to visit keeping you well, physically or mentally alive. You had no one except us, a man who farmed and two girls whom you sent outside to find a little happiness, as none could exist in our house. As children we never ever saw how alone you were, or how we were orphans living in our house with a mother and father, who could not be alive for us."

"I sometimes think you died of pure loneliness, while doing all the labor that was yours alone to do. I am sorry your life was so hard. The choices you had were few. I am sad to think of your life of isolation with loneliness clinging to your heart like the cobwebs you swept away, and never allowed to be in your house, to keep always neat and tidy. If only your life would have been as neat as your house. If only your two girls would have known your plight."

"What was, and what should have been, was always your secret. You shied away from real life a little at a time, never ever allowing hugs and kisses, which are natural between a mother and child. You became a shadow of the woman you were to be. I realized all this heartache, when I became a wife walking in the path of motherhood."

"I often hear your voice, when as a child it seemed only just talk to fill the room. Your voice has become instructions for life. A life you never ever had, yet knew full well of the existence of a well-lived life and love. This you gave me along with my life."

"When in the throes of life, a Mother's love becomes a guide, even though she is physically gone from our life, her words, and actions become the guidelines for our life."


"One never ever forgets their Mother...
and your daughter, Sarah, is always searching,
listening to my heart, for your words of awareness...

# CHAPTER TWENTY-TWO

# Our Three Boys

Everything happens for a reason. I cannot believe that. Why? Maybe Mother was right. I should have put more strength into my mind, instead of leading with my heart. Now I am lost.

My time is about memories. My thoughts, go to 1848, when Asa was born. We were living in the home of James's Uncle Lawrence and Aunt Arabella with their three children; Asa, 11; Sarah, 7; and Norah, 5; and their father, 80-year-old Samuel Barker, also a 15-year-old boarder, Ann Fletcher. Totaled to ten under one roof. Then of course, as was the way, we made room for Effie, to help take care of baby Asa.

In December 1850 we bought the farm, with more land from Uncle Lawrence for the sum of $1,600. This was to be our start, on our way to success, then the unthinkable happened—our Asa took ill and died. My little one is lifeless.

This is what happens to other people, not to us, and not now. We are just beginning. Creating our new farm life. In an instant all is changed. All is lost leaving my full life to never ever be.

Asa's death creates a tunnel where there is no digging my way out, and all I see is darkness. I hear talking, but the words, I do not hear.

Grief has captured, and swallowed me up. Every time I close my eyes all I see is my sweet little Asa. My heart aches with a throbbing chest. I just want to go, to be with him. Hold him. Hug him tight.

James lost his father at 12 years of age, and I, also at 12 years, was left by the death of my mother. His mother lost two children when he was a boy, so his response is to pray, "God's, will be done. He will be with God, and we will be with him again."

So I looked him right in the eyes, and unloaded, "Do you remember being born?"

James replies, "Of course not." My response, "Then how will you know the dead if you know not the living?"

Then I said exactly what I was thinking, "This child was here, now in an instant, he is dead. Asa is gone from us, and our time is done. Why did God abandon us?"

James looked stricken, "Sarah I know you are grieving. I also know you need to get a hold of yourself with those blasphemy thoughts. Do not let my family hear you question —The Word of Our Lord."

I did not say anything more, although I thought plenty. I am not just going to roll over, and play dead. There must be answers. I am not a bad person. I was a good caring loving mother to Asa. I prayed non-stop as the night unfolded, and what did I get only my child in the cold dark earth; 'ashes to ashes; dust to dust' these were the last words ever said over his little grave.

I felt strife in the form of hatred towards all, so I stayed by myself being afraid, unable to experience life. I have lost my life, as the person I was, before Asa, died. It was as if he took me with him, leaving me as this empty shell, who was not feeling life or love. James seemed too accepting becoming stronger in his faith.

Effie, his mother was no help. She lost two children and her husband. "This will make you stronger. God does not give us, more than we can handle." With the loss of our child, life would never ever be the same for the Stevens family. Why?

The next few days, I cannot remember. Weeks blended one into another. It was as if life stopped. I became swallowed up with thoughts of Asa's lifeless body. I began to have bouts of not being able to breathe, as I walked by Asa's empty bed. My heart would race, and I would faint dead away, most times falling to the floor banging my head.

Perhaps, if I was strong like James, he loved Asa, he does not blame God. He misses Asa and says, "He was our gift.  All of our joy is ours to keep in our heart." My memories do not give joy, just loss, such loss.

James said, "Just remember how blessed we are to have loved Asa, so much that it is now hard to say goodbye."

"Asa is our gift from God, and we will get through this by counting our blessings."

In my mind I saw a grown man talking religious sayings, that are separate, and apart from our family. How is this helpful? It makes me feel like a cocked-up bottle ready to explode!

Quietly I hear my mother, "Life is a journey, and some unchosen paths lead to heartache, you must keep going forward with hope in your heart as you will find your truth and wisdom."

I then decided to put on my poke bonnet, to go for a long nature walk. As I grabbed up my satchel, and headed for the door I called out, "Going for a walk" to no one in particular.

Three years have passed. I am due to have our second child. It is a warm September day with crisp cool nights. I am hoping for a girl, and James is thinking of a boy to join him in the farming. Myself when thinking of another baby boy, this tugs at my heart, as a replacement for baby Asa. It seems like only yesterday he was running and laughing.

Everyone told me to get on with life. "He was chosen to be with God, a special child." And I swallow my thoughts, so as not, to speak them aloud, as I think, do you not know how disrespectful, and careless this sounds. If it was his time, then what am I to do with my time? How will I learn to trust again? Do you know how scared I am for this child, that is about to be born?

My heart has been twisted so I hardly recognize myself. I am not sure how this is going to end up. I loved with all my heart leaving me to feel like I am paralyzed, from moving on in my life. Asa left a huge hole in my heart leaving me forsaken. This is never ever said aloud. Our life as a couple is almost lost as well. There is no joy. I should feel blessed to be with a child. On my walks I speak aloud, "Help us." "Help me love again, and love this new child. I am so lost."

James has gotten on with life. Thanks be to his faith in God. He does not know how devastated I am still, after all this time, although he was very kind, and incredibly tender at the first. Then after time everyone expected life to go on for all. Get up, get dressed, spend your day. Take back your life. Leave your sadness behind. I knew all this in my mind. If only there would be a flicker of light to brighten my heart. Instead I feel myself going further away from the premise of my life. Am I crazy?

I must be for my mother's voice is often in my thoughts, "Love has died like an untended garden. Life must go on. You have your chores, just move about one day, then another day, and the rhythm of life will bring you back to heal your broken heart."

Next day, I got up early and just started walking. Somehow I ended up at the burying ground. There in Asa's corner was a baby stone marker, with his name chiseled onto the stone. Nothing else just ASA. It read the same backward as forward. My legs gave way, and I fell onto my knees.

"When did this come to the grave?" I said aloud.

"It is so permanent. It is like putting a period at the end of a sentence, or THE END at the closing of a book of chapters."

It also is saying, "See you mattered, people loved you, and you are remembered forever."

Not that I feel less mad with God, yet I am feeling the caring grace of my husband to acknowledge our son, for the public to see, how much Asa is remembered, and cherished.

I think of my meadow life remembering, even though I am a different person now, there were lessons learned with life, and death all around. I would pick up a dead bird, and be so sad. I would bury him. Never ever did I mark its grave as it would make no difference, being I was the only one who cared. My son has many loved ones, and a community of people who care. This is the beginning of a crack, to allow light to shine back into my heart. We will be fine. Just much older with the burden of grief.

Asa died at age 3. It has been 3 years, and I gave birth to our little one we called Willie. Another sweet little boy, who soon showed me to have a personality all his own. Then 3 years later in 1857 our Nathaniel (Nathan) was born. We worked the farm and raised our boys. Life was good.


A 3-year-old and a newborn made me glad for the extra help from James's mother, Effie, as we all lived together again. We survived and flourished. James was so happy with his boys, then Willie at age 6 died. Why? I cannot retell this story of loss. We now must bury our big boy, Willie. Our sweet wonderful Willie.

Then we have Nathan who cries day and night saying, "I want Willie to come play with me."

Is this too much? Asa was 3 years when he passed. After 3 years we became parents to Willie, who when 3 years became a big brother to Nathan. Then at 6 years, Willie passed over. Now, Nathan is 3 years old. Is there something to this? Can I do anything to save Nathan? Do I need to save Nathan?

I am now afraid, Nathan will leave us too. I need help.

There is a native, the town folks call a Soothsayer, living on the island in the back near the river. Do I dare go visit with her? Am I crazy? How many changes in our lives? Things that should lead to complete happiness, only to bear false witness, and lead to heartache.

Never ever have my decisions led to complete peace, and happiness. I was not taught, or brought up in Christian ways as James. To me things are black and white, with all shades of gray, which gives depth to all that is seen and felt. I have a premonition.

The number 3 is part of the equation to stop what is to come. Secretly I will need to seek out the indigenous lady on the island, with the intention of saving the child we have left, our 3-year-old, Nathan.

When I have an hour free, I walk to the burying ground to see baby boy, Asa.

I sit there by his stone on the grass, and I remember his sweetness, his little arms, that hug so tight, his laugh over any silly thing, and the bluest breathtaking eyes, to encompass and captured my heart...

Then next to him a stone. My big wonderful fun boy, Willie. Always ready, to play with Nathan, who, now spends his days looking for his brother.

James must miss him most of all, as he was teaching, his big boy farming. This was a happy time of looking to the future. His dream of Father and Son, is now quiet...

# Part I – Afterword

NEVER EVER – Forget Life's Lessons


Sarah speaks by her written words, of her childhood spent in her special magical meadow, ending abruptly with new responsibilities bringing struggles of survival.

Two decades pass before she falls in love, marries, enjoys motherhood leading to the heartbreak, of loss. Time passes quickly, leaving regrets for the life not chosen to be lived— as her life was hidden in grief.

Sarah is trapped in fear, leading her to thoughts of a secret action; to reach out for help at the door of an indigenous spiritual pathfinder, the town folks call a soothsayer.

Sarah's words are thoughts, from her mind, sparking her soul, lingering in her heart forming the writings, of freedom to be...

# Part II

**Poetic Justice**

If only there was a recipe to follow
to enjoy all of our short fragile life...

should fate still throw in a measure of
uncertainty and eventful twists ...

on the quest to find the hidden truths
to bring forth a path to love...

**Never Ever Disavow Life's Beliefs...**

# CHAPTER TWENTY-THREE

# Nathan's Fate

Just three years after Asa's death, our second son, Willie was born, whereas the newness of babies was erased by raising baby Asa. This became a chore, even though, I loved Willie, yet being a baby made me even more discerning about the loss of Asa.

When Willie turned three, we were blessed with our third son, Nathan, this was a good time in our family. Willie was now doing things, little boys do, which was all new for me. I began to appreciate Willie for himself. He was so smart, said cute funny things, and he loved his baby brother, Nathan. We were now getting on with life and we were a happy family of four. Even though my deep-seated joy, which was my way of being in life, was not to come back. It seemed, as if, my joy was buried with Asa. My veiled life goes on, though still feeling wounded, I will do my part to perpetuate love, and preserve all that is ours. This is our time of growing our family farm.

Then the unthinkable happens at age six, Willie becomes ill and has a fever. His breath stops. My heart began racing, my mind was swirling, no not again this will not happen. I became, as if frozen, no tears, no acceptance, no understanding death.

Today I sit alone on the grass of their gravesides just starring at the two little markers; one Asa, my baby boy and one Willie, our big boy. My thoughts are at home with Nathan the baby brother, only wanting his brother to come play with him. I began talking to our boys aloud, "Help me. What could I say to Nathan? If anyone would know, it should be me. What are the words to describe such an unspeakable loss to our lives?"

My heart is so full of holes it is almost more, than I can bear, yet I am stubborn, and I can only hope Nathan, who is three, will be even more stubborn, as it helps when there is no making sense of death. Our stubbornness for living life can push us on. I will be a strong example of no more nonsense. Life is ongoing, and will become whatever we make it to be. We, the living, will be a family of mother, father and son, and never ever forget the ones who have passed on before us. We will remain thankful till the end.

Here on the grass I am thinking. How do I protect Nathan? You are three, then six, if this is a curse of all threes, all things happening in threes. Let us say this is true. Will Nathan succumb to death? Will he be 3, 6, or 9 years old?

I began to shiver with fear. No, we will not lose another child. I am making this my mission to discover a way out of this curse, as I, now firmly believe death, to be a shadow to continue to fall over my sons, including Nathan. We will not have three little markers at this burying ground.

I must be careful not to mention this to any of the family, who already think of me as different. If this was known they would indeed think me crazy. Do I care? I must, it must be a secret, otherwise my faithful husband would be disgraced. I have no choice. I will seek spiritual help from the

Wabanaki Soothsayer, who lives by the river on the island. I will start tomorrow for I cannot just do nothing, and still protect Nathan.

"This is a nice morning. I am going for a walk. Can Nathan stay at home with you?" I said to Effie. "But of course we have lots to do, and he will be too busy to ask questions, that have no answers."

Nathan has asked daily, "When is Willie coming home to play?"

I am so scared to approach, and even more afraid there is nothing in her world that can save my son. Nathan is now three years old. I can not dawdle. I see a sign in her window by the door.

KNOCK 3 TIMES TO SEE ABA; spelled the same frontward and backward, just like Asa, also knock 3 times. It is as though, I was meant to be here, my breath stopped, then taken a big deep breath for courage, I knocked. RAP-RAP-RAP I heard footsteps, the door opened, and there standing in front of me was a perfectly normal looking woman about the same age as me.

She smiled and said, "I am called Aba and you are?"

"I am Sarah, nice to meet you."

"Sarah come in off the dusty street. Sit down at the table."

"Would you like a cup of tea whilst we get acquainted?"

"Yes please, that sounds nice."

"It will be just a few minutes." She gave me a sideward glance saying, "Make yourself feel at home and be comfortable. This took courage for you to come visit with Aba. I am glad to make your acquaintance."

I murmured "Have you been in town long?"

She answered, "All my life ever since I was a little girl. My mother, also is spiritual. We have a gift of sight into the roads of life, and paths traveled. Some believe, some do not, and some pretend. A lot like religion." I squirmed in my seat feeling the religious pretense fit, as if aimed at me.

"Death has brought you to see Aba. The hardest was the passing of Asa, now you have lost your son, Willie." She almost had me, then I thought she lives in town, where women talk of all events.

Aba spoke, "This is common knowledge, but what brought you here today is a secret wish, which we will get to. First, Aba needs to understand your past life, then Aba can help you see clearly to move forward."

"You, as a child suffered with the death of your pet cat after praying your heart out, leaving you hollow. Then you lost your mother, after praying all night. You thought God could not, or would not hear your cries for help. You have not shared these with anyone, with the exception of your parents."

"Aba will get us our hot tea. Later, Aba will read your tea leaves, although you are spiritual, whereas, much of your life is on your sleeve, so to speak."

I felt my face become warm, quick like a flash, while she talked openly of my inner secrets, and I mumbled, "Thank you, tea will be nice."

"Now shall we share, what has brought you to Aba's door today. Asa was age 3, when he died. Three years later you birthed Willie. When Willie was age 3, you birthed Nathan. Then at age 6, Willie passed on. You are scared, and want to protect Nathan, who is, now 3 years old. You want to know, if he will live past 3, 6, or 9 years of age. The numbers of infinity, a matrix, that goes on forever."

I was speechless, and took a sip of my calming tea asking, "Can you help me? I will do anything to save my son."

Aba looked at me with deep compassion saying, "Anything?" She paused. "Of course Aba, can and will help you. It has been put upon my heart. Aba, is so sorry, two of your children have passed on."

"Your son will live. You will live on forever, in a place you choose. There are many details, we will put in place, and I will not worry you at this time.

The most important thing for you to know is Nathan can live, and life goes on with the one child, you have, to remain through out your life."

I felt relieved "Aba this is what is needed to happen!"

"Aba must tell you this will take much time, on your part with seeking knowledge, to gain wisdom. We will take one day at a time.  All, to you, will be worth more than gold. The universe will require a plan, to bring the three of us, to our desired outcome."

"Drink your tea and visit Aba often, once a week for the way to be shown. We will never ever say anything to anyone, with respect to this being a spiritual life matter, not of our making."

"I am so glad I came to see you. I am alone in my belief, Nathan, also would die, and this I cannot share with my family. It is clear I was attracted to come to you, Aba."

"Come next week on Monday. Aba will begin work, on your life's map helping you to ready your path. Your big job will be to enhance knowledge, to bring about wisdom to tell you of the trail to lead you back to the joyful Sarah."

"Aba is shown, as to where you are in your journey."

"We must put trust in our beliefs and each other."

"The ultimate decisions will be yours."

"Aba must caution you."

"Be very careful of what you wish."

"Are you prepared for your wish to come true?"

# CHAPTER TWENTY-FOUR

# Aba Sees Hidden Truths

Can you imagine how shocked anyone would be to know my life's story? No one, except one, will never ever know how fear controlled my life, and ruled my decisions to control the outcome of my life, along with my son's life.

My help is Aba, who is Wabanaki, and lives on the back side of the Island in town. On my walks by the water I had felt enchanted from the first time her place caught my eye. Each walk drew me closer, whereas I felt drawn to the front door, and knew not what lies behind, until last week, when I knocked out of desperation to save my only son. Somehow I knew she was the only one who could help.

She had said, "She knew, and would guide to save Nathan." Now she is my secret friend in adulthood, just as the fairies were my childhood friends.

I knocked three times and Aba, a small native Wabanaki lady, opened the door and in a sing-song voice said, "You come for tea, yes." I felt happy to be there again, smiling widely, saying, "Yes."

Aba went on to say, "Sit, Aba make. You look pretty today, but feel troubled, yes."

She spoke again with a confidence that I could hear, "You need tea to direct your soul, to the next parts of your life. It is essential to go to the front line of your life."

"Thank you ,Aba."

"There are choices as you might know from your extensive time spent with the fairies. The life you have had has prepared you with a place for an ability you have. If you choose to tap into this pathway, there is no changing your mind, once chosen, and no speaking of this formidable path."

"I have never ever known anyone, who can see all my hidden truths, that are kept secret in my heart."

"Most are not prepared to acknowledge this power, that lies dormant in all who live. It is the power to redirect your life, to enhance another's life, thus being your son's life. Foremost in your mind, is to protect him from an early death. You have this power!"

"Are you sure, I have such power?"

"As a child you were given the keys to life. In you, this knowledge lies dormant, yet as real as when you were told by the fairies. Remember what you were told, bring belief back into your life, then you can have what you want for your son."

"This only works in silence, if found out, or known by anyone the knowledge will cast a shadow, and break the pattern, of life ever after. In this case an untold secret is worth more than gold."

"Your son will live. This is what you want with all your heart and strength. You sense this building within yourself, as a way to protect him. There are paths, tests,, and controls which must be trusted completely. Even while we talk, Aba cannot tell you all Aba has seen, because you are not to be influenced. Your life choices must be yours alone. If this decision is good, the test of time will determine. It is rare, that we as human beings can gain wisdom through our knowledge, to choose what is best, yet, true if you are enlightened the choice is yours. Choose wisely."

Her words were still registering and I said,

"Aba, you speak with such discernment."

Without fanfare she said, "Aba is fortunate to have had so many dedicated teachers, throughout my path. Did you enjoy your tea?"

I felt so peaceful and quiet on the inside saying, "I not only enjoyed my tea, I also feel so relaxed."

She answered, "Good. Aba, will continue to map out your way. Aba cannot tell you the complete plan, so to speak as we cannot put the cart before the horse. You will know all, as you are readied with wisdom."

*"This week Aba has prepared a clear quartz crystal for you to take home. Today we will learn our first lesson." Aba said, as handing me a beautiful clear stone.*

*"To make yourself familiar you will need to hold it in your left hand, closed in a fist while breathing deeply."*

*"We as people are shallow breathers, yet our life is in our breath. Breathe in deeply, hold, then breathe out slowly."*

*"Do this several times."*

*"Then open your hand, and continue breathing, as you look at your crystal. Do this a few more times."*

*"Again remember: Do this several times each day to make the crystal receptive to your energy. Each time we meet, Aba will teach you of your crystal's capabilities."*

Aba searched my eyes and with discernment and said, "Next time you talk, Aba, will listen. We all need someone to just listen. This will put your thoughts in perfect order for your life's decisions."

"Aba, can sense you are beginning to trust Aba."

"Yes, I needed someone to help me, for I was so alone in my fear. Now, I look to you for knowledge, and comfort. I am so grateful for your kindness with quieting tea and my crystal. Thank you."

"Aba must again tell you your wishes, may not be what is wanted in the end. Please seek out knowledge to know wisdom, to help you choose the right path."

**_FAIRIES REFLECTIONS:_**

**_Arwen spoke of choices:_** _We must talk of choice to choose the right path to have the key to know life, bringing forth the power that lies dormant until you accept, and know all as you are known._

# CHAPTER TWENTY-FIVE

# Aba's Truth

Today is the day! I will have tea with Aba, to tell her of my amazing crystal. I can not wait as I ready myself for my walk. Nathan is playing with some cousins, and barely has time to kiss me goodbye. "Have fun." I said, hugging Nathan tightly, as he squirmed  pulling away. He is very independent, not unlike his mother, I thought as I went out the door. I am anxious to have tea with Aba, the people of the town call a Soothsayer, who lives by the river.

I am here early, but I can not wait to tell Aba. I knocked three times and Aba opened the door saying, "Sarah, Aba has been anxiously awaiting your visit. The tea is ready.  Today is your turn to talk. Come in, sit, and be comfortable. Tell Aba all about your crystal work this week."

I took my teacup faced Aba and began, "Indeed as you said, I took out the crystal, and put it into my left hand. This was awkward for me because I am a very right handed person. Then I took a deep breath, held it and slowly exhaled. This was also not natural in the beginning, but by the end of the week I was not thinking so much, and found deep breaths to be relaxing."

Then my voice went higher and I spoke faster, "In fact my crystal started vibrating. At first I thought it was my imagination, then with each use it was more prominent."

"Then when I go out of doors into the sunshine and open my left hand the crystal transforms into a rainbow of colors. Primarily red, yellow and blue, which also change to green, purple and orange with the vibrations. I could not wait to come to you today to find out why? What is making my crystal look so beautiful, with all colors as it vibrates?"

Aba said, "Sarah, you have progressed so quickly. The vibration is energy. All that is required is to be receptive to the crystal's energy. Aba can tell you are excited, and a little in awe of the process of the power of the crystal. It is amazing, yes."

She went on to say, "This week you will continue to know your *crystal, adding the affirmation.*"

*"I am centered and at one with my energy. It will be."*

*"Say this as many times as you take your breaths."*

"Aba wants you to see, feel, and know, that you are a part of the vast Universe, and grounded to our Earth. We can not rush your introduction to your crystal, for this will be your key to what you want."

"Aba is so impressed with your progress, and very glad to be of help. Aba, will see you next Monday."

"Remember before your wishes come true make sure they are what is actually wanted."

"Aba before I leave, you remind me ' to be careful of my wish' Why is this?"

"Sarah your wish is a feeling you want to manifest, as a needed desire, to be present within your home. A wish for a successful outcome, which will allow Nathan to live out his life. This longing is becoming a request to behest fulfilment."

" Your wish is something, which today, seems unlikely to be brought forth?"

" As you hope, with your belief in your wish, you will aspire to change the paths with trust, and expression to bring into reality the wish."

"Again Aba reminds you, this is a big wish for your family's life.  Aba wants you make sure of what you wish,  will it be what is wanted for your family?"

### *FAIRIES REFLECTIONS:*

***Arwen concluded:*** *"Daydreams help the fulfillment of  our visions, hopes, wishes, to become reality. Let your mind wander with wishful creation of imagination, enjoying imaginary thoughts as real."*

# CHAPTER TWENTY-SIX

# Aba's Right Hand

Good morning Sarah, you are out and about early." Aba said, as she opened the door. I thought maybe too early so I expressed this by saying, "Am I too early?"

Aba smiled, saying, "Heavens no, as each morning Aba walks across town to the east side of the Kennebec River to watch the sunrise. We from the Wabanaki, are the people of the dawn with our home in the east where the rising sun first greets the land. Aba is not truly myself if, Aba misses the sunrise."

My heart fluttered as I realized Aba knows who she is, and what her life needs to be fulfilled. Leading me to say, "I have no idea who, I am, or what I need to fulfill my life."

Aba squeezed my hand to give me encouragement speaking softly and slowly, "Aba has a very big job of enlightenment where you will come to know yourself, then you will see your choices very clearly. Together with the help of the Universe we will allow your life to come into fruition. You will no longer feel lost in this way. It is true you will know who you are and what is required to feed your soul. Just as, Aba knows what is needed to stay Aba."

"You make it sound so easy to have my life fall into place. The crystal energy relaxes me, and has made me feel more in control of my fears, which has made me feel more confident."

"Aba is glad. This is what is needed to go onward to continue to grow. We are ready now, to add steps to your crystal."

"We will add the right hand, to enhance your receiving the Earth's energy for your mind and spirit. What it amplifies within your own being, will be your light known as your truth. The crystal when one within the power of your mind is a great tool for needed transformation. This is what you recognized in my demeanor. You too will have a life determined by you, as the laws of energy and nature determine."

Wanting this to be my fate, I asked, "Do I continue with what I am doing with my left hand?"

*Aba answered, "Indeed you will for one half your time. The first step is to be grounded to the earth, by holding your crystal in your left hand to invite into yourself the energy and affirm :*

*'I am centered and at one with my energy. It will be.'*

*Left hand, breath and affirm one half your time.*

*"Next you will put your crystal in your right hand to send out, with the second part of your time."*

*Do your breaths and to the right hand confirm :*

*'So it is' or 'so be it.'*

"You are moving along with great speed."

Aba warns, "Keep in mind that not all wishes are what we want them to be, in the long scheme of things in life."

**FAIRIES REFLECTIONS:** *You take pleasure in little things, perceiving the world, as it is...*

**MORIA Thoughts:**

*My roots are deep within Maine,*

*whereas my life — each day*

*is inspired by all things hidden*

*from capture, on Mother Earth.*

*All may look towards the ever changing sky ...*

*each day, to watch with awe — the colorful sunrise*

*see, sensual hues of Orange-Reds-Yellow -Violet...*

*Skies, soothing blue with many forms of white clouds,*

*not one, fails to notice the darkened stormy skies.*

*Then, twilight can show a cry for comfort...*

*with a sunset of Yellow, Orange, Crimson & Magenta reds*

*before a consuming nightfall — to hosts the stary skies.*

*Watching the wonders of nature gives inspiration...*

# CHAPTER TWENTY-SEVEN

## Aba's Pain

Another Monday, I arrive at Aba's place. I begin by telling her, "I also feel such a powerful energy."

"Your crystal is awakening your spirit giving you the earth's energy, allowing discernment as a second nature."

Aba looked sad as she continued, "Aba would like to see more people awaken. People look at me thinking; Aba is like dirt under their fingernails. Aba is not offended. This is because of their lack of teaching. Aba knows I am as dirt of the earth; ashes to ashes, dust to dust, and Aba will one day return my body to the earth."

"Sarah people are afraid of the unknown, also religion teaches to stay away from the ungodly acts of prophecy which is thought of as devised from evil."

"Aba understands and agrees, it is sad to be herded as sheep with no mind of the wholeness of what truly is part of all life. Rather than growing freely to experience life they seem content with illness, and a lackluster being, with their only hope controlled by the men, who run the church as they determine who, what, when, where, and why, people exist. In this church world, they say it is written in the word of God that Aba is to be feared. Whereas in the Universe, Aba is a learning child, learning the paths to grow into wholeness."

"I am glad you are helping me, to find my path."

"Aba's heart aches, sometimes, when Aba sees struggle and unclarity. Aba does want to help but this must be an individual choice, to reach out to our universe. Not all are ready or have been scared away by rhetoric. If they only knew the wisdom of seeking out knowledge. It would be so wonderful if everyone knew the freedom to be. To become as they were created by God."

"This now is my hope, to become." I told Aba.

"When Aba sees you, Sarah, Aba sees your soul. You have walked on earth for many years, in many different times, and not once have you taken up the journey to cross the bridge to understanding. You have learned much about life, yet without the fulfillment of your soul. So you see it is my great pleasure to help you grow wise by enlightening you with the tools."

"Like the crystal, and watching my breath flow?"

"Crystals are the ones we are now using with much success. Aba can not tell you what to do or push you into a direction. This is difficult for me as I can see the paths, and also know what you need. You must see and know for yourself. This is to remain your journey."

"Aba can only remind you to be mindful and careful. There is no going back once chosen the pathway remains yours. Sarah, do be careful. Listen with your whole heart and soul. Our life on this earth is brief. Each time we come, we each have our gifts to sustain us. We must not cast aside our gifts as they are to complete our soul."

"I cannot remember my gifts"

"You are this week to remember, the untethered Sarah of your childhood. You need to become her again. To become whole with all your gifts, then be aware, and use your gifts to grow wise."

"I do not know my gifts"

"Remember your life is a gift to many. I am so happy for your progress. You have grown each week, in less than one month you have understood the use of the crystal. Aba is so elated with your progress, and it makes Aba so very happy."

"I enjoy my crystal time."

*"If your crystal slows, bury it in the soil to change its energy that it stores.*

*— In your left hand say, —*

*'I am centered and at one with my energy.'*

*'See, feel, and know, that you are grounded to the earth.'*

*'With the right hand — Affirm by saying,*

*"So be it" or "So it is"'*

*"Remember, the left hand is the receiver; energy flows in...*

*the right hand is the sender; energy flows out."*

"Trust your inner voice. Do not deny it. Your crystal will allow you to get in touch with your inner self to experience your light, also known as your truth, to then put you in touch with your gifts you have abandoned throughout your lives. This will be your biggest breakthrough allowing you to truly explore your life as it was meant to be."

"Any questions to ask Aba?"

"No, I wrote down the highlights to make sure I do all the steps correctly. This crystal work is not hard for me. I enjoy the deep breathing, and the way it leaves me relaxed." I went on to gratefully say, "I am so glad to have taken the chance, you could and would, help me. I am ever so grateful and thankful for your life of knowledge."

"As is Aba thankful to see you emerge from the shadow which is covering your bright life. It is fulfilling to see you drink in the earth's knowledge. This is just the beginning. Till next week on Monday morning."

I smiled, "Thanks to you I am finding peace of mind, and feeling a lightness in my heart.

"It goes without saying, as Aba sees you as Sarah, embracing your life.

Aba must remind you, as you are leaving, to be careful for what you wish to be true. Remembering life goes on in every unpredictable way."

### *FAIRIES REFLECTIONS:*

***Arwen spoke:*** *"Deep within each person there is a secret place to hold belief, the core is who each one was born to be, so this place no one else would fully understand. Focus your attention on not fighting the old ways you were taught, but in living the new ways, will lead to dreams brought forth to reality. Innocent children hold the key to life. It is not imaginings..."*

# CHAPTER TWENTY-EIGHT

# Aba's Straight Line

Today I am dreading my visit with Aba as I knock hesitantly on the door. I think she will be somewhat disappointed in my progress. I am to find myself, and all my gifts, now there seems to be a barrier as though I do not want to go any farther. I find reasons to set aside my crystal work. Why am I afraid?

Aba looked in my eyes, and exclaimed sadly,

"Sarah, Why do you have a mental block?"

"This week was long and I am feeling less confident, due to my lack of progress" I said meekly. "I find looking closely into my mind and heart as a hard uncomfortable task. It is, as if, a blind eye is looking for that once free and happy child."

Aba did not look surprised and she spoke with such knowledge, "Sarah, Aba wants you to know you have never ever allowed yourself to accept your gifts, to use them to aid yourself or others. Remember fear and routine stops us from moving forward. You must find your strength and break away to freedom."

"Your clear quartz crystal is a powerhouse capable of focusing our energy by absorbing, transforming, transmitting, and expanding all thoughts. The laws of energy and nature determine this function, which becomes especially powerful when combined with the host of our mental thoughts which is what changes our knowledge into energy."

"You need not be so hard on yourself. Stay the course. Keep your pace as you race to the goal line of understanding. You will find all your gifts including the abandoned gifts from the past. You will be so elated with your life. You will be able to see as far as you need to guide your life and those you love."

"Today you are afraid to know the child, who had strong feelings of hurt, was blamed and misunderstood. You must know her, except her, and love her, like she was then; as she is you. If you look hard enough to be uncomfortable with the undesirable behavior of the child then you have seen the real Sarah. Until you know yourself, you cannot make life altering decisions with clarity."

"Perhaps a trip to your old homestead will help you trigger some memories. In due time you will break the barrier. Stay the course and be patient."

"Remember that little girl did not disappear in time. She is still here waiting for you to remember."

I took a few deep breaths to quiet myself as I said, "This then is my fear to know myself. To truly know who I am, what I think, when I lived, where I lived, and why I never was able to accomplish spiritual growth. I know, I need to find myself. I should not be afraid to face this child, who is so full of hurt, even knowing she will tear at my heart is somewhat comforting, as I made it through my life by looking away. You want me to look her straight in the heart, to accept her hurts as my hurts."

"Yes this is what is needed for control of your future. You have your 'spirit helper' the crystal, as your personal tool for transformation. It will amplify, store, send, and focus your thoughts, emotions and desires, ultimately manifesting them into reality."

"When you are seeking the truth, your truth, always remember it is done, and no longer can it be changed or reversed. You just make peace with the person of the past as your time is now."

"Thank you, Aba. I am feeling much better."

Aba went on to express, "When seeking, where you find you are blocked, know it is the memories, emotional pain, and suppressed emotions, that stay in you and block energy flow."

Aba told me, "Next week, Aba wants to know about Sarah as a child from her heart. Remembering all people without full knowledge of their history are like trees without roots, there can be no growth or stability."

"We as people never ever learn anything from hearing ourselves talk. We need to listen to ourselves to know this person we have been in the beginning years, are our roots, that give balance to our lives."

"We learnt lessons as children to know all things. We do have grave consequences teaching us to avoid behavior that brings disruption and destruction. Our lessons, also teach us to use and value the behavior in our life that brings order. There is always a balance in a fully lived life which is in tune with the Universe. This person knows their whole self making decisions accordingly. Your job is to find Sarah, to remember her as a child."

"Keep in mind, your wish will need all of your wisdom, all you know and have known. This becomes your challenge so the path will be known to you, to fulfill your wish and to know if this is what is wanted in the end of time. Be careful. A wish can become a powerful detriment for your life."

**FAIRIES REFLECTIONS:**

**Arwen whispered:** *"God fills the Universe silently without noise; Nature fills the heart and soul of children."*

# CHAPTER TWENTY-NINE

# My Words

This week at Aba's door I paused, then knocked three times. She is always the same, inviting me in, saying, "Please sit, Aba will get our tea. How was your week?"

I answered, "I was able to visit my old homestead, the house Paw and his elusive brothers built, now this house is falling down. The life we shared in this place is all of my childhood, but also, still forgotten, so I am looking for myself in the meadow." I continued to say, "You know that expression, 'You can never go back home'— it is true."

"This is true, today the place of childhood is gone, along with the memories, that should be kept alive, instead they are hidden in my heart. In the magical meadow I was so sure all my friends, who were only the creatures of the field, would still be there to greet me. Instead, how terrible and devastating, that I did not recognize, or feel akin to the place where I spent each and every day of my childhood. In fact I was so out of touch the birds were chirping, and I did not recognize their song they sounded like all birds, everywhere. I left there devastated, as I always thought my meadow was a place of solitude where I could go back, to be at home anytime."

"The only good thing was my white rocks were still there. James offered to gather up my rocks and take them to the farm to make me 'happily smile.' These are the same white rocks the fairies told me to collect. They said in their sing-song voices, 'For as many as you will need; is as many as you will gather.' They never ever told me what I would need with the rocks, nevertheless, I always listened and did as they asked. There was always an enchantment as they were very beautiful and very wise." It was odd to be talking out loud about the fairies remembering I was cautioned not to proclaim they existed, yet I knew Aba had a foot in all worlds, she also knew their works, and she spoke of the fairies in my childhood.

Aba asked, "Tell me one other important thing that the fairies asked of you."

I thought for a second and blurted out, "They said, Sarah find what gives you joy!"

"Then I discovered with my Mother, writing stories gives me joy."

"This is how we are going to get to know Sarah as a child. I think if you would please me with stories of your childhood, we will see the gifts you have been given to reinstate them into your life. This is next week's work. Aba, cannot wait to read your story."

"Good as in my satchel I have the story I wrote of my visit home. Hope you enjoy reading it."

"Very Good, Aba is pleased to get started. Next week write a memory from your childhood. Now remember to be careful of that, that is wished. If wishes were horses, beggars would ride."

"My Paw, also told me this saying, to put my feet on the ground as there was work for me to learn.

My Mother said, "Perhaps you should save your wishes for something you desire or hope to happen. A wish is something you want — to be, something good."

### Need To Visit Home —by Sarah

No one lives on the land. It is growing up with alders and brush. Some-one said, "You can not go back home." I thought of course you can, I love this land, it is magical to me, yet looking over the field there is nothing different from all the fields we passed to get here. All were unkept and grown up with brush.

It is not the way it looks. I do not feel akin to this space where I spent my childhood. This was where I escaped criticism, escaped chores, and escaped schoolwork, my safe place. It was my whole reason for existing. It seems so small now. I look around. I see nothing special. Yet, as when I was a child, my heart would swell with pride, with love for this very land. I carried this love in my memory. It was part of what made me feel independent, and different from all the other children.

I had this special relationship with the green earth, the rocks, the plants, birds, bees, and all the little creatures. I was always part of the landscape, not as a ruler, just a child, who was accepted and allowed to run, to pretend. As I imagined all was in awe of me, and so much happier when I was with them, in their fight and flight for life.

As I looked around, my ears try to listen. I hear the birds chirping as they are singing. I do not understand the purpose of their chirps. No matter how hard I listen, concentrating on their sounds, I still cannot know what the purpose is. I am today a total stranger in the meadow. My childlike innocence is gone. With sadness, I realize my memory cannot capture the joy of life this place held. Looking around it is desolate, and even if it was exactly, as it was the last time I set foot on this land I know in my heart it was the magic of my youth, which allowed me to be part of the table of life. I could hear, see, feel, touch, and become part of nature, in the full sense of belonging in my meadow home.

Now, I find myself an outsider, a grown-up who sees bees, birds, flowers, rocks, butterflies, labeled all of what they are called, and what they do for us. For instance bees make our honey; the birds scatter seeds, eat bugs and sing beautifully; flowers with glorious color produce seeds; rocks keep the soil from washing down the hill; butterflies transfer pollination; the trees, grass, even the weeds, all keep the soil from eroding. Everything in nature has purpose.

As a child this is not what I knew or saw. Every blade of grass, every plant, each tree, the birds, the bees, belong there in the field together, in harmony. There was a peace of just being with purpose. No one thing was more important to the land, each has their role, and cannot do what they do without the others. All were important, this order of life became my playground. It was as an enchantment from my heart, bursting with love from the inside — out, to be running freely, under the ever changing skies.

The fairies were part of my life, as I loved them, believed them. My reality was they would always be. I knew they would help me, and keep me virtually alive and well. They are not today in my life to view with my eyes, yet they will never ever leave me. The fairies taught me there is a time in life for all different actions required for survival. They simply encouraged me to see that nothing lasts forever, in my life which will change many times over. The core of who I am will never ever change. It will be my outsides needing to change, to bring about survival.

As masters of 'The Secret of Knowledge' the fairies, along with a whole host of other spirits are invisible to human sight, and can use their purpose for good. The magical forces that lie at our command are no more mysterious to them, than those natural forces compelling the trees to grow, and the rain to fall to earth, or The Earth to turn on its axis. All goes on through-out eternity.

It was the fairies who told me 'someday your life will be in tune with the white rocks.' Collect as many as you can, this will be as many as you will need. Without question I began taking up the stones and putting them side-by-side over by the big rock, day after day. It is odd how I never noticed the white rocks, then it was unprecedented how many I saw. My job is to gather them together because the fairies alluded that they were to be part of my life. The white quartz rocks are in a pile on my old homestead. How can I move them from Cana to Bloomfield?

This planning to change the outcome of my life and Nathan's, has a shadow of darkness, that comes from keeping all a secret. It is like wishing when seeing a fallen star where it is said, "If you tell what you wished, it will not come true." Only this is a "life or death" real time wish; that once made must come true, and only works if kept secret."

The fairies taught me all of what we do is essential for the time in which we live. Find what brings true joy and make this your life. My joy is in writing.

James nudged me, "You seem to be a bit quiet. What are you thinking about?"

I took his hand and spoke from my despair, "It is true. You cannot go back to your home. There is nothing here for me anymore, except maybe my beautiful white rocks, I collected as a child. Perhaps someday we could bring them to our home?"

He looked puzzled, then answered, "Sure if they are important to you and will make you happier. Anyone you want to see while we are in town?"

"No, this place makes me sad. Let us turn around and go back home. There is no place of home, anywhere here, anymore."

**MORIA Thoughts:** *I too, have known your feelings of devastation.*

# Chapter Thirty

# Today

I walked to Aba's and thought of my blocked memories. I had a story in my satchel, but it was not what Aba asked me to write. She wanted feelings, memories, and life experiences, to find the real Sarah. I wrote about facts, places, and people, that were in my life. When I got to the memories of my magical place, I could not share this, that was my heart, as my heart seems locked.

I knocked three times and when the door opened...

I burst into talking, "I did not write about me, the real me, only about the people in my life, who lived and shared my life. They too did not know me as I was secretive about all that made me happy. I was afraid if they knew of my meadow life they would take away my play time where I spent my days in the peace of enchantment."

"I will need to know what my fear is, now. It is not you. I trust you, Aba"

Aba smiled, "Thank you Sarah. Trust is a good first step. Remember, Aba will not judge how as a child, you navigated your growth. The key to finding you, will be in your childhood. Tea is ready"

I said, "So is the history of my carnal life for your reading. Next week I hope to be able to open up to know my feelings or the roots as you called them. I am calling this time in my life, 'My Hidden Heart' as I know not. What do you think Aba?"

"Right." Aba said, "People with knowledge of their history, not their heart are like a tree without roots, with no way forward to grow."

"Thank you for your story today. Do not worry. With your crystal work and your determination you will overcome this fear. Just remember to be careful about what you wish, be clear about what you want."

***

## Nana — by Sarah

I, being named Sarah, was the first born to the Pitt's family. My father needed a bunch of boys, as they were the future of the farm. Getting more than my share of attention from Nana and Gran Papa, Fletcher, I talked young and enjoyed a childhood of fun and games. At the age of four, my sister Eliza was born, and our mother stayed in bed for a long time. Nana was taking care of us and she had sewn us many clothes. I am told that we were the cutest little girls, yet cute gets old with no permanent position on a farm.

In all the days, my sister and I, shared growing up together, my fondest memory is of the stream with moss covered rocks to wade across the river, feeling of the quick current as the water was flowing around our legs. How much fun, as our feet slipped and slid, as we walked across the slippery moss covered rocks. It seemed not to bother us that snapping turtles shared our waters, mainly because we did not know. Why did our mother allow us to cross the river?

In the heat of the summer there were fields of flowers. At our Mother's suggestion we turned them into beautiful corsages. The green fern was first, next we picked some thorny pink Roses which also picked us. When this looked nice and full, we added Columbine Bells and of course Daisies, tying them together with twine, as we had not pretty ribbon from the dry goods store. Quite often our Nana was the recipient of our gifts of flowers. This gave us much happiness and pride, as Nana seemed pleased.

Nana was very prim and proper always sitting quietly, with her legs crossed at her ankles, along with her dress tucked in closely, as the way a lady should be seated. Her pearls were two strands and worn in the afternoon. She was a wonderful seamstress, who was much in favor, therefore hired by many to stitch together their clothing. In these times the men would have her remove part of the sleeves of their dress shirts for summer wear; in winter time they were stitched back for warmth.

In between paying jobs, Nana would sew my sister and I many new dresses, which were more often than not the same. We not knowing the concept of twins dressing alike, never ever would we give this a thought to the need of being dressed differently. It was an honor to have a new dress sewn by our Nana. These were our best outfits, not to wear playing on the farm. We wore them to visit with Nana. Most of our times on the farm we were in clothes that needed no special care. Sort of like us.

It was out the door to play until lunch time. Play we did. There was this rock in the field by the edge of the woods we would run to, and the grass would scratch our arms, so we ran through the field, with arms reaching to the blue and white sky. The sun would be warm, and off by the trees we could hear the birds chirping like they were happy to see us. When we would stop to rest from running there were butterflies of beautiful colors, and bees humming all around us.

"I need to rest a minute because my side hurts," one or the other of us would call.

I remembered what Mother had said, so I told Eliza, "The wild strawberries will be out soon. When the yellow and orange paintbrush flowers are waving in the breeze, if we look under them we will find strawberries. Mother said since we have so much energy we could pick some for her canning and preserves. Could be fun."

I gave her a nudge, "Are you ready to check out our place?"

"Ready, Set, Go!" We called out together.

Ahead lay our big rock with smaller rocks for chairs. Also an old washtub, with a hole in it, that we found in the dump pile along the fence at the back of the house. Sis and I carried the tub over to the ledge, which was a very hard job. Then we put it upside down making this our proper table, as this was to be our field home.

One day our Paw put up a swing in the oak tree. My sister, Eliza claimed it for her own. She no longer would want to go to the Meadow.

All by myself, it became 'My Magical Meadow.'

This was when the meadow became alive with fairies...

### *FAIRIES REFLECTIONS:*

*So this was the beginning of your Summer days spent with the Fairies, we are friends and guardians as we watch over you, assuring your well-being. We are not always within your visual sight, still you will feel our presence. We are on the earth and spiritual, so always with you helping to learn the many lessons of life without interfering in your childish ways...*

# CHAPTER THIRTY-ONE

# Aba Entrusted With Secrets

Sarah, you have never ever had a person to share your innermost thoughts or to just be with the real you in the Universe, quietly knowing you are not alone. Someone who expects nothing of you, yet knows, and understands everything in your life. You had a sister who was not compelled to be your playmate, you both, lived remotely away from all other children, except for some distant cousins who were seen when at your grandmother's for kinship not friendship."

"Aba can relate as Aba, too was a lonesome child, who never ever had one friend. As the years have gone by Aba has thrown myself into my work.  It has been a real blessing to me. Your words have awakened my loss which Aba felt as a child when others would play games, full of laughter, then Aba would come to play they would become quiet. Aba thought there was something wrong with me. Aba was in adulthood before Aba knew they were afraid of me, afraid because my mother was a Soothsayer and Aba was known, about, as a seeress with great powers of foresight. No one knew how to act around me so Aba was always alone."

This made me feel sad for Aba. I spoke softly from my heart, "I feel your pain very deeply, as you had children around you, who chose to act as if you did not exist, which is more hurtful, than having no children exist, yet we were both always alone."

Aba smiled with an understanding of equivalence then continued, "We are all in this Universe for a reason. I eventually gave in, and accepted my fate. This does not mean we are less lonely, but it helps to have a purpose. Aba was born into clairvoyance, and you were born on a prairie with tasks that involve survival. Our instincts to survive were programmed before we were born, yours and mine. Aba thinks of life as wonderfully made from beginning to the end, and if there is acceptance of all which is deemed good, Aba, also must accept, what is said to be bad or sad, as this is part of living a full life."

"Aba is tribal and cannot fit into most worldly events. You on the other hand could have married a rich man, belonging to high society, only for appearances, as your soul is one of a survivor. Today survival has become your anguish. You see, Sarah we are born to be, then if we try to become someone different, we will not fulfill our souls. To grow wise is life affirming. You have heard the expression, 'Bloom where you are planted.' To me this means, 'be who you were born to be' as this is our life's work."

"Aba, you are so wise, and I think of you as a friend. Is this alright? You truly know my secrets."

"Sarah, Aba is a safe person. You trust me not to judge, and know you can let down your guard. Aba also knows, and believes, in the worlds of nature and fairies. I have experienced this in my ongoing life."

"As for you, Sarah, I can only reveal what pertains to your life. My knowledge has grown with years of learning, there are great and wondrous things, Aba knows that cannot be sharded. These must be lived through to become a part of a person's wisdom. I am honored to be your friend meeting you where you are on your journey to becoming."

"Thank you Aba. I feel the freedom of releasing my secrets to the safety of my only true friend, whom I trust wholeheartedly."

"Sarah, yes we are a very unlikely pair in a secret friendship. We are coping with our sad past, also you have brought me joy." Aba went on to say, "This makes Aba glad to know, together we help one another navigate throughout life."

"Aba, to add to this you have brought me joy, along with hope by encouraging me to seek, then learn much knowledge."

"Today Aba, I know you and I, both learned to live alone. We spent our childhoods alone, and learned to share only what we deemed appropriate for the relationships we have. Never ever revealing all, of who we are in our lives. It is just not safe to proclaim our real lives. We have become friends."

Simultaneously we spoke, "This friendship is happiness..."

"This is a sad story from my childhood I called 'Wash Day Fun.' It shows how my survival skills were abandoned by me, in a moment of play. I am ever so grateful for you asking me to write, as remembering my life is teaching me what was expected of me as a child and why."

"Thank you, Sarah, your words have brought clarity until next we meet you know what I must say,

    Be careful of that, that is wished,

    as what comes to be,

    may not be that; that is wanted,

    they may be two different things."

**Wash Day Fun — by Sarah**

Childhood memories, my first of being a little girl was the extreme pleasure of running out of doors, shoeless, and being happy, so happy it felt as though my heart would burst. Each day after being set free outdoors, this was then where I wanted, only to be. Every day outside was a new discovery with such a big world to explore! The birds were singing so loudly, all at the same time, later to learn they were spring mating calls, this became music to me. Looking across the field where it was a carpet of all green, now flowers were filling in with colorful yellow and orange paint brushes, alongside daisies.

Mother said, "This was a sign that the wild strawberries of the field, were also, at their feet ready to be picked." It takes a lot of berries to fill a pail, which became our first important job to help our mother by picking berries for our family who liked shortcake. I liked it too, but eating berries while picking spoiled my desire to share in the fruits of my labor and labor it was, yet no complaints from me.

This was outdoors where the flowers smelled so amazingly wonderful, the air was still, and sort of too warm, as the sun was getting hotter. My hat needed to be kept on my head as my mother had said, "In the house you go if your hat comes off." Yet, hat and all I loved this time. There was sadness when the strawberries were all picked. We all ate strawberries till they were coming out of our ears and everyone said, "This was the biggest year with the most picked berries ever." My mother made enough strawberry preserves to fill a whole shelf.

Now, my lovely flowers are going to seed for another year, first the paint brushes, then the daisies. My lesson learned; joy is fleeting, and it will be a long wait between seasons. Each season has its special chores, yet picking strawberries remains my very favorite.

Outside our house my mother had pink rose bushes, my favorite color. As a small child I learned to shake the flower to allow the bees to fly off, before smelling the sweet fragrance, which became my favorite. This one time I saw a fairy sitting on a petal. I had never ever seen a fairy before, yet I somehow knew this was only for me to see, as no one else ever said such a thing, and neither did I speak of my first encounter with my soon to be new friends. This was to be our secret.

Mother also had a Peony which upon blossoming would be beautiful, but covered with ants. Perhaps a neighborly farm would give some Dahlia tubers, if she had too many. Nothing was planted that needed fussing over or weeding, as Mother had not the extra time in her day filled with cooking biscuits and food for breakfast, lunch, and supper, all on the kitchen wood stove. This was done all year long, no matter what the outside weather, be it hot or cold. What mattered was cooking, clean-up, and everyday jobs, done on the wood stove. Ready on time.

Then washing clothes was one day a week, all day long. When it rained, water was collected from the roof into the trough which filled the citrons or barrels, as most houses had storage for wash day water. Then the hand crank wash tubs would get set up outdoors, weather permitting with all the laundry was sorted. Aunts and other family members from other households would all get together, usually at my grandmother's place, carting their dirty clothes.

Today was unseasonably hot for a midsummer's day, in western Maine. Mother had the wagon all packed with our dirty clothes. She was anxiously waiting for us girls to finish our chores, so we could be on our way to Nana's farm. We, Eliza and I finished our chores at the same time. Eggs were collected, chickens let out and fed, we brought fresh water for the pigs, goats and cows. I was feeling sweaty, and I know from bad experiences, that this is when I forget things, so I ran back to make sure the fences were secure, as I was not to have anything bad happen on my watch.

Our mother said, "Good you finished your chores quickly. Nana and your aunts will be awaiting us to come to get the laundry hung on the lines early, so it will have time to dry before the thunderstorm we are bound to get with this hot day." Mother always had one eye to the sky as she planned her activities around clear dry weather.

Mother started talking, "Now, I am counting on you two to keep out of our way. Stay outside to play just like you do at home each day, only at Nana's you will have a few cousins to join in your play. Now get along nicely with your cousins. Also, it will be hot in the sun so keep your bonnets on, no matter what the others do. When we get to Nana's, please fetch water at the pump for the horse, then your Grand Papa will put her up for resting and feeding."

This was our adventure for the week. Mother liked her togetherness with her mother and sisters and we cousins got to know of one another while playing.

The process was to heat the water to a boil on the wood stove by lugging it to the house a pail full at a time, dumping the water into a copper boiler that was placed atop the stove. It was heated in the night, and brought to a boil in the morning, as the stove was made hot for biscuits. When the clan gathered they began the job of filling the tubs with hot water poured over a bar lye soap making the water go from clear, to milky white.

"Get back, kids. Not too close. You will get scalded" Nana went on to say, "Out of the way now. Go off and play."

Then the group of women would put their white clothes in and begin to switch them around. I would come by for a drink as playing made me thirsty and notice the wash water was getting gray. "Out of the way now go play." The trick was to wash everyone's whites in one tub, then fish them out with pointy sticks, as the water was still too hot for bare hands, next put them into the tub of clean cool water.  After which, one would take the socks, and other white unmentionables, and undershirts feeding them through the hand wringer made of wood, then another would turn the crank on command, letting the clothes fall into a basket. When the basket was full of wet clothes and was almost too heavy to lug, each handle was tugged on by the two whose turn it was to hang the clothes on the line. We kids knew not to go near the clothesline.

They were serious about keeping the clothes clean while they dried, so here they come with the usual warning, "You kids stay away from the clothesline you got the whole yard and field to play in. Now do as you are told." Did not matter which aunt or person, it was always the same speech and it was a good reminder. As we kids, if left to our own fun probably would end up throwing mud balls at each other with no thought of the hanging wash.

We would go away to the brook. There we could catch some pollywogs, putting them in the canning jars we found in the shed. They were clear glass and very clean sitting in the corner of Nana's shed. All us kids took one.  I took the pail hanging on a nail on the wall, to catch the polliwogs. This will keep us out of trouble for hours.

I knew the wash day routine. I always make it a point to know what is going on, after the whites were in and out, of both tubs, a little water from the rinse tub was added to the wash tub.  Then the light colored dresses and shirts were washed. Water was added to the rinse tub. Then the process would start again ending with work clothes. Each week would be dedicated to a different garment: one week towels, one week tablecloths, one week sheets, one week blankets, one week curtains, and laundry day was every Monday, weather permitting.

Now what will we do with our polliwogs? They need to eat so should we take them home? Then we will need to ask our mothers? Somewhere in my mind this was an uncomfortable thought. I went over it. What would be the problem? What was there to object to, they were just baby frogs, we caught to watch their legs grow on them. Then we promise we will put them back in the brook. I cannot think of any reason we would be in trouble. We talked, all of us kids, deciding, I would make it known we had caught them, and our plans of putting them back. I was feeling confident in our decision to keep them until next week, so I agreed to ask.

It was getting hot. We were sweaty and hungry. We gathered our jars of boggy smelling polliwogs, and walked back to the house. We almost cut across the field where the clothesline was at the other end, then remembered the strong warning so we walked way around. The lines were full and drying in the sunshine. All us kids went over under the shade tree to sit on the granite step, lining up our jars of water and polliwogs. Most of us had two or three in each jar. What a triumph we were soaking wet with bog-water, yet happy as we caught and jarred so many. I was jingling inside out. We did what we set out to do. Was not it wonderful?

Nana's calling bell was ringing calling all us children to lunch. Perfect timing, off we run. My Nana met us at the door. "Oh no you are not tracking that water and mud into my house. Take off your socks, long pants and your skirts and shirts to lay them out in the sun to dry. Then you may take a sandwich, a glass of cider, and sit outside while you eat until you dry." Looking at Nana, she had sweat beads all across her forehead. She was talking fast, like she had no time. This is not the time to ask if we can keep them till next week.

After eating, checking our clothes to find they were not dry, and they were getting stiff where they were dry. This is washday. Why didn't they just wash them? I could hear the women talking and laughing, so I looked in the window. They had the huge square table covered with strawberries which they were cleaning by removing the hulls, grass and all that was not berry. Their hands moved fast and I was so impressed by how quickly they were mounting up one bowl, after another bowl of berries. It took my sister and I, much longer to pick them, though we ate as many as we put in the bucket.

Then I heard my Nana yelling, "Something has happened to the jars. They were cleaned and in the shed, now they are gone. I am sure they didn't grow feet. Get the children." They rang the bell.  I stood by the window, as if frozen. I could not move, and then here came the laughing kids pushing and shoving as if they didn't have a care in the world.

I should warn them. What would I say? "Do not talk about the jars. Do not tell them what we did to get so wet. Runaway!" My mind was racing and now I know why. I knew. The sense I was feeling, the uncomfortable thought I was doing something wrong. Now we are in trouble, big trouble. It is clear I should have known the jars were clean, they were neatly stacked by the door near the kitchen. We had picked berries, next came the canning. Why did I not remember?

This is important to our families. Why did they not yell, "Do not touch the canning jars?" I would have known if we were not having so much fun. To think of my Nana and the responsibilities, would have just spoiled everything. Here are the kids laughing happy to be together, some in fact much older than I, yet they did not know any better. I am looking at them with the same critical eyes of Nana and my Mother, as we stand and they asked,

"What is wrong with you?"

"Why would you take my clean, fresh jars for canning without first asking?"

"To do what?"

"What have you done with them?"

"Do not all speak at once."

The kids were all looking at me, so all the grown-ups with their straw-berry stained fingers, looked at me. Everyone was looking at me, like it was my idea. I can not remember. Was it? We did this together as kids having fun. Now, am I to be responsible? I looked at the kids.  I could feel my lips tighten, as if, in defiance. In my mind I could not think what to say, or do. It was not, as if, I had no investment, in the canning of the berries. My sister and I picked them, so I was mad too.

My mother spoke, "Sarah Pitts, what can you tell me about the canning jars?"

I said, "They are not broken."

My no-nonsense mother said, "Just tell me quickly, then what? We want to know, Sarah."

I spoke softly, "We use them to catch polliwogs. They are out on the steps."

Then I heard my Nana, who is all work and no nonsense, "This is going to set us back one hour at the least." She said to the aunts, "Girls go dump those jars out. Start washing them while I start a hot fire to boil and sterilize. We got to work fast as the berries will spoil quickly in this heat. Gather up the berries putting them outside in the shade. Then cover them over with cheesecloth to keep off the hornets and flies."

They were marching around doing as ordered, and we children did not dare move while the aunts dumped our polliwogs. We still did not move, even after, things were well on the way to preparing the berries.

Nana said, "You see, look and see, all the extra work you kids have caused by not asking permission to use jars. These were not yours to use, yet you took them, to catch baby frogs, to be dumped to their deaths. This was done to fulfill our daily purpose of survival which today was to preserve berries to bring us through the hard winter without scurvy, and to keep us from our death."

"You children need to be more responsible. If you are punished this will be up to your parents. I am old and set in my responsible old ways, knowing not what is appropriate to teach youngsters today. Now, take this box, and go pick up the dead polliwogs. Dump them back into the stream before the yard smells of dead frogs."

With that said, we shuffle off to the granite step to what minutes ago was our joy. Put on our sorta wet stiff clothes. Sadly picked up our dead frogs. None of us spoke. What was there left to say?

There was no time for thoughts of our feelings.

Life is about survival...

A hard lesson we must never ever forget...


**FAIRIES REFLECTIONS:**

**Aspen added:** *"It is the truth. Most children are convinced they have a great imagination, then told not to speak, of what they think, they know. Innocent children hold the key to their life, then lose their dreams by listening to others."*


**MORIA Thoughts:** *This story of your family wash day was enlightening to think of this major household task with the women of the family sharing the burden, to bring all together almost as a fun event. These days of kinship are now lost to the olden days, of survival.*

# CHAPTER THIRTY-TWO

# Sunrise Monday

Today is another of my special Mondays. As I was walking to Aba's I imagined again, knocking 3 times. Aba again, would open the door, again, get the tea ready, again, welcome me into her place. I like the knowledge she is always the same person, letting me feel I can count on her even letting my guard down as she will not judge my actions. Therefore I felt relaxed. I was thinking of the story written for her today. This story was personable as it showed my hesitance of the truth, and lack of leadership abilities. It leaves me feeling vulnerable, but that is the point of writing to know Sarah, the child.

"Good Morning Aba. It was a beautiful sunrise over the field today." I said happily.

She replied, "That it was over the river, we both looked at the same sunrise. We each from our heart saw and felt different things. We are in different places in our journey through life. Aba can accept that neither you, nor Aba, are either one perfection."

I said to Aba, "The sunrise awakes our spirits to continue to be in our quest. It fills my heart up with amazement leaving me speechless. We all know this is not good for a writer to be speechless. Today I will leave with you a short story which shows my childhood character. Titled: 'Birds Of A Feather' Hope it is enjoyable to read.

"How is your crystal time? Is it helping you find young Sarah?" Aba asked. I paused to think then said,

"The time spent with the crystal and breath, is making me confident in myself. It calms me and I feel I am being brought back to who I was born to be, allowing my full destination to find my path of Sarah to achieve my wishes for Nathan."

"Good now, Aba thanks you for sharing your writing with Aba, as you remember your childhood. This will be the key to opening up your life. This takes precedence before you can help Nathan and always remember to be careful with a wish, as it may not be as you want in the end."

***

## Birds Of A Feather — by Sarah

In our family only some were schooled proper. This was mostly my cousin's especially the boys. At our house when the farming was catching up and the chores were somewhat manageable, we were asked to practice our reading and writing, not so much arithmetic, as this was for boys, except for proper use of measurements to be able to cook.

As a young girl one of my jobs was egg collecting and feeding the chickens. I was pecked by them a few times when taking the eggs out from under the laying hens, becoming a little scared of our chickens.

My mother said, "We cannot have that, you being scared of your own hens. Sarah take charge as they are small birds. You are the boss."

I was a boss with many pecks on my hands, yet I grew to love them, and cried as if my heart would break when it was time to cut off their heads, as old hens who stop laying eggs become Sunday dinner. I kept on with the crying.

"We need Sally and Sue, for the eggs."

My mother spoke with reason, that should allow no more to be spoken, "Sarah every two years they will stop laying and we will manage our eggs by allowing some new chicks to grow into laying hens." Who wants to know this stuff? I thought shaking my head back and forth as, no, no, no. I wanted her to know, so I said one last thing,

"I love the hens, and I want them all to stay."

To this my mother replied, "That my dear, is why you should never ever be a farmer's wife."

Chores of the chicken coop being done I was feeling sad.  I went into the kitchen to wrap up a biscuit or two, as I was going into the field for a time of grief. Besides today mother was in a frenzy to spring clean, she has already said, "If you are not helping then keep out of the way."

I could help, should help as I am strong for ten years old, but I know from past experience it would end with my mother being pressed for time and very cranky. I can not know how often I have heard, "If you want anything done right you need to do it yourself."

So, I grab my book, another biscuit to wrap in my dish towel, and off I ran into the wide-open field yelling, "I am off to the rock in the field to get out of your way." I kind of closed my ears just in case there was a protest, and I ran faster without looking back.

I thought why did we not just live out of doors. The rains come clean most everything then the sun dries all. How perfect for creatures that I love. What a beautiful cloudless sky. It is a day people say, "You can hear the grass growing." I am growing too as I sit on the rock and take a deep breath of the fresh air.

What could be any better than this? I am happy feeling at home out in the middle of this field sitting comfortably on this big prayer rock. That is right my Paw said, "Your grandmother was faith filled, before the church was built, she had church right here in the field." As my Paw told me the story, I felt more kin to her, more here than anywhere. She died before my birth, so she is a memory passed on to me by my Paw, and his love for her.

The birds are still chirping, maybe I should give them my biscuits. What a fantastic idea! Unfolding the dish towel, breaking the biscuits into pieces, I then shake them out onto the ground not unlike feeding the chickens. Oh, poor Sally and Sue. I have no power to save them. The wild birds do not trust me so they will not go after the food. I decided to read, sitting very still so they could watch me as to decide, I was not to be feared. After a long time I was feeling hungry and my biscuits were bird food.

I was afraid to run home knowing the routine of my mother and her sisters, they would be still moving furniture, curtains, oversized quilts, rugs, carpets, even Paw's gun, and anything not nailed down, out into the sun where they could beat out the dust. This was going on while another would mop up the freshly bared floor.

I made a mental note: When I am grown, I am not doing this, besides of which my sister would not help. Our time will become known as—

"The Lost Art Of House Cleaning."

Just as my dear Mother often says,

"Most today do a lick and a promise"

And I would say, "Amen"

Just like my namesake, Grandmother Sarah Pitts.

I know, I will go ask my sister to get me a biscuit.

She will be swinging. I am sure she did not take food with her. My mother knows I grabbed food. There she is predictably swinging her life away.

"Eliza are you hungry?"

"Not really." she says.

"I am, but I already took biscuits," I told her.

Eliza said, "Almost time for lunch. It will be a sandwich, already made before the aunts came to begin the spring cleaning."

I looked up at the sun. She was right. It was near lunchtime and my tummy was growling. I guess it was good that I came out of the field. Now we will be waiting to hear the lunch bell.

"Want me to give you a push?" I asked, then added,

"I am strong and can push you to the sky, hang on tight, Eliza!"


***FAIRIES REFLECTED:***

***Aspen continued:*** *"All journeys are connected throughout the Universe, most never ever know or suspect. Think of this as you look to the sky. There is not a moment of any day when nature is not showing a perfectly beautiful scene. Picture the beauty of all, everyone, wherever, and however far away, are able to just look up to see the view. The sky is there for all to see and appeals to the immortal in us. It is essential to the spirit of life and yet, people never ever attend to the beauty of the sky. Extraordinary skies of darkness do cause all to notice as a warning to take cover. The sunrise, or sunset, or the puffs of clouds, in all ways are there to be seen and or, lost in our apathy..."*

# CHAPTER THIRTY-THREE

# My Mondays

Mondays take my week of crystal works and writings to fruition, as Aba clarifies my efforts to learn who, and what I was born to be. I love my Mondays spent with my friend and teacher, Aba.

Rap, Rap, Rap.

Aba welcomed me then asked, "I hope you brought another story as Aba has enjoyed reading very much. Reading, 'Need to Visit Home' there was much wisdom, which, only comes from the truth. You wrote: 'There was a peace, of just being a purpose. No one thing was more important to the land, each has their role, and cannot do what they do without the others.' Also, 'My life will change many times over, nothing lasts forever. The core of who I am will never ever change.'

"In the story 'Nana' The words:

'All by myself, it became

My Magical Meadow.'

"Then in, 'Birds of a Feather' your love shines for all, the animals, also the ones in your life taught to you by stories of your Paw. Your sister who would rather 'swing than play in the meadow' as a your companion, yet you did not resent her, and even 'pushed her swing as high as the sky.' The best yet, 'Wash Day Fun' where you were a child playing allowing fun to shadow your mindset for survival."

"Thank you Aba, I really enjoyed writing my stories. This is a new concept for me to share my words, and have them understood as written. This next one is at the time of my Mother's death. I call it, 'Remembering Childhood' as it is of Mother's ways."

Aba said, "It will take all your past lives with their knowledge and wisdom, along with your reclaimed childhood to make the clear choices needed. Fiskars are impatient with apprentices like yourself, due to your limited knowledge that cannot allow for good strong choices. One can only see clearly the way, if this has been a way, that is familiar."

"Aba will guide you, not to tell you the way, as you can only navigate, what you yourself know. Think of this journey as walking a path to life. If Aba said go forth to build the perfect shelter, and you did not know any building skills, the end results would end poorly built. Your strength is in what you have learned living your lives. Only you can know what you are capable of doing, by bringing your gifts into fruition to continue on your way."

"You gave life to Nathan, you have birthed him, now a rebirth is required to keep the breath of life. You were right to recognize his fate. I am excited to help you because, together, we can overcome his death with much brought forth knowledge. Acting in unison, we will be strong enough to overcome death. Aba is confident he will live. As always, I warn you, careful for what you wish as the outcome cannot be seen until fruition."

"I know Aba there is never ever a way of turning back, one cannot take back choices, we all must live with them. Life is a journey of which there is no utopia. There is a balance. We as people know Joy; so we also know grief. This I have learned, the secret to life is to know a balance of good and bad times, and accept equally all events."

"Aba wants you to know throughout life always keep your true Joy, never ever loose your true Joy. Joy is the heart of one as an individual. It is what we keep coming back to perfect. Sarah, do you ever think of Joy? What do you know about Joy today? I want you to ask yourself these questions, knowing Joy is a gift of fulfillment. Also think of the moments in your life that gave you pure Joy. This is your strength, your gift, that will keep you strong and fulfilled, no matter what or when turmoil pulls to throw you off balance. You stay the course and hold tight to Joy."

"Your wish will put you on a different path. Make sure this is where you want to be."

"A lot to think about, see you next Monday. Thank you for the stories. They are truly wonderful."

***

## Remembering Childhood — by Sarah

I often remember my Mother's ways. My sister and I, along with our Paw, lived in the house. We knew Mother's Housekeepers rules: No tracking in dirt, be on time for meals, no talking at mealtime table, wash your hands and face before putting on night clothes so as not to dirty the sheets, no talking before falling asleep, in the morning take off your night clothes and fold neatly putting them under your pillow, dress in your play clothes, make sure you put the covers up on your bed, the pots should be brought out the back door to the outhouse where they will be dumped, rinsed and put upside down on the rack to dry.

After this we go into the kitchen and wash up, as breakfast is waiting, so all this is done as swiftly as possible. Mother will say,

"Sit down girls. Eat. Your chores are waiting."

Mostly our chores were outside the house, feeding the chickens, watering the pigs, goats, cows, and horses. Once done we were on our own till lunchtime. We thought Paw made the chore's list.

Sometimes I would convince my sister into the field to enjoy my "Magical Meadow" although she was not receptive to any of the things which made me so happy. She could not connect with the sounds, the beauty, the smells, all the things that touched my heart. I tried to show her and share my secret life. I would say excitedly,

"Listen to the birds, they are calling to each other saying,

'Insects in the fir trees, come to feast.'

"Look at their beautiful feathers of all colors. Notice how quickly they fly from tree to tree. I wish, we could fly!"

My sister said, "I'm going home to swing. I don't like this field. There is nothing to do up here."

I countered, "But there are insects to watch, new flowers to discover. It is a special world. Do you just want to mindlessly swing your life away?" Sighing, I said, "It is alright. I will see you at lunch, when the sun is straight overhead."

The house was perfectly clean with the lunch on the table. Our mother said, "Go wash up do not dally." We ate and were told to go play. I miss my mother's careful attention to running the house. It was all about a perfect house. The hot meal, the clean floor, tidy rooms. It was so comforting to have everything done for you.

I truly believed that my sister liked to swing, my mother liked to keep house, just like I liked to commune with nature, mostly by myself. I find it hard to visit with my sister in my special field, so I can understand our mother found it hard to visit with us, in her clean house, and always said her truth,

"If you want anything done right do it yourself."

This sticks in my mind. Mother wasn't a teacher, she was the doer. We clearly were in the way. Our mother has died leaving, only my sister and I, to take care of the house, by ourselves, to be sure, it is not done right...

***MORIA Thoughts:*** *I too remember life in childhood being the only real time of learning the fulness of life, as all seems so perfect when young with no cares within our world. It is as though floating through life without cares and burdens. Perhaps the expression 'the innocence of children' was coined to convey the importance of childhood.*

*Then wanting to share the adventures you have discovered, all the things of nature calling to discover and enjoy, yet to learn, no one else cares to join in your meadow life. The sad thing is, as children we learn to justify the apathy of others, as their way to be. We except and are then alone in the realm of this magical place where each day is an adventure to learn how to be in the universe, yet without the joy of sharing. I feel glad for your adventure and I also know your need, to have shared all these things which brought you happiness, the joy to be doubled in your ability to share.*

*I would have loved to join you in your magical meadow with all of nature putting on its lifetime show... I can imagine sharing this space in the warm sunshine with plants emerging in the spring, quickly growing to sway in the breeze, and birds of all colors to watch, as they gather their seeds. My wish, to be with you to have shared this day in time, within the woodland smells, came alive reading your stories. Thank you.*

***FAIRIES REFLECTIONS:*** *God fills the Universe silently,*
*Nature fills the heart and soul of children...*

# CHAPTER THIRTY-FOUR

# Aba's To Be Guide

A Guide, this is my calling. Aba is to serve by guiding ways to fulfill one's life by showing paths. The people must choose to navigate the way by making all the decisions."

"The cost will be keeping it all a secret. This will become the biggest price. In your case Sarah the secret will be worth much, to be exact your son's life here on earth. Also, your eternity on earth, without the benefit of eternal life, as you have in the past died, coming back to gain knowledge, although as of late you have given up on your growth."

"Aba, what you are saying is amazing."

"This new start with Aba is to learn more of what life teaches. Think of this. How do you instinctively know how to navigate things in your everyday life? Before you were shown, you already somehow knew. Why is this? Is it second nature?"

"In my life, I think, it is called, Aunt Harriet."

"Things such as cooking, cleaning, caretaking and many more personal things. Some call it being gifted, but gifts fulfill emotions not our everyday tasks."

"I never ever gave thought to this concept."

"There are many choices in life which are called paths. The Medicine man and Fiskars are old souls having traveled life's many paths, leaving knowledge living in their souls. We can see old souls, and connect to their wisdom, as they can cut through life's nonsense to the truth. They are seeing clearly with seasoned eyes, acquiring much knowledge from traveling the paths. They have been there then shy away from redoing this journey."

"Aba what do you mean by journey?"

"Life is made up of choices, some bring joy, most bring strife, as knowledge has a steep cost, all lives are the outcome. What we ultimately seek is love and peace, which brings harmony. It is far better to know many things when navigating through life, as Aba can only be a guide of what you have free will to choose. The directions, Aba can share with you as they are a part of Aba, as a well-known trail, allowing Aba to help others on their journey. This is a privilege and an honor."

"So this is what you meant by saying you will, 'map the way' by knowing my knowledge."

"Aba cannot tell you the end results of your decisions as this is determined by many factors in your life's journey. The choice will always be yours. Each person Aba guides helps me grow in my own humanness. We become wiser when we give of ourselves by sharing our knowledge. This is my Joy."

"Yes, but Aba I am becoming impatient to move forward."

"It will take all your past lives, with their knowledge and wisdom to make the choices. Fiskars are also very impatient with apprentices like yourself, do to your limited knowledge cannot allow for good sound choices. You can only see clearly the way, if this has been a way that is familiar. I will guide you, not to tell you, as you can only navigate what you know. Think of this journey as the trail leading to life. Remember if Aba had said go forth on your path and build the perfect life, without any knowledge of the way, as you know not any previous path, the end results would come out poorly. Your strength is in what you have learned along the way living your lives."

"So you, Aba want me to know and see clearly."

"Only you can know what you are capable of bringing into fruition for your gift of life to Nathan. You have birthed him, a rebirth is required to keep the breath of life. You were right to recognize his fate. Aba is excited to help you, together we can overcome his death. Together, we will have strength through our knowledge which will be strong enough to support life and love. Aba is confident he will live. As always Aba warns you to be careful for what you wish, as the outcome cannot be seen until fruition. There is never ever, any way of turning back, you can not take back choices, we all must live with them."

"Aba, your thoughts of Nathan to live is encouraging."

"Life is a journey and there is no utopia. There is a balance. We as people know Joy, so we also know grief. The secret to life is to know a balance of good and bad times. Throughout life always keep your true joy, never ever lose your true joy. Joy is the heart of you as an individual, and is what keeps you coming back to perfect your life. Aba repeats again:

'Sarah, Did you ever think of Joy? Do you know Joy? I want you to ask yourself these questions. Joy is a gift of fulfillment. Also think of the events and moments in your life that give you pure Joy, that comes from within the bowels of your soul. This is your strength, and your gift will keep you strong and fulfilled."

"I never ever knew of joy, as a gift?"

"You have said your stories you have penned give you joy. Again as I read your stories my heart is awakened with your everyday view of your life on earth, and those who shared this journey along the way."

"More wondrous still, they are mirrored as real, every word that you write to tell your stories. In you, Sarah, lives a true writer and in your stories you hide nothing allowing the reader to visualize your mind and spirit. You are a true author gifted in writing for fulfillment, not for recognition. In my culture you are known to be a free spirit. Aba admires your ritual of writing in a secret space, without the knowledge of family or friends, as you write the truth of the light, and shadows of your life."

"Remember to be careful with a wish of time."

***

## Outlook Of Life — by Sarah

My eternal view of what happens throughout my life, was determined by if I sensed despair, or accepted it as a lesson of growth. We as people must learn to accept hardships, as they welcome room to grow stronger with more understanding of what was learned through the process of living life through this hard felt experience, coming out the other side.

Life is a precious gift to be lived, with equal times of joy and suffering, to know all aspects of life. In contrast the more suffering, the more joy will be known. All my sad experiences of life have been made worse, lingering longer, with my total unacceptance of what has already happened. Allowing lingering on loss, to postpone living. I somehow understood loss was controlling my life. It was, as if grief had kept me captive with a blockage to the growth I was on earth to learn. Shadowing me from the many lessons of learning to know of true love.

Love was blocked by my stubbornness of my leaning into the unfairness of my losses. When I was asking, 'Why' I became broken, and my life stopped moving forward. I stayed still, as if in a cage where all this time whittled away my productive years on the earth. The years were moving onward leaving me old, without the benefit of life's experiences to teach me love.

This is what I have learnt of real tangible love:

I am referring to real love, which does not start by seeking to find love then voicing 'I love you' instead it is acquired by lessons, allowing a person to see and feel hate. Once felt and accepted, hate turns to hurt, grief, and broken heartedness, then healing through total acceptance of that, that cannot be changed. Then at the end of all the hurts, dissolution, and untrust, like a rainbow's reflection, is love, along with joy, that surpasses all of our knowledge and understanding, as unconditional love.

This full love, is today within me, and as Aba has said,

"We are coming together through our twin thoughts."

Everything is changing, I accept one day all will be gone.

Learn to not fear or resist change;  nothing is permanent or promised.

Let it go, while holding tight to gifts; as gifts are the hearts joy of life.

"I failed my life by selfishly clinging to grief's sadness, with no movement forward."

We are born unselfish;

we should live unselfish;

we should die unselfish.

"Live for today. It all goes by so fast."

This being the wholeness of life —We love one another...


***FAIRIES REFLECTIONS:*** *The sign of the Universe is love, in a perfect world all humans are each connected to one another through love...*

# CHAPTER THIRTY-FIVE

# Recognize Sarah

Another Monday, in a row of Mondays, and I find myself anxious to talk with Aba. The routine never ever changes. It is comforting to know I am expected to learn how to make my life's gifts part of this life.

At the door I am enchanted by Aba's voice in song. I paused and listened to her peaceful voice, then I heard her speak softly, whereas I could not hear what was being said. I waited for a quietness to overtake, then when sure there were no more sounds, I rapped softly three times.

"Good morning Sarah." She had that famous smile that comes from her heart.

"Good morning to you. Were you singing? Excuse me for asking, I was not truly eavesdropping just ready to knock, and paused as not to disrupt you because you sounded so peaceful. Is this something I could do when I am out for my walks?"

Aba told me, "This, Sarah, anyone can do. Aba lights a smudge to clear my space, whereas walking in nature is full of nature scents. Next pick your voice to develop your repetitive sound, need not be words, just softly use this voice to call, also said is to chant. After a few minutes quietly end with speaking softly of whatever is on your mind. It is very simple, yet powerful. Aba, sometimes holds my crystal to clarify, helping me see all things clearly, allowing me to accept all the good in my left hand, then to my right hand to exit all the bad traits, that are blocking goodness, and are hidden within my soul. This chanting will help you improve your growth, into the real whole gifted Sarah."

"The more you recognize what your gifts are, they can give you the strength, to choose the path's direction. In order for you to be strong, you must be made whole, with all your gifts intact. This will be your hardest task to understand yourself by knowing what are your strengths and know they are alive in you."

"Aba this is overwhelming."

Aba agreed saying, "Indeed Sarah, this is why we take only one part at a time. You have your crystal work, and you are comfortable with how it helps connect you to who you are in the world. Continue this week to expand your works. Next week we will add another step. This will be the beginning of your new life."

I looked to her, finding my voice to say, "I am so scared to live my regular life, while preparing to change my life."

Aba looked me in my eyes and said, "It is quite clear, whereas understandable, as you are overthinking your role. If done slowly and properly, it will be as breathing, an act necessary for life. Trust the process, and enjoy your crystal works. Relax and breathe deeply the breath of life. You deserve to know yourself as you are known."

"Do not be afraid to be in the moment when holding your crystal and breathing each breath, in and out, as the breath is life. In this quiet time your mind is present, and you are fully present. You are not in the past, or thinking ahead to the future. You will be fully here in the moment, mind and body together fully present in the time of now. This allows you to be a force with nature."

"You have noticed your stories of your past, are following our discussions on our Mondays? This being as twins, as we put it, is an attunement of the Universe. We are becoming in tune with each other, bringing us together on the wish of extended life for Nathan."

"Sarah you were brave to recognize his fate, and to further follow up with me, to bring a solution to stop his untimely death which would devastate your family. To lose your third child is an event which you have deemed needless, an event that never ever should happen."

"The Universe does not give up on anyone, as there are fairies, angels, helpers and guides, who work together to help, each, one of us move on our chosen path of life, with the use of all the gifts we were given. They will help you to know all the gifts, allowed to lie dormant. These gifts are yours to use to make you whole to bring much needed strength, to overcome any obstacle in your life's path."

"Your job today is to relax your mind, to find memories in your past, you will have courage for all tomorrows."

"As always to make your wish come true ... You must own, your own way, and remember this way is only for where you are in that moment of time, when you choose to continue life on earth for Nathan. This will only extend his time with your family. This extension of length of life will not affect who he is in his life. He will remain the child of the Universe he is created to be."

"Sarah, your wish will only extend his time on earth with his family."

"Sarah, are you prepared for Nathan, to remain with his family?"

"Think of this, as you will somehow need to have an answer."

"Till next we meet, Monday. May you be still within."

**Fairy Life's Lesson— by Sarah**

We were up early because there is much to do in the month of June. The vegetable garden needs to be weeded, and the second crop of beans will be planted, as it takes a lot of plantings to have food to eat, as well as canning for the long winter. Mother and Paw work hard to get the crops in while hoping for enough rain to promote fast, even germination. Some years are good strong growth seasons with lots of sun and plenty of rain. Then there are other years, slow to start, and have droughts until late summer or fall, leaving our plants stunted to bear smaller crops. Everyone is in a good happy mood, when everything is growing, and producing as planned, as needed.

This year so far has been good for crops, and as we finish our breakfast we know time, or lack of time, is foremost on everyone's minds. Mother is already in the dishpan whereas I am helping by clearing the table. Eliza is too young to help without our prompt attention which is at the moment fragmented by a split second need to hurry. We need to finish up the indoor jobs to go about the work at hand outdoors.

Mother said, "Sarah, you tend your chickens and take care of Eliza. Remember stay close enough to hear if I should to call you. Sarah, are you listening?"

I did not want to watch my sister.  I knew not to say this aloud so I said, "Yes, I know stay close enough to hear you if you call."

We were not expected to help plant as the seeds were purchased which meant they needed proper planting. We were expected to help by keeping out of trouble and staying nearby. I took the bowl of food scraps and egg shells putting some in a small bowl for Eliza to sprinkle on the ground for the chickens. She always laughed as the chicks came to pick at the offerings prompting me to say, "Eliza you are laughing and the chickens are happy with what we are scattering on the ground. We are doing a good job. How would you like to go for a walk? We can see what is growing in the field." I knew if she thought, she would want to swing under the oak tree, yet with Mother in the field too far away, it would be me who would be stuck there all morning long.

"Let us go for a little walk."

We walked, and I knew the limits of how far to go, oh just a little further, we would be in the meadow. This is where I wanted to go, where everything is alive. It is just like crossing over into another land filled with birds, insects, and more importantly fairies.

Eliza tugged on my sleeve saying, "I am tired." I looked down at her and her cheeks were red. She looked hot and tired of walking.

"Eliza we will go over by that tree, to sit in the shade for a while." I checked all around the trunk to find a most comfortable place to sit with moss for a cushion. "Eliza please sit here with me. We will take a short nap in this land of peace and quiet." She fell fast asleep.

I stood up, walking around seeing many new caterpillars, thinking to myself this will be a butterfly paradise a little later in the season. Time went by quickly as it does here. The sun was overhead telling me we needed to go back home. Wait a minute. Where is the tree, Eliza is under?

I had walked away without noticing any signs to follow, to bring me back to her. Should I call out to her? This is terrible!

I find myself running from tree, to tree, and I cannot find the right tree. My heart was racing. I knew I never ever should have left my little sister all alone, then I began to cry. This was my fault. I was too far away from our house. I have left my sister alone somewhere in the meadow. What if she awakens? She will be scared. I have to find her!

I heard a quiet laugh, coming from the most beautiful fairy. "Why are you crying Sarah? Can I help you turn your frown into a smile?"

"Oh, yes please. I lost my sister. She was sleeping when I left her, and now, I cannot find her."

"She is right where you left her. We have been watching over her, as this you neglected to do."

I knew they must be disappointed in my breaking my Mother's trust, so was I, now. I realized how badly, I have behaved. I said, "Thank you, for watching over my sister. It was so thoughtless of me to leave her by herself. She could have awoken, and been frightened to be left all alone. Please tell me where she is sleeping, as I need to be with her."

The fairy wings lowered and she said, "Are you ready to meet your responsibilities, no matter, what is expected of you, Sarah?"

Good they will help me. "Yes, Thank you for your faith in me."

"Good go six trees to your right, and you will find your charge, sleeping, and awaking with a hunger for lunch. Remember you will be needed in many ways in life. If you help by doing good, you also will always be taken care of, just as we were there in your need, when you abandoned your sister, even though it was not intentional."

"It is, what it is, abandonment."

"Thank you for being there for us"

"You are welcome and remember this lesson:

Sometimes what is a burden...

like watching your sister, which is keeping you

from what you love...

**In a little time this burden can become...**

**a treasure to find..."**

**"It is all in the way you view the event of the time."**

# CHAPTER THIRTY-SIX

# Trapped

Today, I walked to visit Aba, for our Monday tea.

I feel trapped. I have felt this feeling before. I first recognized it, when I was twelve years old, and my mother died. It is a feeling of not knowing. I am scared to learn about myself. I must put one foot ahead of the other making myself face Aba, with this fear ever looming.

Aba opened the door, my fear came from this big and vicious life-threatening terror to just an echo of fear, which has become humbled. Was it Aba's life of strength? Was it my belief?

Am I moving into my life, my light, and not backing down?

Aba proclaimed, "We have a busy morning, we will sit to begin with the prominence of the clear quartz crystal. Many medicine men used the crystal for diagnosing illnesses, and as a much-used tool in their healing rituals. They consider a clear quartz crystal to be a living rock, a spirit helper. Crystals that have rainbows within them were held by the dying, and used as a focal point for emerging with the spirits. The dead were buried with the crystal, as a valuable property."

"Aba knows the power of the crystal in the Universe of which the crystal comes. Aba knows we as people of the Universe, are gifted with knowledge of all things. We learn to use the crystal to open ourselves, to the prominence of who we were created to be. Our knowledge then becomes known to us. We are ready to go forward to another plane on our journey, knowing ourselves as we are known by the Universe."

"Hold your crystal to the 'third eye' above the nose in between your brows. It is here that you will deal with being intuitive, having perspective, telepathic, optimistic, meditative, and your visionary. Through the years, memories of emotional pain and negative emotions, stay within your body. This creates blocks to the Universe's energy."

*"Once a week you should set aside 20 minutes of quiet time to do the third eye."*

*"Place the crystal above the nose in between the brows while lying down in a comfortable position, with your knees bent to relax your lower back."*

*"Place your arms at your sides, palms up. Deeply inhale, breathe in positive thoughts, love, good health and happiness. Breathe out all negative thoughts, worries, and anxieties. Let it all go."*

*"If you see a color it will be purple. As you exhale, say out loud or silently, 'My higher power guides me and everything I do.' or 'I am attuned to the divine order of my life.' Repeat this seven times. Then say, 'so it is.' Remove the crystal and hold it in your left hand. Rest this way for a minute before getting up."*

"Next few weeks be aware of Joy vs Sorrow or Woe."

"Tell me what emotions you felt when Asa left you"

"I cried my heart out with sadness. I felt despair. Betrayed by my unanswered prayers. I was filled with disbelief. Why would this happen to a small child? I felt hate for all the people, who tried to help me with their words of encouragement. When he died, I also died a death leaving me empty inside. To this day, I still am not that girl, I was or the mother he left."

"Please write your feelings about Asa's passing."

"Oddly, this is my story for you today. You have told me we are becoming closer to each other's paths, with our thoughts, that will bring knowledge."

"You now must make Sarah whole, whereas all those emotions have taken root. They have left no place for the true Sarah. The Joy is not with Asa, buried in the ground; it is buried within your heart. Joy is your core. You feel it is missing. You allowed the loss of your child to hide away your 'gift of joy.' Asa loved you as a child dependent, loves his mother, and you fiercely loved him. This was your time together this short time was your time."

"Listen to me, Your job is to repair your soul. You did not die. You allowed Hate — to take over your Love. You feel justified, yet it is you, who needs to be made whole, before you can love fiercely as a mother. Then, Willie passed on, and you doubled down on the side of hate. You need to clean your internal house."

***

*To enhance your love as well, let go of hate as it is bad for growth...*

**Love vs Hate – Good vs Bad**

*Be happy and joyous; there is no time for sadness...*

**Happy vs Sad – Joy vs Woe**

*Hold your belief with faith; shun all doubt...*

**Belief vs Doubt – Faith vs Disbelief**

*Where there is peace; there will be blessings.*

*We must not let strife and hardships steal peace...*

### **Peace vs Strife – Blessings vs Hardship**

*Hope brings virtuousness; despair turns into viciousness...*

### **Hope vs Despair – Virtuous vs Vicious**

*Thought leads to knowledge; knowledge leads to wisdom; leaving no room for ignorance...*

### **Knowledge vs Ignorance – Wisdom vs Sense**

"The unlearned are unaware of their gifts, they had upon birth, also being born with gifts, they cannot be taken away. Gifts need to be fostered to grow as they can become stagnant if not used. You must meditate on your gifts to recognize what is yours, to help you get your needs and wishes."

"Sarah I have said this before, Do you know Joy?"

"It is a gift of fulfillment in understanding yourself.'"

"Children are accepting, while at the same time being in awe of what is not known. As we deeply investigate we can all learn, and this knowledge brings happiness of accomplishment."

"True Joy is lived within, as a gift. Your job this week is to remember Sarah, the untethered Sarah of your childhood. You need to become her again in order to be made whole, the person you were born to be with all your gifts, be aware and use your gifts to grow wise."

"Again I say, trust your inner voice, do not deny it. Your crystal will allow you to get in touch with your hidden inner self, and help you reconnect to your abandoned gifts. This will be your biggest, best breakthrough, then you can truly explore your life. Your lesson is to learn, experience and work through your gifts, coming out with Sarah, then we can take the steps to secure Nathan's life."

"If this is your wish?"

"Remember, you must know with all certainty."

***FAIRIES REFLECTIONS;***

***Aspen reflected:*** *"A star danced at your birth, instilling a full sense of nearness to the mysterious fountain of Joy. You take pleasure in the little things, perceiving the world as it is, thus perceive your modest place in it, with a feeling of gratitude for what is yours, and never ever longing for what you have not..."*

***

## My Feelings of Asa's Death — by Sarah

James's belief in God carried him to accept that Asa, his father and our baby, Asa, are together in heaven. The only answer he had for the death of a three-year-old child was "God has a plan."

I on the other hand felt cheated, and as if all this talk of "his time to leave" and "God has a plan" were made up to pacify me so I would not dare to question.

"Why? Why take an innocent little boy? Why not take me?" Whispering in words as an emotional plea to God. This I know better than to do. God is said to be all Wisdom. I do know my husband, his mother and the church would think of me as being blasphemous.

I lay on the bed beside my lifeless son, Asa. I have no one to talk to about how I really feel. No one is asking why?

It is because they accept Asa's death as, "God's will" and "Thou is with him." These believers have unwavering faith.

I have no power to bring back life to our baby boy. I would go against God if I had the power to bring Asa back to life. Asa would again hug me tight, with those little arms, so tight around my neck. We would remain Mother and Son forever...I could not let go...

I remember looking at his still little body, leaving me feeling hopeless. My heart knows, God does not hear my prayers. I am thinking back, remembering, as a child I prayed, as hard, as I could to save my little yellow tiger kitten. I knew God hears all prayer and answers believers, yet my kitten died. The same happened when my mother became ill. How I prayed down on my knees I stayed and prayed, until when she died I could not stand. I was so scared only twelve years old, and left alone without my Mother. I remember being so afraid, and becoming angry, that God did not answer my prayer. Perhaps he did not love me. I just knew prayers of mine, will not be answered by God. This is how I felt. Hopeless…

A part of me left with Asa. This new normal in an instant changed our lives. I am aware of the turning point, yet we cannot go back. I wish I could be the joyous person, I was before Asa passed. I am afraid to want anything, or show love, life, hope, and happiness, as there is no knowing how long these will last. My heart was left full of Fear…

I was not prepared to lose my child. I miss him so much. How could I be prepared to have my little one, and in an instant he was no longer, not a breath did he take. He looked at peace like an angel. He was gone. I remember calling his name "Asa come back, come back, do not leave me." I was in shock. James shook me back to reality, saying, "Asa is with God" I thought, oh no not our little Asa, not our baby boy, come back I fell on the bed crying, "why, why, why, Asa" This is the turning point of my reality, as I knew there was no going back.

He is lifeless…

In an instant our life was changed. James became stronger in his faith, and I became afraid, unable and unwilling to experience life.

The person I was, left my soul. It was as if he took me with him, leaving me this empty shell who was not feeling life, love, or caring. I felt the loss of my child so deeply.

My life would never ever be the same. I was a woman alone with no one to express my true self. I felt hate, sadness, doubt, strife, despair, and woe, of my broken heart.

Before Asa's death I was free. I felt good in all of life with love, happiness, belief, peace, hope, and joy. Now I am angry. I am feeling bound by my great loss. My Baby, Asa.

Why?... Why?... Why?... Why?... Why?... Why?... Why?...

When we were expecting Asa, I would put my hand on my middle saying to him,

"Remember you are with great Love. My wish for you is, that even as a young person you will be self-assured, knowing from within, you are an important part of life. The love of your Mother and Father, your Grandparents and their Mothers and Fathers, makes you special and gifted with great Love."

Asa was born into the fulfillment of all this Love. I think of when first holding him watching him closely. He began stretching his little arms out wide, his sweet little mouth would go into a yawn, hands in a fist to flexing open with fingers wide, eyes closed, and there was a look of pure peace. He was my love. This was our son, our first child of whom we, both deeply loved.

As was common, Asa was named by his father,
after his father, Asa.


Asa remains our precious baby, forever...

# CHAPTER THIRTY-SEVEN

# Judgment

The love you give away, is the only love you keep who, what, when, where, how, and why. It is in the palm of your hand." Aba told me clearly.

"Be still and take a long deep breath, let the air out slowly and continue to breathe long and slowly. Look at your crystal, notice what comes from the area, its shape and the light. Next week you can learn how to enhance your crystal."

"Aba is happy for you to be moving forward, remember you're not alone. Aba shares your goal. Together we will conquer this by putting you in control of your life. Remember a tree without roots cannot have a needed vision." Aba said, "We will whittle away the tree with the help of the crystal, and graft to grow Sarah back again. We will make you whole and strong. Aba is so hopeful. You had a good start in life then you allowed your life to be out of balance. Now you will gather back what you have lost, and let go of what has taken up residence in your sixth sense."

"Let us talk about judging." Aba went on to say, "Remembering first, that judging others is not done out of love, nor out of hate. It is done to be what? Judgmental? Why? By judging others what do you get? Where do you keep this judgment? When do you judge? Who do you judge? Stay uncritical, to be charitable."

"Keeping in mind, yes some are taking advantage of the system put in place to help those who need help. So you can judge them as greedy. That just, is not alright. To criticize others' behavior is not to love or understand, they are at a different level in their life's development."

"Yes, some people become old, and never grow up intellectually. It is all relevant, as you are not your brother's keeper. Your job is you, your growth."

"Aba, I never thought of life in this way. So we all can only do what we know; can only know if we monitor our beliefs. Our knowledge grows, only, as we choose to learn. We cannot bring wisdom to others, we cannot make them whole, we cannot help others grow, each person is responsible for their own soul."

"Remember to judge not; lest you be judged."

"If ignorance is bliss; why do we seek knowledge?"

"Aba, I never thought of life this way, as each is free to become, or not, the choice is theirs. The Universe will meet each one where they are to fulfill the purpose of their life. There are no good or bad choices, only growth without thought, which leads to lack of knowledge, and not allowing to gain wisdom, to continue the work of becoming whole, to be, who one, was created to be.

Seek to 'Becoming the One' who we are created to be, wisdom must be pursued, and fostered to be, through knowledge.

"Remember to be mindful when seeking. Are you ready for your wishes to be true? Ready to go down the path, that will include your hopes for your life?"

# CHAPTER THIRTY-EIGHT

# The Number 3

Today is a Monday morning that is warm with sunshine leaving me to feel alive, and full of hope. Today we are going to talk to understand my nemesis, the number 3, to bring focus on the powerful meaning of what it means in my life.

"Good morning Aba" I say as she opens the door, "It is the kind of day when all seems right with the world."

She as always gives me a beautiful smile, waving to beckon me to come in saying, "Do come in we have much to talk through and think about. We will focus our understanding of your fear, for the number 3 in the lives of you and your boys."

" We need to answer is this fear justified as real?"

" First of all the number 3 is in our existence, we are sure 3 exists."

"We must feel the power of 3 in the same way we can feel the sun warm on our skin."

"Then 3 becomes real with association, where we understand things, in terms of other things."

"This test of 3 is called equivalence where we will need to find an equal in value or meaning that is virtually the same as in function or effort. We will begin by making a timeline chart."

***

## Triad Timeline

**Asa** – 3 years old – crossed over  1x3=3

**Willie** – 3 years later – born

**Willie** – 3 years old

**Nathan** – born

**Willie** – 6 years old – crossed over  2x3=6

**Nathan** – 3 years old – cross over?  3x3=9

**Prophecy:** Nathan will live to nine years of age.

***

"The number 3 is an auspicious sign for anyone, when noticing the number 3 occurring in their experience. It is a sign they are connected with a source of energy, and have the power to manifest their desires, as the number is a numeral glyph, meaning it represents a word or idea."

Aba went on to say, "The number 3 is indicative of someone with creative potential, but little direction. This Sarah you must work to become sure, of your way. Every law, every action, every phenomenon in the world is the result of 3 forces. They are positive, negative, and neutralizing, and can be countered by harmony, wisdom and understanding."

"We may feel now, as if, in simultaneous clutter with so much to sort through, and so we seek simplicity. When we feel in discord, we will find harmony. This may sound intimidating, just remember in your difficulty lies opportunity. If you think you can or think you cannot, you are right."

I spoke with truth, "Today I was feeling hopeful, until now, I am simply overwhelmed and feel discouraged."

Aba laughed and said, "Yes you were hopeful, now the opposite you found discouragement, so you understand the principal. When seeing the number 3, it is a reminder from the Universe of our creative potential. You sense fear when you see the number 3, when actually the number 3, is the number of good fortune. It is the first true number to form a geometrical figure, the triangle. Three, stands for harmony, wisdom and understanding. You of course have heard, the third time's a charm, two times fail, the third will succeed. Energy put into the world returns three times, to that person, be it positive or negative, it is Karma."

"Our beliefs are formed to be as we are children, and are strengthened to draw on throughout life. These ways live forever in the heart. To believe is to have confidence in the truth. Our environment, events, knowledge, past experience, visualizations, can be equivocal interpreted, in more than one way. This is why our knowledge becomes so important, to help us gain wisdom, to equip with abilities. The key to wisdom is knowing, what you do not know. Think of it as good designs are invisible."

"The number 3 is known as a sideway heart, for love and friendship. When we see the number 3 it is a reminder from the Universe of our creative potential, and our innately divine nature. The vibrational frequency of 3 is a sign of our alignment with powerful spiritual forces, that can help achieve our aims. Our crystal is 3 colors red, blue and yellow, which become all colors when vibrating. You will need to use the crystal in your hand, breathe in deeply- hold- slow exhale. When your crystal vibrates the vibration is energy from the Universe. All that is required is that you be receptive to the crystal's energy, adding the affirmation by saying, 'I am centered and at one with my energy. It will be.' Say after each breath. This is to be the key to what you want. Careful what you desire it may come to be, yet will this be what you want."

I was trying to take this all in so I was pausing as thinking of all Aba was saying then I laughed and said, "Who would think of me, Sarah Pitts Stevens, as wise and filled with knowledge, from which I am gaining wisdom, to make life-changing decisions about life ever after, for me and Nathan. Would they be surprised, you just got to laugh."

Aba became solemn saying, "This is never ever to come to pass, as this journey is only activated in the realm of secret silence with quietness and humble tasks, to create a place to be. It is as if to breathe; as to master your own destiny. My expressions to you of knowledge, of the universe, is as seeing things in a book as words. When you ready yourself to know the knowledge of all things, you will remember what you already know; what has been planted in your soul, and you will experience this for yourself in your own world, as it will become real and more wondrously still. Be still and know.

"Seek truth, as the matrix unfolds."

"To a mind who is still — the Universe surrenders."

"Be careful to listen with your heart— to know your wish."

**FAIRIES REFLECTIONS: Arwen continued:** "There is none like you. Looking to be other than self is not going to be who you are at your core. This is to be your task: — **"To Be."**

# CHAPTER THIRTY-NINE

# My Finding Sarah

I came to Aba's door elated and she answered without my knocking. She had a welcoming demeanor, as she recognized my clarity.

"I have spent a great deal of time writing down all my answers to finding Sarah. I had a dawning where I saw, then felt within my heart when, why, and how I turned away. Such time lost when I was not my true self. I am ever so grateful to be free."

Aba reached over and we hugged tightly, both feeling overwhelmed, knowing we were on our way to completeness. Aba has become most important to my life by helping me to believe and believing in me, to become the whole Sarah as I was born to be.

"Today I am not bound by strife, controlled by grief or my sadness. I am aware how I allowed so much of my time to be devoted to misguided grief. Life is full of misguided half-truths, directed by feelings of loss. How sad for me to have thought all this time Asa was taken from me, and I blamed all who tried to help."

"Looking with clarity, I have come to understand, Asa came to choose his parents to find the gift of complete love. This we readily gave him and he departed as fulfilled; it was his time to crossover. When he returns he will know love."

"What a wonderful gift, to love and be loved. This you shared with Asa."

"I felt enlightened by remembering a time I was irritated to watch my sister, who was to be my burden for the day, however when I lost her by leaving her sleeping under a tree, and carelessly not remembering where the tree was located amongst all the other trees. When found, this burden, became the most precious gift. It was how I perceived the truth, to make a burden, and or, a gift."

"You see Aba, the child was the same in both scenarios. "

"Life is in our feelings, which I now know, must be examined to stay on the path, and the way chosen to be; for our true selves to be. I want to stay on this path of love and joy. This is my happy spot, where I feel all is right with the world. This I see in you, Aba, it is your presence; one of peace."

"This is because Aba believes our decisions are our own, yet also, where the outcome is predetermined. In other words I am on the correct path for me, moving forward, as deemed necessary for my journey. To stay on this path, throughout life I must continue to know myself asking: who, what, when, where, then Aba asks, which, why, and how. Aba must constantly be moving forward, to stay on my path."

"I want to stay on this path of enlightenment, where all is right with the World. It is as the peace I felt with the fairies when I was an innocent child with readiness to believe. Then becoming an adult I allowed myself to feel gullible, thinking my childhood beliefs, as not fitting into my everyday life, even at times as not real. Today it is real. The path I am on is moving forward, all is right."

"I also know in my heart, God is the creator of all on earth, nature and the Universe. Love rules the way to wholeness. There is order surrounding all God creates. All we need throughout our life is provided, at the time it is needed, as predestined for the good of the kingdom of God. It is not our understanding of that, that is needed. This is God's knowledge. We in prayer ask for others good health, and or, continued life past their predestined time without realizing this is an ask, not a demand."

"We expect our desires to become a reality?" Aba asked.

"Now, I know to see their love as recognized, in the kind ways which is their life. Lifting up as a prayer in thankfulness, for the love in this person. Thanking God for the treasure this person has become to life. My Mother was such a treasure."

Rather than pray, "Please make her well, to selfishly keep her alive here with her family, to take care of us. It is now understood, asking all night for her to live was selfish."

"I see now I should have showed love, by praising her life, her love and virtue, to have cared for our family, to the best she knew how. My Mother was a person who should have entered Heaven, with praise of our lifting voices sounding on high, of her love and virtue."

"Prayers should be of thankfulness. Today I am ever so grateful to be the mother of three wonderful boys. Praise Be To God..."

"This is a much needed, and timely message, as we need to be readied for your wishes to be presented. Aba is prepared to join you in your decision, if you choose to follow through with your desire, to have Nathan remain on earth to live out his natural life."

"Aba will support your wish. The wish must be yours, and there can be no doubt in your mind or heart. Remember sometimes wishes happen, then they are not what is wanted as time goes by, in time your actions of giving up on your continued growth in favor of Nathan to live past nine years of age, may become your burden. In time you may wish there was a way to reincarnate to continue to grow your life. As solace know that your wish to keep Nathan is bigger than yourself."

"You are a mother motivated by love. No greater love than to lie down your life, for the life of your child. In the future we cannot judge the outcome as good or bad. Always see Nathan; as the child you saved from death. Only you can save Nathan."

"I have found my belief. I want Nathan to continue on his path, and the universe to know his way is to be safe, as I now, am on the joyful path, to bring completion to his time on earth, be it the will of God."

"My thoughts are stirred, so is my joy and I will write forever, being content to be the person I was created to be. Seeing myself as creative, optimistic, inspired, expressive, cheerful, positive, with verbal skills for my writing, helping and caring for those I love, domestic as taking care of home and family, working to make all comfortable and secure. Sacrifice for others is natural, as I am a survivor, who is happier to be on this never ever told journey of my life...

"Yes, I am mindful of my wish...

and will await the answer...

with love of acceptance...

**FAIRIES REFLECTIONS:**

**Aspen continued:** *All journeys are connected throughout the Universe, most never ever know or suspect...*

**MORIA Thoughts:**

*Asa came to his mother for the gift — of love...*

*Sarah found her hidden Joy, when she found love that surpasses under-standing.*

*Love is life — To Be— in The End*

# CHAPTER FORTY

# Wish Truth

Aba says, "If you think in your mind and believe this to be in your heart the wish will become, as this is your truth. Sometimes it comes in a form we have trouble recognizing, till some time passes, and the fulfillment then becomes evident. What I am telling you is to know, our desires will manifest the moment heart and mind agree. This then is the time we are thankful."

"We need not wait for the desired wish to be present as over time it will be involved. Come prepared to acknowledge what you cannot see or experience in the moment of choice. When heart and mind, mind and heart connect, the path is chosen. On this you can depend and be thankful. You know your efforts are never ever in vain."

"Life is mastered with decisions, some seem good, some end as bad, and when decisions are not chosen or the paths are deliberately ignored, still the lack of decision becomes a way on the road of life. This way on the paths of life, however is not what agrees with the eternal voice, which helps us choose what will continue to help us grow. We have an inner core which when on the right path, mirrors from within and leaves us content in our feeling that all is right in our world. We are simultaneously in sync with our gifts, life is good, life is peaceful, life is moving forward, and springing forth joy."

"To be joyous we must make decisions that bond with our soul. Being independent of others as they too will have their own paths to peace. Your life is knowing your soul, your gifts, seeking your path, and being one with the Universe. When you learn more of life your love grows starting with love of self."

"Then from our high place, we become as a judge getting all caught up in others' unjust ways, until there is a pullback to the peace within. Eventually, you will recognize everyone is on a journey, and we are all on paths whether chosen or lost. Know it is not your job to make decisions for others; nor to judge others, your job is to accept them, where they are at their level of knowledge. Be kind, by being real, knowing life is a journey where we are all on different, albeit incomparable levels. Stay true to yourself to become a beacon of hope for others by your virtues. Always be thankful for life, even though, knowing it carries many burdens to teach, to make us to be whole, and to further push us into choosing love and joy."

"When we met I could sense your struggles, mostly your fleeting joy was concerning. Today you are strong, moving forward with the tender bruises of loss, as part of the path work of your life. You have come to accept the child who was so happy just to be in the world. She was innocent with openness to accept all that existed in her life. Then with each of life's disappointments and tragedies, the light in your soul became shadowed allowing your hurts to diminish all, that made you special. We are all born special; the only one like us. We are here in the Universe to live our full joyous life, which if, a joy to others brings them the truth."

"Aba I believe, also I now know all things in life happen for growth."

"We are not meant to stay in one place as we were made to move forward to learn of our life. When we get off track and are not moving, something unthinkable happens to shake up our world. This pushes life out of control causing us not to move, as to seek out a path, then becoming bitter and lost. This leaves the lost, without feeling the need to grow, so life continues out of control This is where I, Aba met you."

" Aba of course could sense your hidden heart, your loss of two children stealing your joy, along with your anger replacing your love. Your soul was shallow with each and every day the same as the next. There was wisdom and knowledge, love and joy, hidden behind the darkness of the shadow, which you allowed to creep into your heart. You even believed that your joy left with Asa, albeit, Asa left with his whole person fulfilling his life on earth, knowing of love. To love and be loved by the mother he chose, and he was your everything."

"Today by allowing your life to shine forth you can see clearly, that Asa was a gift, who taught you the love between a child and a parent, which was never ever a tangible experience between you, and your mother. Now you can feel the love of your mother, not by her hugs and kisses, but her sacrifices, she gave to you, allowing development to the core of yourself."

"When we are ready to look back with knowledge of what love can consist of, gathered with wisdom from experiencing the pain and anguish, we then can recognize from knowing these struggles; the depth of love, yet without discernment of wisdom and knowledge, there becomes a block to the love. This love was never ever able to be felt in your emptiness, yet it was there all the time."

"Aba, to know of love I had to see that the yellow kitten I was squeezing, hugging and kissing was childish demonstrative love. My Mother's love was nurturing and no-nonsense, never ever the lesser of love. Love from the heart of a person has many forms. A person has to have many life's experiences, to be able to know love in all its forms. Today through your fine example I am patiently thankful and grateful to be and be with love, joy and moving forward as you, Aba, showed me the path."

"Sarah, it is my joy to guide. Make sure your wish is what you want at this time in your life. Be clear of what you want to have manifest in your life. It will happen with your energy, and the positive energy from the Universe, in the time to come. Let go and trust the Universe's plan, as this always outweighs and serves the greater good."

"This is not witchcraft it is the 'Law of Attraction' at work to make a manifestation in your life."

I look down at the time chart, my map Aba gave to me.

Next Monday NIGHT? So soon! I am to bring a list of things.

"Spell of Transforming" leading to

*protecting and hiding forever...*

"Envision happens in the dark of night with clarity."

✳✳✳

*The Universe speaks of connection through signs,*
  *all journeys forever*
  *connected to one another, to light, to love, to energy;*
  *to the Universe...*

**TYPE OF SPELL Transforming; Nathan's lifetime**

**Protecting; Spell of silence to protect anonymity.**
**Hiding; Sarah- Spirit** will continue in a setting of her choice.

**White Quartz Rocks-** buried to represent and guide Sarah's spirit... represent core of Sarah, on earth.

**COLOR- RAINBOW of Colors** - formed by the refraction and re-flection of light rays from Crystals

**METAL-** Silver to Represent worth; Baby drinking cup

**DAY-** Monday

**BIRDS-** Eagle, Blue Jay, Cardinal

**WOOD** - Willow

**UNDINES** - Water Spirits   SYLPHS - Inhabiting Air

**FAIRIES** - Woodland

**PYRAMID-** Triangle sides, white rocks, nails, hair

**CIRCLE-** Is Life Mother To Son; As Rebirth

**SYMBOL-** NEW MOON


Write an **Acrostic poem on birch bark**, for each bird inspired by your children:


<u>**CARDINAL**</u>

Crimson in color

Angelic feller

Redeeming with hope

Dignified in approach

Illuminates the sky

Nestles close by

Always in our heart

Love never ever to part... ASA

## EAGLES

**E**veryone is in awe

**A**t the ability to soar

**G**liding high overhead

**L**eaving many fish dead

**E**ating all till fed

**S**hadow exist as greatness led... Willie

## BLUE JAYS

**B**lue in color

**L**oud calling feller

**U**ndesirable as greedy

**E**ach one very needy

**J**oyful when in flight

**A**lways ready for a fight

**Y**ells loudly with out love

**S**ent from up above... Nathan

Bring Crystals, feathers, silver baby cup, lock of hair and nails from mother and son, two egg-size White Quartz Rocks

Spell casting table, Willow wood.

O

O X O

O

Planetary Seal... ABA

# CHAPTER FORTY-ONE

# The Path

We are to follow the path that leads to extended life for Nathan. This is a joyous thought, yes?"

"Then we must address your need to give up life in the hereafter. There will be no afterlife, no coming back to use or strengthen your gifts, as you will be dead to the process of reincarnation. Your life's work will end with this death, your choice, once chosen there is no going back to change things, to fit into the time of where you are in your life. We can never ever change our past decisions, only move on accepting what our life has become, finding our purpose within our past choices. If not choosing to accept your choices, the end will come with nonsense 'what if' thoughts.

"Remember this, 'What is done can never ever be undone.'"

"As you age becoming closer to the end of your natural life I feel sure there will be some remorse, with much sadness as grasping the finality of your gift of time to Nathan. When done you will live out this life, and not fully notice the impact of the path chosen, until your life is coming to a close. At this time to look back seeing all your choices which were made, and also the paths that were not taken. Never ever doubt the path taken, was the only correct choice for the time."

*****

"Now through the passage of time with the growth in our spirits we think 'wish I knew then what I know now' this way of thought is frugal, as our feelings of mistakes made are just that, feelings. In truth doing what you know, with the knowledge and wisdom gained by living life, is what the Universe expects..."

"We can surely be confident the choices made worked for the time, in which they are made for seeking out the clear way of fulfillment. This is what is asked of us to continue to be in tune with our needs, and seek the paths moving forward."

"If a wish fulfilled leads to unhappiness it is not the wish, that came true bringing the unhappiness. The unhappiness is in you. Remember the expectation of what your wish is to bring your family, one thing only; more years to Nathan, for a long life."

"We are taking steps to make this wish become a reality. We will continue to encourage the steps needed, to have your heart and mind come together in front of the Universe. Your wish will come into being, your son will live, past nine years of age, giving you a secret worth more than gold.'

"There are three things that cannot be long hidden: the moon, the sun and the truth, only you will have this truth."

"When you die your spirit will remain wherever you choose to bury your white crystal rocks. Again, I say to you, be careful what you wish as time reveals the complete truth. Be clear what you want for your life's journey."

"You are not going to be alone your guide, Aba will be with you, also all the love you have is within your heart. It is a circle of love to help make a choice to bring family contentment."

"You love your husband, yet you are venturing into a new path by yourself. One that will leave him, Asa, Willie, and eventually Nathan, without you. It is alright you can truly love, deeply love, and be on different paths, as you are now on different levels of beliefs. Your knowledge has led you to the path of selflessness. Given the choice of Nathan's life, versus his passing on, at nine years of age without fulfillment. Is there no acceptable choice?"

"This moment is real and the opportunity for extending Nathan's life has come with us recognizing, now we are prepared to act. Together we can deliver this wish to the Universe."

"Sarah, you, your husband and Nathan will remain a family throughout the decades of your lives."

"This moment in time is interconnected. We will open a never ever thought of action, a spell to study deeply, to contemplate carefully, a turn of work done by one in relief of another, to deliver your wish in harmony with the Universe. Your path is clear and achievable, as you engage to bring life into a full circle of love, between a mother and son; whom will remain on their own paths to journey's end."

"Remember, if at any time you cannot bring your wish through into fruition. This will be your choice. Aba, is always there for you. No matter the choice, protecting and hiding all forever."

I must remember I trust Aba, because this all sounds absurd.


I, Sarah will be doing some sort of spell!

**Sarah's words of the fairies:**

My Fairies spent time with me promoting the ability to perceive what is good and true, having common sense with sound judgement to be processing much to be wise filled with knowledge, bringing wisdom to some day have my desired life, filled with love & Joy...

### *FARIES REFLECTIONS:*

***Arwen advised:*** *"The foundation of life is to believe in work, not apathy, have faith, know your God, know your worth. You were born with purpose; of being. Find your place in life on earth, whether it is big or small, it will be blessed with success, only if you take the path prepared for your life."*

### *MORIA Thoughts:*

*Sarah to have a friend, Aba, who is always there for you— helping to decipher all the hidden, never ever parts of life— to know and to love you, the whole self without judgement. Throughout all it makes me glad to know you had such a treasure of love, in a time of worry and distress. Both were fortunate indeed to have complete friendships— one for the storybooks.*

*Whereas both have complete trust in the other, also loyalty as natural, as if to take a drink of water, with knowledge to know it will be swallowed, with out the thought of choking. It is as if breathing to follow this path to live life each and every day. May there always be JOY...*

# CHAPTER FORTY-TWO

# To Begin Transformation

It is a warm August night with the sounds of crickets singing in the fields, otherwise quietness is all around. I look outside through the open window, a nightly task has been with me as a small child. There are fireflies beginning to show their lights across the field, my heart flutters with amazement.  I look and watch in wonder...

My thoughts creep back to tonight, a long dark walk to Aba's with hopes of life at the end of this walk...

We will, summon anew, the beginning of Nathan's long life.

I am ready to make my wishes known. Aba has always asked me to be sure of my wish. Tonight I am ready to make my wish known...

I will reach for Nathan's long life without hesitation.

Together we will continue on our predestined, yet separate paths with our freedom of choice, to one day know love. This my wish...

James was tired and I knew he would go right to sleep; still I lay quietly listening for the change in his breathing to allow me to know he was fast asleep. My thoughts keep drifting to my long dark walk to Aba's. My heart began beating faster and seemed loud as it was beating in my ears.

I feel a little scared to walk to town in the darkness of the night. I have never ever been out after dark by myself on a long walk. Just the thoughts of being alone on the long night-time walk seems daunting, yet I must. This journey is for my love of Nathan, and the dire need to keep him on earth to continue his journey.

Aba and I, together, tonight will call on the Universe. Laying in bed with my mind racing at the mystery of my journey, to trust the way, my chosen path will keep Nathan safe from death. He will be alive, and well throughout my lifetime.

It is I who will choose to sacrifice my freedom of having an everlasting life. I will never ever come back to learn more, to grow wiser, within the new knowledge, on my path to acquire perfection, in the wisdom of whom my spirit is revolving to be. This is a sacrifice; only I can make for Nathan. I have accepted there is not an option. I now have peace with my decision to move forward. In our family, I alone believe in the way of life, the path of completion, and trust completely, in the rule of God's Universe.

We, Aba and I, will bring my desires into fruition tonight. Laying in bed, my mind is racing with all the mystery of my journey to keep Nathan alive in our future. All the work to learning from my past life to have the child's knowledge, to gain the wisdom, that will allow life, to flow into the present time.

My heart is beating faster as I quietly sneak out of the bed. I must not disturb the sleeping people of the farmhouse. Slowly, I walk down the stairs, hearing the steps creek, so shakingly I try to walk even more slowly, carefully feeling for the way to the old door, letting me outside into the terror of the darkness. This darkness is everything I imagined, and much more still. I of course had my clothes waiting outside, also everything Aba asked me to bring in my bag by the apple tree, awaiting the moment to start my long journey into town. This is a walk I do every week in the bright light of day. It is different tonight with only a new crescent moon, and the small kitchen oil lamp for lighting the way.

Walking alone at night, it was extremely dark allowing fear to touch me. This fear awakened my senses to be scared, feeling alone. The darkness was closing in on me. My heart was beating faster. My ears heard the pounding sound of my heartbeat, making it harder to hear the sounds around me, and the harder I listened, the less that could be heard. I began to stumble on rocks, twigs and plants, they seemed to have sprung up overnight.

I was halfway to Aba's, when my thoughts were of turning back to go home. I began to cry. I could feel the darkness defeating my need to walk on to my desired path, which Aba and I have created from working each Monday. I knew going back home would be just as hard as moving forward. There is a struggle that is living within me.

There is a need to calm myself, pausing, taking several deep breaths, feeling myself tremble. The thoughts that fear was going to control my destiny became clear, allowing me to know what must be done. I must regain composure. I must move on, and stop this imagined fear. It became clear, the only thing that would stop the fulfillment of my wish, would be fear. The only thing important is what I do at this moment. I must do this. Nathan's life depends on me. We, Aba and I, this night will bring my desires into fruition.

The mystery of my night time journey, on this midsummer night under the darkness of the new moon, is to keep Nathan alive in the future, by using all my learnings from my past life. To have the knowledge, to have gained the wisdom needed, allowing life to flow in the present time. This will be the most marvelous night.

There is no turning back. My desire to save Nathan is stronger than my fear of not finding my way on the path into town. After tripping several times, I slowed my walk telling myself I have all night, as long as I return to my home by morning. This is so foreign to me being out in the world within the darkness.

I found Aba's door, and before I could rap she opened, motioning me to come in with one finger to her lips, which meant quiet, as if she too was secretly going out. She whispered, "Are you ready to have your wish come into being tonight?"

I answered whispering, "I am now ready to have my wish, accepting all the outcomes, as wisdom allows me. Moreover, I am ever so grateful for your teachings; be they your words, or your actions, or through your fine example of goodness and love, which speaks even louder than words."

Aba had no disheveled look, I on the other hand was not settled. Aba said calmly and quietly, "We will have tea to calm ourselves, while I will tell you the path of how your wish will come to be, for Nathan to live beyond nine years of age."

"We will take Nathan's and your nail clippings, along with the locks of hair from each, to put in the life's seal. This seal is a triangle made of willow twigs, that are standing upright with the bottoms stuck into 3 shallow holes, and tops gathered together and tied teepee style. Your life's identifiers, hair and nails are placed at the feet of the willow, each in their separate spaces. The third space is for the two small pieces of the white rocks the fairies had you collect."

"Now you, Sarah, will draw a circle around the twigs creating another space to hold the bird feathers with words written on birch bark to represent each of your children, allowing the seal to be complete."

"Then we will breathe. Breathing in and out, following the breath as one watches their shadow, breathing in and out rhythmically, alters our sense of self. This is when we are free to be with the Universe, responding to the freedom, gracefully given through being quiet and attentive, to our breath.

We will be in this very moment of time. When you go within, the Universe can connect with you, finding an awakening of all the senses."

"This allows your mind and heart to connect making your soul awake and whole. Your path becomes clear, as in line with the Universe, Wisdom always wins..."

"Off to the side will be the silver baby cup, filled with river water, not to drink, as it is to represent Nathan's 'cup runs over' to symbolize his blessings of a long life. The water will be poured over the burning seal, to silently proclaim 'So it is done'...

"Sarah, again Aba asks, are you ready, and is this your wish in this day?"

"Aba this is my desired wish, to have tonight a completed life for Nathan, allowing Nathan to fulfill his life. Not for his family for him to complete and grow his life within the Universe.

'What will be, shall always be, with movement forward' this is my growing promise throughout my life."

We have gathered all together to head for our spot along the Kennebec River. I am feeling calm with a sense of purpose so different than just an hour ago when I felt scattered and unsure. Here with Aba, I am settled, and looking forward to joining her to guide me in my pledge to fulfill my wish.

Aba and I sit cross-legged... her way of being humble.

We have prepared every week, each Monday for many days, months, years— to have my heart and mind, ready for the Universe to be in line with affirming life to Nathan.

At nine years, his time to leave us by passing on, is fast approaching. Aba confirmed my fears of losing this son, before I could tell her why I came to the door, of 'the soothsayer' as the town folks called her out, to be. If they only knew how insightful, Aba is, they would then respect Aba's gifts. To me, Aba is my pathfinder... Best is, Aba is always the same humble person.

"Sarah all is prepared. The seal was drawn by me today, readied to except the willows for the burning of the Acrostic poems written on birch bark, along with the bird feathers, nail and hair clippings, the egg sized white quartz rocks will become super charged to hold the aura of the space. This place you choose to be where your spirit will reside, after death. All the rocks you have collected will be brought together, put into the ground within your chosen place."

"Aba,  I am fearful of not knowing what is expected of me."

"What is expected has already been done; the crystal work, the breath of life, now you and Aba will present our gifts to The Universe, as tis is needed for the path to be chosen."

"Aba, you make it sound so easy."

"It is that Aba can see the path is open for your wish that Nathan lives beyond nine years. Never ever doubt your belief, as belief is what makes life possible. Proclaim your wish; life for your son, a gift from the powers that be, also from you as your path will change to give longer life to Nathan. You choose to end your hopes of reincarnating, being free to live your chosen life."

Aba can see with knowledge created wisdom,

what the Universe has in the plan of life

of anybody's journey on earth.

Envision happens in the dark of night...

# CHAPTER FORTY-THREE

# No Clarity In Light Of Day

C larity belongs to the dark night...

My mind begins racing with thoughts and fears raging with "What if's." Maybe I am not ready to do my part in this transition of time. I have done all of what Aba has asked, and perhaps this is too big of an ask, to allow Nathan to live to old age. Me to remain in limbo in the place of my choosing, never ever to pass to come back to live life ever after. I have been reborn, believing this to my core, thus I have learned many necessary things. I have not the courage needed to put all I know into practice.

Tonight, together with all the knowledge of my past lives and my childhood beliefs, all will spur me into having my wish for Nathan to become wholly on top of the earth. To live on, to grow his life, finding his paths to wholeness. To not pass on before his father and mother. We have buried two of our children. We will not bury Nathan. He will follow his path to be...

My thoughts are interrupted by Aba with a reminder of awareness:

"These are our works of wholeness coming together here on the bank of the river. Water is one of the elements needed for life. Look down, seeing the earth below in the dirt, which brings life to all that grows. You can now draw a circle with the twig in the dirt that I will divide by a triangle of willow twigs. See all the things you have brought tonight sitting in their places on 'the seal of life.' Calm yourself Sarah by taken a few deep breaths as you familiarize yourself with what is in your circle of life.

"As you breathe, slowly and peacefully, follow the breath as if you are a shadow. Breathe in and follow, notice where it changes to move out. Be in the present. Breathe freely, and listen to my voice as Aba will talk of quieting your heart, mind, and soul, to bring the quietness needed to go on our journey to the edge of the Universe. Once you are in control of your emotions we freely can act together as your wish."

"Listen to Aba's directions. Close your eyes. Take a deep breath in filling your chest with air, notice as your breath turns, slowly let your breath out of your body, breath in noticing an ever so slight pause, as you follow with a breath out. Keep breathing this way."

"In the air notice the smell of the river, the earthy smell of dirt mixing with water which has been baked in the sun all day giving a scent of murkiness to the air you are breathing. Now, listen to the water lapping the river's edge pushing the water to refresh and settle which it does at night. Just as the quiet night time resets all of life."

"Breathe in watching closely, as if, watching a shadow of the giver of life, breath out feeling the earth below you. Continue breathing in this rhythm following every breath, smell the air, add to this the sounds around you. There in the distance hear an owl with a 'who song' of life, as a night hunter. Listen to the water lapping the shore, listen harder and hear the fish jumping out and back into the river, they too are eating in the cool of the night."

"Tune your ears to the crickets in the fields. There are many that are comfortable out here in the dark. Listen to the silence in the darkness of the night, and continue your breaths. It is through your breaths you can find the truth. Stay interested as you feel the breath fill your body, watch for the quiet time as the breath flows back out. Repeat over and over, always watching with your mind. Always bring your mind back to the breath if it tries to wander into stories. Stay in the breath of life. Follow your breath. Let go, live in the quietness of the breath. Be still to be known from the inside out."

"We are not looking outward for any answers, we are allowing the breath to go inward where we will get clarity as the heart and mind come together within the silence of the breath, in this time."

"Our everyday thoughts are of wishes, dreams, things of the past, dreams of the future. This is fine in our day time of life, we now want to be present in the here and now, within this space we are existing. Stay with the natural rhythm of the breath, in this very moment, this is real, not imagined. When we are completely in this moment the Universe reacts."

"The circle of life is completely drawn on the earth's floor with a willow twig.  Your triangle is in place with all the things — 'Sarah's Spell' —within

'The circle of Life'—

Here on the riverbank is your seal

to present your ask of the Universe."


A dark night; Envision happens...


Aba will be silent for now, as we will seek peace."

My breathing went on and, I lost the sense of my body sitting alongside the river. I stopped thinking, my mind was quiet, my heart was quiet, and my sense of self was gone. I was in my breath, in a moment of time. In the distance was the beautiful sound of Undines singing, as they inhabited the water lapping the shore. Aba was chanting and  peace surrounded my time above all the earth. I felt peaceful, as if I was in a cloud of air filled with fine droplets of water.

Aba and I, each, have our crystals to touch. Whereas when the time is just right, Aba exclaimed they would vibrate, producing a rainbow of brilliance. Then when touched together our crystals would transform the willow, feathers, Nathan's hair and nail clippings; along with mine, also the poems for the three boys written on birch bark. Aba took the lead of touching our crystals together causing the willow to catch on fire. I felt the heat first, then heard the crackle of the burning twigs being consumed by the fire, smelled the smoke, and this all appeared as a dream. I was following breath in allowing my outbreath to allow my body to be heavy, as becoming rooted into the earth. I stayed in the now, no thinking, just the peace of being, as if floating far from my body lulled into this perfectness of peace.

Aba was talking. She sounded far away. Her voice was comforting, soft and speaking with discernment, " When you call out to the Universe for something, you are then bound by what... happens... next."

"Sarah, speak from your heart."

I began to express my wish as my heart's desire;

"Let it be known this is my solemn wish; a never ever

wish of time, to have Nathan not die at age of nine."

"Please allow him to stay with our family. I am not asking as a martyr, I am asking to continue to be his mother. I know, as I ask, I am ready to give up my reincarnations, as a sacrifice. I will give up my returns in favor of keeping my son, throughout the lifetime of his parents, allowing him to continue his journey."

"I respect all I have been given. Thank you for all, and love and patience, I have felt through the fairies and, now, Aba. They have known me before I knew myself, this I have learnt by observing their knowledge. In my many lives I have grown to respect the helpers. I am drawn to them and I feel watched over, as I look to take the paths, prepared for me. I am ready for my wish to be. It is an honor to prepare the way, for Nathan."

"It is my pledge, to lay my quartz white rocks, the fairies asked of me to collect, into the dirt of the ground, in the place chosen to be my spirit home. My life with 'Pureness of Soul' as 'Wish' will be, and be hidden forever, never ever to be thought of, or to be spoken about. Life goes on for each, mother and child. This connection through signs, as the Universe speaks; all journeys connected. Forever connected to one another, and to the light, love, and energy, of the Universe. I am humbly grateful."

Now my wish was spoken, "A Never Ever Wish of time" All was quiet. I was breathing in the smoke. My mind quiet.

In the silence, I heard the distinguishing eerie sound of a banshee, wailing and shrieking, in vocal lament of death. Aba speaks. "Look carefully at Sarah, who is filled with faith, and faithful to all she is given, works within the mere existence of her life, in this time of women's oppression. She has said she lacks courage. I can see a woman, who has no need of this virtue, in this time of silence for all women. Courage interferes with her virtues of humanity, to all which evolves empathy. Sarah is giving up her life, for her son?"

"Is this not courage?"

"In the time being- the earth's dirt will be the outer covering, of Sarah's collection of white quartz rocks, to lay endlessly beneath the ground.  If ever at any time, with all times eternal, the rocks are in the light of day, the rocks will exist to be present or found. In this moment of time; time is, said equivocal, which can be interpreted in more ways than one. All time becomes eternal; time gone bye, time being, time to come; time is existing through, all times. If existing in any time, then the rocks, are found or disturbed, Sarah may be free to reincarnate. The soul is not born it does not die. Life is in the now.'

Let us know with a sign of hope to show Sarah's fate. The rocks will exist to be present or to be found...

Never ever at no time to come, will we speak of Nathan's Fate."

I heard this as if in a real dream, I knew Aba negotiated for eternal life, as always, the truth teller.

"Sarah, are you ready to come back to your body?"

"The path is delivered, and going forward the nature of change makes life impossible to predict. The Banshee, now heralds what is to be our sign, that something important and often good is starting to change."

"Aba my guide, my friend, you have helped me attain my wish. This gift will always remain my great treasure, as is your friendship."

"Aba treasures you too. Let us remain in the now."

"For now we will finish. We have this moment of life; where your heart and mine, are as one. The desires deep within are already known by the Universe. Let go, and be wholly in your being. Take the silver baby cup that runs over with river water to symbolize the full life, holding it over the burnt seal of your circle of life, spill out the water."

Aba at the same time proclaimed,

"Nathan earth to earth; time extended."

"Sarah earth to earth; time...what will be, shall be."

"It is no longer to be changed or reversed. It is done."

"We were catalyst to bring about what was always a path to be chosen, there is no acknowledgement for our efforts for we only moved to the path to be in tune with the Universe, our path To Be."

"Thanks be to God, who gave me faith-filled helpers."

"I, Sarah, remain ever grateful..."

"Look Sarah, there is a butterfly, a symbol of transformation, a sign of hope, as change of ascension, although we as humans think we know reality, where we look to see if there could be any sort of logical explanations to make new happenings, make sense. Not today!"

"This butterfly's metamorphosis is the sign of hope. A promise to you Sarah, from the Universe, and the powers that be — at some time you, too, will be free. This as part of the wonder of life, we have just experienced."

"Never ever to be spoken of again."

*What will be, shall always be...*
*when movement is forward...*

# CHAPTER FORTY-FOUR

# Aba My Dear Friend

Aba wants you, Sarah, to know you have truly touched my heart which has led me to think of the needs of my people.

Also, Aba wants to thank you for trusting Aba to guide you."

"Aba will now be helping my Wabanaki people to shine, and grow under the sun. In the Universe, we, all people each have several significant gifts. Aba will come, as the 'Breath of Life' for my people to be complete. Aba will help make whole and wonderful all, on their way to become. Celebrating them, and their gifts. I am asked to help preserve, help grow, and foster, my people to be to become what they were created to be."

"Wabanaki" means "People of the Dawn Land." We as natives have a culture with pride of ownership, through the tools our ancestors passed down to their next generation, their culture lives on in the history of time. In fact, Aba's family has known a rich history passed down to generations, to follow along the paths of life."

Aba taught me well by her fine example of living her beliefs, and sharing her gift of sight. Aba's gift has a renewed strength of spirit, as she was called to invest in the youth who are losing sight of their ways. Most never ever feel the need to be creative after leaving childhood, so it is a great loss of art. Aba's spirit is in need to connect with the youth helping them to remember their pride in Wabanaki, connecting the gifts of culture, to pass on to the next generations, to live on past their time.

As Aba talked of being Wabanaki...

I found myself daydreaming of being native and upholding my culture with its richness in history. I see myself as sought after for mentorship with my great attention to detail. I would be an honored native sharing my ancestral works and artistry to keep our great history alive and flourishing. Mine would be known as "Artifacts Made of the Earth." Even with me not being native, Aba connected her thoughts with success. Aba is a great guide, teacher, and will mentor the youth into owning who they were born to be. Aba did this for me, helping me to see my life as I was born to be.

Aba asked me, "Have you ever tried to remember any of your other lives? Aba has seen in you much compassion, and empathy for one this young. These traits are learned also the swift learning of control of your breath, and how quickly the crystal became alive in your hands. It is as if done by you before, if so this would have been in another life. Sometimes past lives touch present lives, with compassion for all things known well by a life, shared in the past. This gives a sense of belonging. You know of a life where you should know nothing, yet your heart swells with compassion and pride, as if ownership of ways to live this life. This allows for daydreams and knowledge in this way of living life. Could this have been a path you once was on moving to become the Sarah you are today?" Aba thus enlightened me to own my past, hidden in the present.

Aba became my one true friend, knowing me as no other, the real complete me. Aba knew my beliefs, my heart, my loves, and my struggles. Aba opened up my secrets I knew even as a small child. I am in awe of Aba's Spirit, she practices throughout her life. She nurtured me, and helped me find my path to my whole self. Aba guided the way as I made the choice although she always warned me, "Sarah, be careful of what you wish, and never to lose sight of your joy."

"Aba's true spirit is to connect to the youth to help them remember their pride in Wabanaki, knowing the gifts of culture to pass on to live past their times. To use nature to their benefit. This is our way of life. What lives around us becomes our culture. When we die, Wabanaki, we become what lives around us."

"Gifts of nature full circle."

"In the Bird, Animal, Plant World, each species has its own strength, pride, and beauty, to honor. To see a plant blossom with many colors then grow, producing seed makes my heart grow."

"To see majestic trees, with needles and leaves growing together, along-side, one another, makes my heart grow. To see a birds soaring close, in feathers of all colors of the rainbow, swells Aba's heart."

"Knowing, Aba is a part of this lifeline fills me with awe. We with choice need to help to bring forth what comes naturally in nature. We need to be reminded of our spiritual life, as to who, we were born to be. Aba is so filled with deep feelings, so much love, tempered with pride, so deep it changes Aba for the better."

I was happy for Aba to be living amongst, and helping her people, and sad to see her leave as she was the only one on earth who knew me, the real me, then gave me acceptance as I am. She is my only friend.

Aba told me, "The Earth has always existed;

The owner; Grandmother created people, animals, and all natural things, as rocks, trees, whereas each has its own spirit. Our villages are located near water. Each man has different hunting territories inherited through his father, as the Wabanaki are patrilineal. Traditionally, ancestors worshiped spirits of natural features. Tribal beliefs persist as folk religion. Our language is Algonquian."

Wliwni nokemes {Thank you my Grandmother}

Wliwni nid 8 baskwa {Thank you my girlfriend}

"Thank you Aba. I see your joy, and I am happy. I will miss you when we will never ever see each other, yet as I see my favorite bird, or have my calming tea and the best time ever will be when we watch the sunrise, then the sunset."

"Aba looks to the Universe — each day is a gift for joy...

Being happy is an act of courage.

This my life to be — such is an honor."

"Aba has a proficiency for you Sarah, one for you to remember when the end days draw near. The strength of who you are is your empathy. Be careful in remaining true to the whole Sarah as you will be blindsided by those you trust and love. It will be hard, and you must let your forgiveness surpass your understanding, remembering always, love exists without needing reciprocation. Also in your last days you will feel alone. This must not steal your dignity. Remember, as a child you found joy in being alone in nature, in the end days create a space of solitude. Stay true to all that makes you, Sarah."

"I love you, Aba. No matter where we are in life you are, as my dear sister, we are bonded to live on in each other's hearts."

"True Sarah, we will never ever lose our love. This too is true, your life has brought me strength to accomplish what is important. My guiding brought me to see the steps, for you and for me. I want you to know, that you have helped, Aba to choose ways to help others. You thought you found me. Aba thought I was to help you."

"The truth is the Universe brought us together, and we have learned from each other in this environment of love that we share."

"It was to conquer the fears we both had; you of losing your son, and Aba of not knowing my place in this life. These fears were laid to rest, as replaced with trust through love, leaving us to see clearly our choices. We both have been successful in moving forward.

This holistic gift; is a journey greater than us. Our relationship is important to us, as we live separate lives, we will never ever lose our love."

"Always trust in the Universe, as all comes together as needed."

We hugged a long goodbye, knowing we would never ever lay eyes on each other.— "Aba, we will lead separate lives apart from each other; in our hearts we will always be together, as dear friends and sisters of The Universe."

"Remember, our everyday thoughts are of wishes, dreams, things of the past, dreams of the future. This is fine in our day time of life, now we want to be present, in the here and now, within this space we are now existing. Stay with the natural rhythm of the breath, in this moment that is now real, not imagined...

Then when we watch the sunrise

We are completely in this moment...

The Universe reacts... love connecting — Aba  & Sarah."

This was our last conversation. Each Monday, I miss Aba, and make tea to honor her place of home in my life, also to honor her place in Wabanaki history as a successful spirit guide. I sit alone watching the sunrise, that fills my senses with awe, my heart swells with my love for Aba, my dear sister of the Universe...

I say, "I was looking for you."

I feel her love and hear Aba answer,

"It makes Aba happy — when Aba finds you too."

Then together we watch the sky —  Aba and I say,

"Being happy is an act of courage."

# Chapter Forty-Five

# To Mother

I remember our days together Mother, you were busy with housekeeping. My sister who was annoyingly noisy and was always swinging. On the other hand I was a serious study on anything of nature surrounding me. Like the leaves setting on trees in the springtime opening so fast, I thought, I could hear them unfurl with their fresh yellow-green tint shown even more beautiful under the crisp blue sky. I would become so excited, to see the onset of my meadow awaken from the long cold barren winter.

What peace I felt being on the bare ground free from snow, allowing the meadow flowers to poke through the warming soil. When the flowers poked through the soil, some days I knew they grew inches, and if I missed a few days of being in the fields, they became big tall plants swaying in the breeze.

I would take a deep breath smelling the fresh air of spring, and think how wondrous to be here experiencing the newness of life, coming forth from the dormancy.

How glorious was my wonderful life, Being a small part of this 'My Magical Meadow' brought contentment, a feeling of being part of the Earth's show of 'Nature's Beauty' created for all to enjoy.

Never ever did I understand when told by the fairies, 'this was only an early chapter in my life.' They said 'One has to experience a change in mind and heart, to move on to the next path which will be pulling with a desire' then, I somehow knew once destiny started taking over, 'it would be like falling down hill and rolling, and rolling, until my destiny was reached.' What will my full destiny be?

I have figured out, or should say, have been told life is put together in chapters, some good, some bad. Beginning to the End.

" Mother, I am thankful for the beginning you gave me, allowing me to be. Thus letting me grow into my heart and mind. You gave me and my sister, a choice of life, a great gift of freedom. To you I am grateful, as I like the independent woman, I am, so thank you for loving me enough to let me, be me."

"James and I have only one son Nathan, who is book smart, not a hugger or anything at all like his parents. I have learned to respect this as his choice. I know each person is where they are in their lives, as each will live out their own story. It is their life."

"I have come to see more clearly your plight of not disappointing your mother, sisters, and husband. Your selfless world was hard to exist in, and took all your time. I am sorry, we did not come to know each other better."

"Today, I better understand your life by seeing you through my own journey. My life's journey has opened my heart allowing me to see the things, I did not know were hidden within the dark corners."

" When torn by events, it is your voice of wisdom I hear. You have never ever left my side, all while helping me navigate life's choices."

" May your presence be with me throughout the rest of my journey, as your words of loving sensible spirit, are essential to bring about understanding."

"My life has been somewhat of a mystery, when being surrounded by events, that were never ever thought to be possible, or even exist."

"My life's path is to stay thankful and joyful. This I do with my writing, thanks to your lessons, and your belief in my gift. You could see, what I did not know was in my heart, this desire to tell stories."

"As I get older, I miss you Mother, more with each passing year."

"I know without one doubt you were the Mother I needed.
The one I had chosen."

"Thank you, Mother for sharing my life's journey."

"I have come to know,  I have always loved you."

"Your grateful daughter, Sarah.

**MORIA Thoughts:**

*A dear friend always said,  "One never ever forgets their Mother... Over there is my mothers favorite bird, a Robin..."*

# Part II – Afterword

**NEVER EVER – Disavow life's Beliefs...**

Sarah's Quest is to remember her true self, hidden in the past, to accept herself allowing wholeness to be at one within her heart, to be her truth, all leading to complete love.

This she needed to bring alive her deepest wish, into the reality of the chosen path. Aba, the indigenous pathfinder enlightened Sarah to remember her knowledge, wisdom, love and joy, bringing courage to ask the universe this unheard wish.

Aba always spoke to be careful for what is wished, warning this was to remain their spiritual secret.

Aba and Sarah befriended each other as life long friends,

as sisters forever...

love — ever after...

# Part III

**Poetic Justice**

If only there was a recipe to follow
to enjoy all of our short fragile life...

could even the most accurate measurements
go completely askew, such is my life...

All are on their own paths, to be
searching for a lifelong journey to wholeness...

**Never Ever Tell Life's Secrets...**

# CHAPTER FORTY-SIX

# Mother-in-law's Secret

Over time James bought the farm whereas his mother, Effie was to remain housekeeper. She recently has been ill, so reluctantly she asked me to temporarily keep the house in order, just until her strength returns.

I asked James, "What do you think? Could we send a telegram to your brother, Nathaniel? Maybe your mother would get better with a visit from her family. I think it bothers her that they are so far away, especially the grandchildren, whom she has not laid eyes upon."

James said, "Good idea. I will send one today." My thoughts of Nathan's time on the farm, alone and not happy, prompted me to say, "If they came Nathan would have cousins here and Sarah is his same age. Maybe he would like the farm life better with kids to help with the chores and play games."

"Oh, Sarah, do not make plans because my brother is not one to make commitments. Hopefully the news of Ma's failing health will bring them home for a while anyway."

"James as we are talking of the homecoming, I can not stop myself from becoming excited to meet your brother, his wife Phoebe and our nieces and nephews. If I am getting excited, just think of your Ma, able to finally hug her grandchildren."

"We will tell Ma and Nathan when they reply with a yes."

We heard from the family. Yes, they will be coming home. We were all excited, and dwelling on making everything perfect for their visit. I of course began planning all things to do with making their stay special, after all, they will have traveled for a long time to come back home to the farm. There was even a newspaper article written proclaiming 'Nathaniel returns' from gold mining in California, then a move to Australia, where he married and began a family.

In the afternoon Mrs. Stevens, Effie becomes quite talkative and talks freely about her life. A past love she calls, "Her first true love" whom she says, "I named my boy after." This is what she goes on about. It seems she has forgotten time has passed, and old loves are in the past, not to be spoken of again. It is like she exists in the past, leaving her time in her present day life. In some ways it is as though she does not know who I am, and talks excessively about his love for her. "It is beautiful to be so loved."

"Remembering back at the age of 19 years, I was betrothed to Asa who was 24 years, and was known as Capt. Asa, who was back from the service. He was a good man. I came to care for him, thus I remained his wife until his death, then remained his widow. He needed a wife, my father needed a marriage to accomplish one less mouth to feed, my mother said, 'There will be time enough for love talk when properly married.' They struck a deal. I had worked with my Ma, and knew all of the housekeeping tasks needed for Asa's farm, well down south in Bloomfield. Yes, this very farm."

"He was hoping for a family, especially boys. The 1st born was Evelyn Matilda, my sweet girl, then Elijah, our first son. Your James, Benjamin,

Edgar, Eliza Ann, Edward, Nathaniel, then the two who died as infants, Edith May and Christian. Asa was a good man, and I came to care for him. I remained his wife with offspring climbing out the windows."

"At this time my regret in life was I was born too early, meeting my one true love too late in my days. We met, and I knew instantly he was to be the one to hold my heart. He was all I thought of along with my regrets of being tied by marriage to another, when we could have had all the happiness love brings. He would talk, and I would listen; I would talk, and he would listen with the more we talked and talked, we both felt an energy of longing. We had to be with each other, even if it was to be in secret. I led a double life; as wife, mother, housekeeper, and then we would meet where I was to become the beloved, cherished, beautiful Effie. 'My Effie' he would call me. He was very handsome, and becoming a prominent man about town. I married with children would not be in his future. So we took whatever happiness we could in secret."

James's mother seemed to have a perfect understanding of what she was telling me. "These were challenging times as the Corbeils did not approve of our being together. They were desperate to break up our love. It was unfairly overwhelming to be treated as an outsider, when we had a son, named after his father's family. The family chose to look the other way. I had my son, and we would be taken care of by Asa Stevens. He became the one to claim the child, yet I did not give up my love for my Nathaniel. He was still my whole life. My heart was always with him, as I had given it to him."

"My wonderful Asa deserved better than a woman who was always pining for the man, who captured her heart. I tried to live my life as a Stevens, but all the while I was living a lie. Asa and I had many children yet, in those days my love for Nathaniel was always in my heart, hidden away from all people, never ever to be spoken aloud, and always present. I accepted my fate, also I knew my place. I pretended to have a normal life. We were all robbed of our truth."

"Now here I am sick, possibly dying and I will not keep this hidden. My family must know their rightful place in the Corbeil family. We were young doing as we were told, only now I am old, fading away with thoughts of the truth, trying to surface to free us all, by exposing the lies that have become my life. How long before Nathaniel gets home from Australia? He needs to know who he is, and what I always agreed to Asa, to say of his life. I hope he forgives me as I had no power to live a better life."

"Back then Asa looked in pity, he was a good kind man. He loved his family and me. He was an angel, as he was full of life's righteous ways, also regrets. I was never ever meant to feel any disgrace, and I was always welcomed by the family of the Stevens'."

"I consider myself blessed. I was suffering silently due to my heart being guarded, and me always searching for my love. Nathaniel was much harder to clear from my body. This is now my son, Nathaniel's legacy. I must tell my son before I go to my grave. I am telling you so just in case my life ends, all of this will not be lost. It is terribly disheartening to know a secret has taken on a life of its own. It is what it is and must be known, as the truth will be better, than to be misled of their parentage for all their life."

"I will enjoy telling him the truth. To let him know his place in this world was guarded. Sarah please listen, do not interrupt and say nothing of what I tell you. First of all, I trust you. My reason for telling you, my daughter-in-law is clear to me. You will hear without any judgment, you will see the truth, without hiding what it means. I am going to tell you of my hidden life, my real life, and how it affects all in my life."

"In my family some of the children are Corbeil's. You may have noticed I chose the middle name Corbeil, for my boys who are Nathaniel's sons. I do know, respect and admire the Corbeil's family life. They do not drink, swear or disrespect any about town. They have been community driven, helping our town grow richer by sharing their wealth and knowledge, being very prominent even without an attendance of our church. Most people think when they first hear my son's name Nathaniel Corbeil, it is to honor our towns wealthiest, foremost family. What they do not know is he was named for his biological father. My son is a Corbeil. His father and I, have shared a long hidden life."

"I was cast aside by his family, not to be suitable for their son. It breaks my heart to know I lived in such a semi-normal life, and how much I risked living two separate lives. My heart has been crystal clear. I have not compromised my love. My life has become a secret from all, but Asa. I allowed myself to have moments of what I felt should have been my life. Today, I am old and dying with the full effect of how alone I am, as I have no promise of till death do us part. I have no rights as we were never married."

"Yes, the Corbeil boys exist; they are not the bastard sons of Nathaniel as the Church or town folk, if known, would have made them out to be. They are the sons of Nathaniel Corbeil, and need to share their Corbeil family. Even with the scandalous truth, their life should be easier with the truth of their lineage. It is their Birthright. I can not take this to my grave, so I am telling you. If Nathaniel does not get home before I leave this world, my question to you, will you share with him this knowledge?"

My mind is whirling. My heart is beating fast. Did she say her boys with the Corbeil middle name? Would this also include my husband James? My mind was racing. This would not be a good thing for James. Perhaps, Nathaniel, who has not been a homeboy, would want the truth, after all he has spent his life in San Francisco, then married in Australia, even today is coming home by ship, which will take three months. He seems a worldly man, who could deal very well with this knowledge. James, on the other hand, would not accept his whole life has been a lie. His father was not his real bloodline. Nathaniel Corbeil, and his mother were not married; she laid with him out of wedlock. She was that type of woman?

James is deep-seated in faith. His love for God has led him to work hard, and also, to have the knowledge to accept what is given to you, as always you will never ever be given more than you can handle. James's purpose is to make an honorable life; people would look up to, as being real and genuine. The most important thing for him is the respect his way of life has brought him, along with an unspoken acknowledgement of a well lived life by all who know him.

I said, "You are tired, rest and we will talk another time." It feels like the world is standing still, to await the moment her secret is out and all it entails, involving those she loves. In my thoughts: I felt protective of James, who must never ever find out, and our son, Nathan cannot know, as he would take advantage of all things Corbeil. My mind is racing. Who else knows? Will someone at sometime tell James? This is catastrophic. Asa, even with his unrequited love, kept their marriage with their secrets. James is his father's son. Asa is the father he knows and loves.

Kissing her on her cheek, I gently squeezed her ring finger on her left hand saying, "You rest now, your secret is safe with me. I will sit with you awhile." I reassured her with a smile while requesting, "I just ask, as you tell Nathaniel, have him promise to keep it to himself until he comfortably accepts what this means. It could change his life for the better or the worst."

I am thinking he being from mostly away may have a fresh perspective, maybe even a worldly way to deal with an awkward acknowledgement of his namesake. I do not know her son. I do know James, who must never ever know the truth. He quotes "the truth will set you free" this being his belief. How would all, he believes of a normal life in Skowhegan with his mother, Effie and father, Asa, who died when James was a child of twelve. How would knowing his whole life was a lie, set him free. He who loves

God, his church, in this town where the people have known him his whole life. A life lived without a hint of impurity, a source of pride. That pride would fall when these secrets come out into the light of day. They are best left untold or swept under the rug where anything uncomfortable stays in hiding.

These choices our heart leads us into, are the ones our minds cannot control. There is a great deal of desire that takes us all on a journey. Not all however have the courage to expose their choices, their secrets which can create fear and anger in people who are affected and a lot of vulnerability. Some people are disappointed feeling let down, also reminded of times when their own judgment lapsed into desires of the heart. I know not one person who has not had, but at least one secret. Untold Secrets are valuable; as there is no scrutiny.

Effie was anxious to keep talking as if afraid to leave anything unsaid she asked, "Sarah is there something you would like to know?"

I said, "I have given thought to your secret, which is now our secret. Could I ask you a question, pertains to James? He has the Corbeil middle name. Does he also have Nathaniel, as a father, and does he know?"

She told me, "This is something I know and James cannot know, as he has always had a much beloved father." She looked at me reassuringly and said, "I never ever have told him anything about Nathaniel. He may have thought it was strange on my part, yet never ever did he question my choice of his middle name. You want to know if James also is a Corbeil? The answer is yes. Will I tell him? No. I just do not want to take this life changing truth to the grave."

"Asa died so young, after which in my heart I thought Nathaniel and I could become a couple, as there were sons with his bloodline amongst my children. I had grown older, less desirable, and life had taken him on a different journey. Perhaps he now saw me as unsuitable. The woman his family saw quite clearly. We had a love for the record books then time and life has ebbed away the lust and longing, leaving two people who have nothing in common, except for the boys. Today I would not take him into my life, not even on a 'silver platter'. Now, I can clearly see, I have lived my life in folly."

"Asa and I had two children die, one was Christian Corbeil, an infant. However to be honest I did not want these little ones, so dying at birth was in my favor. Is my honesty shocking you? I do not think they were neglected, I just could not love them, and had little care of them. They withered away. Asa was saddened by their deaths. He loved children, growing them into great farmers, and down to earth people. This is how we got by on the farm.

I am tired. We will talk tomorrow. It is nice to have a listening ear. I feel I can tell you my life, and you are not judging or criticizing my choices. This quality you have makes me feel comfortable to talk, of the unspeakable things. You bring peace to me."

"Thank you, Sarah. Come visit me tomorrow."

If she only knew my choices and the direction my life has led me. This I could never ever, and would never ever tell. These life choices will go with me to my grave as valuable secrets. If I should ever weaken I will just remember the dire truth telling from Ma Effie, as for me knowing her secret has been a living nightmare.

I can sense if not living through the events of the past, the story becomes facts without any of the accompanying feelings, and without the feelings it all sounds absurd.

I love James's mother, but what she tells me is not the Ma I know.

I also, am not new to secrets, and can not imagine how shocked she would be to hear my life's story. Only one, Aba, my dear sister will ever know the direction I took through fear of losing my son, Nathan, to an early death. No greater love.

I can never ever tell of my secret friendship with Aba, a native Soothsayer. We together found the Sarah I was created to be then used this strength of life, to the purpose of redirecting life for my son Nathan.

Aba is a special person with gifts of discernment. She accepted my plight, calmed my fears and listened to me as an equals, on separate paths, neither one perfect.  I was always in awe of her knowledge and wisdom, also she led me to move forward on my path.

In the end before she traveled to help her tribe continue on the paths of their ancestors, she told me the Universe brought us both together, to grow into, each of our life's purpose. Aba led me to feel accomplished, as to pen stories bringing my long hidden 'gift of Joy' back. Do you know Joy as a gift of fulfilment?

Aba is my secret friend,  all our needs in life could only happen in silence.

From Beginning to The End —

we are devoted to our lifelong friendship.

Today, I love and miss seeing my humble friend, Aba.

We are on different paths,

where our love connects each day

through the Universe within nature...

Aba asked me to think of Joy. Do yo know Joy?

The answers to living a 'JOY filled LIFE' is to monitor feelings, and not to get caught up in a tangent of one thought. To look at life through eyes, only, brings unclarity, to look with only the heart brings an unrealistic fulfillment of love. To lead with the mind leaves an unsettling, as thoughts come and go. Our feelings can put us in touch with things that make sense, until reviewed from another prospective which can change the whole view into another realm.

Discernment is needed to align our thoughts to our own beliefs, the core of who we are meant to be. All knowledge created wisdom, is responsible for discernment, fulfilled in each day of life for our time—To Be— spent in JOY.

### *FAIRIES REFLECTIONS:*

***Aspen added:*** *"The sign of the Universe is love in a perfect world all humans are each connected to one another through love. Those who have lived in your heart, will remain, as loves within the heart, and in your mind are their words and deeds to comfort."*

### *MORIA Thoughts:*

*Sarah your outlook on secrets; 'they should never ever be told' has brought this as truth into my heart. Why tell of an event of the past, to proclaim the truth of a time which no longer exists in the lives of those who did not share in the decision, to leave this secret without a reveal is a kindness. Secrets, some hide shame and whispering words of a secretly hidden time will not bring closure, or understanding, or love. 'It takes more strength to never ever tell a long kept secret — protecting all with quiet reproach.' This you have taught trough your writings, as an act of real love.*

# CHAPTER FORTY-SEVEN

# The Ultimate Betrayal

After my restless night I again listened to the next part of my mother-in-law's story of the love of her life, while she was married to Asa until — 'death do us part.'

She went on to say, "I needed help. I could not keep up the work of three small children, along with all my housekeeping duties because I was frail. My family did what they could, but it was not enough, therefore we hired a girl from the workhouse, an Irish waif whose name was Hannah. When we could no longer pay her, she asked if she could stay for a while to work for her keep. She became like a sister to me, and as a mother, to Evelyn, Elijah and Edgar. Hannah was a helpmate to Asa, whereas in my naiveness I could see a connection, still never ever thought much of this until she became full with a child."

"Asa insisted she stay on with us for the child's sake. I felt like the girl was out to steal my place, although, legally I would remain the wife and the fool."

"I took many walks to clear my head of the feeling I had lost my husband, and upon these walks I would always say hello to Nathaniel. Sometimes he would slow, walk beside me. I felt unattached, so I made sure my looks were well groomed, graceful, dignified, also I felt pretty to appeal to the handsome Corbeil. Looking forward to our walks and talks, this became as if a courtship where he became the light within my heart. My first true love. We had love without anyway to live this love, as I was married to Asa. My heart's desire to be Mrs. Corbeil was quelched before the thought had properly entered my mind."

"Effie, I understand how hard this must have been." I quietly said, "All things in Universe happen for a reason, It seems only in books do people get to be 'happy ever after' within their life's choices, although James and I are the exception."

She smiled and asked, "Sarah are you sure you are ready to hear the sad tale of Effie Stevens? Your old mother-in-law's woes, of my shameful desire to love and be loved."

My answer to this mother figure in my life, "I know you and your kindness to me during the loss of our children. I see how you drew strength from your past, and gave it freely to me which could not have been easy as I was as a prickly pear without reasoning. You studied my mind allowing me to mourn my children encouraging me to see my pain through. Coming out on the other side where James was awaiting my return. You have been a good and steady person in my life. Of course I will honor your need to voice your time of discontent and unrequited love."

Then to comfort her I added, "I will not and cannot judge. I have been taught through my years of living, judging only harbors hate in our heart, and leaves little room for love. We need all the love given, to bring peace and forgiveness to ourselves, and or, other's. All families have their share of what could be deemed scandalous, when in truth it is people working through their lives on paths they have chosen and, or, not chosen, albeit real. No one sets out on events to hurt or demean others, and, or themselves. There is no book on how to live a perfect life. There is the Bible that gives structure of goodness, yet the feelings stirring deep inside our innermost heart filling us with deep longings, bringing uncontrollable desires to mount up with untold action, bringing shame in the end. This lust has no guide, although as we get more of life's experiences we can then look back, and see the path not taken in the past, would have detoured all the heartbreak, and the unnecessary pent-up shame, which has taken over your thoughts today. Hiding what felt shameful, is now, bringing you shame. It is alright to proceed, I am listening, not judging."

"How hard it was to accept a betrayal from my friend Hannah. She was living in our house helping out, whereas we treated her as family. I loved her, and to be truthful, I still love her. She was my only friend. After her child was born I was torn between love and hate; hate and love. Hannah ran off with a hired hand taking Asa's child with her. She came in like a gentle breeze, and left as a whirlwind upending all of our lives. The children cried for her to come back. Asa was left, suffocating in guilt. I found my true love which left me longing for what could have been. Nathaniel and I were expecting a child and Asa and I, had no relationship. So me being with a child was like an Immaculate Conception. Asa wanted to be known as the father to move onward forgetting all, that challenged our marriage. It was not so easy for me. Nathaniel was still here, not like Hannah, who left. He was in town, also must have wondered about the child. We had talked of my home life, and he knew Asa and I were husband and wife, in name only, now with another child in our family named James Corbeil Stevens."

"Asa was so proud, so glad to have a boy. Time healed our void, only now, I knew how real love felt. I realized Asa was never ever my love. I respected his strength, his sense of doing right by me, his love of his family. These I saw from the outside looking in. With Nathaniel I saw the man I loved from the inside of our hearts looking out, covering over imperfections, our love made it easy to overlook. Thus being blinded, he seemed perfect for me. We were so much in love, life plays tricks on young invincible love."

"Settling into the farm life and family, of four children, I lost hope of ever being anything other than Asa's dutiful wife, housekeeper, and mother of our four children. In time all our discussions became like a fog, as they were not the focus of our life. We had another boy. Asa was happy. I was putting one foot ahead of the other doing my duty, best I could, while my heart ached."

"On my walks I hoped to see Nathaniel again. Both our hearts were still as one, and lust was in the air tugging at my mind. I found myself thinking of how I would like to touch his face, hold his hand, kiss his lips. This never-ending longing to be close was in my mind daily. One day we gave in, he being single and I being married, yet not to him, found ourselves together with our love and feelings out of control. When I was pregnant with another child I knew Nathaniel was the father, so I told Asa."

"He knew Nathaniel would never ever be able to be a father to the child as he was becoming a prominent man about town and these things, these terrible transgressions are things, not to happen in family life. We had to look for proper ways of accepting the life we had together within our marriage this was our truth, and proclaimed untruth. How my heart aches watching my Corbeil boys growing without their father. Asa loved them, taught them farm life. Loving Asa, as their father, life was always good for the family, the father and sons."

"My days as a woman were scorned. Leaving me to make the best of my days, by staying busy to bury my broken pieces of my heart. Then I saw my love, Nathaniel. He was there in front of me. Our eyes met, and next was as if we had talked just yesterday. I told him of James and Nathaniel, and how strong, smart and capable they were becoming. In time he will be glad to have fathered, and to be the father of such boys. Our love was too much to harness, so I was to have another child. I named him Christian Corbeil, this name I picked to cut into his heart, as this is his brother's name with whom he lived. I wanted to send him a message of how much he was missing. How unfair our life was to me, the unfaithful, and he the bachelor, with another man raising his sons."

"When this Corbeil was born I became depressed. I saw my life as it really was. I felt used. I knew my love for Nathaniel was real. At this time, I also knew he would never ever come to my side. My heart broken, and my mind sees my normal life as anything but normal. How can a man proclaim love, then not the care that goes along with loving another person. How can he claim as he proclaimed to me 'I am his one and only' when he makes no effort to be with me. I think I went crazy for a while, remembering moments in my life, when I was close to Nathaniel made me unaware of all my troubles.

My weakness to be loved, led to having Corbeil sons, whom I proclaim to love as only a mother can love her children. How could I leave this earth, leaving them not to know their heritage? They were born as farmers, to join the only Paw they ever knew, he died to leave them to bear the hardest of life's works. In truth they are Corbeil's silver spoon sons."

"Christian was a weak baby, needed much care. I knew and I did not seem to care. My heart was dying, my mind was not functioning. My family took turns to help me out with the children, but little Christian needed a mother, not this woman without a heart, or a mind. He died in infancy. Before his death I let go of my dreams, my hopes, my loves, all was quiet within."

"I came to this realization: I have wasted my life chasing after the shadow of Nathaniel, who was always thought to be my true love. My love's desires left me cheated with disappointments, to ebbing away the love, allowing my heart to feel what my mind came to know as desire. My great love became a hollow untruth. I could see him, as not my true love. I grieved, the disappointment of being fooled by his false love. After all was said and done, I realized this relationship was false. This love mattered to me, whereas, for him our love was an untruth, leaving only me, to feel the loss of love, as in a death. I do not expect you to understand, because I do not myself understand. All I know is I was captured, and nothing else mattered, only our love. Today our great weaved spell of love, no longer exists. I do not love or hate Nathaniel."

"I felt the presence of death, then the mourning of loss, then the grief, so deep and painful. The grieving was not just from the loss of my baby, it was the recognition of the death of my love for Nathaniel. He let me down, and did not honor my love. He left me to work my way through all the things our love left in our wake. Finally my love died. I was free of the hold our love had on my life. We are now two; he is a bachelor, as for me, I am a housekeeper, and sole caretaker of the children, on the Stevens Farm, on the Middle Road, way down. This is my place."

"I regret my deeds more than I can say. Most of my life was upside down and sideways. When my husband died I felt the loss of the years, our best years spent in oblivion, I stole from our marriage, being fooled by my need to be loved."

"Now, I know my love, my real love was Capt. Asa. He was ever there with help and courage, to face life with understanding and goodness. I was his wife and my needs were met with unveiled compassion. He never ever criticized or thought less of me because of my bad choices. He knew his love would win in the long scheme of life. It is now, too late, as I know my true Love was Captain Asa Stevens, who has died. How ironic to be betrayed by my own heart."

"Effie, I have listened. You do have a big secret, likin to a double edged sword; to some happiness and prosperity, to others sadness and loss. I can only say to you, to be careful, who you tell, the long hidden truth of time, lost."

James's family came, and his brother wanted to stay on the farm with their mother. They had funds to buy the farm, and Effie was happy with the premise of Nathaniel staying on the farm. We were fine with James's brother buying our farm for we knew we could not make a go of farming with our only son not wanting to be a farmer. Also, James was elated to have his brother living back home again.

We were looking to move into the newly built village. The house we wanted was sold. Then it came up for sale again and while we were getting the funds together, it was sold again. This purchase was for resale. I have heard the expression, 'Three times a charm.' James bought the house, albeit it cost much more than was feasible for this property.

Effie never ever mention her secret again to me. I assumed she was able to tell her son. Perhaps this is why they stayed on at the farm, regardless we moved to our house that became our home forever.

Our house was not a mansion to anyone's thoughts or imagination, always in my mind and heart it was more than money could buy. It represented peace by giving freedom of choice, to go about being our own family. A time in our lives when we were well and able bodied, not yet, put out to pasture. Remembering with happiness of the times shared under the roof of our new home.

These memories to be a corner stone of our lives...

# CHAPTER FORTY-EIGHT

# End of Day

When we may die to be buried in the Southside burying ground, I am to be alongside James, my sweet sensible husband, our 1st born, Asa who only lived to be three, our son, Willie who passed at six years, also, our son Nathan and his family. We will all be together, on the Stevens lot as it was prepared.

Only now, as I was able to change my plight, I will lay in the grave as a body only, with my spirit remaining in the house James bought for our new beginning, on what they today call Main Street. This is where I buried my white quarts rocks to be, as was my foretold predestination, as was confirmed foreknowledge by Aba, and my fairies, whom had me collect the rocks. This was always to be.

When this was the path chosen by me I was so full of hope to save Nathan from certain death. Our son would be able to continue his path to the end of his journey without forfeiting his right to be. We could not lose another son. All I needed to do was enhance the belief, that was laid at my feet when I was a child. Aba and I, had the path planned to completion of Nathan's rebirth of his spirit. I needed to give him my spiritual life, in turn for his ongoing journey on earth, as our son. When this secret path was chosen by me, I was full of hope of ongoing life.

Choosing our house as the resting place of my spirit was perfect. In spirit, I would be in our house, which will be Nathan's birthright. I could be there with him, until he died. Forever I would be tied to hosting my spirit, which could never ever move onward, except if the white crystal rocks, somehow became uncovered, then I could become born again. This plan gave me peace as Nathan's life was going to be the answer to a perfect life for James and I, as we could not bear, the grief, of the death, of another son. No one will never ever be told. This will remain a life affirming secret.

In time the error of my heart became clear. I set out to save him from death. This was accomplished, whereas he lived, and existed on earth, but there was no love in him. Nathan was his own person with free choice to be himself as we are all born to be. He was not the boy I saw or the man I imagined he would become, and he was so much different from James.

Instead Nathan was self-centered, uncaring, self-serving individual with pretense to the public. Seeing this trait in him I tried to teach him to think of others which in turn seemed to instill in his actions, only the motions of caring by making use of the wording to let people think he cared. He used my words of compassion to design sentences of just, what should be said at different times to assure others that he understands. There is not a chance he is sincere. It is not in him to know true words of peace, hope, and love, with true understanding. No empathy exists in Nathan. This breaks my heart, as I knew his father to be  full of compassion, love, faith, and goodness, leaving me with thoughts of 'the apple would fall close to the tree.' This is not true. I never ever thought they would be so different, or he so unlovable.

It must be the generation as Nathan's cousin Sarah also seems indifferent to the fact that she survived off the sweat of her parents. This generation did not go to bed tired and worrying, if they indeed would survive the long winters, with the wind howling and blowing in cold air, making it almost impossible to heat our modest living space. The survival burden of managing life on the farm was taken away from this new privileged generation. They went to a new school in town, and prospered through learning, not working on the farm, which made them indifferent to the struggles that defined us, making us thus thankful.

We also, abandoned farming, now spend our days working to provide funds to pay for all this new way of living, requiring us to purchase what is needed to live this life. This house with no land for farming, in town, where learning a new way of survival, has became daunting. James was learning a new trade, pluming and heating a much needed business in town. I sold cakes and cookies, also seasonal pies made from the receipts of my own handwritten cookbook.

To this day, James never ever spoke of his sacrifice of leaving our farm or of how farming was what he liked, and did his whole life. We were getting older with the farm work getting more taxing. We became the old Aunts and Uncles, where time is not our friend, because we have spent more days of this life than we have left, making us aware we have lived beyond the halfway point. Death is inevitably near as we are to become old friends with this uncertain time of life. I am so unprepared to accept my real age, because it may make me feel at times like the end would come, meanwhile my mind is still on writing and living.

In the past, there have been times when Nathan has tricked me into getting what he wants, also times when out of his darkness he has tried to get me in trouble. He told his father I was down by the backside of town at the soothsayers. My own son, who I love, and sacrificed to protect with my life. I am used to protecting my choices and beliefs, so I, just said, "Delivering cookies to my loyal customers. I am glad it is the cookies they like best as I can make a big batch, and deliver them more easily than cakes and pies and every penny helps."

Was this a bold lie or a witty cover to protect James from my choices? That was the day that I learned how far Nathan would go to get the upper hand on his own mother. How could he do that to someone who loves him, in spite of what is known, of selfish ways, a mother will always, love her child.

The time becoming our most hurtful was when our son put our very home into peril by borrowing money. We were just barely getting by with our house being all we had for value, yet James took out a mortgage. Nathan always needed funds for schooling, he went to Colby College-Delta Kappa Epsilon Fraternity AB degree, then onto The Boston University Law School. He studied law in town, received admission to the bar then left for partnership with J.B. Harrison in Minnesota, of which required funds. He left us broke and in 1896 married in Washington D.C., a talented musician, Lillian Keziah, who, also had a widowed sister, Phyllis, as her companion, and only living relative.

It has been eight years since Nathan has been home or sent mail by way of letters, perhaps an occasional postcard with a generic message. Postcards come more often, now he is married.

I know James is missing his son with the years soon to be a decade. This time leaves one to wonder if we never ever will see him again.

If we leave Nathan's visiting up to his own volition, James may not see his son again.

I knew what needed to be done, there was no choice.
James is doing poorly, being a family man he needs his family.
This done, to bring him strength, or a peaceful end of day.

The next day I sent Nathan a telegram:

> *Your father's health is poor.*
>
> *It is not the same not having you here with us.*
>
> *Please come home to say a proper goodbye.*
>
> *As soon as possible.*

This was done and made James's longing to see his son and his new wife even stronger. I on the other hand knew Nathan and what havoc he could bring to the last days of James's time here on earth especially if there was a benefit for Nathan. Then of course he will bring two ladies with him that I will need to make comfortable. Perhaps he has grown, is no longer spurious, and is what he claims to be. Could he be genuine?

Then I remember the boy who took all our funds from us to get all that was needed to promote his school and work life. Even borrowing from our home. It all comes flooding back. It was a past due loan brought due by the Sheriff's deed representing owed funds from J.B. Harrison, James and Nathan to Second National Bank. Our name Stevens was posted on a pole downtown telling all, our house would be auctioned due to lack of payment and James was much disgraced.

I would lose my resting place. I was so scared to be without this house, my place would be lost. I know not what would happen to my plight. Would I still be in this house upon death? Even if the Sheriff sold our house at auction? My mind was always racing. What do we do? What can we do with no money? How can we keep our house? The questions had no answers, they hovered in my thoughts and in my heart.

We received a letter from Florence Corbeil stating, "We know that you stand to lose your home, this would be a travesty of untold hardship not to mention very unjust. Let me buy the house. You can pay me back when you get the money. I do this to honor your mother, as she is also is the mother of Nathaniel, who is like family to us. Please do not hesitate on my offer. I will start the paperwork almost immediately and James, Sarah and Nathan shall remain in their home. I want no quarrel with any of the Stevens' about the terms."

James was perplexed. I could only take a deep breath. Then looking at James I remembered, "God moves in mysterious ways."

He said, "Amen."

We got to stay and continued to live in our home. We knew the debt was there to be repaid down the road when we got the money. James would say, "They like each other and have taken my brother and his family under the Corbeil family wing or the mystery of it all was they just happen to like each other and the Corbeils like to help out where they can."

"Thank God."

Who would ever expect a blood connection. I have heard more than a few stories in my time, but this one was too close to home, and too much time has gone by for me to speak the truth. It must remain a secret, anyway it is not my secret to tell, although it lives within my heart and mind.

We as people learn to justify happenings, so we came to the conclusion that Ms. Corbeil bought the house loan, as a favor because of the love the Corbeils have for Nathaniel. This seemed likely.

We owed for our house, even though it was sold months before from a bid, at the held auction. Somehow James sold the house to Ms. Corbeil, who holds the mortgage where we live, with our promise to pay back the loan.

This was a great timely gift,

shall never ever be forgotten by us, James or I.

# CHAPTER FORTY-NINE

# Nathan's Return

Today is the day our son Nathan will return home after years of being away. He will bring his new wife and her widowed sister. The rooms are made ready, all is clean, and dinner will be a big special meal of welcoming.

James is anxiously anticipating his son's return. He has missed their talks and Sunday's at the church. James lives for this family time. He knows, not the son I know. Nathan also would know, I would not tell his father, any of the problems in our relationship. My husband is a good loving father who sees no obstacles or discretions in his son.

The last few hours I have been making sure all the house was ready to invite the party of three to be at home. The carriage pulls up outside and in my excitement I yell, "James, James, come quick, Nathan is here." Out the door we go after years of being apart. I am sure Nathan is noticing how frailness has consumed his father. It saddens me to look at my husband, which makes me extremely happy to see our son.

We hug and he is anxiously introducing his wife, "This is my father, James and my mother, Sarah. This is my wife, Lillian and her sister Phyllis."

We said our hellos with hugs ending by me saying, "Let us all go in, as you must be tired from your travels. If you need anything at all please make yourself known. It has been a good long while since we have hosted, and I am sure I have overlooked something. Please make yourself at home."

Bags in hands, except for James, who led the way opening the door, his face beaming with pride and joy. Nathan's return will help him become well again. This is my hope.

Dinner went well and I did not ask any prying questions, instead I listened to their conversations. They went to the parlor to keep James company, while I did the kitchen clean-up. No one offered to help, as was the custom after a big meal. I was prepared in my mind to say, "You have had a long trip, go relax. I will get this job done quickly. Then come and join you." No need for such chivalry. It was, as if, they were used to being waited on during meals. Perhaps they have servants in their household. We are yet to know their plans or the length of the visit, and or perhaps, this is a return home. As the saying goes, 'First impressions are lasting.' Finishing I join them in the parlor.

James caught my eye saying, "There you are Sarah, could you dust off my suit for tomorrow. We are going to church on Sunday. I can not wait to walk in, as a family with our son and his wife and their sister."

Nathan's returning home is reviving our Saturday night routine to ready ourselves for church. I hope this remembering, will continue lifting James's spirits, bringing back his strength with his wellness to return. His health seems better already.

He is talking of his Plumbing and Heating business, "Father and Son owned. It will be great, now we got to get busy as time's a wasting." Hearing this is like having a runaway horse, as I have no control of his business situation, or the decisions that will be based on the hopefulness of James's wishes to keep Nathan from leaving. What a dire position we could be in, but this relationship is necessary to bring back James's health; anything even, as perhaps sacrificial will be borne to get and keep my husband well.

Sunday came. We walked to the church as a family of five; James, Nathan, Lillian, Phyllis and I. We were happy to be going to church together, then every now and again we stopped to allow James to catch his breath. This was a lot of walking for a homebound man, who was determined as there would be no stopping him.

"I will be fine once we get there. We have a lot of living to catch up on, eight years since you have come to our church, now here you are with your wife and sister-in-law."

"We have a lot to be thankful for today."

"This is a great day the lord has made."

"We are thankful for your return son."

# Chapter Fifty

# Sunday Blessings

We were blessed today. Church was good with the timely message of 'Family and Strength' to live a good life.

After church the congregation crowded around to say hello to Nathan and his family, and also, how glad they were to see James back in church.

It was a good worship service bringing us together as in the past. On the way home I decided to walk ahead to get lunch laid out as the time was getting late due to our after service visiting. Nathan said, "You go ahead. We will walk slowly home to enjoy this perfect day."

This made me hopeful to see James happy, and Nathan acting support- ive as a caring son. Maybe he has grown up during his absence.

We were fed and visiting in the parlor, when I noticed James looking tired. Not wanting to change the mood I said, "Your Dad and I should take a nap, to revive ourselves from such a busy day. Feel free to visit the neighborhood. I am sure they will be happy to see you and yours. Do not hurry your visits, as we have not been going to church, or anywhere for so long, we may fall asleep for a nap, and end up sleeping through the night."

As they were leaving I stood by the doorway saying, "Nathan, Thank you for bringing your strength to your father. May he gain strength to enjoy his life again. Church today is just the beginning. Make yourselves at home."

James said, "Our boy is home. I think he is home to stay. This is what we needed in this house some young blood, with new ideas and lots of energy. Sarah, is this not wonderful." I felt his desire to live for the first time in a while so from my full heart I said, "That it is James, wonderful. Each day, will be a new surprise and exciting, like our Sundays."

"Let us go take a nap while we have the time."

Over time they decided to stay, and the three of them joined our First Baptist Church here on Main Street. Nathan took a temporary position in the shipping room of The American Woolen Company. His wife, Lillian Inez Keziah was prominent in music circles, and was appointed director of the choir at the First Baptist Church. She was an accomplished vocalist and instrumentalist trained abroad and in the United States. Later on she founded the First Maine Philathea Class with seven other women, who had interest in quilting. Joining the Missionary Society, the local women's club, all this left no time for traditional housekeeping.

This left Phyllis home with me working, as if she was their maid, cleaning their room, washing their clothes, making sure their life was tidy and comfortable. When Nathan came home she was happy, and immediately brought his boots outside to brush off the street mud. I noticed her demeanor was one of belonging. When Lillian came back from the church, often I would hear her say, "Phyllis would you be a dear and clean the dirt off my boots." She would pick up the boots with a swiftness and almost hostility, of which she was careful not to let show to Lillian. It was not my active imagination, sensing her desire to please Nathan, who was oblivious. The little nuances were not what pleased Nathan. The work and care of Phyllis was expected for she was in their charge, and this was a way of showing gratitude for their making her a home with them, whereas she had no other family or home. What pleased Nathan was flaunting his wife's accomplishments, this was his pride of ownership. This was important because with Lillian on his right arm, he was looked on as a better man for his marriage connection, in the church, and about town.

The next day Phyllis and I finished our housekeeping chores at the same time. I asked, "Would you like to go to the trading post, then the market to pick up a few things they may like to make their stay here more comfortable."

As we walked to town we talked genetically of the surrounding towns, as I thought it not proper to ask personal questions. This is what I believe. If people confide in me with words or actions, then I could converse on these subjects, until then it was not my business. We were in front of the post, in no time as she was like me, a fast walker. When inside, Phyllis asked shyly, "Do you think Nathaniel would need shaving soap?"

My thoughts, I think what Nathan needs, Nathan gets. At the question she asked I said, "If not it would be good to have on hand."

She picked out a few more things for Nathaniel, as she called him and nothing for Lillian. Prompting me to say,

"You take such good care of your family."

She smiled then, toting her affections in her voice,

"They are the best."

We had a nice day. At the end of this time, I knew my assumptions were true. She was Nathan's champion. Little did she know the real Nathan was only impressed by what others thought of you. For instance Lillian has musical talent, was much accomplished which brought charisma, and placement to Nathan Stevens.

There was no competing with success. No matter how well she took care of him, he would never ever notice as this was a menial job which no one toted as important. He was still enamored with being important, and demeaning work would not be on his list of accomplished people. I was not thought to be high on his list. I was a housekeeper with a baking trade, so he literally could attend school and achieve credentials. He never ever wanted to be a regular person, with no promise of earning more than enough, more than the town's wealthy Corbeils.

I am glad they brought Phyllis with them as she is warm, and quietly assumes her role in the life she lives. There is no complaining or sadness, instead she is thankful and glad.  Leading me to feel in need to reach out to help her.


Phyllis is to me as a daughter, I never ever had in life.


### *FARIES REFLECTIONS:*
***Aspen added:*** *" The sign of the Universe is love, In a perfect world all humans are each connected to one another through love..."*


### MORIA Thoughts:

*In my life I am not familiar with people who care as much as, you, Sarah. When learning the ways of Phyllis — the mother in you becomes protective, and sees her as a lost bird with a broken wing, whom needs your help— for if not you, who will make sure Phyllis —is happy.*

*This is important to you, Sarah, as Phyllis has become, as a lonesome bird to take under your wing, as family.*

*May we all, be intuitive to be there for others with love.*

# CHAPTER FIFTY-ONE

# Teaching Cooking

The challenge was to help Phyllis to become happier. Learning to cook may give her a sense of accomplishment with pride in her life so perhaps being able to remove herself from her sister's shadow. She would then make choices for herself. This could lead to finding what is out there for her full life.

"Phyllis how would you like to join me in the kitchen to learn my Aunt Harriet's well taught cooking skills? I never ever had a daughter to teach, and have missed sharing all my accomplished skills."

She looked stunned then laughed saying, "Thank you, I would like to learn a cook's skills, and you are a good, no I should say a most wonderful cook. Only please keep our cooking time to ourselves as this will be my challenge, and  if not successful it shall remain my failure for me alone to bear the failure."

This statement was telling, allowing me to see that her confidence was shallow. "This will be your success or my name is not, Sarah Fletcher Pitts Stevens. When we are comfortable with our apprenticeship we will shine at church suppers. Only when we are ready, no pressure."

"Thank you again for offering to teach me cooking, as a little girl I wanted to be a cook with the knowledge of knowing my food was good tasting. My mother however had not the skill, or patience to teach baking."

"You are more than welcome as cooking is a passion of mine, especially making new recipes. It is rewarding to make up different ways of putting foods together which must be easy, so they do not eat into the time allotted for cooking. This I learnt when living on the farm where everyday activity was done by the time given, by the clock which left no time to dawdle over cooking food. We are spoiled today, as chores for women living in the village are half of what we did on the farm."

Phyllis chimed in with, "I never lived the farm life. Times have changed in the city, also."

"Tell me about your life, only if you would like."

"Sure, there is not much to tell. I went to school. I married a wonderful man, who died and my parents also died leaving, only me and my sister, who was studying music abroad. When she came back she insisted we live together, all we had was each other to count on. City folks did not recognize my sister's music degrees, without a husband there was no recognition of her talent. They passed her over for less talented ladies, who were married. She met Nathaniel at church, and compared notes. They discovered he also was being overlooked as he was not married. They talked over the events in their lives realizing they would be better together."

I thought of what she shared asking, "So it was not love at first sight? It was an arranged marriage for mutual growth."

She said, "Yes," with a little laugh. "Marriage was a way to redefine their lives to fit into society, and their new success has made them each very happy. They are bound together by their desires of fulfilling their individual careers. It is their life's work and goals being accomplished. Nathaniel has been very accepting of me living with them for as long as I am single, I am welcome. He is a very wonderful man. I wish him and my sister every success in their appropriate careers. Is it, not odd, she is now more talented, married, than when single? As Mrs. Lillian Stevens, she is now recognized."

"Yes, it is true the pulls of society forms most of our lives. What matters is if we have happiness in our life."

"I know you must wonder about my life. I am content to stay quiet and out of the spotlight, also content to be, as if, in the shadow of my talented sister. I do not have the personality to be a people pleaser, in fact when my husband was with me I was most content to run our household, and not seek out attention from the outside world. This was my happiest time, and I do so miss our quiet life he provided. My sister knows me, yet wishes I had something in my life which I also enjoyed. Perhaps it will be cooking, yes?"

"Yes we will begin your new desire of cooking."

"I really like you, so I will share my secret receipts, written to be shared with my daughters, who were never ever born. Full of hope, I wrote my girls a cookbook, which I will give to you if cooking is your pleasure."

"Let us start at the beginning with 'my favorite' cookies. They are perfect and can be eaten whenever hungry, made ahead they will keep for days especially if made with molasses and spice. What a wonderful treat."

We accomplished this mission teaching her all my secret tricks to great baking. She was surprised to see my cookbook, written before I was three decades old, and further established, when I thought I may have girls. I told her she would get a copy upon our successful completion of what a good cook knows, and puts into practice.

We talked generally of our lives, never ever sharing our deepest thoughts which would reveal who, she and I were in life. She never ever spoke of Nathaniel in an inappropriate tone, not once did she slip, and mention her sibling rivalry, it was there in the undertones. I immediately respected her silence on her life, and I very much liked Phyllis as she brought new life into our home. I knew her in my heart. She was loyal to Lillian and Nathan. They were fortunate indeed to have such a person in their lives. I could see she did not resent her place in life, and was not looking to pursue a better life. She was content in her role as keeper of the Stevens' family.

"Phyllis I respect your ways of caring for your family, also I respect your privacy, with all you share to help fulfill their lives they are fortunate to have you. I hope this is enough to fulfill your joy."

Phyllis smiled saying, "It is I, who is fortunate, indeed."

I said, "I love Nathan, as a mother's love for her child, which means I am not blind to his faults. There is no approval for all he has done or does, yet my love never ever fluctuates, we will always have the mother-son relationship. Could I ask you a personal question? Why do you love him?"

Phyllis stared at me, there was a long pause.

"I see him as a man struggling with the need to fulfill his desire to be known as successful, working each day to build schemes and scenarios, to proclaim the power that follows success. Therefore, he is lost in the motivation to gain success, and this is why he is with my sister. It is as a step up to a convenient path to help him be recognized. I somehow think any manner of success, will spur more of a need for more, and I do not think it is about becoming wealthy. It is knowing he is on top of the heap, looking down. This is his all consuming fate. I have come to clearly see him, enough to feel saddened by his desires, which drive his life's choices."

"Do I have a romantic love for Nathaniel? No. A person cannot have a great or wonderful love, if there is no hope of love's return. Two separate people moving in different directions, do not end on one path. He is perfect for my sister as they go hand, in hand, and each seeking to reach the top."

"Phyllis, I am impressed with your ability to grasp the truth of who Nathan is becoming, and I sadly agree with all you have acknowledged. I do hope for a smattering of success to fill his void, allowing for contentment to settle in, with strength to then open his desire for love. My mother's heart knows the loneliness, of being amongst people, attached to no one. It is a lonely life when a person is one."


***


I am glad to have shared this time with Phyllis. I have come to love and respect her as a person who has chosen to serve those who are family. I taught her a new skill. When I am gone, I have passed on my cook's knowledge, making me a known noteworthy cook. All cooks are only as good as their shared accomplishments, to be shared by other cooks to preserve a baking generation.

"Thank you, Aunt Harriet, today I gave your gift of cooking to a wonderful person who has become a member of our baking family, and I feel her to be as my own daughter. Wish you were still here amongst us, and we could visit."

"We both would enjoy one of your special hugs."

# CHAPTER FIFTY-TWO

# Cook's Secrets

**POETIC JUSTICE**

If only there was a  recipe to follow
To enjoy all of our short fragile life...


Would we seek out just the right ingredients
As to make a fulfilling perfect life —
Or
Should fate still throw in a measure
of uncertainty and eventful twists — to


Make even the most accurate measurements
Go completely askew — such is my life...

***Cook's Secrets*** are for you to enjoy the art of cooking, then to pass all on to a new cook. The ingredients will come together to form a recipe. Cooking to create your own versions of baked goods; such as cookies, [*my favorite*] also cakes, pies, and breads. To master baking is to know the foundation of the ingredients which are the basics rules.

**Starch**: which is the flour of many types

**Leavening**: baking powder- soda, cream of tartar, yeast,

**Tenderizing**: rendered fats, butter, lard, eggs

**Sweeteners**: sugar, brown sugar, honey, molasses, maple

**Liquids**: water, milk, cream, fruit juice, tea, coffee

**Eggs**: can leaven, tenderize, bind – add color and flavor

**Pantry Spices**: cinnamon, nutmeg, ginger, cloves

**Dry Ingredients**: sifted together for consistency

**Wet Ingredients**: mixed- combined with dry ingredients

Once the liquid is added it is important to quickly put item into a hot oven to begin the rising especially if using baking soda as leavening, which also needs an acid: Vinegar, Buttermilk, Sour milk or Sour Cream, Yogurt, Molasses

One thing I have found whether living on a farm or in the village is that the available ingredients may change, yet the basic rules of cooking remain.

Once learned and understood you will be a most accomplished, treasured cook...

One more important thing, "waste not - want not."

This has been my life's teaching so if I am not happy with the outcome of the final product I will turn it into  an adventuresome made to order surprise, on request, I can never ever recreate.  It is a "one and done."

Baking will become your domain, never ever to be questioned, as all will be delicious in the end.

Each and every morning when at the farm I started my day with baking, whether it was plain biscuits or dressed up with cinnamon or fruit depending on time. Also, muffins.

**Basic Biscuits:** Bake hot oven  [450 or hotter

Flour measured in cups, 2 cups

3 teas. Baking powder

1 tea. Salt

1 tablespoon Sugar

Sift put in bowl cut in   ½ cup Butter

Add:  ¾ cup Milk

Mix gently, pat out and cut or drop onto pan

**another version:**  1 Egg lightly beaten add

1 c Water & 1 c Milk... mix

Sifter filled —-  4 c  Flour, 1 tab Salt & Sugar

4 teas. baking powder — cut in 2 tab Lard

There are many recipes just remember work fast a

Hot oven, sharp cutters, do not overwork dough.

**Muffins basics:** Bake hot oven [400]

2 Eggs, 1 cup Milk, ½ cup oil...mix

3 cups of Flour, 4 tea. Baking Powder

½ tea. Salt , 1 cup Sugar......... sift

Gently mix there will be flour lumps

**<u>Scones</u> basics:** Bake [375] 15-18 mins.

1 ½ Flour, 1/3 cup Sugar, 2 tea. Baking powder, ½ tea. Salt...sift

¾ cup Cream ...add, stir together

Add fruit, nuts, peels, spices, etc.

Pat in a 7" circle and cut 6 - 8  pie shaped

Wedges. Brush with Cream, sprinkle Sugar


**<u>Pancakes:</u>** pan fry when bubbles appear, turn

1 ½ cups Flour, 1 ¾ baking powder,1 tea. Salt

1-2 Eggs beaten, 3 tabs. Butter, 1-1 ¼ cup Milk

Quickly mix dry and wet ingredients, add fruit


**<u>White Bread</u>** start at 400-15 mins. 375- 25 mins

1 cup milk scald... add to 1 cup water, 1 tab lard,

1 tab butter, 1 tab salt, 2 tabs sugar

1 package yeast, ¼ cup warm water stir together with 3 cups flour adding

3 ½ more flour.

Knead Well until smooth place into bowl cover let rise.  If time permits,

rise to double again, shape dough.


**<u>No knead white rolls:</u>** Bake 375 12-15 mins

2 packages of yeast mix with ½ cups water, hold

¾ cups butter, ¾ cups sugar, 1 cup water, boil

1 cup cold water, add to hot mixture also add

2 teas. salt, 2 eggs slightly beaten, then add

3 cups flour mix until glue like  then add flour to make a soft dough that

does not stick to the sides of the bowl, can be covered and kept cold. Take

any amount and let rise before baking. Rolls, cinnamon rolls or loaves.

**<u>Bread Pudding</u>**: Bake 300-350  30mins.

Save heals and any stale bread  break into pieces add to buttered pan

May add fruit, nuts, raisins, spices,  etc.  mix custard to cover

Using 1 egg to 3/4 cup milk, vanilla

Serve with whipped cream...or any topping.

## **<u>Cookies  {my favorite}</u>**

**<u>Hard Gingerbread</u>**  Bake 350  20 mins.

1 cup butter, 1 cup sugar, 1 cup molasses... cream

2 eggs, 2 teas. Vinegar....add

5 cups flour, 2 teas. baking soda, 1 teas. Ginger

1tea. cinnamon , sift, mix dry and wet, cut dough into 4 parts. Flatten

each part into a 2x 10 bars

Of ½ inch thickness Score with a fork may sprinkle with sugar.  Put in

oven right away to get the rise from the Soda.

**<u>Molasses cookies</u>**  350  30 mins.

1 c Sugar, 1 c Molasses, 1 c sour Milk, 1 c Lard

2 cups Flour, 1 tea. soda, ½ tea. ginger & cinnamon

Sift , add wet and dry... mix... drop... bake.

May add: raisins, dried fruits, anything at all

**<u>Molasses drop cookies</u>**  375 8-10 mins

1/2c sugar, 1/2c molasses,1/2c butter, 1 egg,.. mix

2 1/2 cups flour, ½ teas. Salt, 1tea. Cinnamon,

1 teas. Ginger, sift  mix 2 teas. baking soda with

½ cup boiling water quickly mix dry and wet drop

By teaspoon sprinkle with sugar add fruit or nuts

**<u>Lumberjack cookies</u>...** bake,  pan fry, doughnut fry

6 cups flour, 2 tsp salt and baking soda,  3 teas. Baking powder, 1 teas. Cream of tartar, ½ teas.

Nutmeg, cloves, ginger, 1 tea. Cinnamon...sift

1 cup butter and lard , 2 cups sugar, 1 cup molasses

1 cup milk, 4 eggs, mix dry and wet, add 2 cups dry oatmeal, 3 cups raisins...make ½ recipe still plenty


**<u>Sugar cookies</u>**...375 8 mins. 410 6 mins

2 ½ cups flour, ½ tea. Baking powder, salt, sift

1 cup butter, 1 cup sugar, cream.. Add 1 egg

Vanilla and almond ... mix dry and wet


**<u>Gingerbread dough</u>**......375  8 mins.

1 cup sugar, 1/2c water, 1/2c molasses, 1 tab ginger

2 tabs cinnamon, 2 tabs cloves...bring to boil...

1c soft butter in large bowl, pour over hot syrup

4 cups flour, 1 ½ teas baking soda.. stir into wet

Roll and cut out shapes


**<u>Round Molasses cookies</u>** .....350.. 11 mins.

½ cup butter, ½ cup lard, 1 ½ cups sugar.

cream ½ cup molasses, 2 eggs mix in

4 cups flour, ½ tea. Salt, 2¼ tea soda + ginger

1 ½ teas. Clove + cinnamon mix dry and wet

Roll in 1 ½ inch balls.. rolled in sugar.... bake

**Orange cookies**.....350....20 mins.

1 cup butter, ¾ c sugar, cream...add 1 tea. Vanilla

1 cup cooked mashed carrots, or pumpkin or yams

2 cups flour, 2teas.baking powder,1/2t Salt.. mix

Add ½ raisins, nuts or dates,

### **Cakes:**

**Molasses cake**..... 9x13 pan..350..30 mins.

2 ½ cups flour, 1 c sugar, 1 tea. Baking soda

1 teas. Cinnamon, nutmeg, salt, (½ tea. ginger)

2 eggs, 1 cup molasses, ½ c fats ,add 1 c hot water


**Old  Molasses Cake**...9x13 pan..350..30 mins.

2 cups flour, 1tes soda, salt, cinnamon, allspice, sift

1 cup molasses,½ cup brown sugar,½ cup fat.. mix

1 cup hot water... sir in quickly  (no eggs added)


**Gingerbread by Claire**..350..25-35 mins cast iron

2 cups flour,½ cup- sugar, brown sugar, butter, molasses,   1 egg

cup  milk,  cloves,  ginger,  zest


**Pound cake**...300-325 1 hour 25-30 mins. Loaf

2 cups flour,1 tea. Salt, ½ tea. baking powder...sift

1/3 cup butter,1 ¼ c sugar, 2/3 cup milk, flavorings

3 eggs one at a time ..mix. good with nutmeg...

<u>**White cake**</u>... 350 30 mins.  2 pans- 9 inch

3 cups flour, 3teas. Baking powder, ½ tea. Salt

½ c butter, 1 ½ cup sugar, cream ...

2 teas vanilla, 2 teas. almond ,add to

1 cup milk... add alternatively to dry

4 eggs slightly beaten.. Mix in

*'This cake is known as the brides cake'...*

<u>***Carrot cake***</u>  350 40-45 mins  one 9 inch

1 cup flour, 1 tab, 1 cup sugar,½ tea. Nutmeg

1 tea. Cinnamon  Sift

¾ cup melted butter,2 teas. vanilla add dry - wet

5 raw carrots grated, ¾ cups apple, mix in

Also:  could add nuts, pineapple, coconut etc.

Frosting... beat  8 mins.

½ cup butter, ¼ cup lard, 1 cup sugar, 3 tabs. flour

½ cup warm milk, 2 teas. Vanilla

**<u>Nana's Old World Cinnamon Crumb Cake</u>**

1 ½ cups flour, 2 ½ teas baking powder... salt sift

¾ cup sugar,½ c melted butter, 1 egg...mix.... add

½ cup milk, ½ cup sour cream, 1 tea. Vanilla

Blend dry and wet... put ½ batter in 8 inch sq. pan

Streusel topping:

½ cup brown sugar,2 tabs cold butter and flour

1 tea. Cinnamon.. combine.. Put ½ on top batter

Add remaining batter on top of streusel topping

Add streusel topping on top of batter

Bake 350 25-30 mins. Add nuts, dried fruits, etc.

**<u>Dutch babies</u>** 425 15 mins. Cast iron fry pan

4 tbsp butter melt in pan

1/3  cup flour,¼ teas salt, ¼ teas nutmeg... sift

2 eggs, ½ cup milk...beat gently stir dry and wet

Pour batter into fry pan on top of butter-  bake

May add fruit on top or anything you fancy...

### <u>Pie crust</u>

5 cups flour, 2 teas. Salt, 1 lb. lard ...cut in

1 egg mix with a fork add water to make 1 cup

Mix gently dry and wet... roll .. bake 450 12mins

This basic recipe is good with meat pies also..

Tart Fruit... pies require more or less sugar

**<u>Custard  Pie</u>**   475 5mins. Then 425 10 mins.

4 eggs, ½ cup sugar, ¼ tea. Salt, 1 ½ tsp vanilla mix

then add,  stirring  2 ½ cups scalded hot milk

Pour into pie shell over the back of spoon to prevent

a hole in raw crust  Dust with Nutmeg

**<u>Strawberry Rhubarb pie</u>** 425  50 mins.

Prepare pie crusts for top and bottom

2 cups strawberries 2 cups rhubarb  add...

1 ¼ c sugar, ⅓ c flour, mix all put in shell

2 pats butter.. Dot on fruit... add top crust

Water on top of crust sprinkle 1 tbsp sugar

**<u>Apple pie</u>** 375  45 mins...

Double crust or top with streusel or lattice crust

4-5 cups of thinly sliced apples, placed in a shell..

⅔ c sugar +or -,  ¼ c flour, ½ teas cinnamon,

¼ tea nutmeg, ...mix ..springle over apples

2 tabs. Butter...dot over apples...choose top..

Experiment with sweeteners and thickening

amounts ...Also fruits, berries, etc.

**<u>No roll berry pie</u>**  350 50-60 mins. 9 inch pan

½  cup butter, 1tab. Sugar, ...melt... add 1 c flour

Press into the pan add 2 cups filling of choice ...

Topping: 1 egg, ½ c sugar,¼ c flour,¼ c milk- mix

**<u>Apple pie</u> Magic** 350  45 mins.. grease glass pan

Fill ⅔ full, cut up apples,4 tabs sugar, 1tbs brown

Sprinkle over apples... ¾c butter.. melt... then add

1 cup flour, 1 c sugar,1 egg.. mix pour over apple..

**<u>Date bars</u>**  325  45 mins. 1 ½ cups flour,

1 ¾ cups oats, ¾ c butter, 1 t soda

1 cup brown sugar,... mix.. press ½ of dough in pan

2 cups dates, 1 cup sugar,1 tab heaping flour... add

1 cup boiling water cook until thick ..spread on dough in a pan

covered with another ½ dough... bake ...cool... cut ... yum!


**<u>Clafoutis</u>**  350  45-60 mins. Greased pie pan

3 eggs, ⅔ c sugar, 1 tab butter... beat 2 mins

1 ¼ c milk, ⅓ tea salt, 1 tea vanilla, ½ c flour..

Beat in.. batter will be thin pour in pan...

2 cups cranberries spoon on top

"Delicious for Holiday"

**<u>Cringer</u>**  375  30 mins.  Sheet pan

1 cup flour, ½ c butter, cut in. add 2 tab water

Make 2 balls,  press into 2 strips on sheet

1 cup water, ½ c butter... bring to boil

1 cup flour... stir in 3 lg eggs... beat in one at a time...

Add vanilla... spread on top of strips.. Bake

1 tab butter melt ¼ cup flour stir in over heat

1 cup cream add to create pudding add vanilla &

¼ c maple syrup or honey Cool .. spread on top


**<u>Self filled Honey-bun</u>**  400 30-35 mins sheet pan

1 1/3 c flour, ½ c butter cut in... add..3 tab water

Form a 10 inch circle to form crust

½ cup butter, 1c water melt and bring to boil

1 cup flour add all at once, add 4 eggs one at a time ½ c honey, 1 tea

vanilla... stir in.

Spread batter to 1 inch of edge of crust...


**<u>NO  eggs, milk, or butter Cake</u>**  350 1 hour

1 cup water + brown sugar, 2 cups raisins,

1/3 c lard, 1/4 tea salt + nutmeg, ½ tea cloves,

1 tea cinnamon... boil.. cook 3 mins... cool

2 c flour, 1 tea baking soda, ½ tea baking powder

Stir together all, pour into greased  loaf tin

**<u>Brown Sugar Chews</u>**   350   18-20 mins   8x8 pan

½ cup flour, ¼ tea salt + baking soda...sift

1 egg, 1 cup brown sugar, 1 tea vanilla ...mix

Add:  dry to wet... mix in ..1 c chopped walnuts

Cool in pan ...cut in squares

*"Brown Sugar Chews were served to my now husband*

*the 1st time he called on me..."*

**<u>Apple Squares</u>**   350   25-30 mins   8x8 pan

1 cup flour, ½ tea baking soda + baking powder¼  tea salt, ½ tea

cinnamon...sift½ cup butter,½ cup sugar.. cream...add 1 egg

Add dry to wet...pour over 3 cups thin sliced apples

**<u>Ratatouille</u>**

In a heavy iron skillet brown meat.. remove ..add

1 cup water stir to make a dark gravy... add

Sliced potatoes, onions, salt, pepper... put meat in

Cover and cook or bake slowly till potatoes tender


***A Favored Bonus — Drink—Serve Cold***

***<u>HAYMAKER'S SWITCHEL-</u>***

8 cups water- 1 cup sugar- 1 cup cider vinegar-

½ cup molasses- ½ tsp- ginger, cinnamon

Heat all until sugar dissolves... cool & serve

{"Serving this...     My Heart fell in love"}

Living on our farm we only ate our own cooking. On rare occasions my Mother, my sister and I would travel to my Nana's farm for a gathering. We would bring food back for Paw who was working on the farm. I would notice the foods, their textures and flavor. From the hardy ordinary everyday foods, to the extra good sweets — my interest began.

I have noticed, over the years there have been many  good cooks in my Mother's family. I am writing out long hand for you my favorites of all things made with sugar. It is these sugar filled foods, that can be made with unexpected changes of  ingredients making cooking fun. Never ever fear to use what you have in your pantry to make a sweet as there are no expectations. You are the Artists, there are no right or wrong ingredients.

As a young girl of twelve years I began to cook with the help of my Aunt Harriet. At the first lesson, and the hard part was heating the black iron cookstove to the right temperatures. After conquering this my interest went beyond eating, to creating different versions of baking, biscuits, Breads, cakes, pies, and cookies. 'my favorite' This booklet is one, for my most baked recipes...

Enjoy, ***Cook's Secrets*** is my gift to you...
Sarah Fletcher Pitts Stevens

# CHAPTER FIFTY-THREE

# James's Home Life

H ave you been at the farm?" I asked James, noting his tired appearance. "How are things on the farm? Sit here while I get you a drink. You must be plenty thirsty after your trip."

I hurriedly got a glass of water, and set it on the table in front of him. James said, "Sarah, sit at the table with me so we can talk about the things I have learned being at the farm most of the day."

He looked uncomfortable, as if, he had carefully mulled over what he needed to say, to prepare me for events that would likely change our lives, within our home in town. "Just tell me, what is going on at the farm?" I prompted.

"Alright, but do not say anything until I tell you everything," he began. "I will start with Nathaniel. My brother is leaving again, and wants Ma to sell the farm to his son, James. To sell it to her grandson, living with them, although she has not the strength to start over with the uncertainty of a younger couple. Ma does not want to live with them on their farm."

He continued, "Uncle Lawrence also lost his buildings on the farm, after investing in the Axe Factory, and the business failed. The church, through their town welfare program, gave Uncle Lawrence the house next door to us to support his family. Now, Ma wants to come live here with us."

James paused. "There, I think that sums it up. Sarah, please say something."

I responded with calm reassurance, "Do not get caught up in the facts. Just know we will be fine. It will work out in the end. It has been nice for us spending time together in our own home. It will still be my job as head of household, as I know it is important to give me freedom, and us fortitude, which to me means courage with a resilience of spirit to confront, what cannot be controlled, and strength to endure."

My voice softened as I continued, "As of late, watching you struggle to walk, when even your breathing has weakened, leaves my heart feeling wounded, causing tears to come to my eyes as my heart aches. We have always been strong with our lives together, making us a complete couple. One should not leave the other. I have no way of stopping your failing health and cannot pretend all is well. We are on the pathway to one day become separated. Seeing this happen with my aching longing heart is the hardest task I have ever had to do. My love for you is from my heart, not my thoughts, and I have no control of my heart of which you remain a big part."

James spoke of his mother, "Ma will just be ours to look after because she says we are the ones where she feels most at home." I reached across the table taking his hand, "James, it is not the place; it is the people who make a home. I love you, and together we will welcome your, Ma, Effie, to stay. Her life has always been close to you. After your father died, you were her loyal son, always there for her. Yes, of course she would be the happiest here with us."

He continued, his voice filled with compassion, "I am glad, and she must know she is always welcome with us. We will make room in our family for one more."

" Yes, this special one who has earned a time of being pampered, also looked after by her family. I am glad she will be here so we can now look after her needs. I cannot bear to think of her worrying about where and who, would look after her. You tell her we are happy to have her. She can move in anytime she wants to share our home."

Reflecting on family, James added, "As for my brother leaving we should not be surprised. He has always been a rolling stone. For us, living as this would be undesirable, but for them, it is a way of life. With the exception of their children—our namesakes James and Sarah—who seem to have found roots."

He paused, then remarked, "As for my, Uncle Lawrence, to stay afloat is a lifetime battle. You remember how it was living with them."

James squeeze my hand saying, "Sarah, you are my strength, putting all in perspective. I love you. Tonight here with you, I feel peaceful, even knowing in my heart, my time with you will soon come to an end."

I responded, "I know how you feel. We are the old ones, as they say, with one foot in the grave."

"This is why I love you," James said. "You are undaunted by life, of which death plays a part. It is more than realizing death is coming; it is knowing it has begun the process of slowing me down. I am changing and I find myself weaker each day, with a feeling of being somewhat ready to die."

"James, the day, we found each other, in the hot dusty hay field, was the highlight of my life. Now, each day,, we share is less for us, with more care to keep you comfortable. You are slipping away, leaving a void to be filled with emptiness, with a longing to have what we are to each other, as each day you seem less yourself. My heart senses, you are not here with me, as you are on your own journey, moving away from our life. I know you, with your pride of conquering every obstacle put before you, yet no one avoids death."

James remembered, "It was through the deaths of Asa and Willie, our saddest. Then I gave up farming, unheard of in my lifetime leaving me sad for awhile, until the benefits for us became a new life, of which I would not change. The saddest is thinking, of leaving you alone. My death will end our togetherness, as you cannot go with me, not until God calls you home. Do you have any regrets, Sarah?"

"My regrets are few whereas one is big; it is the long time of morning our boys, without understanding my grief. It was love, I did not know what to do with, when my loved ones were gone from my life. This left a sinking hole with nothing to grasp but memories. Today, I feel better equipped to grasp the reality of death, as the miracle of one who has fulfilled their purpose, of completion here on earth. This I learned with my time within the shadows of death."

"I regret we were not blessed, with a wagon full of children. Sometimes when I sit outdoors, on the stoop, there in the distance I can hear the squeaking of the wagon wheels being pulled by snorting horses, and to my delight there are excited voices, of all the children in the wagon, talking all at once as children do. They seem so happy, and unaware of my presence. I regret we never ever had our girl and more children. I was blessed to be the mother of three boys, and grateful we got to be parents to Nathan. How much strife we have suffered, then came the joys, allowing us to forge onward overcoming the sadness. I love you Mr. Stevens, as much if not more than, the day we met."

"I love you Mrs. Stevens, 'What will be shall be' always remember."

"I want you to know, I do not want you to leave me, but more than this know I understand when it is your time to pass. I will not try to hold you here, instead I will sing your praises with thankfulness for your life. In my heart I will hold your love tight with a knowing peace, for we were one throughout our long lives, and neither have any regrets within each other as we have lived our quiet love story. James when ever you leave this earth, if you pass in your sleep,, or with the family all around, know I will be celebrating the wonderful man who became part of my life. We will be together in the end as we have always lived, you will remain my one true love."

"Sarah my life with you has been somewhat of a mystery. I know we love each other, yet you have an aura of mystery, I could never ever phantom. Your childlike splendor of independence makes me captivated. I sense your spirit of being strong and free. Never ever have I spoken of this out of respect of your person, knowing your childhood was formed by your own specialness and it is enough to love you without knowing all your thoughts."

"James, I know I fall silent as my shy nature makes sharing my ways, thoughts, and feelings, hard for me. What I am thinking is, when you get to heaven and if you see me sitting out on the door stoop watching life pass by, if it is possible please send me a sign. Perhaps one of the happy children in the wagon would notice me with a wave, as I love you always in all ways Mr. Stevens." I stood up reached out my hand saying,

"Let us now go to the farm to make plans with Ma."

"You look sad, Effie. Are you feeling aright?"

"No. I am an old woman who has lived out her usefulness, and I am not needed by my family. Nathaniel has so much love for people, yet he does not know how to care for those he loves. He is like his father, as there is no foundation, so their love is floating in the air, and not much anchored to anyone. It comes and it goes, leaving a person afraid to trust their love, to be real."

"Oh, Effie, I know your son loves you, and do not speak for us. We miss you, and want you to come to our home. You are as a mother to me, and James will not want you unhappy. He's a wonderful generous man who wears his heart on his sleeve. You will know you are loved with him around."

"Do you think I should leave the farm?"

"Yes, just ask James when he comes in, and he will say you should be with us. With your son James you will be cared for, knowing how much you are loved, without never ever needing, to hear the words. I would be so pleased for you to share your days with us."

Unfortunately, Effie was not long with us. Fortunately, her last days were peaceful, filled with love.

# CHAPTER FIFTY-FOUR

# February 13th 1823
# April 19th 1896

**T**hreescore, One Decade, Three Years

Today our James left the earth, leaving us. I am in our bedroom, alone, at last, with no more condolences, not a sound. It is silent. I feel, with my hand, where my chest hurts with an ache of the unbearable loss of James, my soulmate. I walk slowly to the bed, somehow knowing, I must not lay down, with my broken heart, as if to give up. So instead, I let myself, slowly sit, on the edge of our bed, rubbing the blue blanket, with my thumb, as my hand rested on the mattress. My mind begins to race. I feel myself quiet. I begin to think of life in general.

A life well lived is up to each individual to decide. This happens as all people grow from their own childhood with all different types of influences, giving much to pick and choose. If we are curious and clever, we investigate to notice if our parents see things one way, and we another, and our grandparents, still another. We may disagree with both, as they are of different generations. At the same time the core of who we are is already within our body waiting for us to choose the path that feels right. This choice may be condemned by others. Remain true to yourself; we all have the freedom to remain true to ourselves, and never ever expect others to be like us, as we are all different, and moving forward with the lessons, in a balanced life. This was James & Sarah. Always respecting the other's person.

It is harder to deal with the heartache, when we are thus involved with much compassion, and a deep commitment to each other. I know in my mind that we all die. In my heart, I have to accept this. My James is gone.

I am alone. What I now realize, is this is hard as I am afraid of making decisions. I am feeling the burden of carrying his honor by speaking for him, as I am known in all of my days as James's shy wife. Deep within me I know this man, and I miss his quiet way of saying, "I love you Mrs. Stewart." I miss the life we shared, and this makes me so alone. This is our bed, now my bed, this is our home, now mine alone. I am so alone, as I fidget with the soft blue blanket.

I think to myself be strong, telling myself, 'Sarah, buy James, a gravestone to engrave this stone, so as to tell all he is loved, and his plight is now with God.' This James showed me; with Asa, and Willie, as their gravestones tell all who see them how much they were loved, along with their place within their family.  James was loved, and loved by God. His gravestone will tell how much he is loved. This was always his testimony for all to see. They will know of his great wonderful love."

We shared our life, now I must learn to go on. I must learn to go on by myself, with all of this love, for James. Go on in the brightness of day, then please, let me be engulfed by the darkness of the night.

Last night, I lay to sleep, without a wink, as I was truly alone without the breath of James to fill the room. We kept each other, and looked after one another, all our married life over fifty years. I have been loved, and love this man who made me feel like I was coming home within our relationship. This all ended yesterday. My heart aches as if wounded. I lay all night remembering our time. I had promised James, I will not feel sorry for my loss, when at this time I was not knowing the true weight of feeling truly alone. This loss of my husband and best friend, who has been with me throughout my life allowing me to know how fortunate and rich we were to share a great love. This exists, now, only in my heart.

I cannot stay held up here in my room basking in my sadness, accepting all plates of food, and the sympathy, which tries to overtake my desire to carry on. I had promised James. All this taking from others will steal my life from moving on, never ever allowing me to be independent. I need to get up and cook the night time meal, as my giving to others will fill up my life so I can move on to the next steps on my path, to own, my inevitable end.

I remember when we were in the prime of our lives at a time when all was as a dream, being happy and joyous. These times we planned, then my mind goes to the sad, grief-filled days, that came to us without any planning or thought. Things we never ever could think would have happened to us. It almost stole all the joy, and this is not to be again.

My Mother was a different kind of mother, encouraging with many words, and allowing freedom to investigate nature. She once told me, "If my heart was in rule, more attention should be given to my mind." Today, the path from my heart to my discerning mind, is a long journey, without James...

The next day, I was watching the horse-drawn carriages, on the contemplated dirt street that was slippery with the mud of spring. There in the back was a cute little boy, who saw me, then gave a big smile, and a wide unmistakable wave.

My heart swells as it makes me think of James,

and our conversation when I said,

"None of the children took any notice of me."

I wave back thinking with my heart,

'James my love, hello.'

'You are always to live in my heart.'

' I will never ever be without you, Mr. Stevens.'


This became the light of my days and I think,

'There is a Spring and Summer, of those days,

sitting on the stoop in the warmth of the sun,

watching the wagons — come and go,

awaiting an extra special wave of hello.'

I cannot help, but think of my Love, James,

thus sharing with him in this moment,

my joy, my everlasting love...

### *FAIRIES REFLECTIONS:*

***Arwen spoke of darkness:*** *"We must talk of death, with the sense of darkness that floods all the heart and mind, shadowing the love that never ever leaves. The light of wisdom gives power to gradually overtake gloom, leaving the darkness to be overcome by the early dawn. The sunrise becomes day, with the full light of the sun, our life is exposed with a call to move on, as we live our life..."*

# CHAPTER FIFTY-FIVE

# Ode to James

I want to start my writing as if a fairy tale, for none of this seems real to me today:

Once upon a time, on a small farm lived a child named Sarah. Her mother, Mary had another girl child named Eliza, and together with their Paw they were the only ones to live on the farm. Sarah was full of curiosity, and explored with a watchful eye towards all of nature. She felt drawn to running streams of water with its full life; of fish, turtles, and more hidden forms of water creatures.

Back on dry land, she lived for her time in the land of flowers, butterflies, and rocks, especially fond of white quartz which the beautiful fairies asked her to gather. This was a glorious time with all the small animal friends, each awaiting her return to their meadow.

The most glorious, to Sarah, were the birds, of all colors and sizes, with their songs, chirping of hope, and everlasting joy. They seemed triumphant, as they naturally lost feathers, Sarah was there to pick them up taking them home, to feel their softness, and wonder what it is like to be free, to fly away, anywhere you want, to be. In no time at all, she could travel around the earth.

Eliza liked to swing, therefore, would spend each day, on the board and rope hanging from the old oak tree. Paw noticed Sarah never got a turn on the swing. "When I get time I will put up another for you," he said. She did not have time to swing as her life was full in the magical meadow watching things grow. She was part of everything under the sun, and told her Paw, "Thank you, but I am more fond of walking than just swinging back and forth going nowhere."

So each and every day was good for the girls.

Then when Sarah turned twelve, a long shadow overcame the small farm. Her mother left, she died. Quick as a wink, just like that, she was gone, leaving a time of great sad change. There was no time to say goodbye to her mother or to her wondrous meadow. She was the one chosen to keep the order of the farm by learning housekeeping.

Ten long years passed, when the girl had no friends, as all her time each day was spent on the farm, keeping order of the house as was taught to her by her Aunt Harriet. Over time, this little girl grew into a lovely young lady, of twenty-two years, when she met a handsome young man who was helping her Paw on the farm.

Their eyes met, then she became aware of him, from this time on he was the one. All her thoughts were on him by day and night. Her heart felt twisted into knots, leaving her face blushing red, and her words would not speak clearly to express the thoughts in her mind. Is this what love does? It was meant to be, as he also felt love for Sarah. They, both, fell deeply in love and married, beginning their life on another farm.

Death took two of their three boys, with only one boy remaining the farm was to be lost. With tenderness and acceptance, they moved to village life with high hopes of succeeding. It seemed like tragedy was always swirling around, yet the good, always outweighed the bad, and the bad became the good in the future, that was to come. This was their life, and they could live anywhere as long as they were together. In their years, they stayed the course, and changed their circumstances, to meet their way of living. Never ever did they lose sight of their everlasting, encompassing love.

We are the old ones now, and all is about to be lost. One of us will leave the other. This is known and accepted, as we cannot live on this earth forever.

Today you left me forever. My life is forever changed, leaving me in my darkest shadow. My soul aches, my heart aches. Death creates a void, that echoes loss, with ongoing thoughts of our life. We have lived in this time, now, abruptly ended.

Sometimes the ones we love the most are taken away from us too soon, as we feel not ready. Even if we see them ill and slipping away, death comes like a thief.

Today I have lost the one I love, my husband. My life will go on, feeling the loss more than anyone can know. Everyone deserves a great love, James was mine. He was my security, protection, my greatest love.

He was my home, holding this place, as his love is etched on my heart. I do not like being away from my home.

The lived life is put together in chapters, beginning to end.

The Circle of Life, however has no beginning or end.

May you, James, rest in peace with the Lord.

I asked on your stone— to be written:

"BLESSED ARE THE DEAD

WHICH DIE IN THE LORD"

James, to you peace and gratitude mattered. People matter whether they are neighbors or family. Belonging was a treasure. I buried my treasure today. Ashes to ashes, dust to dust, he is in the ground, alongside, Asa and Willie. May you all rest in peace.

So many years with my husband, sharing our life seen through each other's eyes, now I am left alone with single vision, and the world does not look, or feel, as though I belong.

Now, I must move forward to try to figure out a new life without James. If I do not go forward, I will end up in this same sad place, where, I sit and write today. Instead, I need to honor my promise, to James, to choose, to take my, chances with changes. This is life's way to be lived, but only if movement is forward.

*I believe there is hope in my future,*
*yet I have been told and shown,*
*to know there is a lie in my belief.*

# CHAPTER FIFTY-SIX

# Home Becomes House

In this day the inevitable is near. I am woefully unprepared. It may feel at times like the end, but my story is not over, yet, I am close to the end. I am so tired. I have even lost interest in my home. This place where my spirit, will remain forever and ever. Even long-lost happier days have lost their place in my heart...

All of my life, the good and the bad, are thoughts in my mind;

All as if an untold story...

Back when this house was my everything...

The first year of living in our new house was like an unbelievable weight was lifted off my shoulders. This was a time of being master of my own space, checking only with myself as to what needed to be done to perfect order. First, I noticed my behavior becoming stressful in respect to my work about the house. I found it a waste of my time to straighten out other people's things that are not put in the right place. Everything in my house has a place, and a coat or shirt thrown over a chair, is not where it belongs. One abandoned shirt becomes another so my new solution is pegs for hanging to promote order.

Still, when the pegs were new it took a while for them to be used, and I found with my quickness I could grab a shirt in midair on the way to the back of a chair, putting it on a peg. Sometimes it seemed I was the only one to be invested in tidiness. Everyone knew when the pegs were used my attention will be put towards another rule, as all things have a proper place. My mother was a master at tidiness, and I learned by her example, as she was the best housekeeper, but I was the stubbornest.

I thoroughly enjoyed organizing my kitchen by putting every cupboard into good use. Next, helping Nathan fix up his own room, even though, he would like to run back to the farm to stay with the children. Next, I made sure everything we owned was in just the right place by working every day after we moved, except Sunday, our day of church with the afternoon for rest. Our house, thus became our home.

Then of course Mondays, I spend time with Aba having tea, as she remains my dearest friend. We do not need to be in the same village to feel the closeness of our love, and share tea. These days were hauntingly perfect. I had my own home and the reality was lost in me, to the fact, time would not stand still. I went about baking and walking all over town to sell my wares, cookies and bars, were my favorite, along with overhearing the town folks gathering to converse. My every day life was perfect.

Today life, is not as it seems in our home as my son pays no attention to me. He has no feelings for me, or, I believe no empathy, or caring for anyone. I sure do wish I could help him enjoy the life before him.

He moved out of our home to complete his schooling. Then back for summers, and off to get his degrees. We paid many bills with our relentless work. Nathan has a conventional life, married, attends church, has college and law degrees, and all looks good on paper. Yet, his real life does not work for him, as he is not able to bring his life into fruition. He is a man without a real purpose, and each day he just goes through the motions of who he is, without any of the ownership of this man he pretends to be.

There are things worse than death...

My heart breaks, seeing he must live unhappily, as this, my purpose was to allow him to live on past certain childhood death, to become. I made this possible with Aba, and I see clearly how my need to have him live, to remain with family, here on earth has worked in as much as he is here, but not the good man I pictured him to be, like his father. I just wanted to give our son life on earth, to move on as he was born to be, so much so that, I gave up my life, my reincarnation, my eternity.

The truth is I could not save him from himself; only save him from the death of his body, not who he will becomes as a person with free choice. It is done.

There are things worse than death. How could I not see that? Nathan is, and always was a closed off person, who only has space for himself. Not for his father, 'God rest his soul' or me, 'the Marta mother,' who did all to save him, and lost him in the end. To Nathan's purpose, I was the acting author of life, yet he remained the person he was born on this earth to be. We, each are born with freedom of will, and our decisions are our own. Thus making the lasting outcome unpredictable, unstable, and or, undesirable.

Nathan, the two sisters, and I live in this house, which stopped being a home when my husband died. Without James and our togetherness, this is just a house. I miss James so much. We talked and shared our days. He talked and mostly I listened as I did not go out amongst the people each day to learn something new or interesting to tell. This was our special quiet time, our way of being together.

I am now abandoned here in my house which I so loved, today it holds no hold on me, nor is it a place I want to be all my days.

We live in this house as virtual strangers. We never ever talk. Not about church, work, or talk of every day events. Nathan's wife keeps to herself, her sister Phyllis is busy with church projects. Each goes their own way. None of the three has any time or makes any time for me. Evening brings all of us together to eat the meal I prepared. We eat quietly, then it is time to due the clean-up of which Phyllis offers her help to get the work done more quickly, so not a time for conversation, as lately she has many church projects, awaiting her attention.

It is good that I am not bedridden, as I would surely starve to death and the worst is no one would notice. I wish this was my imagination of me feeling sorry for myself.

This is real...

I am alone...

In a house that was once my beloved family home...


### *MORIA Thoughts:*

*Sarah your house was a symbol of freedom with love shared throughout to those you loved, making a place to call home. Your house has become home for our family.*

*Your love was felt within our home, each day by me, and led me to find ' Never Ever Days ' then to share your words written in your secret journal, became my humble privilege, along with my detriment felt, as my duty, to allow your words of truth, an audience.*

# Chapter Fifty-Seven

# Nathan's Plans Birthright

I knew, if Nathan had any knowledge of the secret his grandmother had told me, he would not hesitate to exploit the Corbeils, as he is a grandson, and his birthright was to be a Corbeil. His Uncle Nathaniel had worked closely with the Corbeil business and his daughter Sarah, is written in the papers to be a member of the prominent Corbeil family, whereas her husband is a nephew. James's mother and I, never ever talked about the outcome of her secret telling to Nathaniel.

Nathan has lived away, and has no knowledge of what is going on around Uncle Nathaniel. Now, that Nathan lives here in Skowhegan, Sarah would reveal all, she has been told of the Corbeils. He will put together the story. Only hopefully he will never ever know I knew any of this secret. I knew long before they knew, as I was told when they were on the ship to come back to Maine.

James saw, yet he, being James, would never guess the truth. His mother laid with a man, who was not his father, and also, his very own father was not his father.

I knew, then keeping everything from James, as even his mother had said, she could not tell him the truth, and it was always her secret to tell. She knew he would never ever register the truth as real. As it is with most secrets, involving a host of people, who will be affected by the secret, there can be no good reason to share a secret which has been kept from others for a long time. In this time, life has traveled forward, has changed the person, who holds the secret, and these onward times no longer reflect their views. The protecting secret isolates the keeper from reacting with others honestly, but no good can be expected from telling of a family long-kept secret.

Today, Nathan and I will go to the family-run business, 'Heating and Plumbing Business' started by James and Son. I was left with James's shares, as a wife and a widow. I was determined to sell the shares to pay back Florence Corbeil.

Nathan was perplexed, saying, "You need to know."

"Know what?" I asked.

"My Father knew."

"Knew what. Your father knew what?"

"My Father was told by his mother of his real father being Nathaniel Corbeil. He knew and chose not to tell you, so you see there is no need to pay back any of the Corbeils. Besides, they have money to burn." Nathan spoke, I could hear in his voice, the desperate need to stop me.

My mind was whirling. I tried to grasp the words Nathan had just said. I was thinking and grasping at the words to see if there could have been another meaning. Could Effie have told her son of his bloodline? I needed to ask more questions. Perhaps Nathan knows all of this from Sarah. He is just making this up to persuade me to keep the funds, and not pay back the loan. This would be an unheard of trick. I was consumed with a need to know, if James was told and when. If so, I would never ever understand. Why?

I felt disheartened, also not willing to believe Effie did not remember her words, "I can never tell James. He would never ever believe Asa, was not his father." So why would she tell him? I must talk with Nathan. I needed to know the truth.

"We need to sit down. I want you to talk to me. Tell me what you think your Father knew, and you think I should know. Tell me all the details because this is not making any sense. Start with what your Father knew?"

So he began to tell, "My grandmother told me and my father, when she was young, and first married, she met Nathaniel Corbeil. They fell in love. She and he, met often on the outskirts of town, then she was to have his baby. Nathaniel said they could not be together, as his family would not allow him to embark on taking in a married woman. He made Effie feel like a gold digger, out to catch him when she was already properly married. Asa was told, then feeling compassion for Effie, as she was jilted in the worst way possible by believing she was in love. Asa said, 'Let us hope we have a boy, and he appreciates the farm.' This is what he said, to Effie"

"What did your father say when Effie told him this?"

"He said, I have one father, who raised me to know true love. He was always there for me, and made me into the man I am today. I felt his love all my life. Ma, we will not speak of this or the abomination you have made of your life by always chasing after love, that was already sitting at home."

Then he went on to say, "I think you are getting on in years, and are feeling scared to go on to your grave with your deeds not forgiving. Telling them all will not help you. If you seek forgiveness, realize it must come from within you. After all, it was your sins, that have hurt you. Then by keeping all a secret, you have berated your whole life in these lies, allowing the unjustified word of a coward to coerce you into thinking he cared, or in fact loved you."

"There is more I must share, Your brother Nathaniel, is your blood brother, and I told him of his lineage when he returned home from Australia. I could not take this secret to my grave."

"This makes no difference to my life. My father, Asa is in my heart, as a true father and his son."

"Later, as our conversation continued my father said,

"Nathan, I wish Ma had never ever told me any of this, and why would she reveal layers of family secrets with her grandson present. Now, she has upset your whole life, as well with her hidden truth telling. This makes no difference, Asa will always be my father. "As he spoke his voice was filled with emotion, as if he just heard a mockery of his well lived life." This from Ma was as a lie, lived as true, therefore it cannot take my father, Asa away by shinning an unjust light on my birthfather, as if my whole life was a shame. This is furthest from the truth, as I am the son of Asa Stevens in my heart, mind, and soul. What kind of mother lies to her children their whole life, about their life?"

He paused, and put his hand on my shoulder, then spoke with much compassion of a son, who loves his mother,

" I love my mother and Sarah loves Ma, she would be so hurt to know of the sorted truth of whom, she married through Ma's omission of lineage. Never ever tell your Mother. She would never ever accept this as true. How could she? I cannot. Do not tell your mother.  I do not want, to speak of this again. I can assure you I am your father and nothing in our family will change. I am sorry you were told, for the worst is, her secret, has become our secret. This is what he said."

"Nathan I want you to look at me. Try to grasp what I am going to say. Your father trusted you, not to tell me of Effie's secret, yet his being gone from us, led you to decide to dishonor his memory."

"I wanted you to know, to understand there is no reason to pay back the loan. They owe us more, than this house loan, by not accepting the children of Effie and Nathaniel, whom my father was the first born son. When she moved in and told us her secret my father and I talked. He said he knew, it could be quite intimidating knowing we were related by blood to the Corbeils, the most prominent family in town." Nathan spoke with a great admiration of their wealth.

"Listen carefully, my trust is at loss, to know Effie would be so careless as to take away the only father James knew, with the same secret, she kept from him out of love. She knew his love for his father, who raised him. James then stayed loyal to his mother, this means he understood her plight, by sorting through with love.

James never ever told me, and he never ever tried to address his kinship. This tells me he understood, and held fast to who he was with Sg. Asa as his father. Throughout all this time he was always the same, therefore, I will honor your fathers steadfast ways."

Then I paid Ms. Corbeil, in full by cashing in our shares in N.S. Stevens & Co., making Nathan beyond angry. He started by yelling, "She is rich, old, and definitely would not miss that little bit of money. Frankly, I doubt, if she even has memories of giving funds to the Stevens. This is what they do, philanthropists help people."

I looked into his eyes of scorn and said, "We Stevens will know, we did the only just thing. We are paying back the kindness to the one who offered us a lifesaver, in such a time of turmoil, and we owe her more than money. We owe a debt of gratitude."

*Thinking:* 'Nathans needs contributed to the loss of our home, now he is adding to the burden.'

Nathan scoffed, "Speaking as a lawyer, I can tell you  paying out money is a terrible business decision, and I should be consulted as part of the company."

*Thinking:* 'Where did we go wrong?'

"It is done," I replied firmly.

"The house will remain your birthright forever."

*Thinking:* 'I know not, the mystery of afterlife, whereas I hope James was not able to witness the ways of his son. Nathan did not keep his promise, to never ever tell me the secret of his lineage.' He broke his word to James to  influence my decision, to not pay back the debt we owed without a thought to honor his Father's steadfast ways. 'His Father is gone along with his ask, 'to not speak of this again' is apparently forgotten, and not upheld deep within Nathan's heart. Where is his love for his Father?

### *FAIRIES REFLECTIONS:*

***Aspen added:*** *"The sign of the Universe is love; in a perfect world all humans are each connected to one another through love. Those who have lived in your heart, will remain as loves within the heart and in your mind, are their words and deeds to comfort."*

# CHAPTER FIFTY-EIGHT

# Telling Secrets

Justice is what is fair and correct to give balance. This truth telling to James was not just. Why would Effie, do this?  She knew in her heart her son would be loyal to Asa. He was and always will be, James' father.

What did she want to happen? Did she expect James to claim his true birthright? There must have been a reason for her to change her decision. She was never ever going to tell him, because we both knew James, would never ever accept Nathaniel as his father.

Why did she speak this dire secret with our son present? He now knows all the sordid truth of her past. Could she have wanted more pay back to hurt Nathaniel? Just as she named their children by the names of his father, his brother and his namesake, to hurt him?

Is what I have been thinking, really possible? Could she have gotten Nathaniel's niece, Florence Corbeil to buy our house deed? No, this would be so wrong. Maybe Effie felt her secret would get told, and James would deem it as lying. If she told them they could come to an agreement on all of this, with her being blameless. What is left unsaid hangs heavy in the air with more to question, and with no known answers.

My heart is beginning to feel anger, and a root of hate is forming, for Effie being so careless with her son's beliefs. The act of truth telling from James' mother was being careless. Not to accept the burden of a life changing secret, instead she is reaching for a new enlightenment, which cannot be easily accomplished, or achieved, as there is shame in telling secrets of a lifelong journey. Once a person keeps a life altering secret there is no movement forward that includes telling. It is now a lie, has lived, and taken on roots in the lives of all shielded by not knowing the truth. Once making a secret there is no going back, as this ongoing secret has deceived all it protects.

Most secrets involve a host of people, who can be greatly affected by the telling of a long kept secret. The person who holds the secret has gone on with their life, also has changed throughout time, and has traveled onward, so the current time, no longer reflect the views or the need of this secret. Secrets isolate the keeper from reacting with others, when their knowledge of the facts are to remain silent for protection. No good can come from telling a protective secret.

I wonder why, she did not tell me she wanted to tell James? One thing she did for me was not to tell them I knew her secret, for this I am grateful. Effie told of her secret life, making me promise to tell James's brother, if she should die. She made me a secret keeper of her secrets, but then my trust was overturned instantly, when I learned she told the secret to my James and Nathan, without a moment's notice.

James and Sarah for better or worse, in sickness and health, this our destiny. There is an expression, 'You are only as sick as your secrets' I have kept my beliefs quiet to protect; as my beliefs were thought not lawful. We had beautiful days with lovely years which continued in the pretense of truthfulness. James always said, "The truth will set you free, to do, and be, fulfilling our destiny."

We both failed to live our fulfilling life. We shared our lives where neither in the end were our full selves. This is why Effie's truth telling brings tears to my eyes. My James lived his life without reproach. What he said was exactly how he lived. I think of me protecting James, when more than likely the secret was his to know. Not mine to keep; not mine to tell. This put my heart into an untenable position. Now to find out he knew, due to his dying mother's truth telling, and then he in turn, kept the same burdensome secret from me as protecting me from his newly told past.

He told Nathan, "Do not tell your mother, as she loves Effie as a daughter loves her mother, and could never ever understand such a deception, to be, what was my whole life."

We protected one another to the point of keeping the same secret silent. We never ever trusted one another, or we would have shared all the never ever parts of our lives. I could not share my whole self, my beliefs, who I am, which is all I have in the end and worse yet, he could not share the burden of whom, the secret his mother, Effie told him was his birthright. We protected each other through our secrecy, and in the end we robbed each other from knowing who, and what, our lives were, to be. What a sorry thing to have gone through all of our lives in a committed, yet not committed relationship. How allusive!

I remember Aba told me, "In your future there will be a debacle that will test your empathy, and your strength of goodness to your core. Be careful to remain true to the whole Sarah. You will be blindsided, and hurt by those you love, you trust. You must find forgiveness. Your love must remain unconditional. It exists without reciprocation as yours is a true stand alone love. In the end days you will feel abandoned with solitude engulfing all around. You will need dignity, strength, and grace to bring about peace. Remember as a child you were at peace, with solitude all around in your magical meadow. Solitude is a powerful element in your life, it energizes and fortifies, making you a force of nature. Do not fear, courage is not about finishing. It is about believing in yourself enough to begin. It is hard to feel alone, and left out, yet the people, who are alone, and do not feel anything are far worse off. They will always remain in this state of isolation. You on the other hand will make peace with the fact of being left out, and inevitability get on with life. Because you have a restless soul, one who takes comfort in the sights, and sounds of nature. It is out of loneliness, that fulfillment is born."

These words of Aba's brought me to accept the hurts of Effie's truth telling as her choice. I knew, I needed to free up my heart by forgiving Effie. Clear my mind and heart, sweeping away the hurt and resentment, as these will take over, and there is no light or life in resentment. We are as we think, with all thoughts fortified becoming a reality of who we can become. To live without conflict always remember time moves us all, to be, where we can change, as growth happens. There is the moment looking back, where we do not recognize the person we once were, who was so ready to fight for our ways. Therefore we must have 'compassion for others way of living life' as life can be hard to live while striving to accomplish, to be.

All are growing, seeking, changing, and becoming anew. Everyone is at different stages of development. Some we do not understand, and others we do not want to understand. Therefore if any actions by others bring us to anger, quiet down, and remember we are all in flux of change, therefore step back, and check your anger towards others conduct we find intrusive by action or words. This is a moment, in time, to stand firm on our own values, and not let others actions control our character, as we do not let our views, control others.

With,' Aba's words in my thoughts,' I am not saying what Effie did is alright. What I am really saying is. I am not going to trust the fact that life should no longer be logical and orderly. It does not work that way. Make no judgment, and have no expectations, let go of the need to wonder why, things happen as they do. If counting on ordinary justice, remember you will always be very disappointed ,and 'Silence is compliance, with people in flux of change.'

I am hurt over Effie telling, her long held secret to my husband. I am sad James was alone with his mother's disillusionment. It makes me weary that Nathan also was told. This is my side of the told secret - sadness. I do not know Effie's side, I only know deep within my heart, she has told her secret from her beliefs, that formed her life. It is not my place to be critical. It is my place to find love, and keep peace within my own soul.

"I still love you, Effie"

I will never ever understand your telling a secret of protection that involves many people you love. I now, know, the expression, 'Take your secret to the grave,' is a kindness to save the ones we love. Once a long held secret is told, it leaves no peace; for the bearer, of the secret, their families, and or, any others.

Secrets spiral with untold stories...

### *MORIA Thoughts:*

*We are as we think, with all thoughts fortified, becoming a reality of who we can become. Therefore we must have compassion for others way of living life — as life can be hard to live, while striving to accomplish, to be.*

*—Above — Sarah's instructive words — below —*

*A burden; can be a treasure to find— it is how we view the events, of our life at the time.*

*Sarah, Thank you for sharing; words of intuitive insight.*

# CHAPTER FIFTY-NINE

# Thoughts, of No Emotions

I have grown old. My life's memories seem to have changed over time, becoming quiet, so my recognition is veiled, leaving me to be only present in today.

I have recently read all of my written stories. One would think, as I was the one that jotted them down, the emotions would come through as a lasting tribute to my memories. On the contrary, it is as if reading another time in the antics of someone else's life. I have come to the conclusion we can never ever relive the events in our lives, for the person we were then no longer exists. The time being in the past, whilst our views and the way we see life today changes as does our knowledge and wisdom. The events of the past were so passionately moving, marking an impact in the importance to be the future, seem exaggerated in today's views.

Today I am mindful of the reality of death. I am aware that one day life ends. This sense seems to come from inside of my body, as if all senses are included in knowing death is nearby with my time to end. I feel my energy waning. My thoughts are as if in a fog. This is out of my control and scares me. My life is soon closing as the end nears I am here, and present in this moment making peace with death. There is wisdom in acknowledging death, along with, seizing each day to be fully present.

My mind is racing backward to the beginning of a lifetime of memories. When I was an independent child, as a first married adult, when I was middle aged with two children passing on, then one I would not let die young to leave his life abandoned, leaving the farm with three tries to buy our home, and the secrets of Effie. The years have gone by much too quickly. James, my husband has passed on, leaving me alone, heartbroken, and older, as if, one foot is at the graveside to follow.

It is the death of others, throughout my life reminding me to live fully in this moment, this day. To live my fullest life, to create, write, and hold time accountable with love.

This is a regret throughout my life, I should have taken more time for my writing. Upon reading the stories I have penned I would have liked to have written more. When married James was my bliss. I remember being busy with our boys. Moving from our farm life, to our home in the village, baking then delivering the goods about town, this kept me busy, and away from my gift of writing which Aba quietly reintroduced as my joy.

It remains so today, although this desire is somewhat quelched, because my heart is lonesome letting my thoughts drift, and not connect to my tired heart. Is this not a topsy-turvy life, when young with many responsibilities I was pulled away from writing, now I have nothing but time, and my mind and heart, for the most part are quiet in desire. I regret, I have allowed long times of dominancy throughout my writing.

Mindfulness, gives time, time gives choices, made with wisdom, of passing time, which when viewed, gives lessons to become steps, leading to freedom. Never ever to be swept away by feelings as we can respond with an acquired wisdom, bringing us kindness and love, with an endurance to living out our life.

When we are fully whole having no longer falsehoods to control our responses, just when we truly know how to weld love and kindness, just when we have arrived to our fullness as all the lessons have been taught, just when we recognize the purpose of life has been fulfilled; our time has come, and life is all but done. Death will come.

I can feel the success of completeness of my journey; rather than acting out of habit with reactivity, I am at peace. All I am is becoming still with very few words for me to tell as I accept my days are numbered, I accept my death is soon, I happily accept my journey, has made my spirit aware to changes, to know feeling completed is real love.

Today, I have continued to grow into this person, who has changed and interfered with the completion of my path. I have forfeited my realm just as the fairies knew I would, when they asked me to collect the crystal white rocks. I followed the plan without knowing there was a plan. I grew old, lived out my life, and may never ever live on to continue, the glory of wholeness, which is everyone's true destiny.

I have learnt a person must enjoy each and every day, each moment, as this is the only time to be real. We can recall the things we have done, yet not being able to describe or capture the feelings, the surroundings, the smells, all the things, that made this very moment part of our memory.

I think of our wedding day. I can talk of this event even in the writing of this day. Others will, now know, of our wedding, by then describing. It is odd "the feelings of all the joy and love" can only be shared with those who have empathy towards these emotions. This only once lived day, becomes yesterday, with all the special gloriousness relinquished to the past.

The only time that exists is now, this day,  this moment, in time. We can never ever relive our memories with the fullness of our feelings; even though they built the person, we have become today.

All this has taught me; each day, each moment, each and every person, in my life was a gift of our time, to share. I experienced each of life's gifts, for only this time in my life. The memories are of the past, with the messages living in my heart.

Remembering events, leaves me longing for the experience of my life's happenings, these moments only happened in the time when I was present in the past, when created. These are not mine to keep, or, to be able to relive in their fullness.

The people remembered are those who have aroused my love and therefore live in my heart. I remember the love of people who shared my life, as if I spoke with them yesterday, but they are hollow memories with the people and surrounding events long gone. I can only remember, the time as a shadow, without the fullness of life. I read my stories with the feelings of being blessed, while at the same time envious, for I cannot relive those happiest of times, reclaiming all of what I thought was mine. Only to discover with my old age, this was borrowed time to enjoy fully in the very moment. It was never mine to keep. The past is only to be lived one time, one day, leaving the present day to live your life anew.

Live life, each day, noticing all the essentials; love, joy, as fulfillment of the moment, letting the future lie ahead, one step at a time, so not to miss anything in the very moment of this time.

People find what they are open to explore. If your mind is made up there will be missed opportunities to grow, learn, and understand all of life. Enjoy as to remain present, in the moments of your everyday life. This is your blessing. I have walked the paths of my life, choosing many misguided paths, to get to this place of completion.

Today I write from my heart, the stories from my soul. Everything begins and must end, nothing in life has permanence. It is bittersweet to think all is temporary, without any ownership. We say our home, our children, our life, yet the time will come to let all go. There is no ownership in anyone or anything tangible. People only have ownership of choice over themselves, although sometimes we find the paths, we choose are already predestined and moving forward.

Why do we try to hold onto everything as if our life depends on these things? Is it to procrastinate, the inevitable time of death? We fear knowing every living thing has a time to die, which makes us uncomfortable. We can be sad, unlovable, or joyous; We all die.

Sad to have lived my life without a thought of 'What is going to be important in the end?' This now, I realize should have been my emphasis, as looking death in the eye would have spurred my actions into activities. By knowing time is elusive, and moving on leaving all undone with the knowledge, it will soon be too late to conquer my elusive dreams, seems sad.

Whatever time, there is left, I will use to write my good byes, as to honor my loves. My thoughts will visit in the past bringing me blessing bestowed, through my memories of our times shared, further connecting me to the Sarah of today.

Each new day, may I find the strength, to write the joys, of thoughts, to speak truthfully of my life's loves...

Remembering, I know all of life is in today,

as I remember all my loves — of yesterdays...


***FAIRIES REFLECTIONS: Aspen concluded:*** *"Hold these times in your 'magical meadow' as 'happiness memories' alive in your heart, in your very soul; for they will endear life and give a lifetime of love for all the days, yet to be... all your life is to be with you always, you are Sarah..."*

# CHAPTER SIXTY

# Thoughts, of Aba My Forever Friend

If only I could speak, and have tea with Aba" I said to myself as I am the only one here in my room where I spend most of my days. Not knowing when I took up talking to myself, it is just what I do now.

James is gone. I held most of my speaking conversations with him as we spoke about the bits and pieces of our lives, things we did while going about every day. The church, our family, and all we shared in common within our lives each day. I can not believe, a decade since he is gone. To never ever see him again, along with my friend, Aba, my only friend, whom James never ever got to know or even knew I had such a wonderful close friend.

Aba, my dear friend, whom I secretly befriended thirteen years after my marriage to James. She knew me, accepted who I was without pretense, having the gift of sight into the past and the present. The townsfolk shunned and belittled her, as the Indian Soothsayer, living by the river, never ever knowing she had powerful insight. She helped me without judgment. Just the truth in my quest to find my past lives to be at one on my life's journey to find my path that was abandoned a long time ago. Aba helped me to be at peace with my truth, allowing my deepest wish, to become my reality, if so chosen by me, to lead our family into wholeness.

Today I am thankful to God, for my sister and friend in life, Aba. The one person on earth who knew the inner me and never ever judged. Just listened, then encouraged me to be the person I was born to be. It did not matter to her my thoughts were not conventional, or would they be proper for our times calling for a silent generational prudency. At the first, when we met I could see in her deep brown eyes a spirit of peace and true non-judgmental love.

We spent time together each Monday and I came to see Aba had chosen to be this person, as the existence of belief is formed, to be, when children, and forward moving behavior strengthens the feeling of being certain, something believed is true. Then she nurtured her belief having confidence in the truth throughout her life's events including; environment, knowledge, past experience and visualizations. This taught me to look to my childhood for the way of searching for my true self. What I believed to be, 'the actual soul of my body in life.' The truth, the light, the true self or witness to the soul, not the egotistically learned superficial self. The actual self is fostered by self-describing attributes, a person is aware, resulting in set evaluations they need; to be.

I was always my whole self with Aba, as being gifted, she could see my soul allowing me to be free. I have always hid the parts of my life that make me different from the others, and their ways of believing.  This is what I do, who I am in my shyness, not needing to fit in to be so called normal, and never ever able to share who I am.

My writings for Aba took me back to my childhood, a time that was joyous, also sad. A time of living when I was part of what lived around me. My authentic self making me who I am. Today I am ever so grateful to Aba.

I miss her so much each and every Monday, as she moved to be with her people in the endeavor to help uphold their culture with practices, beliefs, values, and ideas, to form the identity of the community with all its rich history.

My stories give me peace because they are my voice. My words are endearing, meaningful and worthwhile, giving me happiness by leaving me a feeling of belonging and being connected. My words became joyous memories written down as stories, whereas reading these times brings me great joy, also sadness, or a desire to start anew, and or, to  change the outcome by choosing different paths on my way throughout life. I know what I have done, is done and there is no going back to do things differently. Everything in my life I have done has been without malice or bad intent. It was all I knew at the time.  I accept my choices as what worked in the time which was representing my life, with my beliefs stirring in my heart.

Writing stories helps me to be fully me, without putting a burden on others. This allowed me to remain as the dutiful wife, mother, and citizen, who knows my place in this community where women have no voice, no rights and are, as expected housekeepers.

My life long friend, Aba is precious...

Aba is as home to my heart...

Sisters with mysteries forever...

" Aba, I never ever knew of your everyday life, now, I wonder how you became educated to read, write and speak with instructed knowledge. Just as I knew not of my past lives and I remember you saying, 'I could of married a rich man to live in luxury.' It is odd for, of late, I have been affected by dreams, as remembering myself with royalty, living in a castle. Snippets of life, I know not, yet clearly know of and have come to believe you knew. I remember you asking,

"If I every wondered or sought to know my past?"

"Aba you are living in my heart as much today, as when my love for you started. We are apart yet, you are always with me.  We know no matter where we are in life there is a place in our hearts, known as home. I love you, we love each other in all ways, as we accept each other just as we are in this moment in time. You are my special sister and we are physically apart. I miss you today. I spend my time in bed falling asleep with dreams of living in a castle, a life not known, yet one I know."

This said, "Aba, may you grow and bring others into your heart. This will be my joy, for you to have much love. No matter where you are you will have much love. This is my happy thought; how I see you living your life, as filled with an abundance of love by those close, and far."

"It is meant to be. My thoughts are of thankfulness, for bringing me out of darkness, into light by showing me my hidden... "joy"

"May you live your life as it is,

each moment as it is,

each breath as it is,

each day to be..."


**"May we be remembered by the tracks we leave."**

I return your words told to me for human accountability,

Much love your sister, Sarah Fletcher Pitts Stevens


***FAIRIES REFLECTIONS:***

***Arwen reflected:*** *" Yes, these memories will be with you always and nothing will take them away from the life they have shown to your heart and soul."*

# Chapter Sixty-One

# Thoughts, of Nathan

Nathan, I think of our times together as a misguided trial, and error events. Mainly me as your mother trying to direct you into a direction that does not fit your personality, and or, the person you were born to be. You as a child were stubborn, standoffish, and a selfish child, albeit, one I love with my whole heart, and my whole life.

I was fiercely protective due to the heartbreak we faced when we lost Asa and Willie, to childhood deaths. You, who was three, also lost Willie crying uncontrollably for your six year old brother to come play. How much Willie adored his little brother by becoming your close companion.

This happening left the three of us a family. Your father was a faith filled wonderful man, your mother an odd woman, who never ever fit into her life, and you our son Nathan so smart and capable in matters of the mind, tops in any class. You were always looking for ways to succeed which to you was to become the type of person regular folks look up to as a leader of society. My heart breaks seeing you working, struggling, to put this life together.

Marring puts your plan, one of prominence, into the mode of becoming a reality. Her life's choices of working to become a musician, a music teacher, and the church choir leader, has given her a place of prominence in town. This is a source of pride for you, yet this is her vast accomplishment and very rare, for a woman to achieve, in this time of men's rule. She must be special indeed, and especially talented to have won over so many with ease of positioning in the church. You picked a mate to assists your desire to be prominent, and you will remain faithful to her, and with her, you are to achieve your lust of prominence. Which equals power in today's world.

Now, if we could come together as a family. I am alone as James has died. I can sense my life is coming to a close.

Yesterday, we spoke of the house, me being anxious to talk about the outcome of the house, upon my death. So I mentioned, "Nathan, time has overtaken my time of life on this earth. I want to be laid beside your father."

Nathan diplomatically said, "Where else, let us not talk of death."

This was my chance to articulate what else was foremost on my mind. I started talking.

"Yes this is a hard thing to discuss, but necessary. This one more thing, please live in the house that your father and I wanted to be your birthright."

His eyebrows became close as to begin a scowl so I quickly said, "Please keep the house. Please do not sell our home."

Nathan looked out the window as he said,

"Alright, I will not sell. Can we never ever speak of this again?"

I agreed saying, "Absolutely, this is all I ever wanted, to have our house prominently held by our family. How is Lillian doing at the church? She is well liked by the church, successful with many friends, and such a great talent."

Smiling ear to ear Nathan says, "That she is."

I see ease so continued on with, "In this town you are going to be quite the power couple. You are well on your way to use all that education, it will not be long before it will pay off in your life. This would please me very much. I only wish I could help you get there faster."

He smiled a real smile saying, "Thanks, we got it covered."

Nathan and his cousin Sarah were close, and she would help him. She and his Uncle Nathaniel found their place in the Corbeil family. She knew his place as first grandson, and would guide him into his rightful place as a Corbeil heir. They, Nathan and Sarah were close as youngsters, almost so to speak, 'cut from the same cloth.' She knows how to get him recognized as part of the prominent Corbeil family. This is the quickest way to get to the top, and I have suspected they are well on their way to fulfill this desire. I know not their strategies or their plan, and this is not a dying woman's business. They are adults making life's choices. I feel he will get his desires met as did Sarah and her father. This is Nathan's struggle.

I am happy as Nathan has promised to keep our house. It means a lot to me, the house will not be sold. What a perfect ending for my life on earth, to have this sense of peace knowing our house; my spirit's resting place will remain with my only loves. I am not afraid of death, it will be as welcoming.

When I look at Nathan I see my child, a young college educated man, and now a married man who presents without children, as they could disrupt his life. In all the versions of Nathan there remains the standoffish boy, who is striving and self searching for success. I know this son of mine better than anyone, with a selfless love, only a mother knows for her child. I see and now understand, no amount of talk, or hugs, or kisses would change his will, to be. The child became the person with the mind, the body, the spirit, which formed from his zeal, before birth. This I understand, he must unfold his will, to be. I love him with a mother's compassion, with a hope and a need for his whole life to fall into place, as he deems rewarding.

Today, I have let him go, to trust in God within the Universe, to touch his life and keep him whole, as he was born to be, even though I do not know this unscrupulous man he has become.

"Throughout our lives Nathan everything that has happened to us along the way as mother and son has been my fault. My having expectations of how, who and what, you should be, has brought me to keep morphing from hostility to caring, from caring to hostility. We were always changing our feelings leaving no feeling as final. We keep moving into new ways of behaving, leading me to a better understanding of you, fulfilling your life."

"Today I have put all this building time aside, as they create a space where there is no time left for me to explore. It is what it is. We are totally different people, each on our own path to fulfillment. There is no way to judge, a right or wrong path as all journeys call for being true to ourselves, allowing for freedom to know and feel joy. This is important to me. Going forward in your direction of wholeness, hopefully will give the outcome to bring about harmony, to realize true happiness, and joy."

"I truly hope, your life brings you, all that you have strived to achieve. You have given me peace, by keeping your birthright."

"I do love you, Nathan."


### *FAIRIES REFLECTIONS:*

***Arwen continued:*** *"There is nobody like you. Looking to be other than self, is not goin to be who you are at the core. This is to be your task; To Be...*

# CHAPTER SIXTY-TWO

# Thoughts, of My Mother

Now, I am full of life experiences, I can see my Mother more clearly. I look back seeing my relationship with my Mother I see my angst of duty. My memories are of not being loving nor helpful; they are, as if, I was all caught up in the woes of doing what was right for me. Doing only what I wanted at this time.

Today I would do, what I never ever wanted to do. Doing the unwanted would have given me a chance to be useful, a time to be helping, side by side with my Mother. Doing this I would have spent time to know more of my Mother, as a unique person, the only one like her. Why did I never realize this?

It is only now, as I look back realizing what I had missed. I did not do the work in all the moments or all the times, I knew I should have helped. These could have been the best times in our relationship as they would be the most honest, the hard times, the struggles, worked through with grace. This memory would bring me much pleasure, instead I feel guilt for not excelling in this moment of need. I would love to be back there and be helpful. It is too late. I cannot redo the past, and I cannot berate myself for what I knew not.

"If only I had known, if only you had told me how to be present when needed." I feel most people keep important needs to their selves, and struggle on the best they can. Very few people will open up sharing their needs. This therefore allowed my selfish needs to be, leaving me with regrets of causing an increasing distance between us, mother and child.

Mother wanted us to have a childhood. Something she never had. If you had met my Nana, you would know for sure, mother and her siblings were taught the basics of work ethics from the time that they could walk and talk, everyone helped on the farm. As not to be defeated my mother took control of her destiny, creating a place in herself to feel the accomplishment of doing all with perfection leading her to feel accomplished in a meager task.

Then she took pride in her work, and it became her whole life. This household work was always expected of a wife and mother. My mother had no choice but to work hard. Striving for perfection made her stand out from the group of farmers' wives. If she had to work herself into an early grave, it would be on her own terms. As the aim is not death, it is the fear of not being in control of your own existence. She would excel in all that was required, all was flawless. Perfection gave my mother pride in herself as if she was working because she wanted to do this work, not because this housekeeping was expected. She sets the standards which gave her control of her life.

Remembering in her lifetime; she could not own property, be equal to her husband, he was the head of the household, the one who owned the farm. Women did not inherit land, they married and it had to have meant something, yet as I look back there was no equality. I have come to admire my mother for her strength. She struggled to remain independent in a world of brutally hard chaotic survival.

By doing the work on her own terms, was how she remained independent and proud. She knew life would not weigh her down if she was in control of all she needed to do by being the best. It fed her strength, and gave her a sense of pride which fed her desire to be even better. How did I not see? My mother was always jumping to the tune of survival taught to her by her mother. Leaving no time for anything not deemed as important.

We were girl children, who would be leaving the farm. No boys all would be a loss, leaving a wake of burden in her failure. This made her excel in all housekeeping skills as this was all that was left to contribute. Hindsight, I see my mother more clearly as a complicated person who was my mother. Somehow I let the perfect be the enemy of the good my mother was always striving to be. This is something I see now.

My mother, as all mothers, wanted the best for their children. Better than her life which she strived to perfect by being the best housekeeper with nothing out of place, and spotless home. Mastering all types of sewing and cooking that was fast and very good. Preserves and canning all were neatly lined up in the basement on shelf, after shelf with jars in order for quick finding, of just what she would send us to fetch. This she allowed as it bought her a few minutes to finish cooking what was the best meal of the day, the one after a hard day's work.

"Mother, looking back I see things I left undone; these now have become my regrets. I never ever expressed my love for you. Today, I know, if you blink twice, life is over, life is fleeting, and looking back we all do the best of what we know. It is always a struggle of will, what you do is your life, in the end."

"A person can only, do as they know, and now, I know how to react differently."

"There is no need for guilt, or for regret, for action done, or lack of action."

"Your love is ever giving, allowing me, to have freedom..."

"This life's knowledge is my freedom..."

"Mother, I have always loved you...

now I will tell you, what I have never ever said aloud,

I have spent my life hiding all things known to me, all things I have thought to be unacceptable, as a bridge to far to speak aloud in our time of life on earth. It was and is to this day how I live with conflicting beliefs. This I say, knowing you know full well, as you have always been with me, after your death it is your voice which comes to help."

"I am grateful for your ever present love..."

"It is fine, all is fine."

Mother said, "Remember there is an end to all of life."

"Love Your Daughter... Sarah Fletcher Pitts Stevens"


## FAIRIES REFLECTIONS:

***Arwen spoke of choices:*** *"We must talk of choice, to choose the right path to have the key to know life, bringing forth the power, that lays dormant until you accept to know all, as you are known. To Be worthy with my gift of JOY...*


## MORIA'S Thoughts:

*"Thank you, Sarah for writing your truth of your regrets in the relationship between you and your Mother. Your words of, "A person can only do as they know, and now, I know how how to react differently. No need for guilt or regret of action done, or lack of action." These words have brought me the peace of understanding, in my life today."*

# CHAPTER SIXTY-THREE

# Thoughts, of My Paw

It is odd when I think of our time together the words were few and far between, yet it was your kindness to the animal always thinking of their needs to show your quiet love. You care deeply for those you love. You're a man who without parents or your brothers, lived alone from fourteen until joining with Mary to grow the farm raising two girls, as again, fate never ever gave the gift of helping boys.

"Paw, living your life was mostly difficult and unfair."

In the time of loss of your wife, leaving you alone again, to run the farm I never ever heard you complain. I learnt of love by seeing you, to be living each day with the hardest of work, farming, and not once acting out as to give up. Your strength and determination never ever wavered, through this I learnt confidence to carry on doing my part in this farming endeavor. I knew we shared a deep love, as Elisa and I were your only kin and you were ours, our Paw.

In your end days, each day we tried to reach out to you which seemed to push you further into a space all your own. You lived with Elisa, yet she was not able to have a conversation. You seemed quieter and your heart had scars from your lifelong strife of being virtually, alone with your only companions to be the animals. Then when Molly died, it was a dark cloud of loneliness grabbing your tired heart. You insisted on digging your horse's grave, and would let, no one help.

Later during the passing through your last days we could not reach you, whereas you were irrational, trashing about, and swearing causing our husband to tie you to the bed to protect you and others from harm. The toil of living this hard life took over, leaving our Paw, someone we knew not.

Remembering we are all born with the tools to change the course of our life. This is the most evident in our childhood. The child is a being of believing, and trusting, with an openness to knowledge. Looking back, I remember childhood's winding twisting road remembering how things looked differently, all of life seemed attainable. Then children must put this aside, some allow work to lure them into survival, where some allow selfishness to rule.

Somehow forgetting life must be lived in the now. Not looking back, or, to the future. Sometimes the past happenings lower our heartstrings, cobwebs fog up our thinking, then we prioritize looking for how our wishes can be brought into fruition.

My Paw always quoted, 'If wishes were horses then beggars would ride'

"You said this to grow me up, as my mind, heart, and soul, was in the clouds with my feet on the ground, where there was work for the farmer's daughter to learn, then do."

"Thank you, Paw for helping us survive as the Pitts Family."

"This was survival. I was stubborn, but not foolish as time was moving forward, leaving only a few good strong years. I have learned through the beginning, and the middle of my life, with you Paw. The only part to come is the end."

"My end comes with a deep look into our love, Paw. This was a true love, with a true stand on your belief, of love is not earned. True love is given quietly with actions to show unmistakable love, by the care freely given allowing each to know this is real love."

"I am thankful to God, for your life of giving your quiet love to your two girls. We were fortunate to have real love given freely from your convictions, learned in living a life, void of love and care, that was your childhood. This was unfair to live most of life alone. "

"May you be forever at peace as it seems, as there was no peace on Earth...

"Paw always holding our love, your Sarah"

### *FAIRIES REFLECTIONS:*

***Arwen advised:*** *"The foundation of life is to believe in work, not apathy, have faith, know your God, know your worth. You were born with a purpose; of being. Find your place in life on earth, whether big or small, it will be blessed with success."*

# CHAPTER SIXTY-FOUR

# Thoughts, of My Aunt Harriet

When my Mother died you reached out to help our family, whereas I never ever heard one complaint from you. Yet, it was an imposition, this understanding I realized when turning the corner to my more experienced self. Thanks to my loving and caring, Aunt Harriet, who taught me most of life's survival skills to be represented in my life. In a perfect world these skills would have been a shadow from the past, instead of an ever looming presence living throughout our lives.

I was a child with hopes of happiness all but lost. My heart was closed when you took me under your wing allowing me to learn, all the things a girl needs to know to live a successful life. This was a hard time for me. The truth of the matter is it was harder for you to teach all in a short time, along with your own looming work.

In the past, when my cat died allowing me to doubt my Nana Pitt's belief in prayer, then my Mother's death taught me, not to trust in goodness for all, only some. You made me feel hopeful of who I could become with your loving encouragement, also with new found hugs. I will never ever forget how you made me feel special, and how my life revolved around your love.

My eternal view of what happened throughout my life was determined by whether I sensed despair or accepted it as a lesson of growth. We as people must learn to accept hardships, as they become room to grow stronger with more understanding of what was learned, through the process of living through this hard felt experience, and coming out the other side.

Life is a precious gift, to be lived with equal times, of joy and suffering, to know all aspects of life. In contrast the more suffering the more joy will be known. All my sad experiences of life have been made worse, lingering longer, with my total unacceptance of what had already happened. By not accepting loss was to postpone living. I somehow understood loss was controlling my life. It was, as if, the grief had kept me captive with a blockage to growth. This growth I was on earth to learn, as the many lessons, that lead to knowing love.

Love was blocked by my stubbornness, and my leaning into the unfairness of my losses. When I was asking 'why' I became broken, and my life stopped moving forward staying still as if in a cage letting all this time whittle away my productive years on the earth. The years were moving onward, leaving me old without the benefit of life's experiences to teach me love. I am referring to real love which does not start by voicing 'I love you' instead it is acquired by lessons allowing a person to see and feel hate. Once felt, this turns to hurt, grief, and broken heartedness, once healed through total acceptance of that which cannot be changed. There is an end; of all the hurt, dissolution, untrust, it becomes hope; this is your love, you gave to me along with your joy, that surpasses all of my understanding helping me to know...

"It was your kindness and love which brought me through the wake of losing my mother. Your hugs, were God sent. You just knew I was fragile needing encouragement."

"To be myself, as this is who, I will be in the end. Thank you."

"As everything is ever changing, I can accept that one day, all will be gone, so to get the most out of every day is important. I have learned to not fear or resist change, as nothing is permanent, and or, promised. Let it go."

"I somewhat failed my life by not moving forward. We are born unselfish; we die unselfish. Live for today. It all goes by so fast. You have passed on and I will soon follow until then...

" I will always sing your praises, I am sure of your love, and my love for you, Aunt Harriet."

" Daydreams are full of your encircling hugs."

**"This being the wholeness of life... Love one Another...**

**FAIRIES REFLECTIONS:**

**Arwen spoke:**" *Deep within each person there is a secret place to hold belief, the core is who each one was born to be, so this place, no one else would fully understand. Focus your attention on not fighting the old ways you were taught, but living the new ways, will lead to dreams brought forth to reality.*

# CHAPTER SIXTY-FIVE

# Thoughts, of Elisa

Here on my bed, in my room, my thoughts are with you in the time of our childhood when we had a strong sense of belonging. We as sisters have this sense lasting throughout our lives, but more so, when we were together, yet alone all of our growing years. Never ever sharing, our thoughts, or feelings, as we both were deeply private on the farm living within the void creating our childhood. We felt secure being together, just knowing we were not alone.

You, Elisa seemed content when outdoors to swing each day, and I thought of this 'as swinging your life away.' My time was to be in the meadow walking around questioning with curiosity everything around me. Though different together we bonded over the fact, there was no one else. Looking back it was you and I, who formed a unique bond of sisterhood. We were different girls living in the isolation on the farm, putting us in the need of kinship. It was enough to know we were never ever alone.

My early years shared with you my sister I realize as my most grateful of events. Without you, I never ever would have been able to do all, that was expected after Mother's death. You were eight, and I was twelve, with a Paw who spent his days by himself. It was almost, as if we had been orphaned, and I was never the less, to be your mother, as well as housekeeper. We already sisters, who slept in the same room, did the same chores and in this way, life carried on giving us a bond, that exists all our lives.

Our lives became a tale of two different people, with the one thing we had in common, was the need to know we were not alone. This knowledge brought stability into our uncertain life, and continued throughout our lives. You are my sister whom I deeply cherish, and together we stood strong, in all the childhood woes. We were there for each other without never ever needing to ask for one, or the others help, and this caring grace has extended into adulthood.

I was glad when you married Benjamin, living on the Steven's farm, and brought Paw. We were known as the Pitts sisters, who married the Stevens brothers; James Corbeil and Benjamin Corbeil. I later found they both shared the same middle name, along with Nathaniel Corbeil.

In our later years, we saw little of each other, unless a wedding or a funeral. Many of our loves have passed on starting with Mother, Asa, Willie, Paw, Effie, Alisher your sweet daughter, due to a tragic accident, also James and Benjamin, along with many aunts and uncles. We struggle in life with its many twists and turns, whereas for some reason we do not want to give in, as to give up.

"Elisa your life has meant so much to me, as you were my playmate, my helper, my friend, who I knew was there when I fell asleep, then awakened each new morning. We bonded just to know we had each other like comrades, in the good, the bad, and sad times. This is our bond, knowing space away, can never ever take away, our love."

"I am eternally grateful for you, my sister, Elisa. Today we are separated by a few miles, which may as well be another country within our olden age."

Perhaps I should send you a postcard?

" If our life as sisters is thought of as spices...

our life today is as a mix of spices,

whereas we cannot pick out one spice

from another,

nor do we want to disturb our perfectly mixed blend

created throughout all our together years...

Grateful this day, to our sisterhood and I love you, Sis."

**FAIRIES REFLECTIONS:**

**Arwen reflected:** *"Yes, these memories will be with you always and nothing will take them away from the life they have shown to your heart and soul."*

# Chapter Sixty-Six

# Thoughts, of Phyllis

Last of all, yet never ever the least of all, is my daughter, Phyllis. She came to live at our home, interestingly as my son's sister-in-law of whom his wife was her only family.

We each were respectful of our shared interests, and our own beliefs, then to have our love form from our shared times in nature walks, cooking together and everyday conversations. We were so much alike in our make-up it was natural to form a strong bond of never ever love. An unbreakable love of mother-daughter relationship brought forth within our shared likenesses.

"Thinking thoughts of you today brings tears to my eyes albeit happy tears to have been given a beautiful daughter."

"Phyllis your way of respect of any person begins with your way of addressing all, with their full given name, never ever using a nickname. This gives homage to the parents, as to be, a reminder of the love given by their parents upon choosing the little ones name. In this way you bring honor to all persons. A priceless, thoughtful gift, to cost nothing, yet deepens awareness".

"How much more delicious, and delightful, was my life with the companionship of my very own daughter. After we lost James it was your benevolence that got me through my lonesomeness by sharing my days with caring love."

"Today as I write my attention goes to my awareness, of a lightness, and ease within your demeaner. I also noticed your days are spent at the church, rather than at home, attending to your works of taking care of your sister and her husbands needs, as you are in their charge. I hope this means you have fallen in love, in much the same way as James and I did all those years ago. I want you to know the feeling of knowing complete love. When you come into my room to check on me, we will share our thoughts as time is closing in on my days.  I would like to share in your happiness."

"My mothers love for you will remain strong, and I want you to know,
I still have the need to share our ongoing love ..."


***FAIRIES REFLECTIONS:***
*When I was a young child, my friends were fairies*
*they told me many things to enable a good life.*
*I remain ever grateful to Arwen and Aspen — they said*
*to promote the ability to perceive what is good and true,*
*to have common sense, with sound judgment, to be wise*
*to be possessing much  knowledge and wisdom,*
*to some day have my desires in life,*
*to have my very own daughter to love...*
***This came true with my untethered love, given to Phyllis***

# CHAPTER SIXTY-SEVEN

# Thoughts of Words

Today is a day of joy. I have been writing about my life. My thoughts prevalent in my mind, heart, and soul, of my loves. Even as a child I could tell a story by what was not said as people when talking tend to leave out the most important truths, these they keep for only themselves to remain their true strength. I realized I have a gift of listening and hearing beyond what is told. I hear the true self not to be shared for fear of rejection. It remains not my place to talk with anyone and share in stories of what is not common knowledge. At first this seemed a burden, today I know this insight is to help another, whom I do not know. Most likely I will never ever lay eyes on any reader of my writings because these are remaining my secret. It is strange to write such interesting bits of life's prophecy, and know it is not for now, but for some future reader. Somehow, someday, someone, who feels rooted in guilt where they can not move forward, nor back will get the message they need from reading my hidden journal, holding my **'thoughts of words'** allowing to find their own words. My words are from living within nature, growing into a person of belief in God and all his Kingdom of natural life and great love. I found my path to fulfillment, even though I now know this path was to be. My words of awareness are not meant to be Judgmental or religious. Thoughts...

I believe there are no coincidences in our Universe. This makes me happy, and reaffirms we all feel the need to believe in something we cannot fathom to our understanding. Such is our life always expanding our knowledge to include a way to betterment. We can take this too far when we stand on our beliefs as the only true way, therefore we can no longer be moving forward, whilst we become intolerant of other people because of their beliefs.

Today in the late **1800's** the most powerful belief is in God's word represented by the churches. Each church is a little different in their definitions, depending on the men who set the doctrine, which usually is depicted by the needs to precure wealth from the people living in the surrounding towns and villages. The church is an organization, a powerful instrument to help folks believe in the 'Love of God.' Together there is strength to bind all people into one way of thought to be based on love. 'Love one another, as you love yourself.' Churches are based on the Word of God. It is all in our family bible from hence we were schooled, learning to read as a child is when I formed my knowledge of who God is in life.

The church has strong views of what is right and wrong. If you do not belong to a church you are scrutinized, thought to be a heathen or worse perhaps a soothsayer, fortune teller, or a witch, all thought of as undesirable, as from the devil. Remembering the Salem Witch Hunt, in the year of 1693, and the intolerance the courts had for those who claimed to be innocent. The accused, many of whom were wealthy and held different religious beliefs than their accusers, were jailed, along with their children, of whom some died in jail also with many adults, who were hung. In the end it was believed religious feuds, and property disputes played a big part in this brutal outcome, as the estates were confiscated, if a guilty conviction. There was also a heightened sense of fear as the people thought the devil was constantly trying to find ways to destroy Christian communities. After all was said and done, many then thought God was punishing them for their lack of justice because misfortunes overtook by means of droughts, failed crops, smallpox and native attacks. <u>(Bible says 365 times) "Do Not Fear"</u>

The church was based on love, yet had no room for blatant disbelief or any other ways of seeking wholeness. This intolerance for others beliefs makes one wonder if the churched members of society, did believe in the power of their God. Does God seek out the believers help in protecting all people, who are of non believers? If the latter is true, where is love?

People are of all colors and eclecticism. Is this not strange to think all their travels throughout the Universe, should all be the same and they would support one church, one religion. This is the one true belief, so prosecute those who do not listen, then seek a utopia, of this one true belief. In the Bible we read, "To Love thy neighbor as thyself" remembering your neighbor is a spiritual being. Could they, also have love of God at their center, with their belief in God?

Is the Bible truly the word of God? We know it is the most sold book, present in most homes, allowing any person to consume the words; as the final authority for faith, and morality, guiding believers in their lives, their decision, To Be, bringing forth, a commitment to love. Then where is love?

Over time when people can be fulfilled believing in their beliefs, perhaps then they will feel safe to share openly with any bystanders allowing all to have the power of choice, to be at the center of love. Time has come — to accept their paths, they have chosen, accept they are at peace with their God, whomever they consider God To Be, accept that God has touched their hearts, and over time guides us all, into the person we are created To Be, as all is predestination. Is it not?

In the year 1693, think of how self-serving to carry out torment, and strife on those whose beliefs differed from their church, even though the churches today have the majority of believers. Where is love when prosecuting people for not believing, the church's message of religion?

In time to come there will be much awareness, and attention may be given to develop into a new order with many leaving our neat passionate church to seek out wholeness. The church will be tested and found to be man's work. A controlling work of leading the people to gain much wealth and prominence along the way; everyone who wanted to prosper then belonged to the church, hearing without listening and believing all of the doctrine, man has prepared to grow and enrich church life.

Each person has a soul, belief, and knowledge, benefiting their way, as they seek a path to fulfill their commitment to live their best life. What if your neighbor is a good community member, by supporting commerce, helping the less fortunate, cares for their family, keeps their homestead neat as they pay their way through society. They do have one fault, they do not go to church. Do churched members assume they do not believe in God? You must save them. In this matter, zealousness to spread the real truth, becomes the most important task at hand. We need to convince them of the love, they do not know, as they have not heard the news. Through God's grace you must tell them of Christ and their everlasting life, to save them. They seem reluctant to agree to invitations to attend the church. Perhaps they have been on the receiving end of people from church, and see what people do during the week, when outside the church. Most people do not realize, how they live all week, is what they have to bring to the church on Sunday, and more importantly what they are telling others on the outside of the church, by their actions, where their hidden self shines through to be their; "truth, way and life. Where is there Joy?"

Therefore when talking to non churched ones it is, as if their choice matters not, at least not enough to allow them to share how and what they believe. Their love for others is obvious with such good qualities which are attached to their way of living, and helping others live. We, if asked, would not be able to say, what each in the family believes. We have never ever asked of their faith, and beliefs as they are of no consequence, because there is only one true God, whose saving grace is belief in his son Jesus. They do not know the good news, which is to have life ever after in Heaven, where all will be whole and joyous. Is this not the vision of what is known to be true. Where then is this truth, this Joy, within everyday life, hiding?

***Psalm — 305*** *The Spirit of Joy, is a Gift from God,. to share with others. Rejoice in every moment. Recognizing this spirit of Joy deepens our connection to God, and allows us to spread positivity in our communities ...*

Yet, most of our church going people, have not the joyousness to convey God's love, shown by the life, of which they live. Most churched believers, do not live a life of belief and are not listening to the truth, not to mention those of the church family, do not care to hear others wrong beliefs. It is blasphemy to not believe the word of God. It states clearly that it is "the way, the truth and the light." Are these good people along with the church, to be lost forever because all refuse to hear, and accept to live a life of belief? No! We must be on the true path of Love...

***Corinthians— 16:14*** *Let all you do be done in love...*

In my life of basic non communication, living the bulk of my formative years on a farm, far away from people there was little to influence my thoughts. Then moving into a village, where, when, outdoors there was communications, and interactions within the community of folks. I sensed the critical nature of others, as they told stories of what was happening, with much slanting of the truth depending, if they liked the person, or felt threatened or jealous. So this was an eye opener to me. People would be critical to make themselves feel better,  more important, or judge. We all want to be thought well of, even though most know gossip as a story from people in the community. To what purpose?

**Now my thoughts into the future:**

" I see people judging, simply one right way, versus the other wrong ways to live life. This is all known to each and every person, all during the same time. There are people talking, all at once all over the world. They tell of their beliefs of how they live, and criticize others as if their way is the powerful future, to happiness and wealth with contentment. It is a place where one voice, if spoken, and listened to often, can deafen the listeners, making all nonsense seem real, as if this idea is what we have been awaiting. Critical thinking is needed, as the tricksters take advantage, with wealth swinging in their direction. We must guard our communities, and our country. Somehow they share untruths to all who seek out knowledge and wisdom. I have no idea of how this is accomplished; or why?"

In the years ahead travel will begin to develop choices, in the lives of people. We will write to message daily happenings, keeping in touch. What I am now sensing is an extreme invasion of privacy, in everyone's life. Where life across the world is shown, all at once to everyone, overloading our senses and allowing choices to be seen, that may work in other communities and countries, as they were brought into being with a beginning foundation. People like some of these ways and adopt the premise, yet know not the long background with success and failures. Look not just to good ideas, reality is a process. Stay true to who you are, and what your belief is, without a waver, as this is your strength and will be your glory in the end. Do you seek to find your path, you were born to follow?"

**Romans — 12:2** *Do not be conformed to this world, but transformed, by the renewal of your mind, that by testing you may discern what is the will of God, what is good and acceptable and perfect —*

"Orient your strength as in this speaking all at once there is much gossip and the truth is hidden, as are the talking people. We only hear voices and know not to whom the voices belong. Which people have our ear is on how they approach the subject, selected to be most important of the time. People are following these thoughts like an over infatuated child, who has not developed thoughts of their own. These untrue thoughts will totally uproot their own course of life, allowing them to give away their path to fulfillment, in a false way. Eventually people will become totality intimidated by the sheer volume of voices, telling stories not so true; as though they are the truth. There will be many voices at once, where I do not know, how, or when, in the future. Emotions will be running high as most of the people will adopt ways, which are chosen by what others say, and blindly try to become what they are not set out to be. We all have an eternal path upon birth, happy, the one who chooses to follow their correct path, their core, to fill their soul. Are you on your path; To Be?"

It will be a time where assumption of good — will become as evil— and evil, will appear to be good.

"Be aware of diversifying words. All words can enlighten minds, to hear is to begin to reason, whereas thoughts take root to move into action, hopefully with knowledge and wisdom for the betterment of mankind. We here on earth need writers, and spokespersons, who can approach subjects developing critical judgment in decision making allowing each reader to evaluate the words on their merit. This will be a gift of surmountable importance. Could this spur the truth?

In fear people are to make choices, in the end will prove, not right, or somewhat wrong for them. It is then they blame others for what was their own free choice. People tell their stories while pointing at the culprit, who by mere words ruined their life. Most importantly they are leaving out of their voice, it was a choice to follow the decisions, that brought on the debacle. You will see them pointing an accusatory finger always pointing away from themselves. They cannot see the three fingers, pointing back at them, the accuser, who acted in free will for whatever the reason was at the time. People will weigh their decisions carefully then choose what works for the present time. If it no longer works in the future most forget their own decision, appointing blame. It is a shame to see people use all their energy on the happenings of the past trying to get justice. What does justice look like?

Will justice  bring about the truth? Only the truth can give purpose, to move forward, clearing away the personal equations which allow a disconnect to cloud over the whole truth. This choice to believe negatively, over positive, will steal your joy, by becoming your truth. Every negative has a positive being which can be brought into fruition by thinking, as thoughts are powerful, and they grow roots, making people to be, as they think. Should people act on transitory feelings?

On the path to be who we were born To Be, the path changes, from left to right depending on how tainted the brain becomes as we listen to others opinions, not allowing for any truth, that may be the facts, of the situation. Let not the thoughts of others become your truth, leaving you in an influx of what is up or down, left or right, with no way to move forward in the truth which will set you free. Is the truth, the foundation to your love and peaceful future?"

Children all seem born with an internal core of love. The child then is watched over by all sets, of different people who are hired with funds to watch over their bodily needs, yet not their hearts. This leaves children not bonded to their parent's ways of living life, and with a strong need to take up for themselves within the criticism, and feelings of fears, of their daily world. Then the unthinkable, an indoctrination to turn the child away from their own being.  Are the children, also under attack?

The people are seeking identities as there has been an abandonment of their own selves. They know not of their goodness by leaving their traits of purpose behind to have their desires to be, and have whatever they want, not caring if their decisions affect a whole nation. Are they to throw God away?

Cruelty to one another becomes commonplace. The people in charge of charity for the needs of all in the land are giving away, freely, so much that they are erasing, the will of the people to work for their own keep. It will never ever do to be idle, which has brought about strife in the form of greed and entitlement. Crudeness is rampant, allowing cruel treatment of other people, including animals. Will humanity be lost?"

***1 Peter—3:8*** *Finally, all of you have; unity of mind, sympathy, brotherly love, a tender heart and a humble mind*

"The touch of these strung together words, from my heart, hopefully will awaken, thoughts of your own words, allowing to be heard that, that lies hidden within your heart, leaving a person with their own thoughts, not the words of the voices."

***1st Corinthians —13:4-5:*** *Love is patient, love is kind. It does not envy, it does not boast, it is not proud. It does not dishonor others, it is not self-seeking, it is not easily angered, it keeps no records of wrongs.*

Faith, Hope, and the Greatest, LOVE...

***Genesis— 1:1:*** *Everything that exists has been created by God. This means the full expanse of the Universe was created by God. So Be It...*

"My belief is in the Love of our God, Who has created everything and is in everything; including the Universe, all of nature and all people."

***Matthew— 6:25-26:*** *See how the flowers of the field grow. Look at the birds of the air they do not sow or reap or store away in barns, and yet your heavenly Father feeds...*

My meadow life taught me the struggle for survival, as the birds are not perched on top of rocks with their beaks open wide to allow the food to fall in from the sky, instead they are in perpetual motion, searching, seeking, to feed.

**Ephesian— 3:20** _Now to Him who is able to do far more abundantly than all that we ask or think, according to the Power at work Within us..._

"Today, Prayer has come to symbolize, asking God

to create something lacking;

in our life, or others lives,

rather than, being grateful for our existence;

a form of love and thankfulness, as everything needed

already exists according to the power, at work within us

when joyously moving forward, on the path to be...

As God Created...

saved by predestination;  belief of Jesus... Amen"


(Bible says 365 times) "Do Not Fear"

**_FAIRIES REFLECTIONS:_**

**_Arwen advised:_** _"The foundation of life is to believe in work, not apathy, have faith, know your God, know your worth. You were born with purpose; of being. Find your place in life on earth, whether it is big or small, to be blessed with success only if you take the path prepared for your life."_

_The only thing that matters is your love..._

_True love has no room for hurts and feelings..._

_it comes from the truth, our light inside each of us ..._

_our love is what life is all about in the light of today..._

# Chapter Sixty-Eight

# The End

A few weeks back I was walking down the front stairway going outdoors, to sit on the stoop. My ears picked up on Nathan's voice explaining, "When Ma dies, I will deed the house over to you. It will be less of a burden for you to sell quickly, and not be delayed, then we will move to upper Main Street with Sarah in the town's most beautiful house. I can hardly wait to have our dream a reality."

I quietly turned, as I no longer had the spirit to sit on the stoop, watching for my wave. I went back to my room feeling shame of what I had overheard, in a moment of complete chance. I was to be the means to Nathan's end plans, as if, by living I was in the way. Is this the betrayal Aba spoke of? All along I thought it was Effie's truth telling. Perhaps it was both, if you live long enough there is bound to be betrayal. I cannot allow this crushed spirit, to stifle my love.

This with my son Nathan feels worse, as I am a wandering old woman, hearing him speak in his own words his plans upon my death. I now see, it is not my imagination. I am, as I feel alone, and lost in this place. I may stay forever. The retreat to my room allows me to hide the truth I now know.

Nathan lied. I have learned I have not the love of my son, the one I gave my all. Aba warned me, "There is no control over another's life, they will be true to their ways, which are not parable to your ways."

I will accept my plight, of being a means to Nathan's desires to move to the home of the Corbeil's of which Sarah is today, holder of the keys, due to a marriage into the family, and of course Effie's enduring lineage.

I was blindsided by these words of Nathan. I know my son, yet it hurts, never ever the less. Then knowing he cannot stand on his words, by honestly saying, as when he was a boy, "I hate this house and I am not living here" instead he led me to believe he would keep the house, while he stared aimlessly out of the window. Should he not speak his convictions? "This house is not grand enough, so he will buy into the Corbeil's upper Main Street grand house with the help of his wife."

The truth is I heard a private conversation that squeezed the life out of me, literally driving me deep into the sanctuary of my bedroom. I feel shame, even at death's door I am being used to gain Nathan's favor in the community. There is nothing I should do. This truth has entered into my heart, wounding my heart, and I will die alone with a broken heart. What is done, is done. I cannot unhear Nathan's truth. May the Lord's love stay within leaving me content, saving and healing my crushed spirit, as I will not judge my son. I also know if there was the monetary means I would give it to Nathan. It is not the selling of the house as a means to have what he wants. It is his words from his lips, "I can hardly wait" as if I am living and in the way. Just a burden to the end. "I am sorry, Nathan. Your mother still loves you, as a mother loves her child, to the end."

The days are long. My heart is broken into pieces. My own choices have led me here to the end of the way. I lived my life, and led myself down the paths to accept only the life I wanted. To be my own person doing what brought me joy, mostly my writing stories. I never ever a thought, I would end up here, all alone, and old, with my life lived out to fulfillment. I have no fame as writing stories is my gift, remaining my secret, to share in another time. My life feels as if transitory, today.

No friends, as my one and only true friend, Aba has moved to a more fulfilling life with her people, leaving me never ever to be seen or know of her life. Here in my heart live her words, "Stay strong leaving this earth with the whole Sarah. You are never alone, your love will remain strong. Remember, Aba has been looking for you."

"I am here in my home where all within is ever-changing with im-permanence, whereas everything will soon be gone. Fear and resisting is all temporary, I will remain with joy of accomplishment of being Sarah. Thanks to you, Aba, my friend, my sister. I love you."

No family, as my son and his wife, with whom I live have no time for the burden I am, or the patience to share my last days of life. It is Phyllis, their sister, who checks on me to meet my needs.

"Good to see you awake. Is there anything I can do for you? Are you feeling alright, you hungry?"

"No, thank you for keeping my water jug filled, and dumping the slop pail. This is more than should be your burden."

"It is not so much of a burden, as you very well know by taken care of Effie. You are Nathaniel's mother and you have been very accepting of me. I have come to think of you as my adopted mother. Quite often I sneak in to check on you. I do not wish to disturb you, so I leave. I do want you to know you are not alone. I am silently watching over you. Always know your past kindness is not forgotten by me. You have become part of my life. Remember anytime, anything that you need, please let me know."

"Thank you, Phyllis. Just knowing of your helping spirits gives me peace. I will lay here, day after day, feeling as if there is no one to mourn my passing. There is no one to bid on my wishes. I have become a ranting old woman, who has the love of none. Throughout my life I let only a handful of people into my heart, most of my loves have passed on with death. I remember hearing, 'The only love you keep, is the love you give away. Love begets Love.' Now I realize this is true."

"Sarah, I am so glad you have been in my life and I love you as a mother."

"I too have motherly feelings for you and are thankful you came to stay with our family. Being alone I have lost my voice, and my thoughts for long periods of time. Just know I love you, Phyllis, as my much beloved daughter."

"Do you think Sarah, I could come in and visit with you tomorrow after supper? I know you do not want to be disturbed."

"I am not good company. I sleep a lot.  My body feels like it is quieting to prepare me to leave the earth. You need not fear. I am happy to see your smiling face. Tell me, why would you think I would not welcome a visit?"

"Something Nathaniel had said of you wanting to be alone, so to be quiet when tending to your needs."

"Nonsense, tell me how your life is going. Are you happy and well and peddling our cookies?"

"Very happy and very well. I use your cooking lessons every day. I want you to know your kindness and acceptance of me will always be within my heart. You have given me many life lessons, just by being you. As of late, I have missed your presence downstairs."

"Thank you, Phyllis for visiting with me, and for taking great care of me. Now do not worry of waking, or disturbing me. As long as I am still able to talk, then to breathe it is nice to know there is one with me. No one should die feeling as if alone, and I want to hear of your life."

"I am here for you. I am so glad we talked." Phyllis bent down kissing my cheek.

I am so grateful for the love of Phyllis, and thankful to your love God. I will give her my most treasured heart necklace, my Paw gave my mother, then gave me, before our weddings.

Also my blank papers... On one I will write "Fill the papers with words of your life's adventures or pen a cookbook..."

The sun is setting creating a reddish gold reflection on the corner of my bedspread. I reach out and touch the sunlight with the thoughts of warmth, only to find the coolness of the day. My hand lingers on the familiar blanket, as I think, this has been a part of my life for as long as I can remember. Lying here in my bed I can see the red glow, of the last of the sunlight of this day. It is peering through my window, bringing a dance of shadows, as it shines through the familiar tree, and moves in a pattern of light across the wall. I am tired and cannot get up to look out my window. It was always my relaxing way at the end of my day. The shadows are as if calling me to sneak a peek, as my tree is waving in the red light of the setting sun. The color is intense creating a reflection of red light throughout my room. All seems well in the world going into night time, in an ever-changing sky.

Not tonight I am too tired."

Let it go, all is temporary. The love will never ever go...

My Mother's knowing voice I hear, "Red sky at night, sailors delight. Red sky in the morning, sailors warning."

There are things worse than death. Ending life as a lonesome life, where you never ever feel you are wanted or loved. Mother and child are both lost in the end. I lived my life, to save my child, then gave my life to save my child. Nathan became the person he was born to be, and I spent my life trying to change his ways. This hard to love, ungrateful, self-absorbed person, separate from all that is joy in life, is my child. His ways are not of his parents and with his father gone, he is now a man seeking his own way of life. I love him, but, not what he does.

Tomorrow when all, have left the house, I must find strength to leave my room to hide my words, which have been written during my time of life. As I lay here now, I plan on how I will accomplish this feat, and I am mindful of how planning has been one of my life's ways to be prepared. I will go from my room down the back stairway into the kitchen. From here I will go into the connecting shed that leads to the barn. I remember the first time in this space. I was so happy then, and hopeful thinking each day would be an adventure in the village filled with people. When in the barn I will get up the wooden stairs, and place my satchel in the corner under the rafters. There my stories will remain until the right curious, special person finds my treasure, of my heart's joy written over the decades of my fast-moving life. It seems like, only yesterday, we moved here, until today. These stories will tell of the time in between and before, all times of my life, the ones I made time to pen.

Today I am mindful of the reality of my death. It seems to come from the inside of my body, with all my senses included in knowing death is nearby, and time will soon end. It is out of my control, and this is what scares me, the unknown. There is much wisdom in acknowledging death, and seizing the time to be fully present. Never ever to be swept away by feelings, when responding with desired Wisdom, that has brought kindness and love, from living life, in childhood, as an adult, and now at my life's end. Just when all has become, fully lived knowing the good and the bad, accepting true love, feeling deep within all lessons have been taught, and the purpose of life has been fulfilled, there is a taste of completeness. If I could stop breathing there would be my death, and I would no longer grasp at thinking from this permanent slumber. Love has put me in this complete place that never ever searches for yesterday, and never ever awaits tomorrow. Today is wholeness of one alive, filled with true love. My body is ready, my mind is ready, my heart is ready, yet I keep breathing. It is though I am not ready to be quiet and in peace. Perhaps tomorrow after I hide all my words, my work will be done, letting my strong breath quiet; this breath is the beginning and ending of life.

Thanks be to my Lord... releasing my wounded spirit, to be, wholly Sarah, giving hope to one day leave this earth with my love for all those who have touched my heart, throughout my life. Today my thankfulness is for Phyllis and our love. May she be blessed...

*Serendipitous; in nature is the gift of the future...*

Soon I will take my last breath here in my place I have chosen...

... To be forever and ever...

...May I be at peace...

...My life has come full circle...

...Where time has chased me...

...To this moment...

...Where there is no beginning or end...

Albeit a... Magical Universal *Never Ever* Life's Circle...

### *MORIA Thoughts:*

**Secrets – Never Ever End,**

Other's secrets come out trapping Sarah's peace letting betrayal bring judgements to cast a shadow on her truth of her belief.

In her life she has been shown, also she believes each are on their own journey to wholeness, each are where they are on their path. Whether they are on their right path is not for her to judge. Remembering all can only do what they know to be; their truth. Each are where they are on their own journey.

There is not one thing to do about what has happened in the past and clinging to unjust hurts will not project anyone forward into a future of compatibility, as our souls desire us to all get along. We can learn from the past, but never ever can we resurrect the past, to be established in the present time. What is done is done. Time has gone and the life of yesteryears can no longer belong, in today, so make peace with the past.

*The only thing that matters is your love...*

*True love has no room for hurts and feelings...*

*it comes from the truth, our light inside each of us ...*

*our love is what life is all about in the light of today...*

"Thank you, Sarah Fletcher Pitts Stevens for writing your secret journal of stories, filled with love, emotions and of thoughts from your days. The end made me feel sad, as needing to say goodbye too soon, although your words linger within my heart, helping me to choose my path.

As the seasons turn, and the decades swiftly pass, love, loss and unexpected times shaped our path teaching the truest journey is not to be on any map. This you have taught to me through words of your world where memory and magic walked hand in hand.

I am ever so grateful for your life, living in a time where words written of the truth of the times, that were not to be spoken aloud were wrote, and hid as your authentic voice . To read today, is to hear these historical facts, as to enlighten our thoughts —impart knowledge and grow wisdom —as each learns to find their path in life, to be."

" Sarah, We will together print your book, written for your words to be heard."

*Aspen added: "The sign of the Universe is love, in a perfect world all humans are each connected to one another through love. Those who have lived in your heart, will remain as loves within the heart, and in your mind are their words and deeds to comfort...*

***Sarah's Words****: "It is strange to write such interesting bits of life's prophecy and know it is not for now, but for some future reader. Somehow, someday, someone will get the message they need from reading my hidden journal, holding onto my **'Thoughts of Words'** allowing each to find their own words."*

***Love — is life — to be — in the End***

# Part III – Afterword

**NEVER EVER – Tell Life's Secrets**

Secrets ambush Sarah's peace, shadowing the truth, letting betrayal bring judgements, causing a struggle of how to be without judgement in a world of selfish unfairness from those she loves and protects. Sarah knows in her own life what is done, is done, with no going back to do differently, all is done without malice, it is from what is known in this time of living.

Remembering, each one can do only what they know. All being, on different levels of their journey, to finding their own paths to the wholeness of life. We are all at levels of understanding, therefore Sarah must denounce this feeling of betrayal, going forth with internal love and understanding.

***What we all seek, and***
***what matters, is love.***
***Love is life, To Be...***

# Epilogue

**MORIA Thoughts:**
**In the year 2010**

In a bedroom on the second floor enjoying the peace and sense of belonging in our home. I was surprised by a decorative box placed on a high chest, not just fell, but was propelled across the room. My mind directed me to the conclusion, of what I had been thinking, there really is a spirit here. I remembered, long ago, reading a book which directed in such cases to 'invite the spirit to leave'.

In the kitchen over the sink there was a window where on the screens left hand corner was a mark, that cleaning would not remove. The windows were cold in the winter, so were replaced, and the mark returned on the new screen. This is where I went to proclaim, "You may go, and no longer need to feel you should remain here, go be with your family. It is time." This was what I thought was to be helpful, to release the trapped spirit.

Then after reading Sarah's story, I knew, how thoughtless, and simple minded I sounded in light of Sarah's plight. Her sacrifice, to allow her son a long life, was to remain here in this place, which may or not, be reversed.

I now think the stain on the screen is her sadness in a mark of time passed with her watchfulness at the window.

***In the year 2021***

To add another connection of Sarah's writings. Our porch needed to be replaced. Our two grandsons, brought over a Geiger counter to investigate by looking for valuables in the dirt, also there was a lose 5 foot iron bar they were plunging in and out of the soil, when they hit something, prompting us to dig with the spade. There was a white quartz rock revealed, then another, with many to follow.

The deeds to our property led me to know the porch was added after Sarah's death. Do we believe in the legend of Sarah? Are these the same white quartz rocks, the ones Sarah buried in the days after the purchase of this home in the *1870's?*

***Now, the rocks lay in the light of day!***

***The mark on the screen is gone!***

All these facts come together to a renewed sense of purpose to know the brown leather satchel — found — filled with the stories, written by Sarah, are believed as true.

I now need to do the ask, from you, Sarah, We will together print your book, written for your words to be spoken, as prompted by your Mother.

***Investigating, always leads to life's adventures, I feel this one led to freedom...***

**THE END**

# Discussion Questions

WMORIA369@GMAIL.COM

1. Could you identify with Sarah? Her secret beliefs, shy/ introspective nature, perseverance?

2. Did setting the book in the 1850's bring awareness of the woman's plight?

3. Would you want to meet any of the characters?

4. Was there a part of the book that stood out?  Why?

5. Did any events make you feel sad? Happy?

6. At what part in the book did you decide if you liked it or not?

7. Did you like the inclusion of recipes?

8. Did you learn, or think more extensively of life in days past?

9. What did reading the life of Sarah help you identify with?

10. Have you read Historical Fiction? Would you recommend others?

11. What did you learn about suffering and grief from the book?

12. Were you invested in Sarah's journey, compelled to read?

13. Were Sarah's Secrets of her life a surprise?

# About the author

AUTHOR.W.J.MORIA@GMAIL.COM

My roots are deep within Maine, whereas my life, each day, is inspired by all things hidden from capture on our earth. All may look towards the ever changing sky, watching with awe of the colorful sunrise with sensual hues of orange-red, or the soothing blue with many forms of white clouds, then twilight can show a cry for comfort with a sunset of pinkish reds, before a consuming nightfall hosts the stary skies. Watching the wonders of nature gives inspiration to design gardens, on the heels of creating paintings, and my favorite organizing groups of things as to create a place known to be pleasing to the eye.

***~My joy is in all things of Art.***

Today my heartstrings are with trying something new, Authorship. Writing **"Never Ever Days"** let me use my creative imagination, fulfilling my ongoing need to design, with words, expressing feelings from living life. Today my words strung together will bring life as "Historical Fiction" to Sarah, the child, the wife, the mother, in a time when women had no voice, no vote, no ownership of self, only to be as Housekeeper.

A person is "NEVER EVER" to old to try; then accomplish something seemingly unthinkable. I get inspiration from Grandma Moses, who began painting at eighty years of age, doing more than 1500 paintings which are recognized, and valued throughout prosperity.

Time is awaiting my next novel **"ENDLESS ESSENCE"** is calling and tugging at my heart. My wish is the long gone-by days,  written as **"NEVER EVER DAYS"** will be enjoyed, also as, a thankful remembrance of survival.